PRAISE FOR ANNE LECLAIRE

The Lavender Hour

"*The Lavender Hour* tells a compelling story about how a very private and beautiful relationship becomes public and misunderstood. The characters are strong and memorable. This is Anne D. LeClaire's best book yet."

—ALICE ELLIOTT DARK, author of *In the Gloaming* and *Think of England*

"In this utterly absorbing novel, Anne LeClaire expertly maps the terrain of love, loss, illness, and family bonds while focusing her compassionate yet unflinching eye on the truth and consequences of the hasty heart. She has created, in Jessie, a complex character who will stay with the reader long after the last page is turned."

—MAMEVE MEDWED, author of *How Elizabeth Barrett Browning Saved My Life*

"LeClaire packs this winning novel with resounding life lessons and a resonating set of romantic relationships." —*Kirkus Reviews*

The Law of Bound Hearts

"Once again, Anne LeClaire has given life on the page to characters we care about. Here is the work of a natural-born storyteller."

—JOYCE MAYNARD, author of *The Usual Rules*

"A lovely novel whose characters surprise us with their humor and strength . . . LeClaire writes dialogue that could come directly from our own real lives."

—JOSEPHINE HUMPHREYS, author of *Rich in Love*

"*The Law of Bound Hearts* unfolds with such precision and power that it kept me turning pages way into the night, spellbound."

—CASSANDRA KING, author of *The Sunday Wife*

"A gripping, emotional intensity and depth of feeling highlight this poignant and lyrical novel, which illustrates how precious life is."

—*Romantic Times*

"Recommended . . . LeClaire has crafted authentic characters and successfully portrays the power of forgiveness." —*Library Journal*

Leaving Eden

"Tallie is a likable, energetic character, a smart girl with big dreams . . . *Leaving Eden* is a light, breezy novel about serious subjects. It's eventful, with a lingering death, a murder, a secret revealed, to say nothing of a makeover." —*The Boston Globe*

"Anne D. LeClaire's wonderful new novel is that rarest of all treasures: a book that breaks your heart even as it makes your spirit soar. Just like life." —SARAH BIRD, author of *The Yokota Officers Club*

"Funny, heartbreaking, and deeply honest, *Leaving Eden* is an intensely moving novel about the complex ties that bind a mother and daughter together." —KRISTEN HANNAH, author of *Distant Shores*

"You won't want to leave Eden!" —RITA MAE BROWN

"Anne D. LeClaire's latest novel is an evocative and moving story filled with women's wisdom. If you liked *Entering Normal* as much as I did, you'll love *Leaving Eden*." —JO-ANN MAPSON, author of *Bad Girl Creek*

"Artfully crafted characters resonate within this emotional novel detailing one girl's ability to face the hardships of her life. This novel simmers with the diversity of small-town life—from the witticisms of the Tuesday senior citizen's club at the salon to the awakenings of a young girl's heart. Ms. LeClaire's ability to make the setting and its characters come alive makes the reader feel like Eden exists beyond the pages of this novel." —*Romantic Times*

"Tallie is an endearing character, and the Southern banter of the ladies at the beauty parlor where she works is pitch-perfect. . . . LeClaire's homey storytelling goes down easy." —*Publishers Weekly*

Entering Normal

"Exquisite . . . a beauty . . . If you love the feel of Anne Tyler's novels, then this has your name all over it." —London *Daily Mirror*

"It's an ancient truth, the axiom that tells us that what life does not offer us in the way of pain, we'll provide for ourselves. Anne LeClaire's fine, deceptively gentle new book, *Entering Normal,* takes that truth, shakes it, cradles it, and turns it on end. . . . This story of a life-changing friendship between generations is so full of risk and wisdom, I'm jealous that I didn't write it myself."

—JACQUELYN MITCHARD

"A deeply affecting novel about the extraordinary ways in which ordinary people struggle to find their share of happiness and hope and love and connection—and ultimately succeed."

—A. MANETTE ANSAY, author of *Vinegar Hill* and *Limbo*

"In rich and limpid prose, LeClaire shifts the point of view . . . focusing on the small acts that get us through the day, or the night, or not. A woman's book in the best possible sense, this will leave readers warmed and satisfied." —*Booklist*

THE
LAVENDER
HOUR

BALLANTINE BOOKS

NEW YORK

THE
LAVENDER
HOUR

a novel

ANNE LeClaire

A Ballantine Books Trade Paperback Original

Copyright © 2007 by Anne LeClaire
Reading group guide copyright © 2007 by Random House, Inc.

Published in the United States by Ballantine Books, an imprint of The Random House Publishing Group, a division of Random House, Inc., New York.

BALLANTINE and colophon are registered trademarks of Random House, Inc.
READER'S CIRCLE and colophon are trademarks of Random House, Inc.

ISBN 978-0-345-46048-6

Printed in the United States of America

www.thereaderscircle.com

2 4 6 8 9 7 5 3 1

Designed by Stephanie Huntwork

In memory of

Morgan Keefe,
David Doane,
and
Arthur Woessner

The mere sense of living is joy enough.

—Emily Dickinson

author's note

Although Cape Cod and its towns are geographic realities, and specific places mentioned do exist, all the characters that people the pages of this book are creations solely of imagination and are not based on any individuals, living or dead. Jessie's story, too, is a conception only of this author's imagination and is not based on an actual incident.

acknowledgments

A LL WRITERS KNOW that no book is written alone, and this one is no exception.

To Gina Centrello, Kim Hovey, Ingrid Powell, Rebecca Shapiro, and the stellar team at Ballantine, a multitude of thanks. To Allison Dickens, my gratitude for your honesty, support, wisdom, and your critical eye. I feel so fortunate to have landed in your editorial lap. And last, but a country mile from least, thanks to Nancy Miller.

To Deborah Schneider, valued friend, champion, and agent extraordinaire, my gratitude is boundless. You deserve to have more than a room named in your honor.

To all those involved in hospice who opened your hearts to me and shared stories that deepened my understanding of sacred territory I have not traversed, my deepest respect and gratitude. This book would not have been possible without your help, understanding, and numerous kindnesses. Thanks especially to Andrea McGee, Mike Walsh, Robert Chase, and Eileen Urquhart, hospice volunteer coordinator of the Visiting Nurse Association of Cape Cod.

To Eunice Reisman, profound gratitude for your support and for sharing so generously with me your history and experience.

During the period in which I was working on this book, whenever I needed information or knowledge, the writing muses sent the right people to stand in my path. I am indebted to each. To First Assistant District Attorney Michael Trudeau, the staff at the Barnstable County Law Library, Lieutenant Robert Melia of the Massachusetts State Police, and Dr. Barry Conant, thank you for your generosity, your patience, and for returning my calls. The knowledge is all yours, any mistakes solely mine.

To artist Anne Wilson, thanks for conversations about the use of hair in art. I also found the *Collector's Encyclopedia of Hairwork Jewelry* invaluable. And certainly the works of Dr. Bernie Siegel proved inspirational.

To James Blake, thanks for the log entries from your transatlantic sail. I am in awe. And to Lyn Mendalla and Carlton Neuben, thanks for the stories.

There exist on this planet havens for artists that provide time and space in which to create. I am especially indebted to the Ragdale Foundation in Lake Forest, Illinois, and the Virginia Center for the Creative Arts, Amherst, Virginia. Throughout the years, both have blessed me with numerous writing fellowships. To the staffs of both, and especially to Susan Tillett and Suny Monk, I offer gratitude. It is not enough.

Thanks, too, to the other writers who sustain and support me: Alice Elliott Dark, Jebba Handley, Ann Stevens, Virginia Reiser, Sara Young, Joan Anderson, Chris Leighton, Paula Sergi, and Jackie Mitchard. Because of you, I am a better writer.

And to Hillary and Hope and Chris, my deepest love. Because of you, I am a better person.

THE
LAVENDER
HOUR

I STILL GO back to that spring. As I recall that particular April morning, I see it clear. I watch myself as I walk through patches of snow toward a lavender door, my boots sinking into thawing ground, chewing a stick of sugarless gum, nervous as hell and wondering what I've gotten myself in for. It seems now as if I am remembering a different woman. And in a way, of course, I am.

Memory.

Mama told me that hard memories soften eventually. I trust that she's right. I mean there's just so much that can trigger a memory, set it reeling in motion, catch you off guard before you can provide against it. Just yesterday, while I was running on the beach, I thought I heard someone shout out his name. *Luke.* But when I turned, I saw it was only a young woman calling to her child and pointing toward a blue heron that soared overhead in glorious, awkward flight. "Look," she called. One word, misheard, yet it was enough to bring me to my knees.

The boy stared at me. "Mommy," he said, "that lady's crying."

Memory.

Faye says that the elderly and the dying live in their memories because it is less painful for them to look back than it is to look ahead. What I wonder is, what past is it that they return to? The poet William Matthews says the past is the little we remember.

Not quite true. The past, the one we return to when there is nowhere else to go, is not the little we remember but the shreds we have bent and shaped and revised until they are formed into memories we can bear to recall. Prudently screened fragments we can live with.

And even then . . .

I REMEMBER that fall and the trial. Sitting in the witness stand while the DA quizzed me about the final day. Looking out over the crammed courtroom, past the only television camera the judge had permitted, scanning the faces of strangers, finding Lily, searching for Faye, thinking about the dark places sorrow can lead us into. Thinking about the glory and tenacity of love and of the consequences we pay for loving.

I looked for Faye and thought not of the final day but of the first. The end from which the beginning followed.

A spring snow. A lavender door. And, waiting inside, Luke.

THE
ENDING

A STATION OLDER than oldies was playing Johnny Lee's "Lookin' for Love in All the Wrong Places," and didn't that make me laugh right out loud in spite of my high-wired nerves. My sister, Ashley, used to say this could be the title song of my life. Hard to argue with that. My romantic history was a string of jagged beads, each broken in a different way.

I snapped off the radio—*time to change that tune*—but, of course, now that it had taken up residence in my head, it would be cycling through for the rest of the day. I checked the dash clock. Late. Late. Late. I could make better time on a banana-seat bike.

The gray sedan in front of me, one in a long line of cars, inched along three degrees short of a dead stop. Back when I was a child vacationing on Cape Cod, traffic like this was a hassle reserved for summertime, but a shitload of change had occurred in two decades. Now roads were clogged nearly year-round, and each month, one more seasonal cottage held in a family for generations was replaced by a place so large, I swear it could exist in two time zones.

I tailgated the sedan, as if that would speed things up. I was beyond late. No excuses. "Jessie Lynn, I swear you'll be tardy for your own wake," my mama used to tell me. Of course, that was back when she could say something like that without looking like she wanted to slit her tongue and serve it for dinner, back before we all became painfully aware that such a possibility could actually loom on the visible horizon of my life.

At one time, Lily used to treat promptness as something of

consequence, along with matters like impeccable grooming and refined manners. *Please, thank you,* and *elbows off the table* were just the day care level. Back when I was a child idolizing her, I yearned to be exactly like my mama, but then, about the time I hit high school and commenced being a disappointment to her, I vowed I would *never* end up like she had, trapped in a small town, checking her roots for gray, her life consumed with tending to the needs of others. Well, couldn't the irony of it just cause a person to weep, for it was as if, in some weird way, I'd flipped lives with Lily. Here I was wearing twenty minutes' worth of makeup and heading off to care for a stranger while Mama was back in Virginia with her hair gone natural, preparing to sail across the ocean with a man named Jan, a semiretired dentist ten years younger than she was. Go figure.

THE DENTIST was new on the scene, and for details, I relied on my sister, who called him "junior" and "the boy toy," as if someone fifty-five could still be considered a lad.

"So," I said during one of our conversations, "tell me about what's his name."

"It's Yawn," Ashley said.

"*Yawn?*" I said.

"Right," Ashley said. "His family's from Finland. Or maybe it's Norway. One of those countries. Anyway, it's spelled J-a-n, pronounced Yawn."

"You mean as in boring?" Perfect. What was our mama thinking? "So what does he look like?"

"He's shorter than Daddy," Ashley said, which gave me a small satisfaction. But how short? Dustin Hoffman short? Richard Dreyfuss short? Or freaky short? I pictured Danny DeVito. Hervé Villechaize.

I RECHECKED the clock and continued tailgating the sedan until I reached my turnoff. I was running a good half hour late, and my nerves were skinned and deep-fried by the time I finally arrived at the address in the file lying on the passenger's seat. I pulled up directly behind a maroon Dodge Ram, the kind of muscle truck that caused me to feel inadequate, its tires so oversized, it would require a forklift to hoist me up and into the cab. The kind that made *me* feel like Danny DeVito. I switched off the ignition and checked out the house. It was a full Cape shingled in gray cedar and featured a front door and shutters painted a showy lavender. A line of lobster traps was stacked along the property line to the north, and a boat was cradled in the side yard, slightly tilted, with a wooden stepladder propped against the gunwale. Someone had started to scrape paint off the keel but quit before completing the job. Except for that purple trim, the house and grounds were like a half dozen others in the neighborhood. I, of all people, knew it was possible for things to look perfectly normal on the surface while, hidden from sight, the extraordinary was in process, but still, even fully expecting it, *knowing* it, there was nothing to indicate that, inside that house, a man was dying.

To SETTLE my nerves, I unwrapped a stick of gum and popped it in my mouth, my mama's manners be damned. When Ginny Reiser, the hospice nurse, called me the night before offering to meet me there and introduce me to the family, I'd refused. Major mistake. I could have used some shoring up. As much to combat jitters as anything, I performed a last-minute run-through of the patient's file, although I had already memorized every detail. Luke Ryder. Pancreatic cancer. Age forty-five. Commercial fisherman. Divorced. (Which explained the lavender trim. Obviously the ex's decision.) One child, Paige Ryder, twenty-two. (*Difficult; can be confrontational; substance abuse?* was jotted in pencil next to her name.) Primary caregiver: Nona Ryder, seventy. Relationship: patient's mother. (*Doesn't drive; no car,* the case supervisor noted.)

The path to the door was sloppy and rutted. There had been a spring snowstorm three days before, and my boots sank into the ground as I picked through the half-melted patches that spotted the way. I barely noticed. Echoing in the back of my brain was a sentence from the first morning of training.

It is never easy to enter the world of the dying.

Well, I knew *that* from experience. I'd had my own world turned wrong side up by death and disease. "Sweet Jesus, what am I doing here?" I said aloud. I caught a flutter of movement behind one of the curtains at a front window. Too late to cut and run. My grandpa Earl's advice echoed in my head: *Don't worry about the mule going blind. Just load the wagon.* I climbed the steps, chewing that gum like a cow hopped up on speed and hoping I looked more together than I felt. *Just load the wagon.* As I neared the door, a formless clutch of anxiety closed my throat, and I combed my fingers through my hair, lightly traced the scar that lay just behind my ear. Then I swallowed and stood tall, my mama's daughter after all.

The woman who opened the door was dressed in a print cotton blouse, navy pants that had seen better days, and a pair of sneakers with slits cut for bunions, the kind of getup Lily wouldn't be caught dead in. But then again, who knew what my mama was wearing those days. For all I knew, it could have been floral print spandex.

This woman was wrinkled and thin, with drugstore-kit-dyed hair and a bent body that signaled osteoporosis and spoke of a far-reaching history of heartache and hard work. Right then, that first time I saw Nona, she touched something in my heart, and I wanted to reach straight out and fold her in my arms.

"You're Jessie?" she said. "From hospice?"

"Yes," I said. "Sorry I'm late. I didn't allow for traffic."

She brushed away the apology. "I'm Nona. Luke's mother." Behind her smudged glasses, her face was slack, fatigue revealed in every pore and line. "You're younger than I expected," she said, although it appeared she wasn't going to hold that against me, for she stepped aside and allowed me in.

I tucked the gum in my cheek and offered what I hoped was a reassuring smile.

"How old are you, anyway?" she said.

"Thirty-two."

"Well, I thought you'd be older," she repeated in the no-nonsense tone of a person who said just what she was thinking. In that way, she was kin to Faye. I wondered if that was something you grew to as you aged. Like you didn't have anything to lose. Or maybe it came from being a born and bred northerner and not having to come at everything sideways.

"You're not from around here," she said, more statement than question.

"Richmond," I said. "Virginia." I'd never thought of myself as having an accent, but since I'd moved up North, it seemed everyone commented on it.

The living room was small, seriously overheated, and smelled so strongly of wet dog and wood ash, I had to smother a sneeze. While Nona closed the door, I took a quick look around. I swear I'd seen more furniture in a phone booth. The ex-wife must have picked the place clean. A faded plaid couch, the kind you could tell was scratchy without even touching it, faced the fireplace and was flanked by a scarred pine rocker. The *Cape Cod Times* was spread out on a wooden lobster trap that served as a coffee table. One section of the paper was folded open to a partially completed crossword. The only interesting object in the entire room was a seascape hanging above the mantel, an oil in delicate shades of gray and blue with a dory that surfaced from the fog only after I had been considering it for a minute or two.

"The kitchen's in here," Nona said, pulling my attention back. We passed by a closed door through which seeped the sound of a television. Nona slowed a step but did not stop. "I just made a pot of coffee, or there are tea bags if you prefer," she said. "And there's soda in the refrigerator. You just feel free to help yourself to anything."

I looked over at the closed door, assumed that Luke lay behind it. At our last team meeting, Faye and Ginny had told me that he was militantly private and had agreed to accept only a limited amount of help from hospice. Translated, that meant my role there was to provide support for Nona, who had moved up from Wellfleet to care for him exactly one month back. Until two weeks ago, Luke had resisted having hospice involved in any way at all, but when his doctor gave him an ultimatum—hospice or a nursing home—he had surrendered. At first, he only allowed visits from the nurse and from the health aide who assisted with his bath and personal needs, but after the social worker spoke with him, he agreed to my inclusion on the team. "It's more for your mother than for you," the social worker told him. "She hasn't been out of the house in days. A volunteer will provide her with some necessary respite and support." According to Faye, Luke's exact words of acquiescence were "As long as I don't have to have anything to do with her. I don't want some goddamned, recycling do-gooder wringing her hands over me." It was a sentiment I certainly understood and had no trouble respecting.

We had been told that the central tenet of hospice care was that since the dying have so little control over their lives, the hospice team was, whenever possible, to grant them autonomy in decision making during this end-of-life period. "We meet people where they are, not where we want them to be," Faye had told me. Still, the more I learned about Luke Ryder, the more surprised I was that Faye hadn't assigned a man to the case. Someone older and experienced, like Bert, a retired FBI agent who has been volunteering for eleven years. But Faye said, "Trust me. I never make a mistake. You're the one."

"Is Luke in there?" I asked Nona.

"Yes. But they've told you that he doesn't want to be disturbed, didn't they?"

"Yes. They were clear about that."

Outside, a horn tooted. Three short beeps.

"Well, here's my ride," Nona said. She looked over at the closed

door, serious second thoughts plain on her face. "Is there anythi
else you need to know?"

"Nothing," I said, all false confidence.

"It's hard to leave him," she said.

For an instant, I swear I nearly told her to stay. Instead, I said,
"Take as long as you like. I have all day. Really."

"Well, I won't be gone long," she said. "An hour at the most."

"Don't worry," I said, regretting the words instantly. *Don't worry.*
To a woman whose son was dying.

"He has a bell. Did they tell you that?"

I nodded. It was in my notes.

"He'll ring it if he needs anything." She hung back at the door, as
if still trying to determine if I could be trusted.

"Go," I said. "He'll be fine. I promise."

I watched from the window as the car pulled away. I was surprised by a jolt of anxiety—it had been months since I'd had an
attack—and felt the telltale prickly flush of heat flooding my body.
I closed my eyes and reminded myself to breathe—*Deep Breath.
Deep Breath. Deep Breath*—repeating the mantra until the flash of
panic gradually began to subside. I told myself anyone would be a
bit nervous under the circumstances. I told myself I would be fine.

THE WALL thermostat read seventy-six degrees, but it felt like a
sauna. How anyone could stand it was beyond me. I was tempted
to lower it but held back. For all I knew, Luke required this kind of
heat, although there wasn't anything about it in his file. I stripped
down to my T-shirt.

I hadn't thought to bring along a book, and even if I had, I was
too nerved up to read. Back in the kitchen, I poured a cup of coffee, so strong it was nearly solid, the last thing on Earth I needed,
then I stood by a window and stared out at the backyard. In that
first, quick glance, I counted fourteen bird feeders. They were
everywhere: hanging from trees, attached to posts, affixed to the

ndowsill, like some miniature Audubon sanctuary. I busied myself by trying to identify the different varieties as birds swooped in
and out. Goldfinch, winter drab feathers already turning yellow.
Chickadees. Blue jays. And a gray crested bird that I couldn't name.
I'd never been much of a bird person.

I turned away, scanned the room. My gaze settled on a picture
of a stunning brunette in a blue bikini that was stuck on the refrigerator with a magnetic plastic frame. Women like that always made
me feel too short, my copper hair too bright. Was this the ex? The
daughter? A girlfriend? I found myself humming a fragment of the
Johnny Lee tune about searching for wrongheaded love.

While I poked around, I kept alert for the sound of his bell,
slightly anxious about whether I'd be able to hear it over the voice
of the television sports announcer coming from the other room. I
sipped the coffee, bitter, and felt . . . What? Let down? This was so
not what I expected.

DURING TRAINING, Faye told us the role of the volunteer was to
provide emotional support and practical help to the patients and
their families. Errands, chores, anything they needed. Read to
them if they wanted. Take them for a ride. Play games. Scrabble was
a popular choice. Take your cues from the patient and his family,
she had suggested. Be willing to listen. There was one entire training session dedicated to effective communication and reflective listening. *As I hear it, you . . . Could it be that you're feeling . . . As I think
about what you say, it occurs to me you're feeling . . .* We had performed
role-playing exercises and had practiced how to talk without
preaching, judging, sympathizing, excusing, or advising. Beth, a retired kindergarten teacher, couldn't understand why we shouldn't
be allowed to offer advice. "Because," Faye said, "without your
meaning to, it can convey a certain arrogance. It tells the person
they don't really understand the situation, but that you do."

Sitting in the basement room where we'd met for training during the winter, it had sounded easier. Of course, if my sister, Ash-

ley, had been here, she'd do more than give advice. Ten minutes
through the front door and she would have aired out the house,
turned down the heat, and informed the man hiding behind the
closed door that he should take his pride down a notch or two and
accept help when it was offered. But I wasn't my sister. Besides, although I wanted to meet Luke, to sit by his bed and have a chance
to tell him that I understood what he was going through, I couldn't
help but sympathize with his desire for privacy. Like I said, I'd been
there myself.

I explored the kitchen, taking care not to be heard, although I
was fairly certain nothing would penetrate the wall of sound gen-
erated by the television. I opened a cupboard door, found several
medicine vials, a box of Cream of Wheat, and a crateload of Ensure. The adjoining cabinet was stocked with packages of prepared
foods. The inexpensive kind. Macaroni and cheese. Scalloped potatoes. Ramen noodles. Cans of corned beef hash and chicken noodle
soup. One thing the hospice staff had been specific about during
our training was the necessity of establishing boundaries, both
emotional and practical. Volunteers, we'd been told, were never to
invade the privacy of the patient or the family and never under any
circumstances to snoop around a patient's home. But I was curious.
Plus, I'd never been strong on following procedures. (Every time a
flight attendant told me to fasten my seat belt, I wanted to un-
buckle it as soon as he walked away. My one-month therapist asked
me if I thought I had a problem with authority. Who doesn't? I'd
asked. Really.)

I wandered into the bathroom and poked around the contents
of the medicine chest. Toothpaste. Tube of hemorrhoid cream.
Electric razor. Antacids. A generic pain reliever and a bottle of vitamins months past the expiration date. Nothing out of the ordinary. Hardly worth the trouble of breaking a rule.

We had been given surprisingly few rules. Volunteers weren't
supposed to stay overnight. Things like that. Mostly it was guidelines. The thing the staff was really emphatic about was that we

were not allowed to give any medications to a patient. No exceptions. No matter what. Shouldn't be any problem with that one. It was hard to give drugs to an invisible man.

BACK IN the hall, I checked out a gallery of photos in metal frames. A studio shot of a little girl in a sundress with blond hair falling in waves to her hips. (What I wouldn't have given to get my hands on that hair.) The same girl—older—in cap and gown, holding a diploma, hair now bleached nearly white. Not smiling. I assumed this was the daughter—Paige—and, recalling the file notations, tried to read signs of bad attitude in the girl's face, but all I saw was the smooth palette of youth, not unlike that of dozens of my high school students who had 'tude to spare. Next was a black-and-white photo of a man standing at the ocean's edge, knee-deep in the surf. The blond girl, no older than twelve in this picture, stood close at his side, her face alight with joy and tilted up toward his. He was darkly handsome in the snag-your-breath-beneath-your-ribs kind of way that I always associated with Irish men. At that moment, I felt a shock of connection that even today I can recall as vividly as if it were yesterday. *I know you.*

I stood there a while longer, trying to understand this flash of recognition, this sense of knowing, but I couldn't get a handle on it. Finally, I moved on to another shot. In this one, the dark-haired man stood by a truck, a black Lab at his side. I lifted the photo off the hook and crossed to the kitchen window, where I could get a better look. I recognized the truck as the Dodge in the drive, a new model, so clearly the picture had been taken recently. The man looked well over six feet, tall enough so he could step into the cab without the least effort. Well, no radar needed to signal danger with him. Love on the loose and hearts on the run. His hair was as black as the retriever's. I'd felt hair like that—coarse but not wiry—held it between my fingers. (Black—true black—remains to this day my favorite hair color. It holds and reflects light like no other shade.) He looked incredibly fit. Even in the picture, you could see that. I glanced over at the closed door, tried to imagine him lying in a bed on the other side. It seemed impossible to believe that the vital man in the photo could be sick, dying. But when had life ever been fair? I had been fourteen when my father died. And twenty-seven when I got cancer.

I replaced the photo on the wall, then stepped closer to the door, stopped short when the floor creaked beneath my feet, strained to hear some sound other than the television. Should I knock? Call his name? Check to see that he was okay? *Was* he all right? My mouth grew dry. Oh God, I thought. What if he wasn't? My heartbeat accelerated, a caffeine-overdose-like symptom that sometimes foreshadowed a spell of anxiety. I inhaled deliberately, slowed my breath. I closed my eyes, steadied myself, wished I were back at the cottage, busy at my worktable fashioning a piece of jewelry. At that precise moment, I would have given anything if I could have gone back and altered the events that had brought me to that room.

two

IF.

When we were much younger, Ashley and I used to play a game in which we rolled life backward, an exercise we found simultaneously thrilling and terrifying. *If Mama's boyfriend hadn't gotten a burst appendix,* Ashley would start, *she would have gone to dinner with him that night.* On cue, I would chime in: *And if she were having dinner with her beau*—our mama's word—*she wouldn't have gone off to the movies by herself.* Ashley would pick up the story: *And if Daddy hadn't taken a new job and moved to her town, he would already have friends and wouldn't be alone on a Saturday night.* Taking turns, we would continue the tale to its end. How if our daddy hadn't been standing right behind our mama at the box office and she hadn't forgotten to cash her check from the day care center where she worked and if he hadn't insisted on paying for her ticket and if she hadn't said yes but only if he would let her pay him back, et cetera, et cetera, et cetera, a litany we knew by heart—how if one of these things hadn't happened exactly as it had, neither of us would have been born. It absolutely unnerved us to think how one incident changed, one particular break in a chain of events—an appendix not burst, a new job offer not accepted, a check already cashed— just the smallest act altered and neither of us would be alive. That was the part that was so scary and remained so even after we'd grown up: The arbitrariness of history. The fragile strand that was cause and effect.

If.

. . .

As I stood in Luke Ryder's house and stared at his closed door, I found myself unraveling the strand of circumstances that had carried me to that moment. If I hadn't broken up with Steve (not exactly the shock of the millennium; *broke up with a guy, broke up with a guy, broke up with a guy,* was the major theme of my love-in-all-the-wrong-places-with-all-the-wrong-men life) and if my job hadn't been eliminated (arts were always the first to go; God forbid any school budget cut should affect sports) and if I hadn't needed to escape the too-heavy weight of Lily's concern for me and my own long history of disappointing her, I would not have moved to the family's cottage on Cape Cod for a year while I tried to sort things out. I'd thought that maybe, in a different setting, I would manage to let go of the fear and the sense of vulnerability that had settled on me since I'd gotten ill and I'd be able to look to the future. As my grandma said, I'd been given a new chance at life. A lot of people didn't have that opportunity. So here I was on Cape Cod. What was it called? A geographic cure? Well, cures come in all manner of guises. I was taking my first steps in a new life direction as yet undefined. I didn't know exactly where I was going, but I was eager to begin the journey.

FIVE YEARS earlier, on the day following my twenty-seventh birthday, doctors discovered a tumor on my brain. "It can't be," I said to the neurosurgeon, even as I stared at the brain scan. Just the previous week, I had run a ten-K and then gone out and partied like a wild woman. Of course, we are never prepared for the things that rush into our lives uninvited. You think life is settled, and then it isn't.

There had been no warning. The few symptoms I had experienced I'd discounted as ordinary side effects of modern life. Who didn't have an occasional headache? Who didn't get a bit run-down? Yes, I'd been tired that winter and had had headaches from time to time, but I was working hard—a full-time job, two craft shows to prepare jewelry for, my running club—and I put the fatigue and headaches down to stress. On the worst days, I'd swallow three Advils or pop a couple of Aleves and try to forget about it.

By spring, the headaches had become so chronic that I mentioned them to the examining physician during the physical routinely required by my health insurance provider. He didn't seem overly concerned. He suggested I try some stress-reduction techniques and said to check back if they persisted. And even when my eyelid seemed to be a tiny bit droopy, this change seemed minor. Nothing dramatic. No pain. We have an amazing capacity to explain things away. Until we can't.

When Lily noticed the slight asymmetry in my face, she insisted on calling my uncle Brent, my daddy's brother and a pediatrician. He questioned me closely and suggested a few tests. Just to rule everything out. Later I learned he had suspected Bell's palsy.

But it wasn't palsy or MS, or the half dozen other things they tested for and eliminated. It was a growth on my brain. *Schwannoma*. A laughable name for a tumor. It sounded like a disease you'd get from riding a bike. Or something Woody Allen would make up. It proved to be malignant.

Now, AFTER an operation to root out the tumor, weeks of radiation, months of recovery, and years of moving on, I truly believed the nightmare was in the past. At my checkup last summer, I had been given a clean bill of health. I had passed the all-important five-year cancer-free mark. I was determined to be hopeful. Possibilities lay ahead. Opportunities I hadn't allowed myself to consider until I had the all-clear checkup. Still, I would catch others looking at me as if I might at any minute have a seizure. Friends, faculty members, students, the boyfriend du jour. Although once they learned of my history, most men proved gun-shy.

"I'm fine," I'd tell Lily when I was overtired and my eyelid drooped and worry clouded her face. And I *was* fine. I was running again. A half marathon last summer. My hair had grown back and was nearly as long as it had been before I started radiation, except for the spot behind my ear the size of a half-dollar where it had receded a bit. But when my position at school was phased out and my latest romance blew up, I saw that I had been treading water. I saw a chance to really start over.

At first, Lily tried to dissuade me, but eventually she gave in. "If you're bound and determined to go off," she said, "why don't you take the Cape house? We haven't rented it in years, so it's just sitting empty."

"Hell," Ashley said, adding her ten cents, "she might as well. She's already gone through all the eligible men in Richmond."

I accepted Lily's offer, and from there, in the perilous cause-and-effect way, one thing led to another, and before a week had passed, I'd packed up my bobbins and worktable and the other supplies I needed for jewelry making—a side business I used to augment my teaching—and reckless for change, I set off for Cape Cod.

Synchronicity. Domino effect.

Almost immediately, Faye Wilson, a neighbor and an old friend of my daddy's family, stopped by to see how I was doing, and within days, I found myself with a surrogate family, which was how I happened to be driving with Faye one rainy day that October on my way to hear a speech by Dr. Bernie Siegel, an oncologist who lectured on mind-body connection. Faye was the volunteer coordinator for Bayberry Hospice of Cape Cod, the event's sponsor, and she'd talked me into taking her extra ticket, saying I needed to get out more. Of course, when I heard that, my heartbeat accelerated. I wondered if Lily had broken her promise and told Faye about my tumor.

In the hotel conference room where the event was held, I remember wondering what Siegel could tell me that I hadn't already lived through. "Diseases can be our spiritual flat tires," he said early on in his speech. "Disruptions in our lives that seem to be disastrous at the time but end by redirecting our lives in a meaningful way." Spoken like a person who has never had cancer, I thought, and began to drift away. But halfway through, as if some part of my mind had been on alert, listening for it, one sentence penetrated my consciousness. I waited until we were back in the car before I turned to Faye. "Do you think it's true, what he said?" I asked.

"What's that?"

"That we learn how to live from the dying? I mean, it sounds good—*We learn how to live from the dying*—but is it true? Do you think we really can?"

Faye concentrated on driving. "What we learn from the dying," she said after a minute or two, "is the one thing we want to forget."

"What's that?"

Faye turned toward me. "That we're all going to die."

Again I wondered if Lily had betrayed my need for privacy. Ashley always accused me of being a drama queen, but, thrust into the center of a real soap opera story line, I discovered I had a limited tolerance for the attention. When I'd first been diagnosed, I had tried to keep it on a need-to-know basis, and one of the appealing things about moving to the Cape had been that no one there knew about my history. I could feel normal again.

"The dying can teach us how to die, Jessie," Faye was saying. "Maybe that serves as a model for how to live. What do you think?"

"I don't know. I'm not so sure watching someone die can give us what we need most."

"Which is?"

"Which is a sign that danger lies ahead, that it is barreling down the track and heading straight for us."

"And you'd like a signal?"

Well, *yeah*. Who wouldn't want some indication, something to give us warning so we weren't blindsided by fate. "Something."

"Like what?"

"I don't know." I looked over at Faye. "It probably wouldn't do me a bit of good anyway." I tried to lighten the mood. "I wouldn't heed it if it hit me full in the face."

"You don't think so?"

"Just ask Ashley. She's always saying, if the road sign says Stop, I speed up."

"Ashley says that?"

"She does. Anyway, if you're looking for a guide to the fucked-up life, I'm your girl." I laughed. "No work. No man. No clue."

"Why don't you have a man?" Faye said.

I considered her question. Why didn't I have a lasting relationship instead of a string of sour romances? I had asked exactly that of a therapist I'd seen for one month on the back side of yet another failed affair and an anxiety attack so relentless I'd had to use up three days of sick leave at school. He had posited that perhaps it was because, if I left a man first, it prevented him from leaving me. "I don't know," I said again to Faye, and then, uncomfortable, I switched the topic. "And anyway, getting back to Siegel's statement about learning from the dying, is that why you work with hospice?"

"I suppose that's part of it."

"Isn't it kind of—I don't know—depressing?"

"No. Sometimes it's sad, sometimes heartbreaking. But not depressing. It's tremendously rewarding. Not unlike what you get from teaching, I'd say. Mostly, it's a privilege."

Privilege. The word settled in my head. Then (needing what?—an anchor, or at least a keel, something to hold me steady as I started anew, or perhaps simply because I possessed Lily's DNA after all and had a need to give back) I surprised myself by asking Faye if she thought I could become a hospice volunteer. And there it was again. Cause and effect. A budget cutback and lost job. A vacation house left vacant. A chance invitation. One sentence in a speech. A butterfly taking to wing in Asia. And now, six months later, following intensive training, there I was, standing in the home of my first client. Lily—the pre-boy-toy Lily, the public-service Lily—would have been proud. Hell, *I* was proud. It felt good to give back. To think about something or someone other than myself.

. . .

I CONTINUED to stare at Luke's door, strained to hear the sounds from within. *He'll be fine,* I'd said to Nona. *I promise.* Who was I to promise something like that? What if he wasn't fine at all? I had a quick sensation, a low, beating fear. What if he was unconscious? Or worse? On the other side of the door, I heard the scritchity ticking of a dog's nails against a wood floor.

"Mr. Ryder?" The pulse of fear grew stronger.

The dog whined softly. The television blared.

"Mr. Ryder? Luke?"

"Go away."

"It's Jessie," I said. "Jessie Long. The volunteer from hospice."

"Go away."

He didn't sound sick at all. His voice was deep, and not in the least weak, certainly not the voice of a dying person. Again I pictured the man in the photo. His was exactly the kind of voice I would match to that man, the kind of voice that stayed in your head for a long time after.

"I just wanted to make sure you're all right."

Nothing.

"Or see if there is anything you need."

Silence. I couldn't shake the feeling I was failing Nona in some way.

After a while, I crossed to the sofa, which was just as scratchy as it looked. I picked up the newspaper. The top left square of the puzzle was filled in. Six-letter word for cavort. (*Prance.*) Completely refashion. (*Remold.*) Old World lizards. (*Agamas.*) Even with the answers penciled in, I didn't get it. Lily and Ashley were crossword fanatics, but I never had understood the appeal. I refolded the paper, used it as a fan. This was so not how I had imagined hospice work during the weeks of training. Bernie Siegel be damned, it was as clear as crystal I'd made a big mistake. How could I have thought I would be of help here and learn something in the doing?

Earlier in the training, I had envisioned how this day would go.

In my imagination, I saw myself sitting by a bed with an elderly patient. The sheets were clean, the room neat. (Although I knew about the messiness and foulness of disease and death, in my visions, the room was always tidy, always smelling of orange oil or lavender like the sprays Lily had used to scent my bed linens when I returned from the hospital after the surgery.) In this sweet-smelling space, I comforted a wise elder and then listened while she talked to me, handed me the road map I had been missing.

Instead, here I was, fighting anxiety and drinking bad coffee in a room so steamy, it could pass for a spa, a paneled-door distance from a very sick man who wouldn't say hello much less let me know the privilege of helping him. It didn't look like I was going to learn the first thing about how to live or find reliable love in that house. Well, it was ridiculous, really. Thirty-two and expecting to find answers to the thorny questions of life from a dying man. Worse than ridiculous. Believing such a thing possible was gullible and naïve, serious character flaws that laid a person wide open to all manner of ruination. This whole thing was a mistake. If, at that moment, Faye had walked through the front door and asked me if I wanted out, I would have said yes instantly and without a second's hesitation. I thought about calling her when I got home and confessing that I could do no good in this overheated, empty house, where I couldn't even see the man I was caring for.

But I did not call her, and that night, I had my first dream about Luke. Not the cancer-riddled patient whom I had not yet even met but the man in the photo with the crow black hair.

I know you.

three

I HAD BECOME a morning person that year on the Cape, something my friends and family back in Richmond wouldn't have believed, for they knew me as a person never fully conscious before nine. But as I was to learn that spring, people can change even the most ingrained habits, release even the most tenacious fears and deep-rooted beliefs. So every day, I was up and dressed by dawn, drawn from my bed by the promise of the soft air and the lilac-rose of early light over Nantucket Sound.

The cottage, built in the late 1800s, was located in the old Ocean Grove Campground in Harwich Port, an area that had managed in large part to escape the notice of nouveau millionaires and their architects, men Faye described as having absolutely no sense and smaller dicks. "It's all compensation," she maintained. "Why else would they need to build these monstrosities that could pass for passenger ships?"

I'd chosen one of the second-floor bedrooms for my studio, primarily because of the view that gave out over the water from the bay window, and had set my worktable in the window's curve. Occasionally, while weaving a necklace or a pin, I would lift my gaze and look out over the water, which, depending on the tides and light, changed colors hourly from a shade so deep, it was nearly black to a silvery slate blue. I liked to watch the early morning walkers, bundled up against the wind and making their way along the shore. I invented stories for them—lives I liked to believe were possible: blissfully uncomplicated loves that traveled a straight path with no blind drives or messy detours; vacation trips to Australia or Greece; hearts that held steady; health that held firm—and then I'd turn my attention back to my work.

That morning, the hair on my worktable was auburn, but it would look dark brown by the time it was twisted tightly into the pattern I'd chosen, a square ribbed chain braid that called for twenty strands, seventy hairs in a strand. I began by affixing slender wooden bobbins to the end of each strand.

Occasionally a client would ask me how I came to make hair jewelry, but I had no ready answer. In life, as in art, there was no accounting for what you liked, what you were drawn to. Something spoke to you, and you couldn't even say why.

The first time I thought about working with hair, I was twenty-four. Up until then, my focus had been pottery, and that summer, during a trip to Wyoming, I found myself drawn to the idea of exploring more substantial pieces. Vessels. Large pots. On a spur-of-the-moment visit to the Buffalo Bill Museum in Cody, I stood before a display of horsehair pottery, mesmerized by the patterns the strands of hair made when laid in clay and fired. A docent pointed out how the hairs of the mane were less coarse than the tail hairs and so created entirely different patterns. It was the first time I had considered hair in any way connected to art. Seeing my interest, the guide led me to another exhibit of belts and bolo ties and wristbands that had been crafted entirely of horsehair. She told me there was a museum in Iowa devoted entirely to hair art jewelry. On the return home, I rerouted my trip and stopped there. I was hooked instantly. I loved how indestructible hair is, how it lasts longer than flesh and bone. Within the month, I had researched patterns and tracked down and special-ordered the materials I would need. I never found the jewelry weird or creepy, as Lily once maintained that she did. Naturally she—and Ashley—made their revulsion plain. "Stick to ceramics; that's respectable, not weird" hung in the air between us, and telling them about the high-society popularity of hair jewelry in Victorian times did nothing to dissuade them. Lily said she couldn't see any earthly reason why I'd want to create something out of another's personal matter.

She had her own hair story, one she told me shortly after I began creating the jewelry. When she was in grade school, the school nurse would appear in the classroom twice a year, armed with a box of wooden toothpicks. The teacher would direct the students to line up in front of her desk, and each, in turn, would be inspected by the nurse, who would pluck two toothpicks from the box and—with narrowed lips and vigilant eyes—separate and lift hair from scalp to check for lice. When satisfied, the nurse would toss the toothpicks into a wastebasket and, excusing the child with a little push on the shoulder, call out "Next." In a silence broken only by the shuffling of feet, the line would inch forward. But occasionally the orderly pattern was broken, and the nurse nodded at the teacher, who would, in turn, usher a shamed child from the room and to the front office. The next day, trailing the reek of creosol, the child would return and for weeks hear the taunts of his classmates. *Cootie-head,* the others would tease. *Bedbug.* "Even you?" I'd asked my mama, recalling that, in our childhood home, name-calling was an offense she didn't permit. Lily nodded. "I cannot tell you how horrible it was to be in that line waiting," she said, as if that explained everything. "I remember in Mrs. Sherman's class— that would be the third grade—I was so nervous waiting for my turn that I peed my pants."

"God, how embarrassing," I said.

"Oh, not nearly as mortifying as being found with lice," Lily said.

"But surely you didn't have to worry," I said. Our grandma was Dutch, and cleanliness was her religion. Lice didn't stand a prayer on her children.

"You just never knew," my mama said.

Occasionally I'd wonder if this old grade school memory was why Lily was always encouraging me to go back to working with clay. Did she associate hair with something dirty, shameful? I had explained the process to her, how I only used clean hair and actually boiled a piece when it was completed—not for sanitary reasons but to tighten the work—and then dried it in an oven. All to no avail. Lily would be happier if I returned to firing clay.

Or maybe not. My mama was once as predictable as a box of saltines, but now I had no idea what she thought or wanted.

As I said, it was its quality of permanence that first drew me to working with hair. It consists largely of the protein keratin, which is insoluble in water, and contains small quantities of manganese, iron, and various salts of lime, properties that make it nearly indestructible. Outlasting flesh and sinew, it has been found in a perfect and unaltered state on mummies more than twenty centuries old.

Although hair jewelry had been created for centuries, most people are unfamiliar with the craft and are amazed when I tell them that, although the technique is difficult to master, human hair can be fashioned into almost any ornament. Over the years, I have created necklaces and earrings, pins and bracelets, watchbands, rings, and lockets. One winter, I made an entire charm bracelet for a woman in Michigan. The charms (a heart, a Celtic cross, a horseshoe, and a harp) were woven using strands of her grandchildren's hair. For another client, I made a wreath of flowers using the hair of five generations in shades so varied, they defied belief, a kind of materialized genealogy. The woman sent me a photo of it, framed under glass and hanging in her living room. I had made a charm for an infant, woven from the hair of his parents, who held to the superstitious belief that this would protect their son. I hoped it would.

But recently more and more of my commissions came from women who were undergoing chemo. While I was at the hospital for my own treatment, word got out through the nurses' grapevine that I made this jewelry, and other patients began to call. Then word spread, and orders started to come in from all over the country. Rather than wait for their hair to fall out, these women created rituals, finding some kind of empowerment in the cutting of their hair, saving it. I understood.

One woman wrote that she'd held a party with her three closest friends. They washed her hair and cut it, each keeping a lock for herself, then set the bulk of it aside to ship to me. I was to weave it into rings for her children. The remaining few strands she had placed out on the porch railing for birds to incorporate into nests. Something I would never do. In Greece, women burned the combing from their brushes, believing that if a bird used it for a nest, their souls would be clawed and torn.

As I worked on these pieces, I wove in hope and something akin, I suppose, to prayer, and sometimes I wrote a note to these women when I sent off the finished piece. I'd tell them that I was a cancer survivor and to hold on to hope, it was what sustained us.

THE AUBURN hair—that of a child who had recently been diagnosed with leukemia—slipped like water between my fingers. I was tying bobbins to the strands when the doorbell broke into my concentration. Automatically I checked my watch, amazed to discover it was already after eleven. I rose and stretched, glad for an opportunity to relieve the tension settling into my neck. By the time I descended the stairs, Faye had already let herself in.

"Hey," she said. "Am I interrupting, or are you ready for coffee?"

"I'm always ready for a break," I said. "Come on in."

"What are you working on?" Faye's interest was sincere. Unlike Lily, Faye was fascinated with my jewelry. At Christmas, I had given her a pin and on her birthday, a bracelet. She seldom went out without wearing one or the other, again unlike my mama, who, as far as I knew, had never worn the loop earrings I made for her. Today Faye wore the bracelet, a narrow band of brown worked in eight-square chain braid with filaments of gold woven in. She carried a box of doughnuts and was wearing sweats she'd probably picked up at the local thrift shop. Faye had more money than Croesus, but she was the most unpretentious person I knew. She was as likely to wear the same faded sweats to a cello concert at the Congregational Church as to the town meeting, where she raised hell over issues of zoning and affordable housing. I thought Faye lived her life according to an inner compass the majority of people seemed to lack.

"Were you always like this?" I asked her one night earlier that winter when we both were one cosmo over our speed limit.

"Like what?" Faye said.

"You know. Not caring what people think."

"Oh, I care, Jessie," she said.

"You do?"

"Yes. I just don't let it rule me."

I didn't think it was true about Faye caring about what people thought of her. I truly believed she didn't give a damn. But there was plenty she did care about. Bigotry. Prejudice of any kind. Cruelty. Suffering. And she held a deep disdain for affectation. In architecture or in people. One Saturday morning, when we were having breakfast at Bonatts, Faye ignored a woman who called her name from a table across the room. "That woman's trying to get your attention," I said. "Well, for God's sake, don't look over or the next thing she'll be inviting herself to join us," she replied. Later she told me the woman was the epitome of ostentatiousness. "She named her house," she said. I said I didn't see why that was so bad. Hell, half the people in town had quarter boards identifying their homes. *Ocean Breeze. Bide-a-While. Sea Reverie. Whale Watch. Gull Cottage.* It's a Cape tradition. "But she answers the phone with her house's name. 'Hello, Ocean Manor,'" Faye mimicked. For someone who was one of the most compassionate people I'd ever met, Faye could have a sharp tongue.

I put on the kettle and told her about the piece I was working on and about the child with leukemia.

"It's curious," Faye said, running a thumb over her bracelet.

"What's that?"

"Our hair is essentially dead, right?"

I nodded. "Beyond the follicle, hair is nothing but dead cells. Same as our fingernails."

"Odd, then, that that part of us which is dead will outlast the living—the blood, body, bones."

"Isn't it," I said as I measured out the coffee. I felt the fingerlings of restlessness that talk of death could engender. (Ashley had told me once that she believed there were only two things that could permanently change a person's life: having a child and killing someone; but I knew having cancer changed you, too. Like genuine love, it leaves you powerless and vulnerable, feelings that never completely disappear, even with recovery.)

Faye didn't wait for the water to boil before she started in on the doughnuts. "What's the latest word from home?" she asked.

"Nothing new there," I said. I hadn't talked to Lily in more than a week, and although one of the reasons I had moved from Richmond was to escape the burden of my mama's concern and her poorly concealed fear that the cancer might return, I was surprised and hurt when her daily check-in calls turned weekly and then even more sporadic. I blamed her involvement with the dentist. I'd heard from Ashley that Lily was still preparing for an Atlantic crossing, a plan that struck me as so perilous that I had regular nightmares about it. Dreadful, sweat-drenched dreams that haunted me in the morning. I couldn't understand why she had agreed to this voyage anyway. Lily had never been particularly athletic, nor had she enjoyed sailing. Knitting intricate lace-patterned shawls was more her style. When I tried to get Ashley to join me in confronting our mama about the dangers of the transatlantic undertaking, dangers that I saw as considerable—we weren't talking about a Sunday sail but a voyage of nearly twenty-five hundred miles from Virginia to the Azores, off the coast of Africa—my sister honestly seemed more concerned about the fact that Lily had stopped coloring her hair.

"Ashley tells me that Lily's started walking to get in shape," I told Faye.

"Good for her," Faye said.

"Well, I think the whole idea is insane. I mean, Lord God, in five years, she'll be seventy. She's too old to be attempting something like—" I stopped short, remembering that Faye and Lily were the same age. I glanced up to see if I'd given offense, but Faye was smiling.

"I wouldn't bet against her, Jessie. People tend to underestimate her, but Lily has always been a determined woman."

I looked for hidden meaning in this statement, but Faye's face was guileless, clear. According to Grandma Ruth, Faye and my daddy had been "an item" before Lily arrived on the scene and swept him up. I didn't know if this was true. Before he died, when we still came to the Cape during the summer, I would watch him every time he was around Faye, but he treated her with the same slightly easy courtesy he showed all women and nothing more. And as far as I could tell, there was no sense of competition between Lily and Faye, although I knew women could be smart about concealing emotions. Once I asked Lily if what my grandma said was true, that she'd swept my daddy off his feet. My mama laughed and said that Grandma Ruth had it all wrong and if there had been any sweeping going on, it had been Lowell who was holding the broom, entirely avoiding the question of whether or not Faye was on the scene prior to her arrival. Back in the fall, shortly after I moved into the cottage and became reacquainted with Faye, I returned to the subject during a phone call to Richmond. "For heaven's sake, Jessie Lynn, that's ancient history," Lily said. And then, "Do you seriously think Lowell would have been interested in Faye Wilson?" In truth, I couldn't picture it, perhaps because my mama had been so beautiful that I couldn't imagine my daddy attracted to anyone else. Certainly not Faye. And the more I got to know Faye, I couldn't really picture her with my daddy, who, while good-looking, successful, and kind, had never been averse to small pretensions.

"YOU'RE DOING good work with Nona Ryder," Faye said, in a sudden change of subject.

"I wish I could do more," I said. After two weeks of volunteering and five visits, I still hadn't laid eyes on Luke Ryder. Except in my dreams, where he had a starring role. I did not mention this to the volunteer group the previous week when we had gathered for our monthly meeting to share our experiences and to air our concerns and problems. (Beth, the former teacher, was already having a slight conflict with the hospice nurse on her case.)

Truthfully, at the last meeting, I had felt totally inadequate. Ben told us how he played gin rummy with his patient, a seventy-two-year-old woman with lung cancer that had metastasized to her bones. Gordon was reading the latest John Grisham to his, a forty-year-old man who had a failed bone marrow transplant. Sal cleaned an oven and did two loads of laundry for a patient with MS. Jennifer drove her cancer patient to his granddaughter's softball game. Muriel was helping a woman with congestive heart failure sort through decades of family photos and arrange them in albums for her children. Listening to them, I marveled at their ease. When they asked how I was doing with Luke, I told them I read while Nona went out on errands. I did not confess to the group that, at odd times in the day, I would find myself preoccupied with the mystery of him, wondering what his favorite food was, what kind of music he liked, if there was a chance he would recover or go into remission, or if it would help him to hear my own story.

Our last group meeting ended with a prayer from the hospice chaplain, and then Faye told us what good and necessary work we were doing. "There is unexpected joy in the terrain of grief, sorrow, and separation," she said, a more poetic statement than was usual for her. She told us we were doing soul work.

. . .

OF COURSE, intellectually, I knew I was helping Nona. There was some satisfaction in knowing that the short breaks away from the house had been doing her good. Her look of exhaustion had eased, if not the haunted shadows in her eyes. One of my former colleagues—a science teacher—had once told me that fetal cells stayed in a mother for twenty-seven years after she gave birth. At the time, I had thought it was one of those amazing facts that defy belief, but watching Nona those days, I no longer doubted it. I even wondered if those cells didn't remain forever, which would explain why she looked as if a real part of her was dying along with her son.

In spite of the difference in our ages, Nona began to confide in me. I learned that Luke was her only child, that he'd been divorced for two years—a fact that didn't break Nona's heart, as she never trusted his ex. "Marcia is one of those women who just can't sit still, always having to be going somewhere or doing something. All that rushing around just about drove Luke mad," she'd told me, adding, "Not like you at all. Anyone can see you have a calmness to you." "One thing no one has ever called me is calm," I had demurred, flustered at the compliment. "Oh yes, you are," she'd insisted. "I can see it in your eyes." Another thing she told me about Luke's ex was that she is not a kind person. "And I'm sorry to say I see some of that in Paige," she'd said. Nona worried about her granddaughter and asked me if I had experimented with pot when I was twenty-two. I lied, thinking that it was more important that she trust me than it was to offer reassurance about Paige.

One day, Nona told me that before Luke got cancer, she had hopes he would remarry. "It came on fast," she said. "Back in January, he was still fishing. I swear I never saw anyone get so sick so fast. You wouldn't believe it." But of course I would. I knew about the shocking swiftness with which illness could derail a life.

I POURED our coffee and got cream from the refrigerator and thought of how the other volunteers helped their clients. "I don't know," I said to Faye. "I don't feel as if I'm making a difference." I ran my hand through my hair, passed a finger over the welt of my scar. I wanted to ask her if there was any hope Luke's cancer would go into remission, but I kept the question locked inside.

She looked straight at me. "Hospice is elegant in its simplicity, Jessie," she said. "We're there for care. We're there to lift the burden. That's all, and it's more than enough."

I wanted to do more. I wanted to help the raven-haired man who sat in self-imposed isolation. "Honestly," I said, as I split a chocolate glazed doughnut and handed her half, "I still can't understand why you assigned me to this case."

Faye licked traces of chocolate from her fingers. "A hunch," she said. Her voice was clear and sure.

"Well, I hope it pays off," I said.

Months later, I would recall this chilly April morning and wonder what would have happened if, while we sat there, eating doughnuts and drinking coffee, Faye had not only heard my doubts but had began to share them. What if I had told her about how preoccupied I had become with Luke? What if, regardless of her hunch, Faye had assigned someone else to volunteer at the Ryder house? Could all that lay ahead have been averted? Or were some things preordained, destined to play out to their end?

four

WHEN I HEADED out for the Ryders' the next afternoon, I was in what my grandma Ruth called a pissy-ant mood. It was raw and drizzly, an absolutely miserable day that had even Faye grumbling. Earlier Ashley had called and had gone on and on about the lovely Richmond weather, as if by living in the North for the past eight months, I had contracted total amnesia about a southern spring. Today was in the midseventies, Ashley said, adding that the tulips were up and the lilacs and redbuds were in bloom. I told her that we were a few weeks behind in Massachusetts but that the crocuses and snowdrops were starting to poke through the grass. I didn't tell my sister that it had been raining for three straight days or that the lawn was still winter-dead brown or that Faye said Cape Cod didn't have spring, just a long, dreary winter that would suddenly be summer one day in late June. I loved Ashley, but from time to time, we fell into this weird kind of one-upmanship over the dumbest things. Like weather. That morning, after we hung up, I found myself growing homesick for the spring Ashley described, and for my mama, and wondered what I was doing on the Cape and what this year was proving. I didn't feel any closer to figuring out where I was heading than I had been back in September. Lately I had found myself missing teaching and missing my students. And mourning the lack of romance in my life. At one of our meetings, Gordon said he was discovering that one of the things about hospice work was that it helped him put his own life in perspective and made his problems seem minor. I was waiting. I had gotten a few leads on jobs from the alumni office at the Art

Institute, where I'd graduated, sent out inquiries and résumés, but so far nothing had panned out. On the man front, I had had precisely two dates since January, both blind dates and both disasters: a widower with denture breath, clearly looking for a new wife to care for him, no thank you, and a guy who'd had so many DWIs that I'd had to pick him up in my car and drive us to the Squire. I was beginning to feel like a nun. When I mentioned this to Faye, she said it seemed to her I had two choices. I could buy myself a vibrator, or I could think of this time as a kind of purifying fast; I told her that celibacy as a lifestyle was seriously overrated.

I had fully expected I would be married by this point in my life. Women in our family married young. My sister's theory—and Lily's, too—was that I hadn't spent enough time and energy focusing on the kind of man I wanted to attract. Not a problem Ashley herself had ever had. The day she fastened the hooks on her first double-A bra, Ashley settled her attention to the qualities she wanted in a perfect husband, portraits that over the years underwent subtle alterations. Even at thirteen, she took these deliberations seriously, no detail too minute to escape consideration. Hair and eye color and build were obviously up for debate, but so, too, were teeth, feet, brains, and the kind of car he drove, often in that order. I swear she actually spent hours contemplating whether smooth hands were better than calloused. In the end, she'd opted for somewhat calloused, just rough enough to add sensation to a back rub. There were certain deal-breakers. Her future husband would have to be elegantly built and slightly edgy, just enough to make him interesting over the long haul. And then Ashley ended up mad for Daniel, a man on the wrong side of stocky who was too kind for his own good. Which just went to show you. The human heart was too fickle to be trusted.

Ashley was right, though, about me. I never spent a lot of time thinking about the particulars of my dream match. When girlfriends asked what my type was, I'd laugh and say male. But recently—running on the beach or in the evening while working on a bracelet—I would find myself daydreaming about a man I could truly imagine at my side. He stood tall and had raven black hair. He drove a truck.

At night, too, I continued to dream about Luke. In one, we were in a boat that carved a wide wake in the sea behind us. We were laughing. It was ridiculous, of course, like mooning over a movie star. And just as far-fetched. I still hadn't met him in person. I was swooning over a photograph. I chalked it up to an excess of hormones and the mystery of the as yet invisible Luke. I reconsidered Faye's suggestion that I get a vibrator.

ON MY way to Nona's, I detoured for my daily run to Dunkin' Donuts. Inside, I filled my Thermos with French roast and on impulse ordered some cranberry muffins—the hydrogenated-shortening, heart-attack-in-a-box kind that the Food Police are always ranting about. Right after my operation, I had been vigilant about what I put into my body. I had cut back on meat and alcohol, eliminated artificial sweeteners. As time went on, I had become less disciplined and slipped back into my old, bad habits. Still, thinking about the fat, I almost put the carton back on the shelf, but then I remembered something else from Bernie Seigel's lecture back in the autumn, a story about a woman who was furious when she learned that she had cancer. "I don't smoke," she told him, as if bringing up a bargain she had struck. "I stopped eating ice cream years ago." As I remembered it, Seigel's point was that there was no surefire prophylactic against illness and death and that it was better to eat an occasional ice cream cone that brings joy than give it up and be angry. Good point, I thought. Maybe that was one of the tricks I was learning in starting a new life. Enjoy small pleasures.

A bucket next to the register was filled with daffodils, six stems to a bunch. On a whim, triggered no doubt by my earlier conversation with Ashley and my sister's picture of spring in Richmond, I bought two bunches.

When I arrived at the Ryders', Jim, the hospice health aide, was already there, earlier than usual. *People think the volunteers are angels,* Faye told us during our training, *but it's the health aides who are the real saints. The rest of us get the credit, but they're the ones who do the heavy lifting. The messy stuff of daily life. This whole program wouldn't work without them.*

I parked by the curb so that, when Jim left, he'd be able to back his green Jeep out of the drive. Nona met me at the door. Her face was splotchy, her eyes swollen and red-rimmed, and the sight unnerved me, for, like Faye, Nona was old Cape Cod stock, stoic and sensible, emotions held in check. Immediately, I feared the worst and my heart rate quickened, but then I heard the sound of conversation from the other room. Jim was saying something, although I couldn't make out the words. There was a pause and then deep laughter. I took a breath. Not a crisis then. Nona was simply worn out. I tried to imagine what it must be like to have your only child be dying, but it was too painful to contemplate.

"We could sure use some sun," I said.

"Welcome to April on Cape Cod," Nona said.

I often felt like I was saying the wrong thing, talking about the weather while, in the next room, her son was dying. In training, we'd been told that ordinary conversations gave families a break from the constant sorrow and brought normalcy to their days. I knew—from experience—that this was possible, and yet it still felt odd to converse about things like the weather. There was another burst of laughter from Luke's room. We both turned and looked at the closed door.

"Jim's good for Luke," Nona said.

"I know," I said. I felt a stab of envy, and then felt small and mean-spirited.

In the kitchen, Nona spent a few minutes combing the cupboards for a vase to put the daffodils in, all the time muttering about how Marcia had made off with everything that wasn't nailed

down. According to Nona, the divorce was a nightmare, and Luke
nearly lost the house over it. I thought that, in some way, she
blamed Marcia for Luke getting cancer. Earlier she had confided
that Paige still held her mother responsible for the divorce. Finally
Nona unearthed a water glass large enough for the job. Watching, I
noticed, not for the first time, how deformed by arthritis her fingers were. I thought of all the work caring for Luke entailed, even
with hospice help. Again, as I had been the first time I saw her, I was
swept by a desire to fold her in my arms and comfort her. I held
back.

"This was sweet of you," Nona said, as she put the flowers in the
tumbler.

"It isn't anything," I said.

"I never see a daffodil but that I don't think of my mother," she
said.

"Did she like them?"

"You should have seen our yard in the spring. It was a carpet of
yellow. Just a carpet. One year, there was even a picture in the *Cape
Cod Times*. There must have been a thousand bulbs in that yard, and
she planted every one herself." She set the flowers on the table and
crossed to where I was standing and gave me a quick hug. This was
the first time we had embraced in the three weeks I had been coming to the house. Then she pulled away and sat at the table. "We had
a fight," she said.

Her words were so totally unexpected that I wasn't sure I'd
heard her correctly. "What?"

"We had a fight. Last night."

"Who?"

"Luke. And me."

"Oh," I said. Words flashed through my brain, the precise
phrases of glib sympathy we had been trained to withhold. *Don't
worry. Everything will be fine.* It wouldn't be fine. Everyone knew
that.

"It was so stupid," she said.

"Arguments sometimes are." I thought about Ashley and the foolish things we clashed over.

"It was my fault."

"Do you want to tell me what happened?" A safe question. Neutral.

"It was stupid," Nona said again, shaking her head. She looked fragile and every minute of her seventy years. "It was about the damn inspection sticker."

"Inspection sticker?"

"For his truck."

I waited.

"It expired last month." She took a little breath.

"And . . . ," I said. We had both lowered our voices.

"Well, he's been all upset about it. There isn't a day goes by but that he doesn't harp on it, saying I need to get it taken care of." She pulled a tissue out of her pocket and wiped her nose. "Leave it to me to say the dumbest thing. I told him there was no point in spending thirty dollars for a sticker when the truck was just sitting in the driveway not going anywhere." She looked over at me. "I probably shouldn't have said that. But I kept thinking of the cost. Thirty dollars. I know it might not sound like a lot, but money is just *melting away* here."

I reached out, touched her shoulder, nodded.

"Well, Luke just started yelling at me. He said why didn't I go the hell back to Wellfleet. He said he didn't need me just hanging around waiting for him to die. He told me to forget about the god-damned sticker, he'd get someone else to take care of it." Nona twisted the tissue in her fingers. "There I was worrying about thirty dollars. What does it matter?"

She looked beaten, exhausted, heartbroken. The last weeks would have been hard for anyone, but at Nona's age, the unrelent-ing burden had to be harrowing. I knew from our training that the stress of constant care often led to illness or early death of the care-

giver. At that minute, I wanted to go straight into Luke's room and
tell him that he had no excuse to be cruel to his mother, that she
was doing the best she could. All the wrong things, of course. For
the first time, it occurred to me that it made sense that most of the
volunteers were retired. They had more experience in life and
knew how to handle tricky situations. I struggled to think of the
exact right thing to say, but before I could come up with anything
that seemed right, I heard the door to Luke's room open and then
close. Jim came into the kitchen, his arms full of soiled sheets. I
watched the effort it took for Nona to pull herself together.

"Hey, Jessie," Jim said.

"Hi, Jim." He was short and solid. James Cagney with a pony-
tail.

"Nice shoes," he said, nodding at my paint-stained and worn-
out Nikes.

"Yours, too." His Doc Martens had to have been born sometime
back in the eighties.

He crossed to the basement door and dropped the sheets on the
floor. "So, Nona," he said, "did you hear about the Buddhist who refused Novocain during his root canal?"

Nona shook her head.

"He wanted to transcend dental medication."

"That's terrible," she said, but for the first time since I arrived,
she was smiling.

"Ya like that, huh?" He crossed and stood behind her, placed his
hands on her shoulders, and began to massage her neck. She sighed
softly.

"Did you hear about the skunk that went to church?" he said.
"He had his own pew."

Nona and I rolled our eyes, groaned.

"Bad," Nona said.

"Pitiful," I added.

"What are you talking about? That's my best stuff." He kneaded
Nona's shoulders. "You ladies are killing me here."

I looked at Nona and froze. Whenever I let a word like that slip into the conversation with her—*death, kill, dying*—it seemed to hang in the air sparking neon until I could cover it with a spew of words. Jim let them out as if they carried no more weight than any other ordinary, run-of-the-mill words. Faye had the same natural way about her. I doubted I would ever attain that kind of ease.

Jim's pager beeped. He checked the number.

"Okay," he said. "You two can beg me all you want, but I've only got time for one more, then I've got to run."

Nona and I looked at each other, shook our heads.

"This guy and girl had sex," Jim started, glanced over at me. "I don't know if you're old enough for this one, Jess."

I grinned. "Chance it."

He grinned back. "If you insist. So he said, 'If I'd known you were a virgin, I'd have taken more time,' and she says, 'If I'd known you had more time, I would have taken off my panty hose.'"

While we were laughing, he leaned over and kissed Nona on the cheek. "See you tomorrow, sweetheart. You've got my number if you need anything before then."

"Honestly," Nona said, after he left, "if he was seven inches taller and twenty years older, I'd make a play for him."

"He's gay, Nona," I said, although—sexual preferences aside—Jim had started to look pretty good to me, too.

She looked surprised. "Do you really think so?"

Before we could get into the specifics of Jim's sexual orientation, a car pulled into the drive.

"There's Helen," she said, and sighed. "I know she means well, but sometimes I don't feel like getting out." She sighed again and ran a hand over her hair. "I must look a mess."

"You look fine," I said. She did look a little better. Jim medicine.

She fished a tube of lipstick out of her handbag and smeared some on. It was a vivid magenta, as much a mistake as the coal-dyed hair. "How cold is it out?" she said.

"It's raw."

She chose a jacket from the coat pegs by the back entry. I got up and picked up the sheets Jim had left by the basement door.

"Oh, leave those. I'll do them when I get back."

"It's no bother."

"Please," she said, "just leave them." It was as difficult for her to accept assistance as it was for Luke. I had told her that volunteers were to help in any way. Clean. Do laundry. Run errands. Write letters. Nona always refused. She said I was doing enough just coming by and giving her a break for an hour. Pigheaded pride, Lily would call it. A Cape Cod native's stubbornness, said Faye, who saw it reflected in herself.

"Plant a potato, get a potato," I said.

"What?"

"Just noticing that Luke came by his obstinacy naturally."

"Don't you be getting fresh with me," Nona said, but she was smiling. That smile made me feel as if maybe, for the first time, I was doing something worthwhile.

AFTER SHE left, I had the customary moment of anxiety at being alone with Luke, but with each visit, it was becoming easier to control. I washed out my cup, wiped down the Formica, listened for sounds from his room. I wondered what joke Jim had told him that caused that deep and surprising laugh. Personally, I thought men's laughter was just about the sexiest thing. God, talk about grim to no prospects. Now I was getting turned on by a short, gay nurse and a dying man. The fact was, I was so horny even widowers with halitosis were starting to look good. Like I said, I'd been giving serious thought to Faye's suggestion about a vibrator.

At the window feeder, a pair of blue jays were feasting. Below, a chipmunk was munching on sunflower seeds that had spilled on the ground. On impulse, I opened the box of muffins, crumbled one. I unlatched the window and tossed the crumbs to the chipmunk, spread a few more in the feeder. Completely wasteful of good food, but it cheered me up and in an odd way gave me hope. I left the rest of the muffins for Nona. Until that morning, when she told me about not wanting to spend thirty dollars for an inspection sticker—what had she said? money was just melting away—I supposed I hadn't fully appreciated the toll Luke's illness was exacting on this family.

Ignoring Nona's instructions, I picked up the sheets Jim had thrown in the corner and took them down to the laundry. I swallowed against the smell of sour sweat and stuffed them in the washer, then measured out detergent, set the water temperature to hot. When the cycle clicked in, I checked out the basement. It was cluttered with fishing gear, paint cans, lawn furniture. A white enameled picnic table and some plastic yard chairs were piled by the steps leading to the bulkhead. There was a coffee can on the floor by the water heater, placed to catch the drips of a slow leak. One corner of the basement had been converted into a gym with a set of free weights and workout bench. I pictured a dark-haired man in cutoffs doing reps, building up biceps, carving out a six-pack. I crossed to the bench. The weight bar was cool beneath my fingers. I lost track of time, standing there and staring at the bench, and then became aware of the creaking of floor joists overhead. Luke's dog, I thought. I had encountered the Lab once or twice when Nona brought him to the kitchen to let him out before she left, though mostly he stayed with Luke or just outside Luke's door. I switched off the light and headed up the stairs, heard a woman's voice from some daytime talk show. I was halfway across the kitchen before I realized it wasn't a TV program but a real voice coming from Luke's room.

I was checking out the car in the drive, an ancient blue Volvo, more rust than metal, when a girl came out of Luke's room, leading the black dog. She wore tooled turquoise boots and low-rise jeans that went so far beyond tight, they could cause internal injury. Tendrils from a tattoo snaked up out of the waistband and disappeared beneath an orange cropped T-shirt. She had hard, dark eyes and yellow hair the wrong side of unruly that framed a slender, strong-jawed face. The total effect was what Grandma Ruth called trailer trash. Over the years, I'd had this type in my classroom. They always looked tougher than they were, and often, curiously, they were the most creative. Usually they ended up being the ones I missed the most at graduation. I held out my hand. "You must be Paige," I said. "I'm Jessie. From hospice."

"I know," she said. She barely brushed my hand with hers before placing the dog's leash in my palm. "Rocker needs to go out." The dark eyes defied me to argue.

The Lab came right to me, sniffed my crotch. I nudged his head away.

"When he's finished," Paige went on, "just bring him in. Then you can go along."

"Nona's gone out," I said.

Paige gave me a *well, duh* look. Obviously Nona was not there. "I'll stay with Luke," she said. "There's really no need for you to hang around." She returned to her father's room before I could get out one word.

Difficult. Can be confrontational. The notes in Luke's file didn't half sum up his daughter. I was thinking more along the lines of *Impossible*. I didn't bother to put on my jacket and got rain-soaked while Rocker sniffed around for a spot to take a dump. (Rocker. What was he? A chair?) While he deposited a remarkably rank pile, I replayed the scene with Paige. No *How are you? Nice to meet you.* Just *Rocker needs to go out.* If Ashley were here, she would demand an apology from the girl, but that was another way I differed from my sister. And apparently from Paige. I tried to avoid confrontations. No doubt Paige felt like she was the only one in the universe to ever lose a parent or to be estranged from her mama. If opportunity presented itself, I would tell her that, in some ways, she was fortunate, in that she could tell Luke that she loved him and he could say it right back to her. At least, they still had time. They had been given that.

Inside, I unclipped the leash while Rocker shook his coat dry, spraying water three feet in every direction. I yanked a couple of squares from a roll of paper towels and blotted my hair and face. While I waited for Paige to reappear, I found a stainless steel mixing bowl, which I filled with tap water and set on the floor. The Lab attacked it with doggy enthusiasm. I found a ballpoint pen and a small pad of ruled paper by the phone and jotted a couple of lines for Nona, telling her the wash was ready to put in the dryer, and tucked it beneath the tumbler of daffodils.

"Are you all set, then?"

Paige stood in the doorway, arms akimbo. I saw in her eyes a familiar expression, one I'd seen reflected in every mirror I had passed during the summer and fall that I turned fifteen, the year my daddy died. Anger and defiance. The twin masks of fear.

A long moment passed before I let out a deep breath. "All set," I said.

"Okay," Paige said.

"I've left a note for Nona."

"Yeah. Whatever," she said, enunciating it in that bored two-word way that drove me nuts. What ever.

I bit back a retort.

She watched as I gathered up my things. *Listen,* I wanted to tell her, *I know what you're going through. My daddy died when I was fourteen. It sucks.* Before I could open my mouth, the girl turned and went back to Luke's room. Rocker looked up with grave retriever eyes.

"It stinks," I told him. "Big time." Even after seventeen years, the sense of missing my daddy hit me hard and left me dry-mouthed, like I was sucking on a stone.

But as I headed back to the cottage, despite my encounter with Paige, my mood lifted. I recalled Nona's smile, her confidences, the birds at the feeder. Small matters, and yet I felt that things were changing. I was making a difference. I could feel it clearly, like spring. Rebirth was in the air.

five

SATURDAY DAWNED CLEAR and beautiful. Earlier that morning, I had opened the south-facing windows of our cottage, and now the air spread around me, heavy with the raw, marly smells of spring. Armed with a cup of coffee and a pad and pencil, I settled in by the phone.

The previous week, I had received an Easter card from Lily, and at the sight of my mama's handwriting, I was so overwhelmed with home-longing that I actually considered flying down to Richmond for the holiday weekend. I'd been trying to justify the cost of the flight on my overstretched budget when Nona called and asked if I would come over on Sunday morning to stay with Luke while she went to a church service, and that settled the matter. For the first time, Nona had actually asked me for something. My feeling of hope was reinforced. We were making progress.

I had planned on picking up a box of chocolates at the Candy Manor, and in fact had been on my way into Chatham, when I had gotten the idea of making Nona the Easter bread that has been a holiday tradition in our family for as long as I could remember. I turned right around and headed back to the cottage, all the while imagining Nona's face when I handed her the bread, an intricate braid of raised yeast dough with eggs nested in the plaits, their shells colored with natural infusions. Onion skins for the yellow, beets for red, spinach for green. "Jesus be, Lily," my daddy said one year as he watched our mama steeping the vegetables, "wouldn't it be a damn sight easier if you just bought an egg-dyeing kit at Winn-Dixie?" His suggestion was so blasphemous, Lily hadn't even bothered to respond; this, after all, was a woman who used a toothbrush to clean the *insides* of the Lucite faucets in the guest bathroom. Dyeing eggs with vegetables was kid's play for her.

As I dialed, I pictured my mama's delight at the reason for my call. For years and years, Lily had been after both Ashley and me to make copies of family recipes.

"Sweetie," Lily said when she picked up, "I was just thinking of you."

"You were?"

"This very minute. Just last night, I was asking Ashley if she'd heard from you lately. I've been wondering how you're doing."

"I'm fine. Busy. Missing you all." I fiddled with the pencil and tried to calculate what was so different about my mama's voice. It sounded like Lily and yet not like her. "I wish I could be there tomorrow," I said. "Ashley's boys must be big enough now for the egg hunt."

"The egg hunt," Lily said, and gave an easy laugh. "Well, that brings back memories."

"It does, doesn't it?" I remembered how Ashley and I would wake at dawn and race outside, our bare feet and the hems of our nightgowns quickly soaked through as we looked for the foil-covered candy eggs our parents had hidden in the tulip beds. Now that ritual had passed to another generation. *Another generation.* Talk about feeling old. "And then we'd have brunch," I said. "With Great-grandma Helfgott's Easter bread." I drew a quick sketch of a circular braid on the pad, added the eggs. "In fact, that's one of the reasons I'm calling."

"Now that was a good deal of work," Lily said before I could continue. "Lord knows I'm not grieving to see the last of that."

"The last of what?"

"The Easter braid. That's what you're talking about, isn't it? God, when I think of all that work. I swear I must have been brain-dead."

"What do you mean the last of it? You aren't making it this

year?" I pictured Lily standing at the marble-topped counter kneading dough, the kitchen fragrant with the scent of cardamom. "I always thought you liked making the bread."

Lily laughed again, and in the laugh, I identified the change in my mama's voice. She sounded lighter. Younger.

"There's a hard way of doing things," Lily continued, "and an easy way, and the hard way isn't always the path to virtue. More often it's a downhill road leading directly to a martyr's grave."

"You're really not going to make it this year?"

"Not if you paid me in emeralds." Lily said this with the exaggerated weariness of a woman who had a whole string of Easter brunches under her belt and didn't plan on one more. "In fact, I'm not stepping one foot in the kitchen. I'd rather herd cats."

"What are you going to do?"

"Jan and I are sailing up to Baltimore for a few days. As a matter of fact, you were lucky to catch me. We're leaving in a couple of hours."

Jan and I. I didn't like the sound of that. Exclusive of others. "You're not going to be home for Easter?"

"Not this year."

"What's Ashley going to do?"

"I'm not sure. I think she said something about how she and Daniel and the boys are going to his parents'."

Lily wasn't *sure* what Ashley was doing? This didn't sound at all like our mama. Our entire lives, she had been hands-on, involved with the daily details of our lives. Perhaps too much so. Our rift had begun when I had started to rebel against the constraints of her involvement. Now suddenly she'd gone AWOL, turned into an absentee parent, no longer interested in keeping traditions. No longer worried about me. No longer checking in daily to circle around her concerns. *Was I tired? Any headaches?*

"So what have you planned for tomorrow?" Lily asked.

"I'm going over to Nona's in the morning."

"Nona?" she said.

I tried to conceal my impatience. "Nona Ryder. Her son is the hospice patient."

Silence echoed on Lily's end of the phone.

I pushed on. "And later in the afternoon, I'm having dinner with Faye."

"Well, that sounds lovely," Lily said.

"I guess," I said, lost. Here was what was bothering me. Throughout my life, even if I wasn't as close to my mama as Ashley—thick as thieves, the two of them—Lily had been the compass I could count on. Ashley could get knocked up, get married, have kids, I could move, date and break up with dozens of men, develop a tumor—*our daddy could die*—and Lily would always be there. Steady. Okay, annoying, too. But dependable. Until now.

"So did you get my card?" Lily asked.

I pulled myself back to the conversation. "Yes," I managed. "Thanks."

"And?"

"What?"

"What did you think?" Lily prompted, her voice again girlish.

I knew exactly what Lily was asking. Tucked inside the card was a photo of a couple in shorts, backpacks, and hiking boots. Scrawled on the back: *Jan and me on the first leg of the Appalachian Trail.*

"You look different," I said. True enough. Although Ashley had been harping on the fact for months, I wasn't prepared for our mama's transformation into a stranger with gray hair. "I didn't even recognize you."

Lily waved this comment aside. "What about Jan?" she said. "What did you think of him?"

"It's hard to tell from a snapshot," I hedged. In truth, I'd dug out a magnifying glass from the desk, the one my daddy used to pore over his stamp collection, and had studied the new man in my mama's life. Sandy blond hair and—if the color reproduction was true—bluish green eyes. Muscular legs. He looked more like a carpenter than a dentist. The photo alone was enough to make me want to fly home and straighten Lily out.

"I really want you to meet him," Lily was saying. "I know you'll be crazy about him."

This I very much doubted. Who knew who this Jan was or what he wanted with my mama. Daddy had been good with money and left Lily fairly well off. It was entirely possible this dentist wanted a meal ticket. You heard about that kind of thing all the time, and Lily could be really naïve. Who was watching out for her interests? I made a mental note to bring this up with Ashley. Okay, maybe I was the one meddling this time, but I was honestly concerned. Lily, alone and aging, was vulnerable.

"He's looking forward to meeting you, too," Lily said.

"You look so different with your hair gray," I said—a deliberate subject shift. I remembered what Ashley had said during one of our earlier conversations: Why would a person deliberately choose to look older? Especially if she was dating someone ten years younger.

"For God's sake, don't start," Lily said. "I get enough of that from your sister."

"And what's this about hiking?" I asked. "The last thing I knew, you wouldn't go across the street without taking the car."

"We've been getting in shape for the voyage."

"So you're still thinking about doing that?" I said.

"Not thinking about it. It's set. We leave early in June."

"I think it's crazy."

"It is kind of crazy, isn't it?" Lily laughed. "I guess that's part of the appeal."

Now I didn't even try to conceal my exasperation. "Why are you doing this, Mama?" I didn't just mean the sailing. I meant all of it: allowing herself to go gray, dating a man nearly a dozen years younger, dropping family traditions. Again I thought about flying down to straighten things out, but even as the idea occurred to me, I knew its futility. Lily had always regarded my input with amused tolerance.

There was a pause. "I don't know if you'll understand," Lily said.

"Try me."

"Because I want to feel alive."

"Alive?" *Alive?*

"Exactly."

I felt the sudden flash of guilt I had had when I learned about the tumor. "Is this about me?"

"What about you?"

When I'd first been diagnosed, I used to feel guilty around Lily, knowing the worry I was causing. Now I wondered if in some way my having cancer hadn't shaken her life in an unhealthy way and led to all of her recent actions: The dentist. This crazy idea of crossing the Atlantic. "You know," I said.

"This isn't about you, Jessie," Lily said. "It's about me. I want to feel excited about something again."

Jesus, I thought, *if she starts talking about sex, I'm out of here.* "Do you have to sail across the world to feel alive?"

Lily laughed. "Would you rather I buy a motorcycle?"

"What, Mama? Those are the choices?" I took a deep breath. "I'm just worried about you. I mean, think about it. You're sixty-five years old."

"I'm perfectly aware of my age, thank you."

"And you're talking about sailing across the ocean. Can't you see how dangerous that is?"

"The truth of it is, I'd rather die sailing to Europe than at home in bed."

Or hunched over a steering wheel, stopped short in the prime of life by something a lot bigger than a red light. I pushed the thought away, got back to Lily's transformation, which I couldn't explain. "This doesn't even sound like you," I said.

"Life doesn't stay the same, honey. People change."

"I do. I stay the same." This, I suddenly realized, was true. In spite of all I'd been through, in spite of wanting a new beginning, I was essentially the same person I'd been before the tumor, before my move to the Cape.

"Maybe you shouldn't."

"What?"

"Stay the same."

I ignored this. "So, what are you saying? You're having some kind of late-onset change-of-life crisis?"

Another pause, this one longer. "Jessie, honey," Lily said, her voice calm, "two things: I love you. And I'm not having this conversation." And then, to my amazement, my mama hung up.

A HALF hour later, I was still sitting there staring at the pad and the doodle of the nest and eggs, immobilized by my conversation with Lily. The sound of the UPS truck roused me.

"Hey, Kenny," I said, as the driver approached with a package. During the last six months, he had made so many deliveries for the jewelry business that we had developed a first-name friendship. He was married with two kids and a wife who worked days at a retirement home in Hyannis.

"About time we had some sun," he said.

"Sure is," I said, as I signed for the padded envelope. The return address was marked Sonoma, California. I recognized the customer's name from earlier correspondence. Another cancer patient.

I carried the envelope up to my studio. The morning's work—the piece for the young leukemia patient—was still on the table. I had nearly completed weaving the braid and could soon begin fashioning the bracelet.

I opened the envelope. Like most of my customers, this one had sent the hair sealed in a plastic bag, bound by elastic. When I withdrew the duplicate order form, I checked for a note and was surprised to find none. People often included personal anecdotes or histories along with the hair, and although many were from women who had cancer, there were other stories, too, like that from the mother whose son had just joined the navy. She sent a strand she had kept ever since his first haircut. Now she wanted it preserved in a locket. (Imagine, I thought when I received the order, keeping those flaxen strands so carefully for all those years. I had held the hair and wondered if I would ever know the terrifying joy of having a child.) A coed at Mississippi State sent her hair braided into a plait as thick as the arm of a child. She wrote that, all through her childhood, her mother had braided her hair every morning, pulling it with a vengeance, so tight that she wept. Now she was setting herself free. A woman from Fond du Lac told me that her hair held all her power. She wanted me to create a "power piece" for her that she could pin on her clothes. A widow from Sante Fe told me the Andeans believed that, after death, hair was braided into a bridge that helped the soul of the dead cross a dangerous ravine to reunite to the body. She had sent strands of her husband's hair, the yellowish off-white of blond gone gray. A natural blond from Washington asked me if I knew that Princess Diana had spent more than six thousand dollars a year having her hair bleached. I hadn't known that but didn't doubt it for a minute.

But, as I said, the envelope Kenny delivered contained only the order form and the customer's hair caught up in an elastic band. I set it aside and tried to concentrate on my morning's work and replaying my earlier conversation with Lily.

LATER THAT afternoon, as prearranged, Faye picked me up, and we headed over to Brewster.

"Okay, what's going on?" Faye said, as she swung out onto Route 28, cutting in front of a pickup and ignoring the driver, who was honking furiously.

"What do you mean?"

She turned to look at me. "Not hard to figure out. You haven't said five words since you got into the car."

"Watch the road," I said. There. Three words.

Faye tailgated the car in front of us, edging left to pass when an opportunity presented itself. Unmindful, the car ahead crept along. LORPs, Faye called them. Little old retired people who flooded the roads, driving along at a pace twenty miles south of the limit, turn signals perpetually switched on, chins held level with the hubs of their steering wheels. Although Faye was saintly in a number of ways, patience while behind the wheel wasn't her long suit. The LORPs drove her nuts. If it were up to her, she'd have them outlawed. Or permitted on the roads one hour per day. Ten to eleven A.M. Max. Her idea was to clear the roads of everyone else and let the LORPs duke it out, which they often did, backing into one another in the post office lot on a regular basis. Last fall, she advised me not to venture anywhere near there until after noon, by which time, the last of them had picked up their mail. According to Faye, most of them drove like they'd undergone vertebrae fusion, unable to turn their heads more than two centimeters left or right. Nights you were safe, she said, since they didn't like to drive in the dark, but days you definitely were throwing the dice.

"You DON'T have to tell me if you don't want," Faye said.

"Tell you what?"

"What it is that's bothering you."

"It's nothing, really."

"Nothing?"

I sighed. "Okay, it's Lily. I talked to her this morning, and I've barely been able to work since."

"And . . ."

"I don't know." I really didn't want to get into this and most certainly didn't want to tell Faye about my mama hanging up on me. Talking about Lily to Faye made me feel disloyal. "I guess I'm just worried about her."

"Isn't that backward? Isn't the mother the one who's supposed to worry about the daughter?"

I bit at my lip.

"Okay," Faye said. "What specifically are you concerned about?"

"Well, it's this man she's with, for one thing," I said. "This dentist person. Who is he? What does he want with her?"

"I think that should be pretty obvious, Jessie."

"You think he's after her money?"

Faye cocked an eyebrow. "I was thinking along the lines of something more carnal."

I stared at her. "Sex?"

"Desire doesn't dry up with the passing of decades, you know."

"Jesus, Faye."

She laughed. "More power to her, I say. I don't know why she didn't start seeing men years ago."

"Not another word, okay. I don't even want to go there."

Faye laughed again. "So what's the other thing?"

"What do you mean?"

"You said you were worried about the dentist for one thing. What's the other?"

"Well it's everything, really."

"Can you be more specific?"

"It's like she's not even the same person." I told Faye about how Lily wasn't hosting the traditional family Easter brunch.

"Well, that's the best thing I've heard in a long time."

"It is?"

"It means she's letting go of what no longer fits. She's changing."

"That wins the Understatement of the Year Award."

Faye looked at me. "Why exactly are you upset about what she's doing?"

"It's crazy. Especially this sailing thing. You've seen her on the ocean, Faye. She doesn't know a boom from a broom handle."

"True," Faye said, laughing. "Okay. What's the worst that could happen?"

I stared at Faye. "Hellooooo? She's crossing the Atlantic. Storm at sea. Death." *Death*. There. I'd said it.

"And that's the worst?"

"Isn't that bad enough?"

"I don't know." Faye reached over and clasped my hand. "Is it worse than dying from cancer?"

I stared at her, again wondered if Lily had broken her promise not to tell Faye about my illness. At the same time, perversely, I wished Faye did know, since I was finding it increasingly difficult to keep from her.

"We don't get to choose our deaths, Jessie. But we can choose how to live."

"Okay, maybe it's totally selfish on my part, but I don't want anything to happen to her. I don't know what I'd do if she died."

Faye slipped her hand free from mind and reached up and adjusted the visor. "You'd go on."

"I don't know." I couldn't imagine life without Lily.

"You would," Faye insisted. "We all do."

I assumed she was talking about her late husband and about all the deaths she had seen in her work with hospice, but Faye surprised me.

"When I was a little younger than you," she said, "I had a dog, an Irish setter named Rusty. He was the most important thing in the world to me."

I thought about Rocker and wondered if the Lab was the most important thing in the world to Luke.

Faye fell silent, then took a long breath. "Sorry. Even now, after all these years, it's hard to remember."

"What happened?"

"He got sick, and the vet said he had to be put down. He gave me a form to sign, and I managed to scrawl something. I didn't think I could bear to stay there in that room—I always believed I was weak that way, avoided funerals like the plague, but I didn't want Rusty with strangers. No one should have to die alone, not even a dog."

I thought of my daddy, slumped over the steering wheel, dead before the light changed to green, then willed my mind away. "That doesn't sound like you. The part about not being strong, I mean."

"Believe me, it was. Anyway, I knew I had to be there with Rusty. I had to. When I went in, he was too weak to lift his head off the table. He had just vomited, and I can still remember the horrific smell. I held him in my arms and talked to him until it was over."

"I couldn't have done that," I said.

"Yes, you could have, Jessie. We're stronger than we know. Each of us. We don't know what we're capable of until we are tested. Look at Lily. She believed she had to be the perfect wife, the ideal mother, and now she realizes she doesn't have to be perfect at all."

"Do you think that explains why she's let her hair go gray?"

"Well, in all the years I've known Lily, I've never seen her without makeup. She even wore mascara when she was swimming."

I laughed, relieved to be off the subject of death. "It's true," I said.

"So she's changing and challenging herself. Can't you see what a good thing it is that she is daring to try something new?"

"I guess," I said. "I just wish she'd choose something less ambitious to start with than a transatlantic crossing."

"It sure is a bold choice, I'll say that," Faye said.

"Again with the understatement."

Faye swung the Toyota into a parking spot off the road. "Well, here we are."

I stared at the building we faced. You could drive right by the little stone mill and miss it entirely if you weren't paying attention. "This is it?" Faye had been building up my expectations for days. I expected something a bit more substantial.

"Have a little respect for history," Faye said. "This mill was built in 1873."

"And this is where the famous herring run is?"

"Technically, they're alewives, not herring. But, yes, this is it. The run starts over there." Faye pointed to the north side of the road, and before I had even unlatched my door, she was on her way. I caught up by the edge of the stream.

"It's early in the season," Faye said, "but in a few weeks, the run will be thick with them."

I concentrated on the stream and, after a moment, caught the glint of silver weaving through water. "I see one," I said, unexpectedly excited. I followed its progress as the silver-scaled body fought its way upstream and over a concrete step, only to be propelled back again and again by the force of the water. "Will it make it?"

"Eventually."

"Do they ever give up?"

Faye shook her head. "They're hardwired not to."

"Amazing," I said.

"Every year they return here to spawn."

"How do they find their way back?"

"It's their home stream. They recognize it."

"By instinct?"

"By smell."

"Smell?" I assumed she was kidding.

"Biologists have discovered that every brook or river or stream has its own distinctive chemistry, its own particular odor."

"Just like people."

"Exactly. And that's how an alewife identifies its home stream."

We watched as the alewife continued with its fierce, determined futile leaps. It seemed impossible that the fish would ever make it over the step of the concrete ladder. I knelt and dipped a hand in the stream so icy it made me gasp. The fish circled in the pool at the base of the step. Without thinking, I bent forward and cupped my hands, prepared to scoop it up and deliver it to the next level.

"Don't," Faye said, reaching out to stop me.

"I was just going to help it."

"I know, but it won't help."

"Why?" The alewife made another futile attempt.

"Just by touching it, you can harm it."

"Oh," I said, chastised. The alewife disappeared beneath the shadow of the water, hidden and quick. "I didn't mean to hurt it."

"To wish to do no harm is not at all the same as not doing any," Faye said. She put her hand on my shoulder. "Things have to find their own way, Jessie."

Just at that moment, the fish reappeared, made a last leap, and in glistening triumph, scaled the ladder. I couldn't describe the elation this small victory brought me.

We stayed on at the mill for another hour, walking the length of the run and then circling the millpond, where gulls swooped overhead, one occasionally diving to capture a fish in its bill.

As we walked, Faye's words eddied in my head like the water swirling at each step of the run. *Things have to find their own way.*

six

EASTER DAWNED WITH a return to the cold and rain. When I arrived at the Ryder house, Nona's friend Helen was already in the drive, engine revving, and Nona was waiting at the door.

"It was good of you to come," she said, "it being the holiday and all."

"I was glad to," I said, and handed her the box of candies I had settled on after all. "Happy Easter."

"Oh now," Nona said. "You shouldn't have bothered."

"It wasn't a bother."

"I hated to ask you to come on the holiday, but I haven't missed an Easter service in thirty years."

I couldn't imagine this. I hadn't attended church since I left home for college.

"I should be back by twelve thirty," Nona said, "but the service often runs late on Easter and Christmas."

"No problem. I can stay as long as you want."

"Do I look all right? This is the only decent thing I brought with me."

Nona wore a dress, her concession to the holiday. Her legs were bony, the shins knotted with varicose veins. "You look beautiful," I said.

She sighed. "It's so hard to go through the motions of ordinary living," she said in a voice so soft she might have been speaking to herself. She looked over at the closed door and gave another sigh.

"Go," I said. "I'll take care of things here."

After she left, I flicked on a lamp to dispel some of the gloom

and stood for a moment listening to the television blaring from behind the closed door of Luke's room. I thought fleetingly about
knocking, then just as swiftly dismissed the idea. I snitched a few
jelly beans Nona had set out in a dish on the coffee table and headed
for the kitchen to pour myself some coffee.

There was a portable sewing machine set up on the table. A pair
of men's pants was folded by its side. I couldn't remember the last
time I had seen anyone mend a pair of pants. Or anything, for that
matter. I trailed a finger over the fabric, sucked on the candy. When
the telephone rang, I was so startled that I nearly choked on the
jelly bean. By the third ring, I'd recovered enough to pick up.

"Nona?" A man's voice, deep, the resonant tone of a disc jockey.

"She's not here right now. Can I take a message for her?"

"Is this Paige?"

"No," I said. "This is Jessie."

"Hospice Jessie?" the man said. "Freckled nose, blue eyes, perfect posture."

I paused, caught off guard. "Yes."

"Hi. Nona told me about you."

"And who is this?" I felt my face grow hot and wondered what
else Nona had said about me.

"Rich," he said. "A friend of Luke's."

"Oh," I said. "Hi." It was odd, but until that moment, I hadn't
thought much about Luke actually having a life beyond the room he
lay in, although I supposed, of course, he did. Certainly he had
friends even if I hadn't yet seen any.

"I'm just calling to check in. How's he doing?"

I paused. "About the same." Faye had instructed the volunteers
that we weren't to give out patient information.

"Well, tell him to let me know if there's anything I can do, anything Nona needs."

I carried the receiver to the hall and looked at the closed door.
"Do you want me to tell him you're on the phone?"

"I don't know. Is he asleep? Don't bother him if this isn't a good time."

I didn't know what to say. I had no idea what Luke was doing in his fortress.

"Listen," he said, "just leave a message that I called."

"Okay," I said, returning to the kitchen. "Anything else?"

"Will you let Nona know I'll be by sometime late in the week to pick up any trash she has for the dump?"

"Trash for the dump," I repeated. "Got it."

"And tell her I'm disappointed."

"Disappointed?"

"She didn't tell me about the accent. I'm a fool for a girl with a southern accent."

I rolled my eyes. "You got one part of that wrong," I said.

"How so?"

"I'm not a girl."

"What part did I get right?"

"Try and take a stab at it." After I hung up, I poured myself a cup of Nona's lethal coffee, replayed the conversation. I knew the type. There had been enough of them in my past. Cocky as hell. Always fishing for a good time by throwing out a line. Half the time, I bit and swallowed, although lately I had been getting smarter. Hadn't I? Or was it just that I hadn't had occasion to be tested?

A faint sound broke into my thoughts. I paused, listened. It took a moment to realize it was Luke's bell. It rang again. The sound I had been waiting for since the first day I stepped into this house.

"Coming," I called, while my heart skipped and pulsed. I knocked and when there was no response, pushed open his door. My eyes went first to the empty hospital bed that occupied the center of the room facing out toward the window. He sat in a wingback chair, his legs covered with a woven throw, the black Lab at his side. He was thin as a wire hanger—his shirt just hung on him—and his skin was jaundiced. He had on leather slide-in slippers, the kind old men wore, and it was the slippers—more than the baggy clothes or the pallor, the hospital bed or the aluminum walker set to one side—that marked him an invalid.

What had I expected? I supposed the man in the photos that hung in the hall, the one I had been thinking about for weeks, had dreamed about. A fisherman with crow black hair, a man who loved his truck and his dog and his daughter. A man who once headed down to the basement several times a week to do curls and bench presses and dead lifts. A man so fit he seemed incapable of weakness or death. I wouldn't have recognized him as the person in the photo. Except for the raven hair.

I tried to conceal my shock but not quickly enough. He turned away, looked out the window, but not before I saw his mouth tighten.

"Hi," I said. "I'm Jessie."

He stared out the window, stroked the Lab's back with long, precise fingers. I gave a quick look around the room, took in the clutter of books, magazines, a couple of plastic jugs of bird seed, a half dozen empty glasses with bent drinking straws. A stained mattress pad scrunched into an oval that served as a dog bed. There was a small telescope by the window and a pair of binoculars on the sill.

"I don't know if you heard the phone ring a few minutes ago," I said. "Your friend Rich called."

He had no interest in small talk. "Look," he said, "I need you to do something."

I hesitated, praying it wasn't anything that would make me queasy, some requirement of a personal nature. "Okay," I said.

He turned and looked straight at me, his eyes daring me to show sympathy or pity. "I'm out of cigarettes," he said. "I need you to buy me some."

You can't be serious, I thought.

"There's money on the desk," he said.

"You want *cigarettes*?" The man was dying. He looked like shit in a shirt.

"Winstons. And a six-pack of Coke while you're at it. The real stuff. Not that diet crap."

"I don't know," I stalled, my voice guarded. "I mean, I don't think I should go out. Nona isn't here. I can't leave you alone."

"Jesus Christ," he said, giving all three syllables equal emphasis. "Do I look like I need a babysitter?"

"That's not what I meant," I managed. "I just don't think you should be—you know, smoking."

His look silenced me. Once, outside a bar in New Orleans, I saw two men fighting, and what struck me—terrified me—was the violence of their rage, a wave nearly physical, so hot it felt like a flame. I saw something akin to that anger in Luke's eyes. And something more, too. His eyes stared straight into mine as if everything I had ever thought, past or present, was laid bare. As if I had no secrets. Never in my life had anyone ever looked at me like that. It was like looking into death. Or truth. *I know you.*

"So are you going to get me the friggin' cigarettes or not?" he said.

Not, I started to say. And then I remembered something Faye told us during our training. *Try to imagine what it's like to be dying,* she urged us. *Imagine that, bit by bit, nearly everything has been taken from you. Your work. Your health. Your future. Your pleasure in ordinary things like a good meal, a glass of wine, sex. Your freedom to do the simplest things, like drinking from a glass. Try to imagine what it is like to be unable to go to the bathroom without help. Or to wipe yourself when you are done.* Then she handed out a yellow sheet of paper with the title "The Patient's Bill of Rights," among which were their right to be angry and to make their own decisions.

I knew I shouldn't leave Luke. Nona was clear about that. But sometimes what a person wants collides with all good sense, and— even when my smart self was shouting that I needed to sit up and pay attention—I went straight with the desire. At this moment, my fiercest desire was to help Luke. I knew what it was like to feel helpless.

"Okay," I said. "I'll get them."

"And the Coke," he said.

I nodded. "And the Coke."

Months later, I would think: That is how it happens. We make what seems like a simple choice, no more extraordinary or complicated than buying a quart of milk, but then we learn that even the simplest decision carries with it ramifications. Consequences that we can never envision. This was my first choice in one of several that I would later have cause to regret.

THE WHOLE thing didn't take more than twenty minutes. Max. I left the engine running while I ran into Meservey's and grabbed the Coke and Winstons. As the clerk rang up the total, I threw in a foil-covered chocolate rabbit, then rushed out, refusing the clerk's offer to bag my purchases. Nothing was going to happen to Luke in the few minutes I was gone. But still.

When I pulled up to the house, I saw the blue Volvo waiting in the drive. "Shit," I muttered. Paige waited inside, her fury pulsing in waves.

"Where the hell were you?" she said. She faced me, arms akimbo.

"Your dad asked me to——," I began, but was cut off before I could explain.

"You weren't supposed to leave him," Paige said, shouting. She all but stamped her turquoise boot. "That's the entire reason you're here. My grandmother doesn't want him to be left alone."

"Let's calm down," I said.

"Don't tell me to fuckin' calm down." Paige looked down at the purchases in my arms. "What? You left him to go get yourself a pack of weeds? I can't fuckin' believe this."

"I left," I said evenly, determined not to lose control, "because your father asked me to run an errand."

Paige eyed the purchases again. "You bought him *cigarettes?*"

"Listen—"

"Listen, shit. Did it occur to you that maybe his doctor has told him not to smoke?"

"Look," I said in the reasonable tone I would use for a student who was acting out, "I'm sorry if I've upset you, but I'm here for Luke, not you. He wanted the cigarettes. It was his decision to make. Not mine."

"Jesus," Paige spat. "Where do they find you people?"

"Paige." We both turned at the sound of Luke's voice. He stood at the door, weight supported by an aluminum walker. "That's enough."

"Fine." Paige flung the word at him. "Go ahead. Smoke. Kill yourself. You're just as stupid as Mom always said you were. Well, just don't expect me to cry at your funeral." She pushed past me and headed for the door, her eyes hot, hard.

"Hold on, Paige," Luke said. "Just hold on."

She stormed out without looking back. I couldn't hear what she was saying, but I could certainly guess. The car door slammed. Moments later, I heard the sound of the Volvo roaring out of the driveway.

Luke turned and made his way back to his chair by the window. I could see the angel wings of his shoulder blades through the fabric of his shirt. "She's been a hothead since she was old enough to talk," he said. He sounded more proud than apologetic.

"Looks to me like she comes by it honestly," I said before I could stop myself.

He surprised me by laughing, and in this moment, for the first time, I could see something of the man he had been before cancer. Handsome. Dangerous. A crash course in the blues if ever there was one. Even this wasted, there remained a sexual energy about him.

He held out his hand for the Coke and cigarettes. I crossed the room, handed them to him. He looked at the foil-covered rabbit but did not take it from my hand. I placed it along with his change on the desktop, embarrassed now that I had bought such a childish thing.

"Is it true what Paige said?" I asked. "Did your doctor tell you not to smoke?"

He snorted. "Doctors tell you lots of things." He slit open the wrapper with a thumbnail and shook out a cigarette. "Want to know the best thing about dying?"

I held back the denial that sprang to mind: *You're not dying.*

"The rules don't matter anymore," he said. "Not one of them matters a good goddamn."

"What rules?"

"All of them. Wear your seat belt. Eat fiber. Exercise. Cut back on fat. Lower your cholesterol." He looked over at me. "Anything you want to add?"

"You forgot flossing," I said.

"Yeah. That, too." He lit up, took a deep drag, deeper than I would have thought possible from the looks of him, and stared out the window.

"To tell you the truth," I said, "you don't look a like a man who has spent a hell of a lot of time paying attention to rules."

He rewarded me with a laugh, that deep laugh I'd heard when he was with Jim, and it stirred something low in my belly. Then he inhaled again, but this time, the drag provoked a coughing fit. "Tastes like shit anyway," he said, grinding the butt out in a saucer.

I looked around, searching for a reason to keep me in the room. I pointed to the binoculars by the window. "You're a bird-watcher?"

"Amateur." He closed his eyes, rested his head against the back of the chair. Beneath the yellow cast, his skin was ashen. The butt smoldered in the saucer.

I resisted the urge to cross over and put it out. "Can I get you anything? A glass of ice for the Coke?"

He flipped the tab top, then took a straw out of one of the empty glasses and poked it into the can. "This'll do fine."

The dog looked up at him, tail thumped against the floor.

"Rocker, right?" I said, nodding at the Lab.

"Right."

"How'd he get that name?"

"My ex," he said. "She said I was off my rocker to get him. Said I wasn't responsible enough to take care of a family let alone a dog."

I kept quiet. How could you respond to that?

"So where are you from?" he asked. "Somewhere in the South, right? Maybe Virginia. Or Maryland?"

"Richmond, Virginia," I said.

"What brings you up here?" He didn't look at me but continued to gaze out into the yard.

"Taking a year off," I said.

"Divorce." It wasn't a question.

"No." For one instant, I was taken by an impulse to tell him everything—my tumor, the operation and treatments, my recovery—but in the end, I simply said, "Lost my job." I waited for him to ask what I did, but instead, he picked up the TV remote and punched up the volume from Mute.

"Close the door on the way out, would you?" he said, the conversation clearly over.

Any other man acted that way, I'd be on the highway before he could draw a breath, but Luke wasn't any other man, and not just because he was sick. I didn't even know him, but I already understood that he was a man I'd bend the rules for without even knowing why.

I returned to the living room and, within five minutes, had polished off the bowl of jelly beans while I replayed every word of our conversation. When I pictured him, thin and ill, the image totally erased that of the strong, vital man in the photos hanging in the hall. I considered his ex-wife's remark that he was irresponsible and wondered again what the story was behind their divorce. Whose idea had it been? Had he been unfaithful? Had she? Exactly what had Nona meant when she said Marcia was not kind? I recalled the words Paige had flung out in anger. *You're just as stupid as Mom always said you were.*

After a few minutes, I got up and began to prowl the house, searching for clues. There was a flight of stairs at the far end of the living room that led to a second floor. In the weeks I had been coming to the house, I had never had cause to go up there. The first few risers creaked, but I found if I stepped on the edges close to the wall, I made no noise, probably a needless precaution. The way the television was blaring, he couldn't hear a herd of bison storming through. Upstairs, a narrow hall opened onto two bedrooms. The first held a set of twin beds. A woman's sweater over the arm of a chair and a robe folded at the head of the bed marked this as the room Nona was using. The second held a large bed but little else, so barren it might have housed a monk. Even with nothing in sight to suggest it, I knew this was Luke's. In the closet, there were more empty hangers than garments. Two pairs of blue jeans, a half dozen flannel shirts, three short-sleeve cotton ones, one pair of chinos. Shoved in the back was a dark gray suit that looked as if it had had little use. A pair of brown loafers on the floor.

I heard a car door slam out in the drive and made it back down the stairs just as Nona came up the front steps.

"How was the service?" I asked. My voice was steady, although my heart was pounding. Had I remembered to close the closet door?

"There was a new minister," Nona said. "A woman. Personally I prefer a man up in the pulpit." She nodded toward Luke's door. "Everything okay?"

"Fine," I said. "Someone named Rich phoned. He said he'd be by later in the week to pick up your trash. And Paige stopped by." I might have told her then about leaving Luke alone while I ran his errand, but before I could, Nona interrupted.

"How was she?"

"Paige?"

"Yes. Was she high?"

"Not so I could tell," I said.

"I don't like her coming here when she's high. She's tough enough to deal with when she's cold sober. Like her mother, that one."

The moment to tell Nona that I'd left Luke alone passed. Well, there was nothing to tell, really. I had only been gone a few minutes. He was fine. He was fine, and we were finally talking.

By THE time I pulled up at Faye's later that afternoon, the sun had broken through. Her house was at the end of the street on a bluff overlooking the sound. A wide veranda flanked the east and south sides. A week before, rushing the season, Faye had set out wicker rockers, and now they swayed in the breeze.

Inside, the house was filled with the scent of roasting chicken. She had pulled a small drop-leaf table out to the glassed-in porch. "I thought we'd eat out here," she said. A mass of purple hyacinths sat on a side table, spilling their fragrance into the room, a bunch so large, I couldn't have contained it in my arms. Thrifty in most ways, Faye splurged on cut flowers throughout the winter. An extravagance her soul demanded, she explained to me.

"Shall we have sherry?" Faye had changed from her usual sweats to a long skirt in a faded blue, a concession to the holiday. I admired the way she crossed the room. In spite of her size, she still moved like the dancer she had been in her youth.

"I met Luke today," I said, accepting the glass.

Faye's eyes widened in surprise.

"He asked me to get him some Coke." I didn't mention the Winstons or the fact that I'd had to leave the house to get the soda.

"And?"

"And we exchanged about five sentences. Then he more or less threw me out."

"Good," Faye said.

"Good?"

"It's a start."

"I guess so. At least I got to meet him." I sipped the wine.

"And to talk," Faye said.

"Well, let's not get carried away here," I said, laughing. "It wasn't exactly a 'Let's be friends' kind of conversation."

"Give him time."

I swallowed. "How much does he have?"

"Time?"

I nodded. "He looks terrible."

"He's not dying any faster than anyone else in this life. This second is all we have."

"You know what I mean, Faye."

"The one thing I know is that you can never tell how long someone has."

"You must have some idea," I pressed. "I mean, what are we talking about? Weeks? Months?"

"Yes," Faye said.

I stared. "What?"

Faye returned the gaze. "Yes," she said again.

I waited, wanting more. Out on the sound, a single gull curved in and landed on the jetty in front of her house.

Faye sipped the sherry. "The truth is," she said after a few minutes, "patients you would swear wouldn't last an hour live on for weeks, and others who you would think still have a great deal of time slip away overnight. A person's will plays a part in it. Sometimes a patient hangs on, waiting for one particular day that holds importance for him. A holiday or an anniversary. A birthday."

"But usually you have some idea, right?"

She nodded. "Sometimes. But the only thing I can tell you with certainty is that every death is different."

"Really?" How many different kinds of death could there be?

"Each death is as unique as the person who is dying. Just like each life is different."

"If you had to guess, how long do you think Luke has?"

Faye poured us more wine. Out on the jetty, a second seagull joined the first. "Best guess?"

"Yes." I held my breath.

"He won't last through summer."

The words sat in my heart hard as a polished stone. My earlier good mood deflated as quickly as it had come.

seven

Ashley phoned later that night, just as I was getting ready for bed.

"We missed you today," she said.

"I missed you, too."

"What did you do?"

"Faye asked me over for dinner."

"That was nice of her," Ashley said, almost concealing the edge in her voice. Earlier in the winter, she had asked me why I didn't find a friend closer to my own age. I thought she was absurdly suspicious of Faye's motives in nurturing our friendship, in arranging for me to volunteer. Ashley thought that my work with hospice was a mistake, that it would be too depressing for me, given my own experience. "Does she want to adopt you or what?" she once asked.

"How was your Easter?" I said. "Was it weird not to be at Mama's?"

"You talked with her?"

"Yesterday. She made it sound like all those years of Easter brunch were pure torture."

"Yeah, that's what she said to me, too." Ashley's sigh traveled over the wire. "I thought the boys would miss the egg hunt, but the truth is, I think I missed it more than they did."

"So do you think this sailing thing is actually going to happen?"

"You mean across the Atlantic?"

"Yes."

"I doubt it. I think it is just a fantasy that will pass."

"What makes you so sure?"

Ashley laughed. "Remember the one time Daddy talked her into going camping?"

"God," I said, remembering how Lily had left the campsite in the middle of the night and checked into a hotel. *If it doesn't have hot running water and a king-size bed, I don't want to be there,* she'd said when she returned home the next day.

"I rest my case," Ashley said.

"I wish I shared your confidence in the matter."

"Can we put this conversation on hold for a minute?" she said. "I've got two nephews here who want to wish their favorite aunt happy Easter."

"At this hour? Aren't they in bed?"

"I'll be lucky if they fall asleep by midnight. Total sugar high, both of them."

Jeffrey got on the phone first. "Hey, Auntie Jess. Guess what?"

"What?" I closed my eyes, pictured his face. The last time I'd seen him, he was just beginning to lose his baby fat.

"Our dad took us to a farm this afternoon. There were baby lambs."

"Baby lambs?"

There was a commotion on his end of the wire. "It is *so* my turn," Jeffrey yelled. "Mom said I could go first."

Another commotion, and then John was on the phone. "Hi, Auntie Jess." In the background, Jeffrey wailed.

"Hi, John." You weren't supposed to have favorites, but John held a special spot in my heart, partly because I'd been present at his birth, but also because I'd felt protective of him after his brother was born. Ashley babied Jeffrey. She expected more from John because he was older.

"I wanted to tell you about the lambs."

"Well, you can tell me, too."

Eventually, after he'd delivered a blow-by-blow account of the day—from every kind of candy in his Easter basket to what they'd seen on the farm—he handed the phone over to Ashley.

"Still want to get married and have kids?" she asked. She sounded exhausted.

"I'd be content to start with the marriage part."

"So what's the score on that?"

I could see Ashley settling in for a long conversation. "Hold on," I said. "Let me get a drink before we get into this."

"So have you been dating?" Ashley asked when I returned, fortified with a glass of pinot.

"Not recently."

"You're kidding."

"Sadly, I'm not," I said, and took a drink.

"What? Aren't there any men up there?"

"Not if you eliminate the retirees and the ones already taken." Ashley laughed.

"I'm not joking."

"This doesn't sound like you at all," she said.

"What do you mean?"

"Oh, you know you, Jess. In town by seven and in love by eleven."

"Yeah, well, not this time around."

"You know what you should do?"

"What's that?" *I swear,* I thought, *one word out of her mouth about how I should get myself a computer and sign up for an online dating service and I'm hanging up.*

"Move to Anchorage," Ashley said.

"Anchorage? As in Alaska?"

"Is there any other?"

"I'm not dating and *that's* your solution? Alaska. Thanks."

"Think about it." Ashley was using her let's-get-down-to-business voice.

"Wait a minute," I said. "You're joking, right?"

"I'm absolutely serious."

"Okay, so it's a little slim on the dating scene, but somehow I don't think relocating to Alaska is the answer."

"Did you know men outnumber women four to one there? I heard it on *Oprah*."

"I'll keep it in mind."

"Seriously," Ashley said, "four to one."

"Yeah, well I don't think ratio is the problem."

"What is?"

I didn't want to get into this, especially with my older sister, Miss Happily Married with Two Kids and All the Answers. "Forget it."

"No," Ashley said. "I want to know. Really, Jess."

I recognized the tone in Ashley's voice. She wasn't about to be put off. "I don't know. Maybe I'm not good at it. Look at Steve," I said. "Would you be happier if I'd stayed with him?"

"Honestly?"

By all means, let's be honest.

"I don't think you gave him a chance," Ashley continued.

"A chance? You're kidding. I mean there was a relationship that overstayed its natural life. It shouldn't have lasted longer than a moan."

"He was good to you."

"You mean he was the only man in Richmond who wasn't freaked out of his skull because I'd had the big C."

Ashley sighed. "I liked him."

"You always like the men I break up with."

"You don't break up with guys, Jessie. You leave town. Mama thinks that—"

It infuriated me to think Ashley and Lily had been discussing me. "Listen," I said. "It's possible to be perfectly happy without being tethered to a mate. Did you ever think that maybe some people aren't meant to be married?"

"Okay. Forget I said anything."

"I just don't like being defined by what's missing."

The sound of mayhem rose on the other end of the wire. "Listen," my sister said, "I gotta run. The boys are at each other's throats."

"Okay," I said.

"I love you, sweetie. You know that. I only want what's best for you."

"Me, too," I said, although I knew we'd never stop wanting different things. I hung up and finished the wine, then—thinking what the hell, it's cheaper than a move to Alaska—I poured another glass.

LATER THAN night, while brushing my teeth, I stared at myself in the mirror, trying to see myself through the eyes of a man. Specifically, I wondered what Luke had thought when he looked at me. As Nona had apparently told Rich, my posture was fine, thanks to constant nagging on my mama's part during my teen years. And my hair was an asset. It was a deep shade of copper that most people believed was tinted. Once I compared it to a swatch in a drugstore hair-coloring display. Standing there, I'd been mesmerized by the infinite number and rich lexicon of shades. Honey, platinum, ash, straw, champagne, linen, almond—and these were just the blonds. The closest I'd found to my own was a shade called gingerbread.

I had never been tempted to alter my hair color. I knew the damage the processing could do. I'd read somewhere that Jean Harlow bleached her hair with a mixture of peroxide, household bleach, soap flakes, and ammonia until it fell out. In Renaissance Venice, they used to use horse urine to bleach hair. In ancient Rome, they used pigeon dung. No thank you to any of it.

So, posture and hair: a plus.

I continued the scrutiny of my face. Unless you were looking for it or I was fatigued, you couldn't detect the asymmetry around my eyes, how when I was overtired, my left eye drooped a bit. My complexion was good—if you didn't mind freckles—but faint lines fanned out from the corners of my eyes. Already. At thirty-two. All those years of mindless tanning before we knew better. Still, feature by feature, there was nothing exactly wrong. I wasn't plain, but I wasn't beautiful either. When I was at the Art Institute, a French exchange student I'd dated briefly told me I looked

American. When I'd asked him what that meant, he'd said, "Good teeth." I'd felt like a horse.

I changed into pajamas and climbed into bed, wondering what kind of woman Luke liked. Tall and built, judging by the photo of the brunette in the bikini. I found myself again wondering why he had gotten divorced. I wondered what his favorite food was. Wondered if he had been an imaginative lover. *Had been.* Past tense. I wondered if he was afraid of dying. I remembered when I'd first begun radiation, one of the other patients I'd gotten to know asked me if I was afraid of death. No, I'd said. It wasn't death I feared but the process of dying. The deterioration of mind and body. That was why, when I was sick, I couldn't stand to watch a plant wither and die. I still couldn't. If I got flowers, I tried to throw them out right before they started wilting.

It was late, but I couldn't drop off. My mind was restless, ruminating on Lily and then Ashley and then Luke. Lately my insomnia had returned, and I wondered if I needed to get back on Xanax. It had seen me through some rough times in the past five years. When I finally fell asleep, I dreamed of a quicksilver fish fighting its way upstream to spawn. In the dream, even knowing it was forbidden, I lifted the fish in my hands and carried it over the steps of the ladder to the millpond, where I released it and watched it disappear into the depths.

eight

I N ANOTHER ERA, hair workers were called spiders because they wove and crocheted and spun human hair into things of beauty. I never found this term demeaning. Sometimes, bent over my table, twisting and weaving human strands, I felt akin to the solitary arachnids whose filament webs were strung in corners of my cottage.

Working with hair brought me to a nearly altered state. It was calming, the way using your hands could be, and settled me. Better than the meditation my doctor had prescribed. When I sat at the braiding table and wove the strands into their intricate pattern, a deep serenity often settled over me. I knew I was part of a history and craft that spanned continents and centuries.

Hair jewelry can be traced back not just to the Victorian age but even further, to the Middle Ages and as early as the Egyptians and in ninth-century Japan. I had read that, in the early 1800s, a town in Sweden had been famous for the hairwork done there. During years when the crops failed and there was a famine, whole families would leave the village and travel to other towns with their craft, thus sustaining all the residents of the town. Another curious fact I'd turned up in my research was that, in the 1853 Crystal Palace Exposition in London, there was a full tea set made entirely of hair. (I could only imagine what Lily would think of that.) I'd heard of an artist in Chicago who chopped hair into fine pieces and mixed it with pigment with which she painted.

With the permanence, I liked the resiliency and surprising strength of hair. One single strand could support a three-ounce weight without breaking. Because it is nearly invisible and lasts a long time, conservators use it to mend textile art. Beyond these properties, I found hair wonderfully articulate, both uncivilized and raw, of a charged nature, and vital and connected to life. Once I'd examined a hair shaft under a microscope; it looked like the bark of an ancient tropical tree.

To BEGIN a piece, I sorted the hairs into equal lengths and tied the ends with packthread, which I then soaked in a solution of water and baking soda and boiled for about fifteen minutes. When it was dry, I divided the hair into strands of twenty or thirty each, knotted the strands, and fastened a lead weight to each. On the opposite end, I tied a sailor's knot using packthread and gummed with cement comprised of yellow wax and shellac. After these preparations, I was ready to begin.

The bracelet on my table was nearly finished, and I was relieved to know I could soon ship it off to the young leukemia patient. When I was done attaching the gold clasp, I rose, and the calmness that had centered me while I worked evaporated. Two days had passed, and I assumed that, by now, Paige or Luke must have told Nona that I'd left him alone. I was surprised that Nona hadn't reported me to Faye. I was due at the Ryders' in a half hour, and as I threw on a clean shirt and put on some lipstick, blush, and eyeliner, I rehearsed the explanation I had prepared to give to Nona. In spite of my anxiety and dry mouth, I found I was also more excited about the visit than I had any right to be.

WHEN I got there, Jim was sitting at the kitchen table with Nona, filling in a records chart.

"Hi, sunshine," he said.

"Hi." I glanced over at Nona but could read nothing on her face except worry and exhaustion, a face full of effort. My heart twisted in sympathy. That morning, sitting at the table, if someone had told me that, within months, Nona and I would become adversaries, I would have found it impossible to conceive.

"How is everything?" I asked, *everything* meaning Luke.

"The same," Nona said.

I waited while Jim finished with the paperwork and gathered his things together.

"So," he said, "did you hear about the duck who went to the drugstore to buy some prophylactics?"

"No," I said, although it was an old joke, one I knew. "I haven't heard that one."

"Well, the druggist asked him, 'Do you want to pay cash, or shall I put it on your bill?' "

A tired smile creased Nona's face. She waited for the punch line, which Jim delivered in a cartoon voice.

"I'm not that kind of duck," he said.

Even knowing the joke, the way Jim told it, I had to laugh. It took Nona a moment to get it, and then she laughed, too.

He stood up. "Ready?" he asked her.

Nona nodded. "Jim's taking me to the Stop & Shop," she said.

I looked at him, raised a brow in question. This was not part of his job.

"I have to go anyway," he said.

I suspected this was untrue. "I'd be happy to run you there," I told Nona.

"You stay here with Luke," she said. "He mustn't be left alone."

I looked at her, trying to determine if there was a hidden message there, but Nona was picking her handbag up from the counter. "Anything I can do while you're gone?" I asked.

Nona shook her head. Jim took her arm, opened the door for her. "Oh," she said, remembering. "Rich—the man you spoke to on the phone the other day—he might be coming by to pick up the trash." She pointed to a pile of trash bags by the back door. "I didn't set it outside because of the raccoons."

"Got it," I said.

. . .

JIM'S JEEP had no more than pulled out of the drive when I heard Luke's bell. My heart gave a queer jump. I combed my fingers through my hair, felt my scar, tucked my shirt in my jeans. He was in the chair by the window and looked thinner than I remembered. I recalled Faye's response on Sunday when I'd asked how long he had to live. *Weeks or months? Yes.*

"Hi," I said.

He stared at me, and again I had the queer sensation he could read every thought my mind had conceived. "Where's Nona off to?"

"Shopping," I said.

"So does it make you feel good?" he said after a minute, his voice gone flat.

"What's that?"

"Coming here. Being a do-gooder."

"Yes," I said straight out. "In fact, it does." I think my acknowledgment surprised him. "What? You'd rather your mother didn't get any help?"

"I don't like taking charity."

"So you'd feel better if you had to pay me?"

"Feel better?" He gave a mirthless, hacking cough of a laugh. "No. I'd feel better if I wasn't lying here waiting to die."

"Yeah, well I'd feel better if I had some kind of life myself," I said, and then immediately regretted the comment.

He opened his eyes and looked straight at me. "What exactly is it that's so bad about your life?" he said.

"Nothing," I said. "Just talk."

He gave me that piercing, truth-seeking look.

I sighed. "You don't want to know."

"Why?"

"Trust me. It's boring."

"I'm listening."

I looked around, wanting to get off the subject. We had been told not to sit and talk about ourselves when we visited. "Church visitors" Faye called the people who came to the room of a dying person and filled the air with talk of their grandchildren and their most recent trips. *You go there to help,* she'd told us early in the training, *to offer the comfort of being less alone, and to listen, not to talk about yourselves to someone in the last portion of his life.* Scanning the room, I saw a small oil painting on the wall that I hadn't noticed before. A dory pulled up on the shore with similar subtlety of composition to the painting in the living room. "I like that," I said.

"You want it," he said. "It's yours."

"I just said I liked it."

"Guy I knew in college did it. What? You thought I was a high school dropout?"

"I wasn't thinking anything, really," I said, although that was exactly what had gone through my mind. "I mean, I don't know any more about you than you know about me." Not true, and he knew it.

"What did they tell you about me? What was in my chart?"

"That you're forty-five and a fisherman."

"Was," he said. "I *was* a fisherman."

"Let's see," I went on. "You're divorced with a daughter. You didn't want hospice coming in."

"Really? Well, they didn't tell me a damn thing about you."

I knew this wasn't true. The caseworker had given both Nona and Luke some information about me. Without waiting to be asked, I crossed to the chair by the bed. "I'm thirty-two," I said. "I was born in Richmond, Virginia. I have one sister who's two years older than I am. When I was fourteen, my daddy died of a massive heart attack. Lily—my mama—is still alive. I graduated from the Art Institute in Chicago and taught high school art until last year, when the school district eliminated my job." I paused to take a breath.

"You finished?"

"Not quite. I'm not married. No children. I make jewelry. I guess that's about it."

"Boyfriend?"

"No."

"Why not?"

"I don't think I'm capable of it," I said, surprising myself with this answer.

He studied me for a minute, and I felt a flush heat my chest, spread up to my throat. And then he smiled and said, "Do I know you?" in a way that made me smile, too, like we were both discovering a long, shared history we were only now remembering. It was that kind of eerie moment of recognition that could make a person believe in past lives.

"So," he said, "do you know how to play backgammon?"

"It's been a while," I said.

He indicated that I was to pull up a chair by the card table. While I set up the board, he ran through the basics, reminding me where to place the stones. For a time, while the two of us sat there and played, I swear I could nearly forget how ill he was. I was a tentative player; he was ruthless and lucky, throwing so many doubles, I accused him of cheating. We played three games, and I lost them all, crying "enough" after the third. He put the stones in their storage slots, then closed the board. The Lab, who had been curled up on the makeshift dog bed, rose and crossed to me. I rubbed his ears and the ridge of his spine, felt the coarse and oily fur of a water breed.

"You like dogs?" he asked.

"Sure."

"He's my third. All from the same line. This one was the pick of the litter." He looked over at the Lab. "Isn't that right, boy?" Rocker thumped his tail against the floorboards.

"He's beautiful," I said.

Luke stared at the dog. "There was this famous actor out in L.A. who owned a horse," he said.

I waited, wondering where he was going with this.

"So this actor, he got cancer."

I focused on the dog, unable to meet Luke's eyes.

"He'd been born somewhere out in the Dakotas, and that's where he wanted to be buried." He stopped and stared out the window at something I couldn't see. He fell silent, and I wondered if he was thinking about his own death and where he would be buried.

"Private funeral," he said after a moment. "Then he was cremated. Those were his instructions."

I waited, petted the Lab.

"Families don't always do that, you know. They don't always do what a person wants." It was like he was talking to himself. I didn't interrupt.

"Well, about a week later, a few of his childhood friends and what family he had left all met in his hometown in the Dakotas. About eight of them in all. They rode on horseback out to this particular site where he wanted his ashes buried. One of them led the actor's horse along with them. When they got there, they braided the horse's mane with flowers they had picked, and bunches of sage. They said whatever it was that was in their minds to say and buried the actor's ashes."

I could actually picture it. The circle of people and horses beneath the endless sky. The vial of ashes. The solitary horse, his mane bedecked with Dakota sage. Luke's next words took me by surprise.

"They shot the horse and buried him there, too."

I stared at him, too shocked for words.

"That's what the actor wanted," he said, as if I had argued.

"God." My fingers tightened on Rocker's fur. "That's terrible."

"Yes," he said. "Yes."

He laid his head back on the pillow, closed his eyes.

I felt that he had told the story deliberately, to shock or test me.

He opened his eyes and looked at me for another moment or two, then picked up the remote and flicked on the tube, my signal to leave.

"I understand, you know," I said.

"Yeah? Understand what?"

"About being sick. Having cancer. I know how you feel."

He gave me a hard, dismissive look. "I don't think you know the first goddamned thing about it."

I crossed to his chair, knelt on the floor, bent my head forward until my hair fell forward over my face, revealing the bald circle and smile-shaped scar. After several minutes, I got up, flipped my hair back.

He was staring out the window, his face set. "What happened?" he said.

"A tumor."

"When?"

"Five, nearly six years ago."

"Malignant?"

I swallowed. "Yes."

"So you had chemo?"

"Radiation," I said. I had refused chemo. Lily and I had fought for hours over this decision, but I wouldn't cave. I wanted a future that held the possibility of children. I didn't tell Luke this. "Did you have chemo?" I asked.

"No. What was the point? To go through that to gain what? Another month or two? Forget it. So your cancer, did they get it all?"

"Yes."

"What do they call it? Clean edges?"

"Yes."

He turned away again. "Then you can't possibly understand how I feel."

"No," I said. "You're right. That was presumptuous of me." Still, something had changed between us.

"So is that why they sent you here?" he said. "Because you're a *survivor?*"

"No," I said. "They don't know."

"Who?"

"Anyone here. At hospice."

He stared at me, studying my face. "Is that a fact?"

"Yes."

"So do me a favor?" he said, his voice neutral.

"What's that?" I said.

"A friend of mine is supposed to be stopping by to pick up the garbage."

"Rich," I said. "Nona mentioned it."

"If you're still here when he comes, tell him I'm asleep, will you?"

"Company might be good for you." The words escaped before I could contain them.

He snorted. "What would be *good* for me is to be back out fishing, earning a living. Having a life."

His eyes told me everything. *Would you want your friend to see you looking like this?* "Please," he said. Just that. He needs me, I thought, and with that knowledge came the end of any good sense I ever had. Up until then, I'd had no idea of the mighty seductiveness of being needed, feeling essential. I reached out then and circled his wrist with my fingers, startling myself as much as him. It was the first time I had touched him.

"Okay," I said. "I'll tell him you're asleep."

I WANDERED back to the living room, my hand still remembering the bones of his wrist, the grainy coolness of his skin, the beat of his pulse beneath my fingers. I cupped my palm to my face, inhaled, but smelled only the familiar almond scent of hand lotion. I didn't completely understand the impulse that took me then, but it drew me upward, up the stairs and straight to his bedroom, to the closet in his room. I opened the door and pulled one of the flannel shirts from its hanger. It was green plaid—the kind of moss green that flattered Irish black hair, dark eyes—and was soft with wear and washings. When I slipped it on, it hung nearly to my knees, the cuffs concealed my hands, suggesting the man Luke once had been. When I took it off, I didn't return it to the hanger but folded it carefully and rolled it into a tight cylinder, the way Lily had taught me to pack for a trip so that clothes would not wrinkle. I brought it back to the kitchen, and, in one more action I would later have cause to regret, I put it in my tote. I didn't stop to question why I was taking his shirt. (*Stealing* his shirt, I would later hear.) I knew only that I had this irrational urge to take something of his. I wanted some part of him for my own.

LATER I heard a car pull into the drive. Expecting Jim's green Jeep, I was surprised to see Paige's rusted Volvo.

"Hi," I said, determined to be cordial. Paige looked tired and like she was returning from a night spent hard. That long blond hair could have used a decent brushing. She tracked in mud.

"Hi," Paige said.

"Look," I began, "about last time—"

"Forget it." The girl's voice was sullen but not openly hostile, as if she had decided on a workable truce. She looked toward the closed door. "Is he awake?"

"I don't think so." I'd heard the television switch off a half hour before, then nothing but silence from Luke's room.

"Damn," Paige said, peeling off a tattered sweatshirt to reveal a cropped T. "How do you stand the heat in here?" Without waiting for an answer, she began rummaging through a cupboard, shoving aside cans of Ensure. I wondered if she behaved this way with everyone or just with me. Twenty-two going on sixteen.

"Doesn't Nona have any Tylenol around here?"

"In the cupboard next to the sink," I said. Even standing three feet away, I could smell the stale, sour-skin smell of a hangover.

Paige found the bottle, shook out three capsules.

"Long night?" I asked.

Paige flashed a quick, surly glance in my direction, checking for condemnation. Whatever she saw reassured her. "Wicked," she said.

I retrieved a can of ginger ale from the refrigerator. "Hydrate," I said. "Most hangovers are caused by dehydration."

Paige reached for the soda. "What are you, a nurse or something?"

I laughed. "Just the sorry voice of experience."

"So you're what? An alcoholic?" Her voice rose. "Great. They sent an alcoholic to take care of Luke."

"Relax, will you? I'm not an alcoholic, just have my own history of hangovers."

Paige held the can against her left temple, then her right, and then she flipped the tab and took a swallow. After that, she downed the capsules. Too many, but I knew enough to keep my mouth shut.

"Where's Nona?"

"Jim took her to the Stop & Shop. She should be back soon."

"Jesus," Paige said suddenly. "What's all that doing there?"

For one frozen moment, I thought Paige was looking over at the counter where my tote sat, flashing neon with the bulk of Luke's shirt inside. Then I saw the girl was staring at the pile of black garbage bags stacked by the back door.

"Trash," I said. "Rich is supposed to come by today and pick it up."

"Ah, Rich," Paige said, and took another swallow of soda. "Rich the Wonder Man. Have you met him?"

"Not yet. Why?"

Paige whistled and then pantomimed blowing on her fingers, extinguishing a flame.

"Hot?" I said.

"Torrid."

I recalled the sound of his voice the one time I'd heard it.

"We're talking off the scale," Paige said. "Posi-fuckin'-tively radioactive."

"That bad, huh?"

"Or good, depending on how you look at it. George Clooney before he went gray. I don't go for older men, but I'd seriously consider jumping his bones."

"Really?"

"Like that's going to happen."

"Why not? He's what? Twenty years older. That's not impossible."

"He's Luke's *friend,*" Paige said. "It's too creepy to think about getting it on with my father's friend. Ya know?"

I nodded, thinking, *this child wears her id right on the surface.*

"You might be tempted, though," Paige continued.

"He isn't married?"

"Rich doesn't marry. His women live with him until he moves on. So, are you interested?"

"I don't think so." Gorgeous cowboys who hadn't grown up were the last thing I wanted. God knows, I'd had my share of those in Richmond.

"What? Are you married or something?"

"No. Just not interested. Let's just say I've already had more than my quotient of bad boys."

Paige laughed out loud and raised the can in a mock toast. For a moment, things were fine between us, almost as if I were sitting here with Ashley or a younger friend talking about the age-old, ageless topic of men, but then, wanting, for Luke's sake, to forge a real connection, I spoiled it.

"I know what you're going through," I said. "With Luke."

"What do you mean?" Paige narrowed her eyes, distrustful.

"I lost my own daddy. He died when I was fourteen."

Paige made a soft sound that I misunderstood for sympathy. "Heart attack," I said. *My daddy slumped over the steering wheel. Daddy? Daddy? What's wrong?* "I never got to say good-bye or tell him that I loved him. So in that way, you're fortunate to have this time with Luke."

Paige jumped up so violently, the soda sloshed on the table, splattered my jeans.

"Well, shit," I said. I crossed to get a sponge and wipe at my pants, and then began mopping up the mess.

"You people don't know the first goddamned thing you're talking about," Paige yelled.

"I only—"

She grabbed the sponge from my hand. "Forget that, for Christ's sake."

"Listen, I didn't mean—"

"Luke's not dying. You got that? He's not dying."

I heard Faye's voice in my head: *Know and understand your response to anger. Keep your inner calm.* "I'm sorry—"

"Just get out, okay. Just go."

I wouldn't take this behavior from a high school student, and I sure as shit didn't want to take it from Paige, but again I heard Faye: *Accept the person's right to be angry.* My anger cooled and grew a skin, like set pudding. I picked up my tote. It weighed heavy in my hand. "Tell Nona I'll call later," I said.

"What Ever." She wouldn't look at me. Of course, she was right to distrust me.

That night, I slept in Luke's flannel shirt.

nine

T HE NEXT MORNING, I phoned Faye and related the details of the confrontation with Paige. I was afraid she might already have received a call from Nona and planned to remove me from Luke's case, but Faye said all the right things to comfort me.

"But what about what Paige said about Luke?" I asked. "Doesn't she *know* her father's dying?"

"Of course she knows," Faye said. "But knowing and accepting are two entirely separate things."

"She was furious with me," I said into the phone. I looked beyond the window out toward the horizon, where the blue sky blended into the sound so seamlessly, the line of demarcation was impossible to discern. I thought of young John Kennedy and how he had flown his plane straight into the sea, then deliberately willed the thoughts away.

"She's furious, period," Faye was saying. "And she has every right to be. Remember, anger is often the first reaction of family members."

Of course we had been told this during the training sessions, but nonetheless, I hadn't been prepared to have the rage turned on me. "I kept hearing your voice," I told Faye. "All the things you told us about dealing with anger."

"Good work," she said. "That girl's a handful, but you're up to the task."

A handful. That was what our daddy used to call Ashley when she was sixteen and stirring up trouble. But he had made it sound cute, which Paige most surely wasn't.

"You asked me the other day why I didn't put one of the older volunteers with Luke," Faye was saying. "Well, Paige is the reason I assigned you to this family."

"She is?" I twisted the phone cord around my wrist.

Faye laughed. "Can you imagine Beth trying to deal with her?" she said. "Or Muriel?"

I had to smile.

"Right now, Paige is hurting. Four months is not a long time to come to terms with what she's facing."

Four months. Sometimes I forgot that Luke had only been diagnosed in January. According to Nona, that was when he finally went to a doctor with a digestive problem drugstore remedies weren't touching. Nona said it had taken six weeks of tests (CAT scan, blood work, MRI, endoscopies), of infuriating misdiagnoses (Crohn's disease, depression, celiac disease), before they were told he had pancreatic cancer. His doctor said that he had probably had it for months even though he hadn't experienced pain, explaining that the pancreas was deep in the abdomen, which made it difficult to detect and treat. He said the organ didn't have nerves of its own to carry messages of pain and that Luke's pain signaled that the cancer was spreading, pressing on nerves. An operation wasn't an option.

"One reason Paige is angry is because her father's not fulfilling his contract," Faye said.

"What contract? I don't understand."

"He's her father. He's supposed to be there for her, to care for her."

Like Lily, I thought, my mind suddenly flashing to my mama. Okay, it was ridiculous, I suppose, but I felt abandoned. Lily had taken care of Ashley and me after my daddy died, and she'd been there for me all through the period of my illness and recuperation, and then she just disappeared. Off on a new life with the dentist.

"And Paige is probably feeling guilty, too," Faye was saying.

I pulled my mind back. "Why should she feel guilty? You mean because of the drinking?"

"Because Luke's dying."

"But why would she feel guilty about that? It isn't her fault he's sick."

"No. Any more than it was your fault that Lowell had a heart attack."

I tightened the phone cord around my wrist, breathed against the tightness in my chest.

"After Luke dies," Faye continued, "Paige will need someone to talk to. I think she'll turn to you then."

After Luke dies. The words stung. I pushed them away.

"How are things going other than that?" Faye said.

"Okay, I guess." What would Faye say if she knew about the shirt I'd taken?

"Well, cheer up," Faye said before she hung up. "You're doing fine."

DURING THE next weeks, neither Luke nor Nona mentioned Paige to me. When she stopped by to see her father, the visits never coincided with mine, though I didn't know if this was by accident or deliberate design. I would have liked to have seen her. After the conversation with Faye, I felt softer toward Paige.

Over the days, I gathered and hoarded the details of Luke's life, as if preparing for famine. I learned that it was he who completed the crossword in the daily papers and that he had majored in literature at a small independent college in Vermont but had left before getting a degree. "Too much sand in my shoes," he told me. "I had to come back to the Cape." Nona's version was that Luke treasured his independence too much to work for anyone but himself. "Just like his father," she said. Nona had been divorced for years. Luke's father was currently living in Santa Fe with his third wife. "So far away from the ocean," Nona said in disbelief. She didn't know how he could stand it.

I was spending more time with Luke. My hospice responsibility required two visits a week, but almost from the beginning, I stopped by more often. We rarely talked about his illness. He continued to take delight in besting me at backgammon. He told me that his great-grandfather on his father's side had immigrated to Prince Edward Island from Ireland. I'd smiled when he told me that. That black hair.

Sometimes we listened to music. Marvin Gaye. Crosby, Stills, and Nash. Neil Young. Other times we'd sit in companionable silence. And then, for no particular reason, he'd start talking. He told me what it was like growing up on the Cape. He'd started fishing when he was thirteen. Never wanted to do anything else. He said he only went to college to please Nona. She'd been saving for his education since he was born, working every job she could find.

When Luke knew I was coming, he would leave his door open. Occasionally I read to him. He liked Steinbeck. After I finished *The Red Pony,* I got a copy of *East of Eden* from the library, but he wanted to stick with the short stories. He never said it, but I believed he thought he didn't have enough time left for novels. I refused to accept this. Some days he just wanted me to sit with him. He said I brought a calmness to the room, and, recalling what Nona had said about his ex-wife's inability to sit still, his words would make me happy. I could not admit, even to myself, how deeply I had come to care. When I remember those blessed days when things were still relatively good, I remember all of this, and I remember the background song of the birds.

Luke was different than any man I had ever known in many ways but especially in his connection to the natural world. One day he told me he was going to teach me how to recognize birds by their calls. Blue jays. Grackles. The bossy English sparrows. Nuthatches. And the titmouse—as gray and timid as the name suggests, a tiny, feathered nun. At first, all I could hear were tweets and trills, indistinguishable one from another. "Close your eyes, clear your mind, listen," he told me. At first, I learned the easier ones. Catbird. Cardinal. Chickadee. He told me that instead of a larynx, birds had a syrinx, two-sided so they could sing several notes at once. When we sat and talked like that, I could almost come to believe a future was possible.

"Birdcalls differ from their songs," he told me one day. "Calls are innate to each breed, but songs have to be learned." I quizzed him about the difference, and he said calls were to signal danger, to claim territory, things like that. "Then what is song for?" I asked. "For joy," he said. "Simply for joy."

I wondered what birds did to show grief. But perhaps, unlike us, they knew only rapture, not sorrow.

So the days passed, filled with questions and struggle and punctuated by occasional moments I would later come to think of as nearly sacred. It was hard to tell the blessing from the curse. Sometimes he dozed while I read. He was getting morphine now and was noticeably weaker. And frequently the room smelled of foul emissions that embarrassed us both until Jim rescued us by making a joke about how Luke's farts were industrial-strength, so bad even Rocker wouldn't stay in the room with them.

More than once, while Luke slept, I sketched him, memorizing the bones of his cheeks and brow and jaw, his elegant hands. The planes of his face stood out like farmland in the spring, before it was softened by crops. His pain and my giving him comfort created a growing intimacy between us, and therein, of course, lay the danger. He recognized this more often than I and would pull away, draw back into himself, but I would wait patiently, tend to him, and he would come back. Occasionally, nights when I was alone at my cottage and struggling to sleep, I allowed myself to fantasize that he would go into remission.

Like Luke, Nona too was losing weight. And aging. Her roots had grown out a good two inches, and the white stood out in stark relief against her dyed jet hair. She seemed to have shrunk another inch in height and constantly smelled of arthritis ointment. When we sat at the kitchen table, I'd catch her massaging and kneading her hands, working her thumbs across misshapen knuckles and wrists. When I left, I would embrace her, and lately she had started to hug me back.

ONE MORNING, Nona met me when I arrived and looked so distressed, nearly ill, that I was instantly alarmed.

"Nona," I said after a quick embrace, "what's wrong?"

"I don't know what do to anymore."

"What's going on?" A knot of anxiety thickened my throat.

"Luke's not eating. Last night he asked me to make him some of my macaroni and cheese. His favorite thing as a child. But he only ate a bite, and even that he couldn't keep down."

"Oh, Nona," I said.

"He's just wasting away, Jessie. Not eating enough to keep a flea alive. Fluids are about all he's managing."

Panic edged in. *Weeks or months? Yes.*

"What about those milkshake things?" I asked, remembering the cans of Ensure stacked in the cupboard. "Have you tried them?"

"He won't touch them. They cost about as much as a good sirloin, but he says they taste like chalk. All I know is that he has to keep eating. If he goes on like this . . ."

"Maybe you could try something different," I said. "Like smoothies." Toward the end of my six weeks of radiation, I had pretty much existed on smoothies.

"What are they?"

"Yogurt and fruit drinks," I said. "They're easy to get down. And yogurt has acidophilus."

"What the hell is that?"

"Acidophilus? It's the good bacteria that makes a healthy climate in your intestines."

"He sure could use *something* healthy in there," Nona said, smiling a bit. Jim had gotten us all joking about Luke's farts.

"I'll bring a blender tomorrow," I said. "And some fruit. What does he like best?"

"Blueberry," Nona said. She looked better, hopeful.

I felt a flash of guilt for my part in Nona's optimism. We had been told to offer courage and hope—whatever the stage of disease—but we had also been cautioned against offering false promise. I found the line between the two was slippery. But false or not, looking back, I know that I was clinging to hope as tightly as Nona. Hope is so strong. So unwilling to give up. Even now, I marvel at its power. It carries us sometimes. It had held me through the worst of times, and, of course, it was hope for a new beginning that had led me to the Cape in the first place.

"Where are you off to today?" I asked. Members from Nona's church had set up a driving schedule. Someone drove up from Wellfleet and took her out so that she didn't have to rely on Helen for everything. I couldn't imagine being so reliant on others. I had asked her once why she never got her license, and she said when she'd gone for her test years ago, she'd driven right up on the sidewalk and sideswiped a fire hydrant before she'd even pulled out of the registry parking lot. The inspector had failed her on the spot, and she never got up the nerve to try again.

"Oh, I guess we'll ride around for a bit." She had run out of errands. "You know what I'd like to do?"

"What's that?"

"I'd like to go home. I miss my house." It was the first time I'd heard her offer one word of complaint.

"Well, why don't you go there for the afternoon?"

"I don't know. That would mean I'd have to ask someone to drive me there, and then bring me all the way back here. That's an hour for the driving alone."

I spoke without stopping for one moment to think. "Why don't you go back for one night? It would do you good."

"How can I? I can't leave him alone."

"I'll stay here."

"I couldn't ask you to do that."

"Of course you can. I'm not doing anything else. It will do you good." I reached out and stroked her head. "Get your hair done. And you could use a night of undisturbed sleep."

"I don't know," she said, but a bit more convincing was all it took. Within twenty minutes, she had packed the few things she'd need. Luke was sleeping and she wanted to wake him, then decided against it, reluctant to draw him from sleep. Recently, sleep and drugs had been his only sure escape from pain. She scrawled him a note instead.

I saw her off, then went to Luke's room and sat by his bed, sketching him, happier than I had any right to be. As soon as he stirred, I flipped shut my pad, set it on the floor. I told him Nona had gone back to Wellfleet and would return tomorrow. He read the note Nona had left and then studied me for a minute, not saying anything.

"You won't be alone," I said quickly. "I told her I would spend the night."

He turned and looked out the window, his face shut down, as withdrawn as he'd been the first time I saw him.

"Unless you want me to call someone else," I said, now nervous.

"Don't you have anything better to do than sit with a dying man?" he asked. He still wouldn't look at me. I could see he was slipping into that separate place he went to, the closed-door, loud-television place of isolation. He did that without warning, switching from trust to withdrawal and, occasionally, to bitterness. Once he referred to himself as the rubber plant. "Just set me on the porch and water me," he said.

"Look," I said, in a cool, no-nonsense voice, knowing sympathy or pity would only drive him further away, "if you would rather have someone else here, I can arrange it, but Nona hasn't been home in months, and she needed to go there. She's tired. She needed a break." I thought I had lost him, but he came back.

"Sorry," he said. "I'm being a perfect asshole."

"Nobody's perfect," I said, and was rewarded when he gave a small smile.

"It's just . . . ," he began.

"What?"

"Yesterday. You didn't come."

I perched on the edge of his bed. "Luke," I said, "I wasn't scheduled to come yesterday." We both knew the schedule was a joke. As I said, I was dropping by four or five times a week.

"I know," he said. He closed his eyes, sighed. "It wasn't that you didn't come. It was that I missed you when you didn't."

I picked up his hand, unable to suppress the joy his words gave me. "And that's a bad thing?"

"Yes," he said. "Given the circumstances."

"It doesn't have to be."

"We both know it does. There's no future in it, is there?"

I turned away so he wouldn't see my eyes fill with tears. "Well, what is it you want from me? Do you want me to stop coming? Do you want Faye to get another volunteer?"

"I want . . . ," he said.

I waited. I knew it would kill me if he said yes.

He sighed a long, deep sigh. "I want to get in your car and take a ride."

"Anywhere in particular?"

"I want to go down by the cut."

I saw he was serious. "Are you sure?"

He nodded. "And then I want to head over to Harwich Port and get a Dairy Queen."

I hesitated. As far as I knew, he hadn't left the house in weeks.

"I want to do something ordinary, something normal."

I studied him for a few minutes.

"Please," he said. "I want to be with you somewhere outside this room, this house. Somewhere where we can pretend for a minute that things are normal."

I FOUND him a clean sweatshirt and shoes, helped him dress. Of course, there was no way we could leave Rocker, and so he came along, too. By the time Luke had walked to my car, leaning on me the entire way, he was weak and out of breath, and I was already second-guessing the outing. I slid into the driver's seat and sat for a moment, trying to decide if we should continue, when he said, "Well, what are you waiting for? A push or a shove?"

I switched on the ignition.

"God, this feels great," he said. He didn't look so great. I wasn't sure how long he'd be able to last and so went directly down Main Street and toward the Coast Guard station and the cut, a break in the barrier beach on the Atlantic. It was a warm day, one of the rare windless ones, and I started to roll down my window when I noticed he was hunched forward, hugging himself. "Cold?" I asked.

He nodded. I closed the window and cranked on the heater. I hadn't thought to bring a jacket for him, since the temperature had reached the midseventies. I pulled into the parking lot opposite the station but kept the engine on. The heater pushed hot air through the vent by our legs. There were about a dozen other cars there. In the SUV next to us, two girls ate sandwiches and drank takeout coffee. I looked across to South Beach, just past the breach where the tides had shoaled the sands, forming a connection from the barrier spit to the mainland, a corrugated arc of sand. Winter-weary walkers were spread out along the beach, strolling along the water's edge. Occasionally someone stooped and retrieved something from the sand.

"What are they picking up?" I asked him.

"Probably shells, maybe a few sand dollars or starfish."

"Really? I found a starfish one summer when I was about five. I still have it."

"Ah, the amazing starfish," he said. "Another question for the poets and Nona's God. Why should the starfish hold the miraculous power to regenerate and not us?"

Of course there was no answer to that. I wanted to take his hand but held back, afraid he'd interpret the gesture as pity. To tell the truth, I'd been off balance since the moment he'd admitted that he had missed me the day before. Again, the air between us had shifted, but I wasn't sure of the new ground. It was as if, over the past weeks, we had been moving and moving toward a certain destination, and then suddenly had arrived but didn't have a name for the place we found ourselves occupying, or even the right to speak of it. I think he felt it, too. He rolled down his window. Rocker sat up and put his paws on the back of Luke's seat and nuzzled his nose to the opening.

"Will you be warm enough with that open?" I asked.

"I need to smell the salt," he said.

We sat for a while, watching the beachcombers. The girls in the SUV finished their lunch and left. A fishing vessel made its way in through the channel, on its way back in to the fish pier.

"God, but I miss this," he said.

"The ocean?"

"All of it."

I focused on the boat cutting through whitecaps, watched it hook around a marker buoy.

"I hate being like this," he said.

I reached over and took his hand then. When I allow myself to think back to my time with him, that afternoon is one of the memories I recall in every detail: the sun pouring through the windshield, heating my chest; the doggy smell of Rocker mixed with the brine of ocean air; Luke's hand in mine. The promise of possibilities taking root in my heart.

After a while, he rolled up the window. I put the car in reverse, and we headed over to Harwich Port.

"You live around here, don't you?" he said.

"In the campground," I said. "Wanna see?"

"Sure."

I took the left fork off 28 and onto Lower County, swung through the narrow side roads that led to my family's cottage.

"I haven't been down here in years," he said. "It used to be mostly summer homes."

"It still is," I said. Throughout the winter, Faye and I had been the only people on our street, although over the Easter weekend, families had started to appear and had begun the annual task of taking down storm shutters and opening up their homes. I pulled up in front of the cottage.

"You have a view of the sound," he said.

"Yes." A picture took shape in my mind: Luke and me in the cottage, where I would tend to him, heal him. I allowed myself to almost believe this pretty dream, a fantasy rooted not in the truth of a reptilian, cunning disease but in a spreading, irrational desire in me, desire built on love, which later in the fall I would hear labeled obsession. But that day I was taken with the dangerous belief that if you loved someone, you could save his life.

AT THE Dairy Queen, we each got a vanilla swirl. Rocker, too. I was feeling happy, triumphant. I turned to say something to Luke, but his face, twisted in pain, cut short my words. And then he groaned.

"What?" I said, meaning, *What's wrong? What can I do? What do you need? Oh God.*

"Home," he managed, more groan than word. I opened my door and tossed what was left of our cones, then sped back down 28. He moaned again—a sound akin to the noises Ashley had made during child labor—then doubled over, cramping. In the rear seat, Rocker began to whine, a back-of-the-throat, nervous whimper.

"Luke? Are you okay?" My chest tightened. My mouth turned dry.

WHEN WE returned to the house, Jim was there in the yard, and I nearly wept at the sight of him. He started toward the car, but before he could reach the door, Luke lurched out, took two steps, and then fell, retching and puking, spewing vanilla swirl soft serve all over the grass.

"Steady," Jim said.

Luke retched again, and then a brown stain spread over the seat of his pants. Shit rolled down his legs, pooled in his shoes. Rocker jumped from the car and ran to Luke, pushing against his legs.

"Get a leash on that dog and keep him away," Jim yelled.

I sat in the car, hands clenching the wheel.

"Now," Jim shouted. He was supporting Luke, half carrying him toward the house.

I swallowed and swallowed, frozen, unable to move.

"Jess," Jim hollered, "get hold of the damn dog."

I *wanted* to move. Didn't he understand that? I would have if I could have.

"Jess?" Jim yelled again. And then a pickup pulled up and a man got out, and amazingly that broke my paralysis. I crossed the lawn and grabbed hold of Rocker's collar.

"Need a hand with that?" the man asked.

"Christ," Luke said. His face twisted into a spasm of pain. Or anger. "Don't let him see me," I heard him say to Jim. He pushed the words out between clenched teeth.

Jim jerked his head at me, indicating I was to intercept the man in the pickup, then he lifted Luke and took him into the house.

"Need some help there?" the man asked again. He stood by the truck.

"We've got it under control," I said. *Under control.* My hands shook.

"Jesus," the stranger said. "Is it always like this?"

My voice returned. "Not this bad."

He turned toward me. "I'm Rich."

"Jessie," I said.

"Doesn't look like a great time for me to be stopping by," he said.

"No." Rocker pulled against the restraint. I got a good look at the man now and thought, *This is Rich?* He was built square and was darkly tanned, like all the men who worked on the sea. Too much sun, and probably liquor, too. Still, he possessed the kind of raw energy that some women—women like Paige—found attractive. And he knew it. I took a step back, put some distance between us.

"I'd better go in," I said, "see if I can help out."

"Should I come?"

"I don't think so."

"Right," he said, relieved, I thought, not to have to go into that house. "Tell him I'll call later." He started to say something more, but I had already turned away, headed inside, not letting go of the Lab.

IN THE kitchen, I listened to the sounds from the bathroom. The running of the shower. A toilet flushing. I waited while Jim got Luke bathed and changed and settled. Finally, he came out of Luke's room, closing the door behind him. He carried an armload of soiled clothes. I could smell the stench across the room. He dropped the pile by the basement door and turned toward me.

"Just what the hell were you thinking?" He was furious, a Jim I had never seen.

"He wanted to go out," I managed to say, thinking, Oh God, don't let Luke be too bad. "We're supposed to do what they want."

"You're *supposed* to have some sense, to use your head," he said.

"I'm sorry," I said. "He just wanted to see the ocean." I started to cry. "I'm sorry."

"Hey." He came over and slipped his arm around my shoulder. I managed to take a breath, tried to get myself under control. The stench from Luke's clothes was overpowering, like a third presence in the room.

"I'm going to go take care of this stuff," Jim said. "I'll be right back." He headed to the basement. I heard the rumble of the washing machine starting up. By the time he returned, I had retrenched.

"Will he be all right?"

Jim looked at me, his gaze steady. "He's not dying today, if that's what you're asking."

The stone sitting beneath my breast shifted, lifted. Jim crossed to the sink and washed his hands. There was a smudge of shit on his shirtsleeve, and he rinsed that, scrubbing it out.

"Should you phone the doctor or something?" I asked. I couldn't erase the picture of Luke doubled over, caught in spasms of diarrhea and vomiting.

"I'll give Ginny a call," he said. "He's lost a lot of fluid. She should probably check to make sure he's not getting dehydrated."

"Should I get him some water?"

"In a bit. Let him get quiet, things settled down. Is there any Coke or ginger ale in the house?"

"Both."

"Try the ginger ale. Shake it until it's flat, and then give him a little at a time. When I say a little, I mean a teaspoonful."

"Okay," I said, glad beyond measure for something to do.

"I'd like to wait for Nona to get back, but I'm already late for my next appointment. Will you tell her she can call me anytime?"

"Okay," I said. I didn't mention that Nona was in Wellfleet for the night, afraid that he would phone her and she would insist on returning. Even then—after all that had passed—I wanted to stay with Luke. To have the night with him. Later I would see that, from the beginning, I wanted too much. Wanted too much in a fierce and violent way that could only lead to trouble.

LUKE SLEPT for hours. I sat in the chair by his bed and watched. After a while, I retrieved my pad and sketched his face. Over the days, I had done dozens of drawings but not nearly enough. Sometimes I just did quick lines, the suggestion of him. Or his hands. His face angled away, shadows falling across his jaw.

When I looked over, he was awake, watching me. I flipped the pad shut and set it aside.

"Haven't you done plenty of those already?" he said, causing a flush to heat my cheeks. I wondered how much he had observed during those times I'd thought he slept.

"Do you mind?" I said.

He didn't answer. I reached over to the table and picked up the glass of ginger ale. "Jim said you should have some fluid." I offered him a spoonful. He sipped, swallowed.

"What time is it?"

"A bit after seven."

"I hate to ask you," he said, "but Rocker needs to be fed. And walked."

At the sound of his name, the Lab crossed to the bed. He followed me to the kitchen. I measured out his kibble, then took him outside, walked him around the perimeter of the lot. Back in the kitchen, I ate a few spoonfuls of macaroni and cheese, cold, straight from the fridge. When I returned to Luke's room, he was sitting on the edge of the bed.

"Do you need something?"

"My medicine." He nodded toward the kitchen. "The bottle's in a cabinet by the sink."

The one firm and certain rule that had been drummed into us during the training was that we were not to give medications. But surely there were exceptions. They couldn't expect us to stand by and see a patient in pain. "How many?" I asked.

"One should do," he said.

I shook out the pill and carried it to him, watched him wash it down with a swallow of ginger ale. It seemed a harmless thing to do, the right thing. I turned on a lamp, just the one. When the phone rang, we both started. It was Ginny, calling in to check. I handed him the phone, listened to him tell her he was okay now, that he was getting liquids, that he had someone with him. "About a seven," he said into the phone. I knew he was telling her where he was on the one to ten pain scale.

"Is she coming over?" I asked after he hung up.

"Tomorrow. She said just keep on with the ginger ale and call if I needed to."

He shifted his position.

"When I was little and sick, my mother used to make ginger tea for me," I said. "She would serve it in a special china cup. When I finished the tea, she'd give me a back rub." Lily had done the same thing when I had been in the hospital, the day after my surgery. I could still recall the comfort of her touch.

"Sounds nice," he said.

"The tea or the back rub?"

"Both."

Without asking, I reached for the controls and lowered the head of the mechanical bed until he was prone. "Here," I said, "turn over."

I half expected him to refuse, but without a word, he slipped off the sweatshirt he slept in. I was grateful he had turned away and could not see my face. I had to catch my lip between my teeth. There were patches of raw skin. Bedsores, in spite of Jim's care. Each rib, each knob of his spine, was raised in relief, bones so tight against his skin, it seemed a wonder they hadn't pushed through. I had seen photographs of skeletal bodies like his staring out from the pages of textbooks and newspapers. Brown-skinned children with flies crawling at the corners of their eyes. Gaunt-faced people clad in striped pajamas, so emaciated it was impossible to tell their gender.

His skin was dry, as if filmed with powder, with a yeasty, etherish sharpness to it. I traced the ridges of his bones with my finger, smoothed my palms over his broad-shouldered back, comforting, memorizing. I tended to him in this way for nearly an hour. Even as wasted as he was, I could see how muscular he once had been. He was long past due for a haircut, and dark curls formed at the nape of his neck. I allowed myself to touch them, and they felt exactly as I had known they would, soft, not wiry like some.

"I know," he said. "I need a haircut. It's been driving me crazy."

In the gentle glow of the desk lamp, I memorized the terrain of his body, traced the L-shaped scar on his right shoulder blade— nearly two inches long—and wondered what its history was. When I finished, he turned over and pulled up the blanket. In the moment before he could conceal it, I saw his penis, erect, pressing against the leg of his pajama bottoms. The air spread around me, and I lost my sense of direction. I felt the knife edge of desire, a longing so intense, I thought that it surely held the power to stop my heart, and then, just as swiftly, a sorrow marrow-deep.

"Thanks," he said, his voice guarded. "For the back rub. That was nice." He reached for the bed controls and returned to a sitting position. I unsheathed a fresh straw and set it in the ginger ale, watched as he took a sip. When I was certain my voice would hold steady, I asked if he wanted the television on or for me to read to him, but he said no to both. We sat and watched the patterns that moonlight drew on the walls, sat for so long the moon inched across the sky and out of our line of vision. At some point, he reached for my hand. Then he surprised me by reaching up and stroking my hair. He asked if he could smell it, and that simple and unexpected request nearly undid me. I bent to him, let him press his face into my scalp, felt desire stir again.

"You have beautiful hair," he said, his voice a whisper.

The air shifted again, leaving me disoriented, confused. "I know a girl whose hair saved her life," I heard myself say, my head still bent to him.

"Rapunzel?"

"No, a real woman, someone I knew in college." Why had this story surfaced now? Why was I telling it to him?

"And . . ."

"Well, she was hiking in California with a friend. They were well into the forest when a breeze came up and lifted her hair, blew it across her face. She said that her hair smelled of smoke." I told Luke how the woman had leaned toward her friend, bending her head so she could smell her scalp, and the other woman agreed that her hair did in fact smell of smoke. They both turned into the wind, but neither of them could detect anything in the air, only in the one's hair. The other woman wanted to keep hiking, but her friend insisted they go back, she couldn't get away from the smell of her hair, as if it had been singed. That evening, a fire broke out deep in the woods. "And so she was saved by her hair," I said.

"True story?"

"True."

"Your hair," he said, "smells of sweat."

"Jesus," I said, pulling away, embarrassed. "I'm so glad I let you take a whiff."

"No," he said. "I like it. It reminds me of the sea."

I was absurdly pleased.

"Jesus," he said then. Beneath the outline of the sheet, he again had an erection. He shifted his weight. I pretended not to notice.

He asked for more ginger ale; I got a glass for myself, too. I set both tumblers on the table by his bed, then turned off the lamp, asked him if there was anything else he needed.

"You don't have to stay in here," he said. "There are beds upstairs. Or the couch."

In answer, I slipped off my shoes and, suddenly bold, lay down beside him. "Okay?" I asked, afraid he could hear the silent commotion of my heart.

He edged over to give me more room. We lay there, and within minutes, he slipped into a drugged sleep. The room was hot, the bed narrow, and I couldn't sleep. I thought about the scar on his shoulder blade, wondered again about its origin. I listened to him breathe.

At least I'll have this night, I thought. *After.*

Sometime near dawn, I fell into a gray dreamless place. I woke to the creaking of the bed. Luke was sitting up. Rocker scrambled up and stretched, performing a perfect yoga pose. The morning sun flooded the room, robbing it of last night's intimacy, as if it had never been.

It was morning, and he was still alive.

ten

On Thursday, I rode with Faye to our volunteers' twice-monthly meeting. She had baked a pan of brownies, and the car smelled sugary with chocolate.

Our group met in the Methodist Church in a cinder block basement room used on Sundays for church school. There was a framed picture of a blond Jesus—all pastel piety—hanging from a nail that had been drilled into the concrete block and an old upright piano that I imagined was used to accompany the children's hymns. *Jesus loves me! This I know.* At Lily's insistence, Ashley and I had attended Sunday school in a room almost exactly like this.

Including Faye and the hospice chaplain, there were nine of us, gathered, Faye told us, to offer "a circle of support for one another." Early in the training, I had felt shy around the others. Beth and Ben and Gordon. Sal and Jennifer and Muriel. Although I knew there was no such thing as absolute virtue, at first I attributed the purest motives to the other volunteers, ascribing them goodness approaching sanctification. But as I got to know them and with greater clarity, I saw them as they were. Flawed and ordinary people with free hours in their lives, wanting to be of use and to do good in a world that surely needed it and in return finding satisfaction in knowing they were helping. Lily would have been happy in their company. Later in that fall, they would divide and take sides—for or against me—but that spring, they were without exception kind to me. I thought I reminded them of their daughters.

We sat in the folding chairs Faye had set up in a circle, and the chaplain opened the meeting with a quote by Leonard Nimoy, of all people: "The miracle is this—the more we share, the more we have." Beth, the former teacher and most anal of the group, asked him to repeat this; then she took out a pencil and wrote it down in round Parker penmanship. I could picture it affixed to her refrigerator with a magnet.

Next, Faye tended to some business. A new e-mail address for the hospice. The date for the next meeting. And then—going clockwise—we went around the circle, each taking a turn. Beth was still having issues with the nurse on her team, who, she maintained, was just short of being rude and seemed to resent her presence. Faye listened, and then said, in the most nonjudgmental voice imaginable, that occasionally some of the nurses developed proprietary feelings for their cases. "Remember, it all comes out of caring," she said, which appeared to mollify Beth to some degree. Sal reported that he'd built a wheelchair ramp for his patient with MS, and Muriel said she was still working on the photo album with her patient, the woman with congestive heart failure. *Her* patient. A slight smile crossed Faye's mouth at the use of the possessive.

Jennifer said her son couldn't understand why she wanted to be around dying people, didn't she find it depressing. "I told him that to participate in one of the most important days of someone's life, to be close on the final journey, is a transcendent experience," she said. The others nodded. When it was my turn, I told them about Luke and the Steinbeck short stories and backgammon. There were things I was unwilling to share, things I wanted to hold private, so I didn't tell them that he was teaching me birdcalls or that I had given him a back rub or how, when we sat in the moonlight, he had held my hand. I certainly didn't mention Luke's having an erection. "Any problems?" Faye asked. I told them about the hostility I occasionally felt from Paige. I didn't say a word about taking Luke out for a ride and the disastrous consequences. And of course I didn't say anything about my feelings for him. Faye's gaze held steady on my face while I spoke, but I avoided her eyes, fearing she would read in them all the things I was omitting. I suppose if I had shared more, they wouldn't have felt so betrayed later.

It was Gordon's turn next, and he paused several moments before he began. He had to swallow a couple of times and kept saying sorry while he gained control. He told us that Roger, the forty-year-old man with the failed bone marrow transplant, had slipped into a coma. He wasn't expected to last the night. Gordon had brought his cell phone with him, although this was usually discouraged at the meetings. He struggled to keep from crying. Sal laid a beefy hand on his shoulder, clasping it in the hearty way men did when they wanted to offer support. Gordon leaned forward, his elbows propped on his knees. He stared at the floor. "I have such mixed feelings about going there if they call," he said. "I'm sixty-seven, and believe it or not, I've never seen anyone die."

Faye asked how many of us had been present at a death. Ben and Muriel raised their hands. I didn't, and Faye looked over at me but said nothing, although I was fairly certain that she knew I had been in the car with my daddy when he'd had his attack and died.

"What are your memories of that moment?" Faye asked Ben and Muriel.

Ben spoke first, his voice low. "If you mean the precise moment when my father died, I missed it," he said. "I was there in his room, but I missed it."

"It can come so fast," Muriel said, nodding in agreement. "You can be waiting and waiting, and then, in the time it takes to draw a breath, it's over. It's not dramatic, like you might think, but gentle. A sigh. Like an inhale, except it's an exhale."

"Yes," Faye said. "The moment of death is very much like giving birth. There is a contraction, and then a release. And as in birth, the labor of death comes in the days and hours and weeks before."

Or it doesn't, I thought, remembering my daddy. *It just comes. Sharp and sudden as an arrow made of lightning.*

Faye continued, talking about what our patients might think during this period. She said, "This can be a time to turn inward and ask the existential questions that can provoke great anxiety: *What makes a good person? Has my life been worthwhile? How many unresolved conflicts am I taking into my death?*"

The chaplain nodded. "What we are doing," he said, "whether we know it or not, what it is our great privilege to do, is to bear witness."

For nearly two hours, we sat on hard metal chairs and drank coffee and ate brownies, and beneath the benevolent gaze of a church school Jesus, we talked about dying and death. When the last of us had finished, Faye spoke of our need for self-care. She reminded us that, as part of a hospice team, we, too, were under a certain degree of stress and urged us to practice loving kindness to ourselves, to engage in stress-release activities, and to develop strategies to maintain well-being. "I recommend chocolate," she said. Everyone laughed and reached for another brownie.

"Don't forget," she said, "hospice workers need respite, too. Let your team members know when you need some time and distance." Again, I felt her gaze settle on me.

Just before the meeting ended, Gordon's cell phone rang. We all fell into silent waiting. "Roger's going," he said after he hung up. "The family asked if I could come now." We hugged him, even the men. Faye told him to call her later if he needed to talk, no matter how late it was. "Love is more powerful than fear," she told him. "Remember that. The most important thing you can give to the family is a sense of no fear." Gordon slipped out; the chaplain closed with a prayer, but I wasn't listening. I reflected on Faye's words and wondered if it was truly possible to get to a place beyond fear. Could you grow beyond the fear of pain and deterioration, of separation and loss?

We stayed on after the others left. I folded and stacked the chairs while Faye rinsed out the coffeemaker. "How do you stand it?" I asked. "How can you keep doing this?"

"Remember, I was a pediatric nurse before this," Faye said. "Believe me, this is easier."

"Easier?"

"This is natural," she said. "Death is natural."

"Even for someone like Roger? I mean, he's only forty." I blinked back tears. "Shit," I said. "Don't you ever get tired of the suffering?"

"There's value in suffering," Faye said.

How Buddhist of you, I thought, suddenly angry. "Tell that to Roger," I said sharply. Or to Luke. Or Nona.

"That is something I suspect Roger has already learned," Faye said, her voice calm in the face of my outburst. "Our job is to witness the suffering and remain compassionate, but not to get overly involved in it."

Right, I thought. My heart didn't know the first damn thing about detachment.

eleven

I T WAS PAST nine by the time Faye dropped me off after the meeting. When I opened the door, the phone was ringing, nearly causing my heart to stop. *Luke,* I thought. And then, *Please God, no, not yet.* The receiver shook when I lifted it.

"Where were you?" Ashley said. "I've been calling for hours."

"I had a meeting," I said, able to breathe again.

"What meeting? That hospice thing?" In past calls, Ashley had shared with me her theory that one of the reasons I currently had no love life was because my volunteer work was morbid and depressing. Better to be making phone calls for United Way, she had said. I thought of Jennifer's comment at the meeting about how she told her son that hospice work was a transcendent experience.

"Yes," I said, "the hospice thing."

"Damn, there goes my fantasy of you on a date. Little sister, you've got to get yourself a life."

"I've got a life," I said.

"I'm thinking, maybe not so much," Ashley said.

"Don't start."

"I'm only saying—"

Well, I knew where this was heading and cut her off at the crossroad. "How's Lily?"

"In love and acting like a teenager. She's dying for you to meet him. She wants you to come for a weekend before they set sail."

"I have a photo she sent. Mama and the Walking Yawn."

Ashley laughed. "Whatever floats her boat, and take it from me, Jess, it's obvious the boy toy knows a thing or two about levitation."

Why, I wondered, did everyone *insist* on sharing her opinion of Lily's sex life with me? "Well, what do you know about him?" I said. "Has anyone checked into his background? I mean, Daddy left Lily a chunk of money. For all we know, the Yawn could be after that. Think about it. He's taking her on a trip across the ocean. Just the two of them in a boat. We both know Lily is clueless on a boat. Doesn't that sound just a tiny bit suspicious?"

Ashley laughed again. "Do you think you can ratchet down the paranoia a degree or two?"

"Go ahead, laugh," I said. "I still think it would be a good idea if you have Daniel check him out."

"What? You mean hire a private detective or something?"

"Yes."

"Jess, honey, you've been overdosing on the DVDs. He's a *dentist*."

"That doesn't mean anything," I said. "Maybe *you* should watch the news."

Ashley ignored this. "So, listen," she said. "Aren't you curious about why I'm calling? Aren't you just the teensiest bit interested in hearing about who's back in town, asking around about you?"

"You're going to tell me anyway."

"Bill," she said.

"Bill who?"

"I can't believe you've forgotten," Ashley screamed. "God, for months on end, you bored the rest of us to distraction with your talk about Bill this and Bill that and guess what Bill is doing this weekend. *Bill Miller*."

I remembered then. Bill was the lacrosse player I dated my senior year at Thomas Jefferson. I'd heard he had become a lawyer.

"He's moved back to Richmond," Ashley said.

"Really?" I said, thinking *ancient history*. "I haven't been keeping track."

"Maybe you should have. We're talking tall, dark, and divorced."

I thought of Luke—tall, dark, and dying. Sorrow hot as bile burned in my throat.

"Helloooo," Ashley said. "Anyone there?"

"I'm here," I said.

"So here's my plan," Ashley said. "You fly down for the weekend, and I'll set up a dinner party. Casual. Not anything huge. Three or four couples. No, let's stick with three. I'll ask Nan and Bob Davidson. You remember them. And Bill, of course. Not back in town one week and asking about you, Jess. He's seriously interested. Interested and eligible. So what do you say?"

"About what?"

"Jesus be, have I been talking to myself here? The dinner party. We can't do it this Saturday. That won't give me enough time to set it up. How about next weekend?"

"Next weekend?"

"Jeez, Jess, are you smoking something or what? Yes, next weekend. You could fly down on Friday, hang out here. The boys miss you. They haven't seen you since Christmas. I miss you. We can visit; you can see Lily. She'll be over the moon to hear you're coming. Hell, maybe I'll even include her and the boy toy in the dinner so you can meet him. No, that won't work; we want to keep it fun, no parents. So we'll do lunch with them Saturday at the club and save the evening for Bill, a romantic dinner, candles, but still casual—I'll farm the boys out for the night—and then you can fly back on Sunday."

I let her run down. "I can't," I said.

"The following weekend, then. You don't want to waste time. He's fresh meat on the market, but Lord knows he won't last out there for long."

"I can't," I repeated.

"Why not? Is it the plane ticket? Listen, I'll send you the money."

"It's not the money."

"What, then?"

I hesitated. "It's Luke. I can't leave him now."

"Who the hell is Luke?"

"Luke Ryder," I said, barely concealing my impatience. I'd told Ashley his name, told her about Nona. "My hospice patient."

"The fisherman with cancer?"

"Yes."

"And you can't leave him for a weekend to meet your future husband, the future uncle to my boys? I don't mean to sound callous, Jess, but have you lost your mind? Just get your ass on a plane and get yourself down here. So you'll come, right? I can count on it?"

I didn't answer.

"What?" Ashley said into the silence. "What's going on?"

"I just can't, Ashley. That's all."

My sister gave a little laugh. "Have you fallen for this guy or what?"

The wire hummed between us.

"Oh God," she said. "You have, haven't you?"

I struggled to keep my voice light. "Oh, you know girls like me. That's what we do. Remember how you used to say I could create a relationship standing in line at the grocery store."

"Oh, Jess, honey," Ashley said, not fooled at all. "Don't do this to yourself."

I started to cry.

"Oh, baby," Ashley said. "Listen, would it help if I came up?"

"No." I inhaled, concentrated on making my voice steady, persuasive. "I've had a bad day, that's all. Really, I'll be fine tomorrow."

Ashley wasn't convinced. "Tell me," she said. "Tell me you aren't in love with him."

"I'm not in love with him," I parroted tonelessly.

"Oh, Jess, you sweet, foolish baby. There's no future in this. You know that, don't you? Come home. Promise me you'll at least think about coming home."

"I'll think about it," I said. A lie, and we both knew it. I thought suddenly of that one-month therapist who'd said I had to fall in love with a guy before I could break up with him. Would he consider this progress? For the first time in my life, I wasn't going to leave a man before he could abandon me.

I TOSSED in bed half the night, Ashley's words echoing in my head. *There's no future in it.* Well, I *knew* that. I wasn't completely stupid. Later, in the fall, I would tell myself I *should* have resisted when in fact, I did the exact opposite, gave myself over, *flung* myself straight into the heat of desire. But this wasn't about being smart or foolish. Some things you couldn't control. *I couldn't help myself,* people said when rushing headlong into folly, as if possessed of madness. And it was a kind of lunacy, a passion that took over, erasing reason, wanting only to be fed. In retrospect, I would see that it was inevitable. It is always what lies beyond our grasp that we lust for most.

twelve

R AIN LASHED AGAINST the windowpanes, and it was a moment before I understood that it wasn't the storm that woke
me but the phone.

"Jessie?"

"Yes."

"Can you come?" Nona's voice was so weak, it took me a moment to recognize it as hers.

"I'm on my way," I said. I threw on the first thing my hands
landed on and rushed off without stopping to wash up or brush my
hair. On the way over, I whispered every prayer I knew. I switched
the wipers on high, but their metronome beat was half that of my
heart's, thumping inside its cage of ribs. As soon as I turned onto
his street, I saw the ambulance, its flashing lights, greasy and my-
opic through the rain-blurred windshield. "Oh God," I said for the
umpteenth time, my heart beating even faster, though I wouldn't
have thought it possible.

No siren. That was a good sign, wasn't it? *Wasn't it?* I jumped out
of the car—key in ignition, door open—and caught sight of a face
peering from behind curtains in the neighboring house. I tore past
the ambulance idling in impatient silence and ran to the house. A
paramedic stood inside the door, jotting notes on a clipboard.

"I'm from hospice," I said, the words so rushed they came out as
one. "Where is he? How is he?"

The EMT stared at me. I must have looked frantic, mad, my hair
so wild it looked electrocuted. And then I saw Nona. She was
stretched out on the plaid couch with two paramedics bent over

her, so big and burly, their presence filled the room. One knelt at her side and was strapping a blood pressure cuff around her arm; the other was rooting around in a defibrillator case.

"Nona?" I said, confused. Luke sat at his mother's feet. I crossed to him. "What's going on?"

"She woke up about an hour ago with chest pains. Some dizziness. She was having trouble getting her breath."

I lowered my voice. "Heart attack?"

"They're not saying anything."

The man with the clipboard turned to us. "She's stable at the moment, but we're going to take her up to the hospital," he said.

"What's wrong?" Luke asked.

"Her blood pressure is elevated, and her pulse is slightly irregular."

"Has she had a——"

"Like I said, things are stable now. The best thing is to get her up there where she can be evaluated by the doctors."

"And then what?"

"They'll run some tests, take it from there."

Two of the medics returned with a wheeled stretcher.

"Luke?" Nona said.

"Right here," he said. "How're you doing?"

"Such a ruckus over a little dizziness," she said. "I shouldn't have called them. Just a foolish old woman."

"You did the right thing."

"I hate all this fuss over me."

"They're going to take you up to Hyannis, to the hospital."

"Oh Lord," she said, her eyes panicky. "There's no need of *that*."

"Just a precaution," he said.

"I feel so foolish. All this *commotion*."

I took her hand. "Do you want anything to take with you? Your handbag?"

"Oh yes. I'll need that," she said. "And my watch. My glasses. Everything's upstairs." She clung to my hand, pulled me closer.

"What is it?" I said.

"My teeth," Nona whispered.

"What?"

"I'll need my teeth. They're in a glass upstairs."

The medics moved a chair aside to make room to bring through the stretcher.

"For heaven's sake, I don't need *that*," Nona said, sounding for a minute like her old self. "I can walk."

"It's regulations, Mrs. Ryder."

Luke rose unsteadily. I ran upstairs and got Nona's black plastic purse, her watch, her glasses, found the dentures in a glass by the bed. A partial plate. I had to close my eyes while I fished it from the solution, wadded it in tissue. On the way down to Nona, I used my shirttail to clear the film from the lens of the glasses. She took the purse from me, tucked the glasses, teeth, and wristwatch in an inside pocket, then pulled me close again and whispered in my ear.

"What is it, Ma?" Luke said.

Nona released my hand and reached over and patted his cheek, as if he were a boy. "Now don't you go worrying about me."

"Should Jessie go with you? Or follow the ambulance up to Hyannis?"

She turned to me. "You stay here with Luke."

"What about you?"

"Oh, you know hospitals. I'll probably be stuck in a cubicle somewhere; they'll take their own sweet time before they get to me."

"You shouldn't be alone. How will you get home?"

"Will you call Helen?" she said. "Oh, and Paige. I suppose someone should let her know, so she won't come by and go hysterical when she hears where I am."

One of the medics indicated that it was time to go. They lifted her, hefting her from couch to stretcher as if she weighed no more than a Christmas ham. She gave a last, nervous look. Within seconds, they had her out the door and in the ambulance. The siren

screamed to life, startling me. We didn't speak until the last echo of
it had vanished, leaving a hollow emptiness in its wake. I helped
Luke back to his bed. When the phone rang, he indicated that I
should answer. It was a neighbor. She had seen the ambulance and
wondered if there was anything they could do. I thanked her, promised I would call if we needed help.

"I'm sorry about all this," Luke said.

"All what?"

"Getting you over here. Nona should have called Jim or Ginny
or one of the staff. She shouldn't have burdened you." *Burdened.*

"That's ridiculous," I said. "I was glad to come. You know that."

"This is too much for her."

"Has she had heart problems before?"

"Not that I know of, but she wouldn't tell me if she did. I didn't
learn about her cataracts until after she'd had the operation."

"I still think someone should have gone with her."

"Would you call Helen? What time is it, anyway?"

I checked the kitchen clock, amazed to see it was only a little
before seven. I felt as if I had been up for hours. When I got through
to Helen, she was clearly shaken and asked about three hundred
questions, none of which I had an answer for. Before we hung up,
she promised she'd head directly to Hyannis and said once she'd
seen Nona, she'd call with an update. Luke decided there was no
point in phoning Paige until after eight.

I put on a pot of coffee and made hot cereal for Luke. I found
half a loaf of bread in the breadbox—the white, squishy kind I
hadn't had since I was a child—and dropped a piece in the toaster.
I found a tray and brought the cereal to him, nibbled the toast while
he pretended to eat the Cream of Wheat.

"What did she say?" he asked.

"Who?"

"Nona. Before they took her. What did she whisper to you?"

I smiled at the memory.

"What was it?" he said.

"She was worried."

"About me?"

I shook my head. "About her legs. She hadn't shaved, and she didn't want the paramedics to see her hairy legs."

He stared at me. "You're kidding."

"Cross my heart."

We started to laugh, breaking the tension.

After breakfast, I did the dishes and cleaned up the kitchen. It felt cozy there, the two of us, the rain outside. When I was finished, I went back to Luke. "Do you want to get shaved?" I asked. I had never shaved a man in my life, but I wanted to now. It seemed an intimate thing, as personal as bathing.

"Jim's coming around eleven," he said. "He'll take care of it."

"Anything you need?"

"I could use a Dilaudid."

"One?"

"Yes."

I didn't hesitate but went to the kitchen and opened the prescription bottle, handed him the orange tablet. He turned on the *Today* show, and we watched together while the rain lashed against the window. At eight thirty, he phoned Paige, but there was no answer. "I wonder where she is?" he said.

You don't even want *to know,* I thought, but said only, "Probably sleeping with the phone turned off."

"I worry about her. She's had a tough time of it. First the divorce, and now this."

"She seems pretty strong to me," I said.

"You think so?" I could see he wanted to believe it.

WE WATCHED the rest of Meredith and Matt, and then turned to a game show. A little after ten, Luke asked if I'd bring him the walker. He needed to use the toilet. There was a portable commode in the room, but he was embarrassed to use it. "Call me if you need me,"

I said. I was afraid he'd fall while in there. I wasn't strong enough to lift him. I was fretting about that when Helen phoned.

"How's Nona?" I asked.

"I'm right here with her," Helen said, and passed the receiver to Nona.

"Luke?" she said.

"It's Jessie," I said. "Luke's in the bathroom right now. How are you? What did the doctor say?"

"All the folderol they put a person through. You wouldn't believe it."

"Are you okay? What did they say?"

"I'm just fine," she said.

"But what did they say about the chest pain, the dizziness?"

Nona snorted. "They think it was an anxiety attack. *Anxiety*. I swear, they make me sound like a nervous old lady. I told them I've never had an anxiety attack in my life."

"Will Helen be bringing you home now?"

"They insist on keeping me overnight. For observation, they say. If you ask me, they just want the money. Do you have any idea how much it costs? I hope to heaven Medicare takes care of it."

The bathroom door opened. "Wait a minute," I said. "Here's Luke. Let me put him on."

"Well, she sounds better," he said when he hung up. "Like herself." I could see he was relieved.

Jim arrived shortly before eleven, and I explained the situation.

"It doesn't surprise me," he said. "She's been under a hell of a lot of stress. I'll take a run up there tonight and check on her. Have you made arrangements here for Luke? There are respite nurses who can come in for the night."

"Everything's taken care of," I said. "Listen, while you're here, I'm going to run out and pick up a few things. It won't take more than forty-five minutes."

He checked his schedule. "Let me make a couple of calls. Then I'll be able to stay here for an hour."

. . .

THE CAR door was still wide open—a reminder of my frantic run into the house earlier—and the driver's seat was rain-drenched. Water seeped through my jeans as I drove back to the cottage. I took a quick shower, shampooed my hair. I didn't take time to blow it dry but wrapped a towel, turban-style, around my head, then dashed about gathering some things: my overnight bag, scented candles, lotion, a set of sheets from the linen shelf. I had a quart container of chicken soup in the freezer, some that Faye gave me back in March, and I grabbed that, too. My hair was still damp when I headed back to Luke's, driving through the haze of rain much faster than was wise, although the torrential downpour of earlier had changed to a steady, near-silent soaking. I left my things in the car, figuring I'd bring them in the house after Jim left.

"He's sleeping," Jim said when I went in.

"That's good," I said.

"I've called the hospital and checked on Nona. They've given her something to calm her down. Probably a good night's sleep is the best thing in the world for her right now."

"They're sure it's not her heart?"

"As sure as they can be. All the tests are negative."

"I was so worried."

"How about you? Are you okay to stay here until Faye lines up a replacement? My schedule is full until after five, but I can swing back by before I head up to Hyannis."

"There's really no need. But I know it will mean a lot to Nona if you see her."

"You sure you don't want me to call Faye so she can arrange for another volunteer to spell you until the night nurse arrives? You have arranged for that, right?"

I felt a breathless flutter in my chest. "I've taken care of every-thing," I said.

· · ·

SOMETIME AFTER three, the rain stopped. I brought my things in from the car.

"Jessie," Luke called.

"Be right in." I ran upstairs and found a towel and single sheet in the upstairs bath closet.

"What's that for?" Luke asked.

"You'll see." I dug through my bag, retrieved my comb and a pair of scissors. I shook out the sheet and draped it over his shoulders before he could refuse, tucked the towel around his neck. I set the comb and shears on the table.

"Wait a minute. You're giving me a haircut?"

"You got it," I said. A mindless rhythm vibrated in my chest.

"You sure you know what you're doing?" he said.

I snipped at the air with the scissors. "How do you think I made drinking money all through grad school?" I said, although, in truth, I had given only one other man a haircut, a Buddhist from Cambridge who had moved to Richmond seven years ago. We'd met at a flea market and were lovers for about two months. The one thing I remembered about him was that he once told me that yearning was at the center of all human experience.

I hadn't thought of the Buddhist—Paul—for a long time. His hair was sandy, and although he was only twenty-seven, it was so thin as to be wispy. Nothing like Luke's. I combed through his hair, dampened the thick clumps of curls with water. His head was beautifully shaped. I couldn't get enough of touching him, as if I could store it up. Slowly, working from front to back, I cut and trimmed and shaped. He didn't move. Black chips of hair fell onto his shoulders and pooled in his lap, vivid against the white sheet.

"The last time I had a home haircut, I was about four," he said. "I think Nona used a bowl."

I resisted the impulse to stroke his cheek, to bend my face to his scalp. I took longer than the job required. Finally I was done and stepped back to check. "Lookin' good," I said. "Yes, sir, you are looking mighty fine."

He rubbed his palm over the back of his neck and up over his scalp. "I have to admit it feels better."

"Want to see? I can get a mirror."

He shook his head. "I'll take your word for it."

I carefully folded up the sheet, taking care to scoop up the cuttings. "I'll be right back," I said. "I'm just going to shake this out."

"Want to take Rocker with you? He hasn't been out since morning."

"Come on, boy," I said. "Does he need the leash to go in the backyard?"

"Just keep an eye on him. If he starts to head for the road, call him back."

I stopped for a moment inside the kitchen door and, on impulse, reached inside the folded sheet and withdrew two ebony curls. I twisted them inside a paper towel, which I tucked in my bag.

Outside, the Lab ran in a frenzy of joy at being loose. He sniffed the ground and ran laps around the yard while I shook out the linen. Luke's hair twirled though the air; the longer strands floated down to the grass and lay there like black commas. I imagined chickadees or a titmouse swooping in and carrying the curls off for nests and, remembering the Greek myth, felt an unreasonable flash of fear. I should not have shaken the sheet there, but it was too late now. Once things are released to the wind, it is impossible to recapture them. I refolded the linen and waited while Rocker peed on a shrub, called him to me, and returned to the house.

THROUGHOUT THE afternoon, Luke dozed on and off. He asked me to stay with him, even when he slept, said my presence helped keep him steady, that he had never known anyone like me in that regard. Of course, I would have stayed by him even if he hadn't asked. Later he tried to call Paige, and again, there was no answer. "She must be off at work," he said.

The sun had reappeared earlier, after it stopped raining, and now it slid toward the west. Inside the house, it felt cozy, almost as if this were an ordinary day. While Luke watched the early news, I slipped out and performed housewifely chores: a load of laundry, a quick dusting of the living room, emptying the trash. Around six, I went in the kitchen to start dinner. I set the chicken soup on low. While it heated, I found two matching bowls. I put some saltines on a plate, poured two glasses of ginger ale. I could only find paper napkins and regretted I hadn't thought to bring cloth ones. I ran outside and cut two lilac stems and put those on the tray. When everything was ready, I carried it in to him. Rocker roused himself and came to the bed by Luke's side.

"You didn't have to bother with this," he said. He snapped a saltine in two and fed the halves to Rocker.

"It wasn't any bother."

He reached over and touched the tiny bells of the lilac blossoms. "They're in bloom already."

"Tulips will be next," I said.

"Spring works so hard to come," he said. He sounded tired.

I dipped a spoon in the broth and raised it to his lips. "I can manage," he said, and took the spoon from my hand. I knew he would make an attempt, pretend to eat, as he had at breakfast. It didn't seem possible that someone could exist on so little. "It's good," he said. I didn't tell him Faye had made the soup.

"What's your very favorite meal?" I asked.

He shrugged. "It's hard to remember the last time I really gave a damn."

"Well, what's the thing you would choose if you could only pick one?"

"You mean like the condemned man's last supper?"

"Not exactly the analogy I had in mind."

He laughed. My chest pinched at the sound. "The one thing?" he said. "Just one favorite thing?"

I nodded.

"That's tough. It's a toss-up."

"Between what?"

"Chicken Parmesan made with a thick, red sauce. Or rib roast, end cut, rare, and a baked potato on the side, heavy on the sour cream."

I smiled.

He fished a chunk of chicken out of the bowl and fed it to Rocker. "But, of course, on a hot summer night, watching a ball game, nothing on earth can beat a pepperoni pizza and a beer. What about you? What's your favorite?"

"Me? Oh, I like everything."

"You have to pick one, remember? Your rules."

I looked out the window at the growing darkness, unable to face him when I answered. "This," I whispered. "This. With you. This is my favorite meal." My words fell into silence. Finally I dared to look over, but I couldn't tell if he was angry or sad. An ache spread like a stain through my body.

He put the spoon down. The room was so still and empty, every movement drew notice. He stared out at the gathering dusk. "There is nothing here for you, Jess," he said.

"I don't care," I said.

"Don't you get it? I can't give you anything. I have nothing to give."

"I don't care," I repeated. "Let me give to you."

He rubbed his eyes, a weary gesture. "Why are you doing this?"

"I can't help it," I said.

"We can always help it."

"No. We can't. There are some things we can't stop. Some things that can't be helped."

"You're wrong," he said. "This is a mistake."

"It's not. I don't want anything from you." A lie, I knew. I was reduced to this single, feverish want. To receive. And to give, too. I couldn't remember ever having such a deep desire to give to a man.

"You're making a mistake," he said again, and turned from me, looking off into a middle distance.

"Luke?" I said.

He wouldn't answer for a minute. Then he said, in a voice so soft I had to lean close to hear, "It's impossible."

"Why?"

His mouth twisted in a bitter smile, but he reached for my hand. "I think that's pretty obvious."

"Is it?"

"Let's just say our timing's off."

I felt the harsh truth of what he said, felt the unbearable pain of knowing what might have been but couldn't be.

"Do you have any feelings for me?" I said.

His fingers tightened around mine. "That isn't the question."

"But do you?"

He wouldn't meet my eyes. "You know I do."

I held the words close. A quiet joy hummed in my chest.

"I wish . . . ," he began.

"What?"

"I wish you could have seen me at my best."

"I am," I said. I thought about his gentleness, his hand stroking Rocker, how carefully he listened to the birdcalls, how patiently he taught me to do the same, how much he loved the ocean, how calmly he faced what lay ahead. "I am."

"Liar," he said. He brought my hand to his lips.

AFTER A while, he again dozed off. I went to the kitchen. I cleaned up the dishes and dumped the rest of the soup into Rocker's bowl. He came in and lapped it up. I pulled on a sweater and got his leash, for it had grown dark, and I couldn't risk letting him run free. Outside, the air smelled the way it did after spring rain. As if the earth had been cleansed. Renewed.

You know I do.

Back inside, I carried Lily's sheets upstairs and stripped Luke's mattress. It had the slightly musty smell of a bed long unused. I re-made it with the soft linens; then I went down to him. He was awake but had not switched on the lamp, and I could not see him in the dark. "Do you mind if I turn on the light?"

"If you want." His voice was neutral, as if our earlier intimacy had not been.

"What's your routine at night?" I asked, carefully matching his tone. "Do you need to use the bathroom? Or to change?"

He looked down at his sweatshirt and pants. "I can sleep in these," he said, "but I need to use the john."

I helped him up, guided him to the toilet.

"I can take it from here," he said, and smiled. I was so grateful for that smile. When he was back in the bed, he asked for and I gave him another Dilaudid.

"I appreciate everything you've done today," he said. "This must have screwed up your day."

"No. Not at all."

"Is someone coming in later for the night?"

I shook my head. "I'm staying," I said. "I made up a bed upstairs. I can sleep there." I wondered what he was feeling. Maybe he wasn't feeling anything.

"You've done so much already," he said.

"It's not a problem. Really," I said carefully. "Do you want the TV on?"

"No."

"Here," I said. "Let me rub your feet. It will help you go to sleep." I was afraid he would refuse. *The center of all human experience is yearning.*

"You don't have to," he said.

"I know." I sat at the edge of his bed and folded the blanket back. His feet were long and thin, like his hands. Webbed bones outlined against sallow skin the color of buttonwood. Back in Richmond, my closest childhood friend had been Catholic. A crucifix hung over her bed, and when I stayed there overnight, I would fall asleep looking up at the body of Christ, the thorn crown, bowed head, impaled hands and feet. Feet like Luke's.

"Thanks," he said when I was finished. "That felt good." His voice was heavy from the pain medication.

I shifted on the bed, sat closer to him. The house felt solid and safe around us. I watched the sinking and rising and sinking of his chest, and a river of grief took me with surprising force. I bent and kissed him on the lips. It seemed as if that was all I ever wanted. I kissed him again, felt his lips open beneath mine. When I pulled away, he made a soft sound, like a bird calling to its mate.

His hands, when he reached for me, were unsteady. "I don't want . . . ,"

"What?"

"I don't want your pity."

Pity? How could he think that? "Trust me," I said. I brushed his forehead with my lips, then his mouth. "This isn't pity."

His face twisted, an expression close to disgust. "I know what I look like now."

"You're beautiful," I said. I had never before said that to a man, but it was true. I kissed him again, felt him respond, surrender, moan that birdlike sound. I kissed his chest, inhaled the yeasty, medicinal scent of him. I had once read somewhere that everyone had a deeply individual smell, a personal bouquet comprised of diet, hormones, hygiene, and health. I tried to imagine what Luke's was before he became ill. I thought of the herring finding their way home, guided solely by the smell of the water. I understood. I felt as if, after a long battle upstream, I had come home. My body was weighted with desire.

I slid my hand over his shoulders, his chest, the hollow of his stomach.

"Oh God," he moaned, and pulled me closer.

When I was six and afraid of thunder, I would climb into bed with Ashley. There I felt safe and protected from the storm. I felt that way that night with Luke.

He reached up and stroked my face, kissed me again. Everything felt new. First time new. That first time new. The moment felt near holy. And hopeful, that, too. The impulse toward life is so strong, I remember thinking. Even close to death, we reach for life.

I MUST have dozed off, for I woke to hear him retching, deep and racking convulsions. Vomit stained the sheets, his clothes; the reek of it filled the air.

"Christ," he said, managing speech between spasms. "I'm sorry."

"Shhhh," I said. "It's all right." I got the wastebasket and brought it to his side, held his head while he puked, tending him naturally and easily, as if this were something I had always known how to do.

When he was done, I stripped away the soiled linen and his shirt, then I washed him and found him a clean shirt from a pile on the dresser. While I tended to him, he tried again to apologize, but I shushed him.

I had just finished putting fresh sheets on the bed when he began to shake, trembling so violently, his teeth rattled. "Hold on," I said. Upstairs, I ripped the blanket and quilt off Nona's bed. I piled them over him, then crept in and lay beside him and let the heat of my body flow into his. Gradually he quieted. "I'm so sorry, Jess," he said once, but I stopped him, pressing my fingers against his lips. And then he slept.

I waited until he was deep in sleep, and then, too restless to sit still, I rose and switched off the lamp, wandered into the kitchen, made a pot of tea. I checked on him again before finally settling on the couch. I didn't want to go upstairs to the bed I'd prepared, afraid I wouldn't hear him if he called. I didn't believe for a minute that I would sleep, but I woke later from a dream. I was in a hotel somewhere out west. Las Vegas. Somewhere like that. I had become separated from my friends and could not remember my room number. As I got into the elevator, I was joined by five men, all strangers. I stabbed the button for the second floor—still unsure of what room, what floor—but the car shot up, zooming sky-

ward so fast, we were all thrown off balance. Up and up we went in
an elevator out of control. I woke in the panic dreams could pro-
duce, unsure of where I was. And then I heard Luke call my name.

"What do you need?" I asked, at his side in minutes. "Another
pill?" Light leaked in from the night-light in the hall. He stared at
me in its glow.

"What is it?" I said.

"I'm not going to go bit by bit," he said.

"What?" I was still in dream confusion.

"I'm not going to sit around and die by degrees." His voice was
so steady, he could have been asking me to take Rocker for a walk.
"I'm not letting it kill me off piecemeal."

A chill ran through me, a seizure of fear. "Don't——"

"I don't want to hang on, drag out the inevitable."

I tried to hush him, but he wouldn't stop.

"I'm not afraid of dying, you know. I just don't want to be
alone."

I REMEMBERED suddenly what Faye said about the time she had to
put her dog down. *No one should die alone.*

"I want you to do something for me."

"What?"

"There's a bag in the bottom drawer of that desk. Would you
get it?"

I crossed to the desk, opened a drawer.

"Not that one," he said. "The bottom one."

I closed the drawer, opened another. "What am I looking for?"

"A plastic bag."

I rooted around. There were several manila folders, a small
photo album, a stack of canceled checks. "I'm not finding it."

"Turn on the light. It's in there."

I switched the lamp on, tried again.

"You're sure it's here?"

"Positive. Reach in back."

"Got it." I held up the bag. It contained two vials. "What is it?"

"Seconal," he said. "And an antinausea medicine."

"Why?" I said, already knowing, refusing the knowledge.

"For when it's time."

"Where did you get this?"

"That doesn't matter."

I shoved the bag back in the drawer.

"I know what to do," he said. "I'm just afraid of waiting until it's too late. Until I can't manage it. I need to know there's someone who'll be there. To help me if I need it. I could never ask Nona," he said. "And Rich——Rich could wrestle a bear, but he isn't capable of this. I tried to talk to Paige once, but she walked out of the room. Stayed away for a week."

"Shush," I said. I couldn't listen to this. I closed the drawer.

"Will you——"

"Shhhhh," I said. "Don't talk now. In the morning. We'll talk in the morning." *Things are always worse in the night,* I thought. Everyone experienced the dark hours of doubts and fears and anxieties— terrors that were eased by the light of dawn. I would negotiate for each minute, each day. I remembered what Faye had said about patients who willed themselves to live. For one more anniversary. A birthday. A holiday. I would give Luke a reason to stay. Through the power of pure desire, I would make him will himself to live. Truly believing this possible, I sat with him until he fell into a fitful sleep.

Of course, later I would see that, in that moment, I was no different than Paige, locked in militant denial fueled by desire, blindly refusing to see the truth because it was too terrible to bear. Not listening to Luke's need because my own was too great. And because I believed I could never bear to do the one thing he had asked. To sit with him while he died.

thirteen

I WOKE TO the sound of birdsong, insistent and exuberant, and for an instant, my heart rose in response, and then I recalled the elevator dream, a vision that clung like a wine hangover the way dreams could, and I recalled the midnight conversation with Luke, which—in the confused half sleep of that waking moment—seemed as unreal as the dream. Moving slowly, I got up from the couch as if drugged. Voices came from his room.

"Good morning," Ginny said when I went in. I watched while she checked Luke's pulse and took his temperature. "I tried not to wake you when I came in," she said. "You were out to this world." Luke stared at me, his gaze unflinching; I knew then with swift and chilling certainty that our conversation in the night had not been part of any nightmare.

"I'll let you finish up here while I put on some coffee and get breakfast started," I said, and escaped to the kitchen. Rocker followed, and I let him out, watched from the door as he tore across the yard and lifted his leg to pee against a tree stump. Ginny came into the kitchen as I was calling the Lab back into the house. Although it was early in the day, she already looked exhausted. She sat down, flipped open her patient's record book, and began jotting notes.

"Luke told me about Nona," she said. "He said you stayed all day, and then through the night."

"Yes," I said, my throat dry.

"You should have called, you know. They would have arranged for a night nurse."

"It wasn't any problem. I was glad to do it." I was surprised the truth wasn't plain on my face: I didn't want anyone else there.

"How was he in the night? Any problems?"

"He woke up once and was sick, but after that, he slept through."

Ginny asked a few questions about the vomiting, made a notation.

I wanted to ask her the things I couldn't ask anyone else. I needed to know if there was hope for a miracle, or did cures and complete remissions happen only in fiction? Did we hold on to desire, even to the end? Was that the last to go? Ginny was a nurse. She would know those things. "How does he seem to you?" I asked.

"About as expected."

Which means exactly what?

"He tells me Nona is coming home today."

"That's what they told us yesterday. They were supposed to be keeping her just for the one night. For observation."

"These past months have been a terrific strain on her, as you can imagine. I'll call Faye. See if we can arrange for some more help here."

"I can stay," I said. "It isn't a problem."

"You've already done too much," Ginny said. She finished up writing in her notebook and rose.

"Can I get you some coffee before you go?"

"No. I'm behind schedule. Story of my life."

After she left, I made Luke tea and hot cereal and fixed coffee for myself. I toasted a slice of the soft white bread, smeared it with jam, and brought it into his room with my coffee. I might as well have been eating Styrofoam the way the toast caught in my throat. He watched me, and although neither of us mentioned the midnight conversation, it hung in the air between us like the acrid aftersmell of an extinguished candle. *You want too much of me.* Not quite true. I would have given him anything, anything but the one terrible thing he had asked.

I bustled about the room, folding the blanket and quilt I'd

brought down from Nona's room, straightening the pile of newspapers, clearing away a half dozen empty glasses, fussing about like
a deranged maid. Yesterday's cozy domesticity—Luke's haircut, the
chicken soup, the house secure against the storm—all that seemed
long ago.

As if my activity had attracted it, the house suddenly came alive
with more commotion than it had held in weeks. The neighbor,
who'd watched from her window the previous morning as the ambulance came for Nona, appeared, bearing a tuna casserole and a
pineapple upside-down cake. Luke's door was open, and she
marched right in before I could head her off. As I carried the food
into the kitchen, I was surprised to hear Luke talking to the
woman, as if overnight he had decided to end his self-imposed isolation. Then Paige called, stunned to learn Nona was in the hospital. "Is she going to be all right?" she asked, her voice suddenly
young and stripped of attitude.

"She'll be home today," I said. "It was an anxiety attack." Paige
asked if Nona needed a ride home from Hyannis and promised to
come right over. Then Betty, another hospice worker, arrived and
pretty much took charge. When I left, she was settling in to read to
Luke.

"Tell Nona I'll see her tomorrow," I told him before I left. I
wished we were alone. I would have kissed him good-bye.

He nodded, reached for and squeezed my hand. "See you soon,"
he said. A long finger of sunlight fell through the window and lit his
face. His words were heavy with an intention I could not bear.

I thought I had long ago learned all there was to know about desire, but the longing I felt for this man—this *dying* man, I made myself remember—shook me. It transformed all past relationships
into childlike diversions. Things I once had thought important were
now meaningless, as insignificant as a rice grain. I tried to convince
myself that my feelings for Luke had been born out of my loneliness, coupled with the intimacy of the times we shared when my
ordinary defenses collapsed in the face of his utter vulnerability.

The cliché of a nurse and patient. That was an argument I might have made to any friend who came to me in this situation, but it was not true. What I felt for Luke was inexplicable and extraordinary and terrible. Never had I felt so possessed. Or so lost. Much later, when I looked back on that spring, I did not—*could not*— think of my feelings for him as some twisted obsession, although many people would come to voice exactly that opinion.

"See you tomorrow," I agreed.

fourteen

ALL THAT WINTER and spring, even on the wildest of days with winds near gale force or fog so impenetrable I was the only one foolish enough to brave it—those days when I sought escape from boredom, from fear of an unsettled future, from a formless, free-floating anxiety—I would head for the beach at the end of our street, a narrow strip of sand with stone jetties that jutted out into the sound every thirty feet, and I would walk. That stretch of beach held the power to bring me some measure of calm, some semblance of peace. After I left Luke, I drove straight there.

Although it was still cool for June, I kicked off my shoes, peeled away my socks, and rolled up the cuffs of my jeans, then walked across the sand to the jetty and, progressing carefully from one to the next, made my way to the large gray boulder at the very end and folded myself down, perching like a herring gull. The tide was low, and the water lapped in the crevices between rocks where barnacles and periwinkles clung. In the distance, Monomoy Island lay flat on the horizon like a mirage. There was a light onshore breeze, and I inhaled its salt, closed my eyes against tears. This was where Faye found me.

I hadn't heard her approach, and the first I knew of her presence was her hand on my shoulder.

"Are you all right?" she asked.

"I'm fine," I said, although a blind man could see the blatant untruth of this.

Faye lowered herself to the rock. "Lily called last night."

"Mama called you?"

"Just after midnight. When she couldn't reach you." *Just after midnight. When Luke was telling me he had no intention of dying piece by piece.* "She's worried about you."

I searched Faye's face, wondering how much she knew, how much she had guessed. It occurred to me that Ashley might have called our mama and repeated the details of our last conversation. That would explain Lily's call to Faye; certainly she hadn't been worried simply because I was out after midnight. There were times in my late teens when I hadn't come home until morning, and Lily had long ago given up trying to control my behavior or my morals. Or maybe she was afraid I was sick. Why else would she call Faye?

"I stayed overnight at Luke's," I said. "Nona was taken to the hospital. They thought it was a heart attack, but it turned out to be anxiety."

"I know. Jim caught me up on everything." Faye waited for me to say something, but I stared out at Monomoy. The island shimmered in the sun, and although it had been deserted for decades— the last of the beach shacks long ago had surrendered to time or fire or vandalism—some deception of the eye made buildinglike silhouettes seem to rise above its shores.

"Jim was under the impression you had arranged for a respite nurse for the night," Faye said.

"I don't know, that seemed kind of silly when there was no reason for me not to stay. I wasn't doing anything."

"Still," Faye said, "you should have called. You know volunteers aren't supposed to spend the night. We would have called one of the staff nurses."

"It seems a silly rule," I said. "I didn't have anything else to do. It made sense to stay. I didn't see any harm in it."

"You know, Jess," Faye said, "hospice patients and their families come to us at the worst possible time in their lives. They're tremendously vulnerable."

"I know," I said, dismayed that I couldn't keep the emotion out of my voice.

"And . . ."

"And?" I echoed.

"And it's pretty easy to get overinvolved."

"Am I in trouble for staying there?" I dug my fingernails into my palms, afraid Faye was going to take me off Luke's case. I turned away, but not before Faye saw my tears. Of course she misunderstood them.

She put her arm around me, pulled me close. "You meant well, Jess. I know that." Her voice was steady, comforting. "But in the future, let's stick to the guidelines. Okay?"

"Okay," I said, so relieved I would have promised anything. The breeze intensified, lifting my hair.

Faye shivered and drew her jacket tighter, then put a hand on my shoulder and used it to brace herself as she stood, reminding me that, like Lily, Faye was no longer young. "Shall we walk back together?"

"I'm going to stay here a bit longer," I said.

"Maybe dinner, then? Later?"

"I'd like that."

I watched Faye walk back down the jetty, stepping from boulder to boulder in slow but sure-footed progress. As I often was, I was struck by her grace despite her size and her age. When Faye reached the sand, she cupped her hands to her mouth and called back to me. "Don't forget to phone Lily."

"I won't," I hollered back.

I PHONED Ashley first. I needed to know what my sister had already told Lily so I would know what I was dealing with.

"Have you changed your mind?" Ashley asked as soon as she heard my voice. "Are you coming down?"

"I'm thinking about it," I said.

"Jesus be, Jesse. Don't *think* about it. Just get yourself back here."

She sounded so exasperated, I had to smile. I could picture my sister clearly. One hand on her hip, a full eye-roll. Ashley, the queen of eye-rolls.

"So I heard Mama was trying to reach me last night," I said.

"I know. When I told her I'd been trying to talk you into coming for a weekend, she said she was going to add her voice to the choir. Naturally I didn't tell her about Bill and the dinner party idea or she'd take right over, and the next thing we'd be in for a formal dinner for sixteen. You can thank me for that later."

I laughed.

"So when are you coming?"

"My exact plans are up in the air right now, Ash. I'll try to work it out."

"What's to work out? Get yourself on a plane and get here. Do you want me to take care of the reservation, or shall I give you my card number so you can do it? What's easiest for you?"

"Like I said, things are a little unsettled right now. Nona is in the hospital, and so Luke's alone."

A sigh traveled down the wire. "They're not your problem, Jess."

"I know, but I don't want to abandon them."

"Jeez, Jess, exactly when did you turn into Mama? God, do you remember all those Thanksgiving afternoons when our friends were watching football games and we were standing in some food kitchen ladling out sweet potatoes? Is that how you want to end up? You need to get away. Get some perspective."

"It's not that simple."

"Snap out of it, Jess. What you need to do is head for the nearest place where there's a man—an eligible and *healthy* man—and create-a-date."

Create-a-date. Our name for our ability to walk into a bar or a party and, within five minutes, walk out with a man and a plan. Had we ever been so confident, so detached?

"Listen to me, Jess. How long has it been since you've gone to bed with a guy?"

"You mean sex?" I remembered lying next to Luke on the narrow mechanical bed.

"Of course I mean sex. How long has it been?"

"I don't know. I don't exactly keep a calendar of these things."

"Ballpark."

"Last fall, I guess."

Ashley did the calculation. "Nine months? *Nine months.* Sweet Jesus, no wonder you've got yourself all messed up. You need to get laid, honey pie. Give those hormones a healthy workout."

"It's more complicated than that, Ash."

"Jess, trust me. It's not complicated. Come home."

"So did you tell Lily?"

"About what?"

"About Luke," I said.

"You mean about your infatuation with a man who's on his last legs? No way, José. I didn't think that was something she needed to hear. All it would do is upset her."

"It's nothing that is that *upsetting,*" I said, although I was relieved Ashley had not told Lily.

"Jessie, sweetheart, the very fact that you can say that the situation you've gotten yourself into is 'not upsetting' is pure proof that you've lost your mind."

"You don't understand," I said.

"Promise me, Jessie. Promise me you'll come home."

"I promise," I lied, too worn to argue further. I'd straighten it out later.

LILY ANSWERED on the first ring, as if she had been sitting by the phone and waiting.

"Hi, Mama," I said. "Sorry I wasn't home when you called last night. I hope you weren't worried."

"I gave that up a long time ago, sweetie."

"Good," I said. "How are you?"

"I'm fine. Fit as a fiddle, as your grandpa Earl used to say, although what is particularly fit about a fiddle, I have no idea. How are you? When I talked to Faye last night, she told me how much she's enjoyed your company this year."

"I'm enjoying hers, too."

"I must say, I can't picture spending the winter up there. I imagine it must be terribly dreary."

"Not really."

"Ashley tells me she asked you to come for a visit, even offered to pay for your ticket, but you declined."

"Right now isn't a good time, Mama."

"She misses you, Jessie Lynn. We all miss you."

"I miss you, too, Mama."

"Your sister's really disappointed. I am too, honey. It's not like you have a job or family there or any reason you couldn't come back for a weekend."

I felt pressured, manipulated. "You know why Ashley's so fixed on me coming back? Bill Miller is back in town, and Ashley has some idea that because we dated in high school, I should come running back now that he's turned up again, divorced and eligible."

"Bill's back? I had no idea."

"Well, he's ancient history. And I'm not interested. End of subject."

"I was hoping you'd come back for more selfish reasons."

"Like what?"

"Jan and I have upped the departure date. We're leaving in two weeks. I'd like to see you before we go."

"Before you go? You mean the trip? You're still set on that?"

"More than ever."

"I'm against this, Mama. You know that. I think it's crazy."

Lily sailed right on, as if I hadn't spoken. "Friends are throwing us a bon voyage party this Saturday night at the club. It would mean the world to me if you'd come. I so want you to meet Jan."

"I'm against this, Mama," I said again. "It's insane, and I won't come and celebrate it. For God's sake, Mama, you're sixty-five."

"I am constantly aware of that."

"All I'm saying is a transatlantic voyage is the kind of thing suited for younger people."

"I'm not in the ground yet——"

"And who is this Jan, anyway? What do you know about him?"

"All I need to. And if you'd come back down here and meet him, you wouldn't have all these questions."

"Have you thought that he might be after Daddy's money?"

Lily gave the girlish laugh she had discovered this spring. "Money is the last thing Jan has to be worried about, Jessie. And if you'd just come home and meet him, you would know who he is."

"Oh, Mama, I don't want to fight."

"Nor do I, Jessie Lynn. But I mean to do this thing—this wonderful and wild thing—and I would like to see you before we leave."

Why can't you come up here? I wanted to cry. Why do I have to go there? "Okay, Mama," I surprised myself by saying. "I'll come."

fifteen

AFTER DINNER THAT night, Faye and I curled up in the wicker rockers on her porch. She brought out woolen shawls and brandy to warm us, and we watched the magenta-tinged afterglow of the sunset turn to night. We sat in companionable quiet. Nona said I was calm, but Faye was more comfortable in silence than anyone I'd ever known. Finally I spoke.

"I called Lily," I said.

"What did she have to say? It was so late when she phoned that we didn't chat long."

"She wants me to come back this weekend. Friends are giving a bon voyage party for her."

"Well, that's terrific. Are you going?"

"I don't think I have a choice. She and Ashley are guilting me into it."

"Ashley, too?"

"Don't get me started. She's determined to match me up with an old boyfriend who's back in town. She and Mama are resolved to get me back there."

Faye searched my face. "Do you want to go?"

I shrugged. "I guess."

"Yes. I can see that. Your unrestrained enthusiasm was my first clue."

I laughed.

"So why don't you want to?" she said.

"Oh, I guess I keep hoping Mama will change her mind about

this trip, that if I keep acting as if it isn't happening, maybe she'll call it off. What do you call that?"

"Militant denial," Faye said flatly. A car pulled up outside where the street ended and bleached wood steps led down to the beach.

"Are you expecting company?" I said.

Faye shook her head. "Someone took a wrong turn. Happens all summer long."

I felt a flash of regret that the tourist season would be under way shortly, robbing us of the privacy we'd enjoyed all winter. The locals didn't take wrong turns. We watched the car back around and head out, its beams cutting through the dusk. Faye offered me a dish of shelled walnuts, took a fistful for herself, and then sat back and propped up her legs. Her feet were misshapen, her toes deformed from dancing.

"When does Lily set sail?" she asked.

"They've upped the departure date. In two weeks, she said, but she didn't tell me the precise day."

"Well, here's to her." Faye raised her wine high. *"Salut."*

Reluctantly I leaned in and clicked my glass against Faye's.

"I'll send along a gift with you. Although I haven't the foggiest idea what one gives a woman who is setting sail across the Atlantic with her lover."

The word made me cringe.

Faye chatted on. "I suppose something small and sensible— there's scarcely room for you to sneeze on board a boat—but I was thinking more along the lines of an utterly impractical gift."

Was I the only one who thought the venture not only dangerous but completely insane? "I'll only be in Richmond for two days," I said. "Just the weekend."

Faye leaned over and held my knee. "It will be good for you. You haven't had much fun this spring."

"Do you think anything will happen while I'm gone?" I asked. "With Luke, I mean."

"Are you asking me if I think he is going to die?" she said.

I nodded.

"He's in process, but I don't sense he's near the end yet," Faye said.

"I don't think I could leave if he was." I caught my lip between my teeth, afraid I had revealed too much.

"Well, there are no guarantees," Faye said. "For that matter, your plane could go down."

"Well, Jesus, Faye, thank you for that cheery thought."

Faye laughed and flexed her damaged toes. Shortly after that, I finished the wine and, pleading exhaustion, slipped home.

THE WIND had died down, and it was warm, the air soft on my skin as I walked back to the cottage. The moon was midway across the night sky, laying a narrow silver swath across the sound. It looked like the illustration in a picture book I had had as a child, a story about a girl who rode to the stars on a spotted rocking horse. What had Lily done with all the books we'd had as children? Given them to Ashley for her boys? Time marches on, my daddy used to say. The thought did not bring comfort.

In spite of what I'd told Faye, I wasn't ready for sleep. At grad school, we used to call my condition *wired and tired*. I headed up-stairs to my workroom. I was seriously behind on orders—all the time I was spending with Luke—and hadn't even chosen a pattern to braid for the locket my client from Sonoma had ordered.

Earlier that afternoon, I'd brought the paper towel with Luke's hair up to my worktable. Now I unfolded it and fingered the raven locks, still intact and curled, like the tips of spring ferns. I thought of the woman with the son in the navy and the clippings from his first haircut that she'd kept wrapped in tissue all those years. I understood that, understood the metaphysical power a lock of hair possessed. No wonder the one biblical story almost everyone can recall is the story of Delilah cutting Samson's hair. But I hadn't

wanted to rob Luke of the little strength he possessed, only to possess something of him. I hadn't taken enough to fashion into a ring
or even the smallest charm. Just the two curls, something that artist
in Chicago might have chopped finely and used with paint or that I
might seal under glass in a locket. Or eat. A bizarre thought, I realized, even as it came to mind. I found an envelope and wrote his
name on the front. *Luke.* It gave me pleasure to write it out like that
in cursive. I slipped the hair inside and tucked it away in the top
drawer of the desk. Determined to get some work accomplished, I
sat down at the worktable—a stand actually, as round and cylindri-
cal as a hatbox—and flipped through a book of patterns, searching
for the perfect one for the woman from Sonoma, but my attention
kept straying, and after a while, I gave up and went downstairs.

I wandered restlessly from room to room. Twice I picked up the
phone to call Luke but each time set it down before dialing, caught
in a push-pull of desire and despair. The third time I lifted the receiver, I dialed the airline and made a reservation for a round-trip
flight between Boston and Richmond. The price was exorbitant
because it was last-minute, but I charged it on my card, too proud
to use Ashley's. Committed to the trip home, I grew even more
wired. There were dust-coated bottles of liquor in the back of a
kitchen cabinet—remnants of summers past. I pulled out the Tan-
queray and found a bottle of Schweppes. When I opened the gin,
the piney sharp smell of it rose up in a wave, overwhelming me
with memories: late summer afternoons on the porch, the skin on
my shoulders tight with sunburn and salt, sipping a lemon Coke
while my mama and daddy drank gin and tonics and played games,
the slap and click of dominoes on tabletop, in the background the
sound of Ashley's boom box—a cut from a Queen album or the latest from the Cure—and the shuffling of my sister's feet as she
danced, oblivious to us, me feeling simultaneously safe and slightly
bored. That summer had been the last of such contentment. The
next year, our daddy was dead and Lily had switched from G and Ts

to white wine coolers. Ashley had a part-time job at the Clam Bar, and I began to live on the edge of reckless adventure, sneaking beers and losing my virginity on a sand-gritty blanket to a Connecticut boy who lived two houses down and whose name I'd long since forgotten. I twisted the cap back on the gin, as if doing so could stop memory, could stop pain.

sixteen

NONA CALLED EARLY the next morning. She was back at Luke's and asked if I would come over. When I arrived, I recognized Rich's pickup in the drive. Nona was in the kitchen, washing the breakfast dishes. Luke's door was closed.

"How are you?" I asked, hugging her tight. I think she had grown to enjoy getting these embraces as much as I enjoyed giving them.

"Me? I'm fine. It was all a bunch of foolishness."

"You had us worried," I said.

"Foolishness," Nona repeated. "They said it was anxiety. Well, the way those doctors carry on, making such a big deal of it, a person would develop a case of nerves just listening to them."

"I'm so glad you're okay." I picked up a dish towel and started wiping dishes.

"Of course they've got me on some kind of pill. Valium. Supposed to calm me down, although it's scarcely big enough to see. Hard to figure how a pill that tiny can do any good, but that doesn't stop them from charging you all outdoors for it."

"This has been tough on you," I said, drying a mug.

Nona turned to me, hope written all over her face. "But you know," she said, "I think Luke's better. I really do."

I tightened my grip on the towel. "He is? Has the doctor been in? Is that what he says?"

"No, but I can tell."

"Oh."

Nona's look of hope turned nearly defiant. "There's been a change, Jessie. One for the good."

I glanced over at the closed door and steeled myself against Nona's optimism—optimism I both longed for and feared. "Really?"

"He had one of your smoothie things for dinner last night," Nona said.

"He did?" A sprout of hope rose in my chest.

"And he's seeing people again," Nona said.

"He is?" I remembered then how, the day before, he'd talked to the neighbor.

"This morning, he asked me to call Rich and have him come over. Can you imagine? It's the first time in months he's wanted company." Nona drained the sink of dishwater and dried her hands.

The dangerous sprig of hope took root.

"Doctors don't know everything," Nona said. "You hear all the time about people going into remission."

"Could he keep the smoothie down?"

"Yes," Nona said, her smile triumphant. A horn sounded outside. "Oh, there's Helen. She's taking me to Orleans to get my hair done. About time, too. I've certainly let myself go. Scare myself just looking in the mirror."

NONA LEFT before I could get around to telling her I was going to Virginia over the weekend. I continued drying dishes and thought about her conviction that Luke was getting better. Could it be possible? I suddenly recalled Bernie Siegel and his book that had been for sale following the lecture. *Love, Medicine and Miracles.* Proof that even doctors knew there was a place for the miraculous. I was nearly finished at the sink when Rich came into the kitchen, leading Rocker on a leash.

"Hello, again," he said.

I concentrated on the glass I was holding and inhaled. He was one of those men who didn't have to say a word to fill a room, just sucked the oxygen right out of it. "Hello."

"Nona go out?"

I nodded, reached for the last glass in the drainer.

He leaned back against the counter and looked pointedly at my left hand. "Luke says you're not married."

"Last I heard, that's not a federal offense."

"If it was, I'd be locked up. So do you ever go out?"

"Sure," I said.

He leaned in, more sure of himself.

"I go to the post office and to the market and to the beach," I said.

"Funny," he said. "So do you date?"

"Not much. I'm pretty busy." I was conscious of Luke in the other room, wondered if he could hear this conversation.

Rich took out his wallet, withdrew a business card, and passed it to me. It was gray with either age or grime, and said RICH ELDREDGE, LANDSCAPING. "Give me a call," he said, flashing a hard brightness of teeth, "you feel like getting out some night."

"Like I said, I'm pretty busy." I was eager for him to leave so that I could go in to Luke.

"All work and no play . . . ," he said.

"Original," I said. I nodded at Rocker. "Are you taking him out?"

"I'm bringing him to my place. Luke wants him to get used to being with me. You know. For after."

That tender sprig of hope turned to bone and lodged in my chest. I knew then why Luke had asked to see Rich, and I didn't want any part of it.

"So give me a call," he said. "I promise not to bite."

"I'm so reassured to hear that," I said, my voice cool.

AFTER RICH left, I made a blueberry smoothie and brought it in to Luke. He was seated by the window, the robe over his lap. He seemed calm, peaceful. I could see why Nona believed he was getting better. I allowed myself to think that perhaps I'd been mistaken about why he'd wanted to see Rich. I felt the sharp, keen bite of wanting.

"Shall I massage your shoulders?"

"Just sit with me," he said. He seemed content with the silence, but I was taken with a need to fill it. The room was oddly empty without Rocker.

"I'm going to Richmond for the weekend," I said. "To see my mama. She and her boyfriend are having a party." We had been told not to bring our own histories and stories to the patients, but Luke and I were far beyond that. I had sat beside him, my hand in his, and told him about my cancer, had told him my secrets. And he had trusted me enough to tell me his.

I told him about Lily and Yawn and the trip to Europe they had planned. I had told him weeks ago about how my daddy had died when I was fourteen, and now I told him that this was the first time my mama had seriously dated. He sat quietly while I rambled on, filling the room with chatter. Occasionally he stroked his fingers along his thigh. Eventually I ran out of words. Our eyes met.

"Rich isn't much with women," he said. I knew then that he had overheard the interchange in the kitchen. "Not much with women but great with dogs."

"Really?" I said.

"He's going to keep Rocker." His eyes were steady, calm. Mine watered.

"How can you give him away like that?" I said.

"I need to clean things up," he said.

"At least you're not having him shot," I said, surprising us both with my anger.

He ignored this. "I don't want to leave everything for Nona to worry about."

I refused to listen. "You look better today," I said. "Really. A lot better."

"Stop it, Jess," he said.

I bit my lip, refusing to cry.

"I'm dying," he said. "We both know that. But I'm choosing the way and time to go."

"Don't say that. Please. It's a way off yet."

"Jessie," he said, "I won't ask you again. But I'd like you with me. If I need help, I'd like it to be you."

"How can you ask me that?"

"Who else can I ask?"

I fiddled with the blanket on his bed, refused to meet his eyes. Couldn't he see that he was asking for the one thing I was incapable of giving him?

"What if I say no?"

He looked at me, the same look he had given me the first time I saw him, as if he knew me better than I knew myself. "You won't," he said.

I couldn't answer.

"When are you coming back?" he said after a minute.

"Sunday night."

"I'll miss you."

"Shall I stay here, then? I can, you know."

"No. You go to your mama's party." And then, "Jesus, I swore I would say this."

"What?"

"I just want you to know . . ."

"What?"

"If things were different, if I could have a woman . . ." His voice dropped, then stopped.

"What, Luke? If you could have a woman, what?"

The words came slow, as if pulled from him. "I'd want it to be you."

Tears welled in my eyes.

"Hey, none of that," he said. "I'll see you when you get back."

"Promise?" I said, holding his gaze steady. I needed to know he would still be there when I returned.

"Promise."

seventeen

I STOOD AT the closet trying to manufacture the least bit of interest in packing for Richmond. It had been months since I had been shopping, and I could not find one thing that looked like it would do for Lily's party. I pulled out a pair of jeans, a couple of Ts, and a pair of heeled sandals I hadn't worn since the previous fall, and dropped them in the suitcase. I would have to borrow something from Ashley for Saturday night.

Early Saturday morning, I drove to Boston. Just before I left, Faye came by with a gift for Lily that looked suspiciously like lingerie. I promised to convey her best wishes, double-checked that she had both Lily's and Ashley's phone numbers, and asked her to call if anything changed with Luke, a promise she agreed to easily, reminding me that everyone on the team is always notified whenever there is a dramatic change.

I left the Toyota in the lot at Park 'n Fly and caught the shuttle bus to the terminal, then grabbed a cup of overpriced coffee and made my way through tedious lines and security checks before finally boarding the flight, already exhausted. My assigned seat was toward the front of the plane, between two businessmen, the one to my left already busy with a spreadsheet, the one in the window seat smiling with the eager-to-connect look of a talker. While we waited at the gate, I pulled the in-flight magazine from the seat pocket and pretended great interest in an article on Virginia wineries, hoping to deflect conversation, but the man in the window seat was not in the least discouraged. He had the oily skin and soft hands that I have always associated with shoe salesmen.

"Are you on vacation?"

"Sort of," I said.

He smiled. "What's a 'sort of' vacation?"

"I'm going to see my family for the weekend."

"You're from Virginia, then?"

"Richmond," I said. I flipped to another page, pretended to read. He didn't take the hint.

"I'm from San Francisco originally," he said. "I moved to Chicago ten years ago and to Boston last year. Usually you hear it the other way around. Most people move from east to west."

I nodded, continued to read.

"My name's Mel," he said. "Mel Wallace."

I nodded again.

"I'm in real estate," he said.

Of course you are. We taxied out, fourth in line for takeoff. As we departed, Boston Harbor receded beneath us, and I felt a flash of panic. The trip was a mistake. I shouldn't have left Luke. I couldn't shake the sense of doom that I'd had since driving off the Cape that something terrible would happen while I was gone, that, in spite of his promise, Luke would be gone when I returned. My hands tightened on the armrest until my fingertips turned white.

"Don't worry," Mel said, misunderstanding my anxiety. "It's a perfect day for flying."

I forced my fingers to relax. "Yes, it is," I said.

"So what do you do?"

"I make jewelry," I said, "out of human hair."

"Oh," he said, visibly startled. I actually felt him recoil. I reclined my seatback, closed my eyes, and for the remainder of the flight tried to fight the sense I was making a huge mistake by going to Richmond, by leaving Luke.

Ten minutes before our arrival, the pilot came on to report that it was eighty-eight degrees and sunny in Richmond. I could feel the oppression of the heat even before we landed.

. . .

I WAS walking into the terminal when I heard Ashley calling my name. The boys, who had shot up since Christmas, enveloped me in sweaty hugs and handed me small bouquets of dandelions. "We picked them ourselves," Jeffrey announced. Ashley kissed my cheek, and then threw her arms around me. "God, I'm glad you came," she said. She looked fabulous in a pink sleeveless dress that revealed toned arms. I felt rumpled and frumpy in comparison. As we walked across the parking lot, heat rose in waves off the tarmac. The boys skipped ahead, pulling my wheeled bag behind them.

"Over there," Ashley said, pointing to a new-model BMW.

I looked around. "Lily didn't come?"

"She's at the house preparing for your arrival."

"Is Yawn there, too?"

"I wouldn't be surprised. They're inseparable. She's just dying for you to meet him."

"Any chance we could stop for a drink on the way?"

Ashley gave me a sharp look. "At ten in the morning?"

"A Bloody Mary won't kill us. I need something before I face Mama and her friend."

"She'll have our hides."

"Just one," I pleaded.

"Well, I guess we could stop by our house and have a quick drink. We could tell her your flight was delayed."

"Fine," I said, wondering why we had to lie.

Once at Ashley's, I dug through my bag until I found the Red Sox caps I'd brought for the boys. "Don't let your father see you wearing those," Ashley warned them. I remembered Daniel was a Phillies fan and immediately went to work teaching them the "Let's go, Red Sox" chant. I suggested they perform for their daddy when he returned from his golf game.

"You're bad," Ashley said, and then sent the boys off to watch television so we could have a few minutes alone before we headed over to Lily's. I sat at the table while Ashley got out the vodka, tomato juice, and Tabasco.

"Not too light on the vodka," I said.

Ashley raised an eyebrow.

"I'm nervous, okay? To tell you the truth, I wish I could see Mama alone first, without the boy toy."

Ashley handed me the drink. "Jan's not a bad guy, Jess. Give him a chance."

"*Not bad.* And that's what? Supposed to reassure me?"

"Will you lighten up, Jessie? Mama loves him. He treats her well and makes her happy, and that's good enough for me."

"I thought you didn't like him."

"I guess I've come around. I don't understand why you aren't happy for her. Don't you want her to be in love? Would you prefer that she be lonely?"

"Of course not." But Ashley's question startled me. Is that what I wanted? My mama not to be in love? I took a swallow of the drink, waited for the vodka to calm me.

"Well, what's the problem, then?" Ashley said.

"I don't want her to get hurt."

"She's a big girl, Jessie. She can take care of herself."

"What about this trip? I still can't believe you're in favor of it."

"And I can't believe you're so against it."

"Let's just drop it, okay?" I took another swallow of my Bloody Mary, which was already half gone. Ashley had hardly touched hers.

"So how's Faye?" Ashley asked, an edge to her voice.

"Older and heavier, but other than that, she's the same."

"Whatever that means. I haven't seen her since Daddy's funeral."

"She's been great to me this winter. I don't know what I would have done without her."

"What is it that you like about her?"

I thought for a minute. "She's fun to be around. She isn't afraid; in fact, she is one of the few people I've ever met who doesn't seem to have a laundry list of fears. And you know where you stand with her. She tells the truth."

"Quite a recommendation." Ashley looked at me. "So tell me about this Luke."

"Not now," I said, and took another gulp of my drink.

"But what's the story?" she persisted. "He's dying, right?"

"He has pancreatic cancer."

"So this thing—this crush you have on him or whatever it is— it doesn't even make sense."

"Not everything in life makes *sense*," I said, an edge to my voice. I polished off the drink. I'd barely been back an hour, and we were already circling close to an argument.

Ashley set her drink—still barely touched—on the counter. "Come on," she said. "I'd better get you over to Lily's before she sends out a search party."

As ASHLEY pulled up the drive to Lily's, I felt that jolt of nostalgia that returning home always gave me. With the exception of a series of rented apartments, which hardly counted, this was the only home I'd ever known. Two-thirds of my history had occurred here. After my daddy died, I'd been afraid Lily would make us move, a groundless fear, since our mama had never even hinted at the possibility, but one I could not shake nonetheless. The house, a brick Georgian, sat on a rise, surrounded on three sides by trimmed boxwood hedges. There were lilacs and dogwoods in the side yard, plantings of hostas and bleeding hearts on the east, a graceful bed of dahlias and peonies and camellias edging the front porch and the wider veranda on the side. I'd helped Lily plant some of those bulbs. Our love of flowers, of gardening, was one of the few connections we had managed to maintain during my teen years, and as I stared at the blossoms, memories, softened by time, flowed in.

"Who's taking care of the house while she's away?" I asked.

"She's hired a house sitter."

"You mean some stranger's going to be living here?"

"Not a stranger. Someone Jan knows from the university. Well, here we go."

I had a constricted feeling in my chest. Then the front door flew open, and Lily stepped out. The photo she'd sent at Easter hadn't fully prepared me. Her hair was not just gray but nearly completely white, fuller and freer than I ever remembered.

"Your hair," I said as we embraced.

"Not one word about it," Lily said. She hugged me, and then held me at arm's length, searched my face. "Are you——?" she began.

"I'm fine, Mama," I said.

She hugged me again, then set me loose. Her hug felt familiar, but different, too. It took me a moment to identify the off note. Lily no longer smelled of Shalimar, the scent I had associated with my mama my entire life. She used to call it her signature scent, but apparently it had gone the way of her monthly color and cut at the Elkwood Salon. What had caused so dramatic a transformation? Why the dentist, the gray hair, sailing across the Atlantic, for God's sake? Had she joined a women's group, started therapy? *What?*

"Come on," Lily said. "I want you to meet Jan."

He'd been there all along, in the shadows of the front hall, watching us, and now he stepped forward. He was solidly built with sandy hair and the burnished complexion middle-aged men acquired playing golf or tennis. Lily took his arm, beamed.

Seeing them like that, side by side, was much worse than I had feared. My face flushed with shame for my mama. Did strangers think Jan was her son? Or worse, a gigolo? I couldn't help but wonder what her friends were saying, if they laughed behind her back. I had a vision of my daddy standing next to Lily, tall and strong and dignified, with that puzzled look he always wore in photos, as if he were the last to get the punch line. I willed myself not to cry. I couldn't understand how Ashley had let this happen. It could be worse, but I didn't know how.

"Hello," he said. "I've been looking forward to meeting you."

"Nice to meet you, too," I murmured dutifully. I felt hot, dizzy.

The drink had been a mistake. Or maybe the mistake was in not having had two.

"Jan wants to take us to lunch," Lily said. She still clung to his side. With her free arm, she circled my waist and pulled me close. "We thought Julep's."

"Sounds great," I said, forcing enthusiasm into my voice, remembering the Sundays my daddy would take us there for lunch, pronouncing their cheese grits the best in Richmond.

"I'll see you all later," Ashley said.

"Oh, you come, too," Lily said. "You and the boys, and Daniel if he's free. It's so seldom we're all together, I don't want to lose a minute of it."

"Daniel's playing golf," Ashley said. "But count on the rest of us."

"I'll have to change," I said.

"You look fine," Lily said, although I was dressed in jeans and a cotton shirt, wrinkled from the flight.

"Really?" I said, recalling the many fights we'd had in the past, the times Lily refused to let me leave the house unless I'd been "properly attired."

And later, at Julep's, Lily didn't say a word when the boys sat through lunch wearing their new baseball caps. It was as if she didn't care anymore about things like manners. I chose a seat between my nephews and listened to their repertoire of knock-knock jokes, rescued from having to make conversation with the Yawn. Lily didn't seem to notice. I kept sneaking glances at her, trying to understand what had caused her to change and why it was so deeply unsettling. Wondering, too, what this man saw in her, a woman who looked every year of her age and a good deal more than his. I remembered when George H. W. had been president how everyone thought Barbara looked like his mother. When the gossip hit about his having had an affair, Lily had said, *Well, I'm not surprised. Why would the president want to be with a woman who looks so much older? She should color her hair.* Had she forgotten that?

Occasionally, during lunch, the Yawn faked an interest in my life and tossed a question down the table, but I pretended to be too engrossed in my nephews to hear. Ashley kicked me under the table. "Be nice," she whispered once. Lily just kept smiling and saying how wonderful it was to all be together, oblivious to any tension.

When the lunch was finally over, Lily and Jan went home to rest up for the party while Ashley and I returned to her house to ransack her closet for something for me to wear. Ashley finally decided on a black sheath with a cowl neck that draped open in the back, nearly exposing my entire spine.

"Smashing," Ashley declared, pleased with herself.

"No one will be looking at me, anyway," I said. "It's Mama's party."

"You never can tell," Ashley said, with a smug look that, if I hadn't been so preoccupied, would have tipped me off.

WHEN ASHLEY dropped me off at the house, Lily was already dressed. She wore a sleeveless linen dress in teal, and even from halfway across the room, I could see the loose skin on her upper arms and throat. It was as if she was deliberately trying to look her age. The Yawn wore a pair of white slacks; a pale blue shirt, open at the neck; and a blue blazer. All he needed was a commodore's cap.

"Jan and I are going to get to the club a little early," Lily said, "so we'll be there to greet the first guests, but there's no need for you to be there early unless you want to. Ashley and Daniel can pick you up."

"I have to shower and change," I said, "so I'd better ride with them."

"See you there, then," Lily said, and hugged me again, as if she couldn't get enough.

After they left, I roamed through the house in a time warp, so little had changed, and I found some comfort in this. Even my bedroom had remained as I'd left it, right down to the ivory trim, blue-flowered wallpaper, and matching blue spread on the bed. I wondered if the house-sitting professor had a daughter, if she would be sleeping in this room. I took a shower and slipped on the black sheath. I pulled my hair back in a knot. I hadn't thought to bring earrings and crossed the hall to Lily's room. I raided her jewelry box, choosing a dangly sapphire-colored, cut-glass pair. On the other side of the dresser top, there was a man's tie clip and a short black comb. The photo of my daddy that had been there as long as I could remember had disappeared. I was both mad and sad to see it gone, exactly the way I'd felt earlier when I thought about anyone else living in this house.

I was ready by seven, and when the phone rang, I was watching for Ashley's headlights to sweep up the drive.

"Hey, Jess, I'm running late. The babysitter's sick, and we haven't been able to find another. Daniel's going to stay with the boys. I'll pick you up in ten minutes."

"No problem," I said. I checked the clock, wondered what Luke was doing. All that day while I was teasing my nephews and picking out a dress with Ashley and having lunch and talking with Lily, he had never been far from my thoughts. My mind flashed on the plastic bag in the bottom drawer of the desk. I wished I had thought to hide it before I left.

I picked up the phone, dialed his number. "Nona?" I said when she answered.

"Yes."

"It's Jess."

"Jessie? But Luke told me you were going away this weekend."

"I am. I'm calling from Virginia."

"Long distance? You're calling long distance?"

"I just wanted to see how Luke is doing."

"About the same. He's sleeping right now."

"Well, tell him I called, will you?"

"He'll be happy to hear that." She lowered her voice. "He doesn't say anything—'course he won't say anything to me—but I think he misses you. We both do. You're good for him, Jessie."

Her words made me happier than I had any right to be. What

the hell was I doing in Virginia? "I'm due back tomorrow night. If I get on the Cape early enough, I'll come by."

I HADN'T been to the VCC since one of Ashley's baby showers. The Virginia Country Club was the site of every important occasion in our family's history: our parents' wedding reception; my mama's baby showers; Ashley's sweet sixteen bash, complete with DJ; Ashley's wedding reception; the gathering after our daddy's funeral. Inside, the party was already under way. Every friend Lily had in Richmond was there, people I'd known since childhood and some others who were unfamiliar. I was no more in the door than Polly Collins—one of Lily's oldest friends—dashed over to say hello, still wearing her blond hair in a stiff bouffant the shape and size of a football helmet. Another time warp. Ashley headed off to say hello to some friends. I made straight for the bar and ordered a gin and tonic—my daddy's drink. Lily hadn't noticed our arrival, and I watched from a distance as she made her way from table to table, the Yawn in tow, laughing and greeting friends. Off to one side of the room, a large easel had been set up with a display of photographs of his boat, a fifty-seven-foot sloop with "Odyssey" painted in black on the stern. Propped on a second easel was a map someone had drawn of the Atlantic, a cutout of the *Odyssey* stuck in the middle atop a yellow line depicting their voyage. There was an arrow indicating the starting point in Norfolk and another showing the journey's end in the Azores, off the African coast. Colored drawings of mythic sea creatures decorated the borders. I could have done without the monsters.

I was just turning away when Ashley appeared at my side, her arm looped inside that of a man. "Well, look who I found," she said in a phony what-a-surprise tone of voice.

"Hi, Jess," he said, freeing his arm from Ashley's and reaching for my hand.

"Bill," I said. I flashed my sister a wait-until-later look. Now I understood why she had insisted on the backless dress.

"I'll just leave you two to get reacquainted," she said, then winked at me and melted into the crowd.

"God, you look better than ever. I was a fool to let you get away."

As if it was your choice, I thought. "You're looking good, too," I said, fulfilling my half of the social contract. Actually, he didn't look so bad. He was thick through the chest, heavier than in high school, but not yet fat. It would be another ten years before he had the bloated look of an ex-athlete. He smelled of English Leather, the same after-shave he had used in high school. He was tan—recently back from Saint Bart's, he explained. I stared at him and remembered the sexual intensity we had once shared, chemistry that had made him the object of my total obsession throughout our senior year.

"Ashley tells me you're just here for the weekend," he said.

I nodded. "For the party."

"That is some trip they have planned." We both looked at the map.

"So everyone seems to think. Personally, I think it's insane."

He was momentarily caught off balance by my response, but he regained his footing within seconds. "Ashley tells me you're an artist."

Ashley talks too much, I thought. "I make jewelry," I said, wondering how soon I could get another drink. If I didn't pace myself, I'd be drunk before dinner.

"Well—" Bill started.

"*William.* William Miller. I thought that was you." A woman with chestnut brown hair swooped in and claimed him with a smile.

"Doe?" he said.

I recognized her then. Dorothy Jarvis had been in Ashley's class and had gone on to Sweet Briar or maybe it was Hollins; Lily used to cochair bake sales with her mama.

"I heard you were back in town," Doe said to Bill. "You *must* come sit and tell us what you've been doing and what brings you back to us."

I remembered what Ashley had said. *Fresh meat.* "Go," I said. I knew enough not to say everything I was thinking.

He shrugged apologetically. "I'll catch up with you later."

Around the room, people were gathered in clusters, and I felt like an alien in their midst. I could imagine what Faye's take on this event would be. Some of the women still wore girdles. *Foundation garments,* Lily used to call them. I took refuge in the ladies' room. Ashley found me there.

"So?"

"What?"

"Don't be clueless, Jess. *Bill.* What do you think? Isn't he hunky?"

I shrugged. "I don't know."

"What's not to know? The man's gorgeous and loaded. And I sensed the chemistry between you two."

"I don't think so."

"You're kidding."

I shook my head. "He's wearing English Leather."

Ashley looked at me as if I were daft. "And that's a crime?"

"That's what he wore in high school," I said, trying to make it sound like a joke. "I could never take anyone seriously who still wears the same shaving lotion he wore when he was sixteen."

Ashley stared at me. "Jesus be, Jessie, when are you going to grow up?"

"I thought I saw you two disappear in here." Lily stood at the door. Her cheeks were flushed, whether from alcohol or excitement, I could not tell.

"See you later," Ashley said in a pissed-off voice, and slipped out.

"What did I interrupt?" Lily asked.

"Oh, Ashley's mad because she got Bill Miller here and I didn't fall at his feet and end up in bed with him, the rest of my life sorted out. I mean, isn't that what you want, too?" I wasn't convinced Lily hadn't had a hand in Bill's invitation to the party.

"Oh, honey, I only want what you want. Whatever makes you happy."

The standard parental lie, I thought.

Lily hugged me. "I'm so glad you came, Jessie. It means the world to me."

"Me, too."

Lily noticed the earrings. "You borrowed them," she said. I could smell gin and saw then that she was a tiny bit drunk.

"Do you mind? I forgot to pack any."

"No. I'm glad you did. They look lovely on you. You should keep them."

"It's a nice party," I said.

"Did you see the drawing Sally Kincaid made? The map of our trip?"

"Yes."

Lily smiled at me, and, in spite of the gray hair, her face looked suddenly young. "I always wanted to travel, you know," she said. "It's always been a dream of mine. I mean in the real sense. I actually used to fall asleep and dream of visiting Portugal and Greece."

Stubbornly, I kept silent.

Lily sighed and then inspected herself in the mirror over the bay of sinks, checked her teeth for lipstick. "You haven't told me what you think of Jan," she said.

"He seems . . ."

She turned. "What?"

"I don't know. Kind of young. Aren't you afraid of what people are saying?" I stared at the crepelike skin of Lily's throat, her arms. "I mean he looks young enough to be your son or something. Aren't you a little ashamed?"

Lily's hand had been stroking her jaw, and now it dropped to her side. She gave me a steady look. "No," she said. She raised her hand, and I drew back as if she meant to strike me, but Lily only cupped my face, her touch gentle, her eyes unutterably sad. "I don't give a goddamn what people think or say, and I am most assuredly not ashamed. Furthermore, I won't let you taint this wonderful thing that has happened to me." Her hand felt hot on my chin. "Can't you be happy for me, Jess?"

I had to look away, and then the door opened and one of Lily's friends poked her head in to tell her she was being summoned. In the distance, I heard the sound of a knife clicking against a glass, a voice raised in a toast, people clapping, someone calling her name. Lily left without another word.

The noise of the party had gone up a notch when I returned to the bar. My plan was to hang out there until the party was over. There was a large vase of stargazer lilies at one end, and their scent—nearly funereal in its heaviness—made me slightly ill. My head felt light, untethered to my body. I still felt the touch of Lily's fingers on my cheek, my chin. I wouldn't have minded getting a little drunk myself.

"Buy you a drink, young lady?"

"Uncle Brent," I cried, and allowed myself to be enfolded in familiar arms. For the first time since I'd arrived at the club, I was genuinely glad to see someone. Brent had always been my favorite relative. When we'd been babies he had treated us for the usual childhood diseases. The summer I was ten, a splinter in my foot had become badly infected, and he was the only one I would let touch it. He had seen me through the whole cancer time. He wasn't my doctor—I had an oncologist—but Uncle Brent was there to explain things the cancer doctor didn't. My heart caught, he looked so much like my daddy.

"Look at you," he said. "You have turned into a beautiful woman. I wish your daddy could see you now."

Unexpected tears flooded my eyes.

"Hey now, none of that." He pulled a handkerchief from his breast pocket and wiped my cheeks, stroking over the exact spot Lily had touched earlier. "What are you drinking?"

"Gin and tonic."

"Two," he told the bartender. When we were served, he carried the drinks to a table off to the side, held a chair for me.

"I thought you were in Hawaii," I said. My aunt Monica had died two years before, and after she died, Brent surprised everyone by turning over his practice to a young doctor and moving west.

"I was. I just flew in yesterday."

"It was so nice of you to come to Mama's party."

"I wouldn't have missed it," he said. I'd forgotten how much he sounded like my daddy. After our daddy died, I used to fantasize that Lily and Uncle Brent would marry. It would be almost like having my daddy back, I'd told Ashley once, and my sister had asked what I planned to do with the inconvenience of Aunt Monica. Oh, maybe she'll get hit by a bus, I'd said with the single-minded callousness of a teenager. Ridiculous, but nearly two decades later, I still felt a twinge of guilt about Monica's death. "So how are you doing?" I asked.

"Well, I keep busy. My golf game's improved. I do some work at a volunteer clinic."

"And you like Hawaii?"

"Love it. You should come out and visit."

"You must miss Aunt Monica."

"More than you can imagine." His voice was raw.

"Maybe you'll see her again," I said, keeping my tone light.

"You mean in another life?"

"Do you believe in that?" I asked. "Do you believe in life after death?"

"You're asking the wrong question, Jessie."

"The wrong question?"

He nodded. "The question is, is there life before death?" He took a sip of his drink and sighed. "Of course I miss her, Jess. Always will. But I know better than anyone that death is a normal part of life. We just forget that. It's the fear of death that's so terrible. It holds us back from life."

"You sound exactly like Faye," I said.

"Faye?"

"Faye Wilson."

He gave the faintest of faraway smiles, as if remembering a sweet moment, and that trick of time happened when you could look at someone and see exactly what they looked like when they were six or ten or seventeen. "God, I haven't thought about her in years," he said. "I used to have quite a crush on her back when the whole family used to summer on the Cape. She was quite a looker. A bit wild, too. She never gave me the time of day. We all thought she was smitten with Lowell. When did you see her?"

"I'm staying at the Harwich Port house this year," I said. "Faye is the volunteer coordinator for the local hospice, and I've been doing some volunteer work with her."

"Good for you. Hospice is a great organization. Those people do amazing work. I don't know how I would have managed during the last months with Monica without them." His eyes focused on some imaginary point, and I knew he had gone off to a place I could not follow.

Off to our right, a woman laughed. Voices swirled around us. "The man I'm caring for has pancreatic cancer," I said.

He leaned in, back in the present. I could sense his professional interest click in. "When was it diagnosed?"

"In January."

"What kind?"

"Adenosarcoma," I said. I had read this on Luke's chart, learned it was the fastest kind of cancer.

"So he must be close to the end, then," he said, accepting the inevitability of Luke's death.

"How does it happen? Death, I mean."

"You mean the physiology of it? The process?"

"Yes."

"Well, basically, the body wastes away. It's a series of losses. Systems begin to shut down, one by one. Digestive is the first. Then bowels and bladder."

I thought about what Luke had said. *I don't want to die piece by piece.* "And the last?"

"Well, the heart, of course. And hearing," he said. "Hearing is the last sense to disappear into unconsciousness."

"It's so hard to watch," I said, swallowing against tears.

"But a blessing to witness, too," he said.

"I don't know if I agree with that," I said automatically.

"Every death is a gift to the person observing," he said. "A tremendous lesson and blessing."

"Even Monica's?"

"Yes." His eyes watered momentarily, and a spasm of pain crossed his face. I realized then that he loved my aunt and that I'd never had the slightest clue about their marriage.

"How did you stand it in the end?" I asked. "When everything was hopeless."

He seemed to understand I was asking about more than Monica. "There's a middle ground you have to find."

"A middle ground?"

"Between clinging to false hope and falling into hopelessness."

"I don't understand. How can there be a middle ground?"

"The middle ground is that space—maybe a few months or weeks or a day, even an hour—that you can *reasonably* hope for."

It wasn't enough. I wanted more.

THERE WAS a roar of laughter from the front of the room. While we'd been talking, Lily had been opening gifts, and now she held up one—Faye's, I noticed from the gift wrap. It was a T-shirt inscribed WELL-BEHAVED WOMEN RARELY MAKE HISTORY. Lily slipped it on right over her dress.

I looked at my uncle and saw him smile at Lily.

"I think this trip she is so goddamned set on taking is crazy," I said.

"Why?" His voice held no judgment. He seemed to honestly want my answer.

"Why? Let's start with she doesn't know the first thing about sailing."

"She'll make a good mate. And Jan's nephew and his wife are flying in from Denver to meet them in Norfolk. Both are experienced sailors."

"That's the first I've heard of it," I said, and wondered why neither Lily nor Ashley had thought to give me this crucial piece of information.

He looked over to where Lily was opening another gift. She looked both silly and spunky in the teal dress and Faye's T-shirt. "Your mother is stronger than you give her credit for, Jessie. She always was the tougher of the two."

I looked at him, surprised, and then realized he was right. Lily had always been the enforcer. My daddy had been the easy one.

"Well, I've monopolized you enough for one evening. There's a gentleman across the room who has been looking over here for the last ten minutes. He seems to be growing impatient. Shall we oblige?"

"In a moment," I said. "You go ahead. Mingle with the widows. I'll be right there. No disrespect to Aunt Monica, but as Ashley would say, you're fresh meat on the market."

He laughed and kissed my head. "You've grown into a magnificent woman," he said before he left. "I always knew you would."

Across the room, I heard Lily give a shout of glee. She was tipsy, I saw now, and nearly stumbled. Jan was at her side instantly, steadying her, smiling at her, as if she were absolutely perfect. I thought about what Ashley had said earlier. *He's a nice man. He makes her happy. Give him a chance.*

Lily caught my eye, held it for a long moment. I raised my glass in the air and smiled. "I love you, Mama," I mouthed.

Lily grinned and blew me a kiss.

I sent one back, and then waited while Bill Miller crossed the room and made his way back to me.

eighteen

M Y FLIGHT LANDED at Logan at four thirty, but we were delayed at the gate because of a mechanical problem with the door, and it was well after five by the time I had reclaimed the Toyota and headed back toward the Cape. I was light-headed with exhaustion, both from the party, which had gone on until nearly three in the morning, and from the emotions of the trip. It had been difficult to say good-bye to Lily. Earlier that day, when Ashley picked me up at the house, I'd had the distinct and unshakable feeling that I was parting from my childhood home for the last time and had been unable to hide my tears.

"I won't have you worrying," Lily had said, misunderstanding.

"I'm not, Mama," I'd said. *I'm sad.*

"I'm embarking on an incredible journey. The trip of my lifetime." Lily had sounded like a child on Christmas Eve. "And I don't want to have anyone dampen it with their tears."

"We'll write every day," Jan said. At the party, he'd announced that he'd made arrangements to e-mail from aboard the *Odyssey* every day of the two weeks the trip would take. Fourteen days seemed both an unbelievably short time to make a transatlantic voyage and a terribly long time to be out to sea. Since I hadn't bothered with an Internet hookup at the Cape cottage, Ashley promised that she'd keep me informed. Our tiff in the ladies' room of the club was forgotten, although she still thought I was crazy not to have latched onto Bill.

Before the party ended, he had asked if he could drive me to the airport on Sunday and mentioned the possibility of flying to the

Cape for a weekend. "I don't think so," I'd said, and saw the flash of surprise on his face before he regained control.

"Perhaps another time," he said, but we both knew it wouldn't happen.

Ashley couldn't understand why I didn't even try. "What's so wrong about him?" she asked.

He's not Luke, I thought but could not say. "Stop trying to fix my life for me," I'd said instead.

"Well, somebody should," she said.

As I headed south out of Boston, I exceeded the speed limit, hoping to arrive back on the Cape in time to see Luke. I was held up again by repairs on the Sagamore Bridge but still managed to make it to the Harwich exit of the Mid-Cape Highway by quarter to seven. I stopped by the cottage to unload my luggage and phone Nona.

"Hi," I said.

"Hi, Jessie," she said. She sounded spent.

"I just got in," I said. "How's Luke?"

There was a pause—long enough for my heart to go flat—before she answered. "About the same."

"I thought I might stop by."

"He's sleeping now," she said.

"Oh," I said, unable to conceal my disappointment.

"Can you come by in the morning?"

"Sure. And tell him I called, okay?"

I rang Faye next, but there was no answer. Too antsy to stay at the cottage, I got back in the Toyota and, with no clear destination in mind, headed toward Chatham, eventually ending up at the parking lot by the Coast Guard station. I turned off the ignition, rolled down the window, and listened to the lapping of waves, remembering the day I'd sat there with Luke. That day seemed very long ago. In the last light of evening, I watched one of the fishing fleet come through the cut. On the sidewalk, two boys skateboarded recklessly past, narrowly missing a family of four just coming up from the beach. The mother and two children were blond; the father had hair as dark as Luke's, reminding me of a story a woman from L.A. once told me. The woman's mother had been Danish and her father Jewish. She and her brother had hair as dark as their father's, and when they were young, their mother colored their hair blond and washed their arms in peroxide to bleach them, too. The woman had sent me her hair to fashion into a necklace. It was wiry and defiantly black. Her story held the entire history of her family, she said. I watched as the family climbed into a green sedan, not even taking time to brush the sand off their feet. I imagined them going off to a dinner of fried clams.

I needed sleep, but I put off returning to the empty cottage. It took all my resolve not to go to Luke's, regardless of what Nona had said. Even watching him sleep would bring me a measure of comfort. On the way back down Main Street, I pulled over in front of the Squire. The first of the college crowd had arrived for the summer, and the bar side of the restaurant was jammed. I found an empty stool and ordered a beer.

"Pretty busy," I said to the bartender.

"It will only get worse," he said, and told me a local band was going to be playing later. I was aware of appraising glances coming my way, and, too exhausted to fend off anyone, I kept my eyes focused on my beer.

The bartender slid a bowl of pretzels in front of me. "Want to order anything from the menu?"

"Not right now, thanks," I said, although I hadn't eaten since noon.

"Let me know when you're ready," he said, and drew a round of drafts for a group at the other end of the bar. He was back in minutes and set a bottle in front of me.

I raised an eyebrow. "I didn't order this," I said.

"Compliments of the gentleman," he said, indicating someone standing off to my right.

I turned and saw Rich. He took that as an invitation and edged his way through the crowd.

"Nice surprise seeing you here," he said.

I used the noise of the crowd to avoid replying.

"Good band tonight," he said. "The Total Strangers. You know them?"

I pantomimed difficulty in hearing him through the noise of the bar crowd.

He picked up my beer and, before I could react or resist, led me to a table. I stumbled once, and he caught me. "This is better, yes?" he said when we were seated.

"I really can't stay," I said. "I just stopped in for a quick beer."

He ignored this. "Luke tells me you're from Virginia."

"Yes."

"I was stationed there," he said. "When I was in the navy. Norfolk."

I pictured the map at Lily's party. The big yellow arrow that pointed to Norfolk, the matching one aimed at the Azores.

"So where exactly in Virginia are you from?"

"Richmond," I said.

"You still have family there?"

"My mama and a sister." I hated this kind of bar talk. "How's Rocker doing?"

"Great. I take him to work with me. Now he thinks he owns the truck."

"I bet he misses Luke," I said.

"I don't know. He seems to be adjusting."

"How long have you known him for?"

"Rocker?"

"Luke."

"About twenty years." He signaled for another round.

"Not for me," I said, but when the waiter came over, he brought two beers. I looked down, amazed to see I'd nearly finished the one in front of me. Aware I had a slight buzz on—exhaustion and no dinner—I resolved to nurse this one. The band came in, and we watched them set up. I wanted to ask Rich a million questions about Luke, and at the same time, I didn't want to talk about him at all. I stood up.

"You're not going?" Rich said.

"Ladies' room," I said. I stumbled again when I took a step, and he cupped his palm on the small of my back. Instantly I flashed on the image of Jan helping Lily at the party in exactly that way. I tightened my fingers on his arm, steadied myself. "Sorry," I said. "Too many beers on an empty stomach."

"No such thing as too many beers."

His arm was hard, muscular beneath my hand. He was not tall, probably five seven to my five three. We would be what Ashley and I used to call pelvic matchups. My face warmed at the thought. Definitely too much to drink. I pulled my hand away. Inside the restroom, I caught sight of myself in the mirror. No makeup. Hair a mess. Looking as tired as I felt. I was not up to a night of fending off passes and decided to slip away through an exit on the restaurant side, but when I came out, Rich was waiting.

"Hey," he said. He narrowed the space between us until I was backed against the wall. His eyes were slightly bloodshot, and he was edging one gear past third on the drink scale. I wasn't far behind. In the background, the Total Strangers began to play, guitar leading the way. He reached over and brushed my hair away from my forehead, then stroked my cheek. Wait a minute, my brain said, protesting. His thumb touched the pulse point in the hollow at my throat. His slightly calloused fingers stroked my collarbone. It had been a long time, and my body responded immediately.

"This is a mistake," I said. *Mistake, mistake, mistake,* my brain echoed.

"Is it?" he said, his mouth slightly curved.

I was aware of music, the buzz of conversation, the clink of glasses, a waitress calling "Coming through," and tried to nod. He held my gaze. I gave myself over to the hard comfort of male arms. It felt so good to be held. Looking back now, I can see that, in that moment, I was lost, confusing grief with desire. I closed my eyes. My lips, traitorous and independent, opened beneath his.

When I opened my eyes, I saw Paige. She was watching us, her mouth curled in a triumphant smile. Like a cat with a mouthful of cream, Grandma Ruth would say.

"Shit," I said, then, "Paige," but the girl turned and walked away.

"Hey," Rich said. "No harm. No foul." He reached for me again.

nineteen

I SLEPT BADLY, my night punctuated with anxiety dreams. I woke with a headache and a mouth made dry by the haunting remnant of a dream, one so vivid that, propelled by an irrational sense of foreboding, I got up and crossed the hall to the workroom. I had not drawn the shades—I seldom did—and the floorboards were awash with morning light. Through the window, I could see people down on the beach, walking the shore.

The envelope containing Luke's hair was there in the desk drawer where I had placed it. Touching it, I was taken with an absurd sense of relief. In the dream, a woman's hands—not mine—had braided the lock of Luke's hair into the shape of a noose. Black and glossy and strong. And clearly meant for me. I laughed at my foolishness—that I'd had to actually *check* on his hair—and returned the envelope to the drawer. Months later, I would recall this morning and wonder at the wisdom of my subconscious. It had sent me the only prescient dream I had ever had.

In the bathroom, I urinated for what felt like five minutes—all that beer—and, remembering the details of the evening at the Squire, grew nearly giddy with relief that I had escaped the close call of Rich. What had I been thinking, letting him kiss me, kissing him back? For I had, I most definitely had. Well, at least I'd disentangled myself after that one kiss, escaped. But not before Paige had seen us. And had Paige not been there, watching us with her lips curved in that strangely triumphant expression, where might the night have headed? Where indeed? Would drunken lust—even in the morning I could recall my body's response to him—have led me to stagger into one more ill-fated romance only to have to flee from it days or weeks or months later? Well, I refused to think about it. I had not gone to bed with Rich. I chose to see this as a victory over past history. I showered, dressed, drank about a gallon of water, and swallowed two aspirin, then headed over to Luke's.

NONA LOOKED exhausted, absolutely shrunken with fatigue. When I hugged her, her breath was a long sigh against my neck before she drew back.

"Well, enough of *that,*" she said.

I knew not to offer sympathy. "Is Helen coming to pick you up?"

"Not today. I'm not going out today. I was up most of the night. With Luke."

My breath caught in my throat. "He didn't sleep?"

"On and off. Mostly off." I read in her eyes the knowledge that this was the beginning of the really bad nights. "The doctor was by earlier. He changed Luke's medication. Put him on liquid morphine. He said that should help, but . . ." She shrugged. Beneath her exhaustion, there was fear.

I closed my mind against the contagion of it. "What can I do? Can I pick up anything at the store? Run errands?"

"Can you just stay here awhile? With Luke?"

"As long as you need."

"I'm going to go up and lie down. See if I can get a nap."

"You go ahead," I said. "I can stay all day if you need."

"I doubt I'll be able to go off."

"Even if you can only get a rest," I said.

"Yes," Nona said. Then, "You go on in. He'll be glad to see you."

THE ROOM was absolutely still. "Hi," I whispered.

He didn't answer, and I thought he was asleep. Then he opened his eyes and stared straight at me.

About the same, Nona had said during our call on Saturday night when I'd asked how he was, but I saw at once this was not true. He had failed in the last three days, more than I would have thought possible. He had shed more weight and was sculpted down to the beauty of bone, the starkness of a Byzantine saint. His hands, when I took them into mine, were icy. He pulled them away. There was an IV tube running into his arm. I noticed a box of Depends in the corner. *Digestive is the first to go. Then bowels and bladder.*

"Can I get you anything? Would you like to play backgammon?" I thought suddenly of those long-ago August evenings when Lily and my daddy played dominoes, a memory I could almost reach out and touch.

He didn't answer.

It was the first real day of summer, already in the high seventies, and the window was open a few inches. I could hear the birds singing in the backyard. "Nona's gone up to try and take a nap," I told him.

He still wouldn't speak.

"What's wrong?"

He sighed. "So I'm being an ass," he said. His voice was weak.

"What?"

"It's just . . ."

"What is it? What do you want? What can I do?" Was he in pain? Did he need more morphine?

"It's funny."

"What?"

"I'm dying. I'm dying, and I still have room for jealousy."

I understood then that Paige had told him about seeing me with Rich, understood the meaning of the smile the girl gave me at the bar. She hadn't wasted a minute. She must have come by earlier that morning or on her way home last night.

"Listen," I said, needing to explain. He lifted his hand and pressed his fingers against my lips.

"Nothing happened," I said.

"I know."

"Really. Nothing."

He nodded. "I know."

Overhead, the floorboards in Nona's room creaked, then fell silent.

Luke laid his hand on the side of the bed. "Lie here with me?"

"Are you sure?"

"I'm cold."

"Shall I close the window?"

"No. I need to hear the birds. Just lie with me."

I stretched out at his side, curled my body to his, smelled the faint odor of urine on his skin. I laid my head on his chest.

"Is this too heavy for you?"

"No."

I stroked his chest and listened to his heartbeat, followed his breathing, patterning mine to his. I thought about the middle ground Uncle Brent had spoken of. The territory between hope and hopelessness that just two days before I'd rejected as not enough. I would take that now. Would take weeks. Days. Anything. I no longer believed that if you loved a person enough, you could save his life, but I needed to believe you could extend it.

"Nona called my father last night," he said.

"In Santa Fe?"

"She thought he should know. In case he wanted to see me."

My chest ached. "And he's coming?"

"No."

"He isn't?"

"I didn't expect him to. We haven't spoken in two years. And before that, we did nothing but fight."

"But still." I couldn't imagine being so angry with Lily or Ashley that I would refuse to see them if they were dying.

He laughed, a sort of hiccup that turned into a cough. "You've got to admire a man who sticks to his principles."

I had no answer to that. There is a lot I can forgive in this world, but not a father refusing to see his dying son. I must have fallen asleep then, for I was awakened by a change in his breathing. A luminosity of sweat coated his skin. I wiped his face with a corner of the sheet.

"Are you in pain?" I asked. I checked the IV bag to see if it was empty.

"Jess?"

"What?"

"The painting." He nodded toward the oil I had admired the first time I saw it. "I want you to have it."

I tried to refuse. I don't want the damn painting, I wanted to scream, but when he insisted, I agreed, although I could not be gracious about it. And even then, he wasn't satisfied until I actually took the painting off the wall and carried it out to my car.

"It's time," he said, when I returned.

"For what?"

"I need to go."

I assumed he needed help getting into the bathroom, but then I saw his face, filled with hard determination and surrender. In that moment, I had a glimpse of a future I was unwilling to see. My heart turned frantic, a small animal. "No."

"Last night, I shit the bed, Jess. Paige had to clean it up." His face twisted at the memory. "That's what I have ahead. Shitting the bed and watching while my daughter or my mom cleans up."

"You can't give up yet," I said, negotiating. I was prepared to bargain—to fight—for each day, for more time in the middle ground. "Aren't there things you want?"

He smiled. "It's liberating not to care. Not to want."

"Surely there's something you want. I was thinking tomorrow I'd get the inspection sticker on your truck. Maybe we could take a ride." I looked out at the familiar sights of his backyard—the bird feeders, the woodpile, the lilac bush—now blurred. *I don't want to lose you.* Looking back later, I would see that he had already gone.

"Two things I'd like," he said.

"What?" *Anything.* I tried to convince myself he would get through this despair.

"I want another cigarette." He reached for the pack; I struck the match, my hands shaking. Neither of us spoke while he smoked. He finished the cigarette, down to the filter, coughing twice, long, hacking coughs. Then he turned to me. "The second thing," he said. "Will you let me kiss you once more?"

I thought about refusing, as if, by denying him this, I could keep him. That middle ground. Ridiculous, of course.

I tasted first the chemical taint of medicine and the stale after-smoke of cigarettes, and then beneath those—as if uncovering the complicated layering of a rare perfume—the faint essential taste of him. *No,* I thought. I couldn't bear it. To have found him only to lose him. The bitterness of it weighted my heart, my bones, my being.

"I don't want you to go."

"I know."

"I love you, Luke."

"Oh, Jess," he said. "Don't."

"I can't help it." My need was so great that I couldn't see his. "It's so unfair." I began to cry. "I've waited my whole life for you, to feel like this."

"Don't," he whispered. "It's okay." He stroked my hair.

"It's *not* okay."

"Listen, to me, Jess."

"No," I said, my voice childish.

His voice was fainter, more labored. "If you can care this much now, you will care this much again. If you can give this much now, you can give this much again."

"You give me . . ." I waited until my voice was steadier. "You give me too much credit. You think I'm better than I am."

"No, I don't, Jess. I see you clear," he said, his voice weak but so full of kindness, it nearly broke me. "You're the one who doesn't know how good you are."

My fear and sorrow shifted, turned to anger. "How can you—how can you be so goddamned calm? Aren't you angry? Aren't you afraid?"

"Not anymore, Jess."

"Don't you feel anything?"

After a minute, he said, "Sad. It all goes by so fast."

"Then why not take what you have left?"

He pulled away, closed his eyes. "I'm so tired."

"You need to sleep," I said.

"I want to," he said, meaning something else entirely.

Outside, I heard the song of a bird.

"Cardinal," I said.

"Yes," he said.

The bird continued to call.

"Did you know . . . ," he said, his voice so faint I had to strain to hear. His breath had become more labored.

"What?"

"Did you know birds practice while they sleep?"

"Practice?"

"Their songs."

"Can that be true?"

"Scientists have proved it."

"That seems—" I wanted to tell him that this seemed like the most wonderful thing.

He reached for my hand. "It's time," he said, his eyes still closed.

I tightened my fingers around his, as if by will alone I could keep him there.

"Now," he said. "While Nona is upstairs."

twenty

I WAS IN the kitchen when Nona came downstairs.

"Did you nap?" I asked, stunned to discover that my voice held steady, sounded normal.

"I didn't think I could, but I guess I did," Nona said. "What time is it?"

"Three o'clock." I feared the pain in my heart showed clear on my face.

"Lord, I must have really dozed off." Nona looked toward Luke's door. "How is he?"

"Quiet now," I said, after only the slightest hesitation.

"Sleeping? That's good. He didn't get much last night." Nona made a vague, indeterminate sound that could have been a sigh and sat at the table. She stared off into the backyard. "I wish you could have seen him when he was a boy," she said. "He was a beautiful child."

"I'm sure he was," I said, now on automatic pilot, as if drugged.

"And good, too. So serious. What was the word one of his teachers used?" She paused, searching memory. "Earnest," she said suddenly. "That was it. She told me he was an earnest little boy."

I didn't trust my voice to reply.

"The word fit Luke exactly." Nona smiled suddenly. "Did I ever tell you the story about his first haircut?"

"No," I said.

"He was about four. I always cut his hair, but he begged and begged to go to the barbershop—like his dad, he said. Those days, he wanted to do everything his dad did—so I finally gave in. Well, he marched right in and sat down on the footrest of the chair. The barber patted the seat and told him that was where he was supposed to sit. Luke looked up at him—all serious—and said, 'Well, where are you going to sit?' His dad and I laughed about that for months." Her smile faded. "It goes so fast," she said, her voice so soft I could barely hear. "You wouldn't believe how fast it all goes." She looked shrunken, old.

Sad, he'd said. *It all goes by so fast.*

"It hurts," Nona said. "It hurts."

I reached over and stroked her hand. She looked at me, really seeing me for the first time since she'd come downstairs.

"Are you all right?"

I nodded.

"You look tired. Lord, look at the time. You probably need to get going."

"I can stay." I *should* stay. I couldn't leave Nona alone here. Not now.

"No. You go along." Nona looked at the clock. "Jim will be along soon."

Of course. Jim. I felt a moment of relief, absolved of responsibility. All wrong, of course, but suddenly I knew I couldn't stay there any longer. "I'll be back tomorrow."

"Yes." Nona gave a weary smile. "Tomorrow."

When I left, Nona was sitting in the kitchen, staring off into the past.

AFTER MY daddy died, I'd spent months in a dazed state, amazed that the rest of the world continued on, as if things remained perfectly normal. I felt the same way now as I drove back to Harwich Port. I pulled into the yard, looked over at Faye's, saw her car in the drive. I couldn't talk to her just then, but I couldn't bear to be alone either—not then—so I changed into a pair of jean shorts sawed off below the pocket and headed for the beach. My mind flitted on the surface. If I'd allowed myself to think of Luke, I would have collapsed.

The beach was crowded with the first of the summer people. Just the other night, Faye had remarked that they came earlier every year. She'd said she could remember back when the tourists didn't arrive until the Fourth of July. And then, she said, sometime in the eighties, it seemed the crowds started to build in mid-June. Now the first of them arrived by Memorial Day.

It was getting late in the day for sunning, but there were still dozens of bodies laid out on blankets, limbs exposed, glistening with lotion and courting melanoma. Two older women sat in canvas chairs beneath the shade of a huge orange umbrella, reading paperbacks. Down by the water, away from the sunbathers, a father and son threw a baseball back and forth. The boy looked about six and wore a fielder's mitt that swallowed half his arm. When I walked by, the father nodded and said hello. "C'mon, Dad," the boy yelled. "Throw the ball." I remembered how Luke had told me about growing up on the Cape, fishing with his dad. I thought of Luke's father then, wondered how he could have walked away, never to come back, not even now.

Although it had been weeks since I'd gone running, I jogged the stretch from in front of the cottage all the way down to Wychmere Harbor and back, taking the loop twice, as if trying to force my legs to take me to a place beyond pain. Then I walked out to the end of the longest jetty and stared out at Monomoy Island. Even the sea breeze couldn't wash the taste of Luke from my mouth or the burden I carried. I was numb with the emotional kind of exhaustion that leveled more completely than physical labor, but even exhaustion couldn't silence my thoughts. Finally, when even the last of the stragglers had packed up and headed back to their rental cottages, I left the beach. At the house, I made myself a gin and tonic, and when the phone rang, I was sitting on the porch, nursing the drink. I rose slowly and went inside to answer.

"Jessie," Faye said. I heard her inhale. "Luke's passed."

I stared out at the street, at the sound beyond.

"Jessie?"

The previous Saturday, my across-the-street neighbors had arrived, and now I heard the sound of their television. The smell of the meat grilling on their barbecue made me nauseated.

"Are you there?" Faye asked. "Are you all right?"

This was the moment, of course, my opportunity to tell Faye everything.

"Jessie? Shall I come over?"

"I don't think so," I said.

"Are you sure?"

"God," I whispered. Then, in a louder voice, "I was just there today. This afternoon." *Now,* I thought. *Tell her now.*

"How was he when you saw him?"

"In some pain. They had him on a morphine drip." I was amazed at my ability to sound normal. "Do you think I should go over to be with Nona?"

"Paige is with her right now. And Jim. He's calling friends from Nona's church."

"Oh. That's good. She shouldn't be alone."

"And the police are there, too," Faye added, an afterthought.

"The police?" This time my voice did shake. "Why?"

"It's routine procedure in a case of an unattended death," Faye said.

I had to sit down.

"You sure you're okay?" Faye asked. "I can come over. I know how hard this can be."

Get a grip, I thought. *You can't break down now.* "Thanks, but I need to be alone right now."

"Call if you change your mind. Promise?"

I made myself another drink—this one mostly gin—and returned to the porch, numb with the knowledge that Luke was truly gone, refusing to think about the future. Sometime after midnight,

I went upstairs to the studio and took out the envelope with his hair. I held the curls in the palm of my hand, ran a forefinger over them, as if that would connect me to him, but they held nothing of him beyond traces of his DNA. As I slid them back into the envelope, I lifted out one of the curls, then returned the other to the desk. I sorted through my materials until I found an empty locket and set Luke's hair beneath the glass dome. Months later, I would wonder what prescient sense led me to save one lock of his hair.

twenty-one

TWO DAYS LATER, Lieutenant Ralph Moody from the State Police called and asked if it would be convenient for him to stop by.

"Why?" I managed, the receiver damp in my hand.

"We're interviewing everyone who was present around the time of Luke Ryder's death," he said.

"Why?" I repeated. Faye had mentioned routine procedure, but nothing about this sounded routine to me.

"Just a few questions," he said.

We agreed on eleven, and I showered, dressed, and roamed the house, too anxious to sit still. I didn't dare try breakfast, afraid I might vomit in front of Moody. He arrived precisely at eleven. I expected him to be in uniform, but he wore gray slacks, a casual shirt, and an unstructured jacket. He was a large man with close-cropped hair, neat at the nape, and a modified gut barely concealed by his jacket.

"I'm surprised the police are involved when someone dies of cancer," I said. My words echoed in the room. I wondered if they sounded as defensive to him as they did to me.

"Actually, at this point, we've listed the cause of death as undetermined," he said. His gaze held mine. His eyes missed nothing. He flipped open a small notebook. "When was the last time you saw Luke Ryder?"

"The afternoon he died," I said.

"That would be June 7?"

"I guess." I made a pretense of having to think back. "Yes. It was Tuesday. If that was the seventh."

"And how was he when you left him?"

"Sleeping," I said. "He hadn't slept well the night before. Nona, his mother, hadn't been getting much rest, and she went up to try and get a nap, and I kept Luke company. We talked, and after a while, he nodded off." I forced myself to shut up.

"What did you talk about?"

"With Luke?" I said, hedging.

"Yes."

"I don't know. Birds, mostly."

"You talked about birds?"

"Yes. He was teaching me to identify different birds by their calls."

"Anything else?"

"No. He was getting tired."

"Did he seem depressed?"

"Of course he was depressed," I said, suddenly angry. "He was dying."

Moody was unfazed. "That afternoon—or anytime—did he ever mention taking his own life?"

"He was depressed, not suicidal," I said. A lie I would come to regret much later, but at the time, I was thinking only about protecting Luke. And Nona.

Moody looked up from his notebook. "And he was alive when you left?"

"Yes," I said, amazed at my calm tone.

"Well, I guess that about wraps it up," he said. "Thanks for your time."

"That's it?"

"Unless you can think of anything to add." The cool eyes were steady on mine.

"No. Nothing."

After he left, I went into the bathroom and threw up. When I was sure I could keep it down, I made tea. I tried Faye at work, but she was away from her desk. I called Ashley and left a message on her machine, called a couple of people in my hospice group, let their words of comfort wash over me. None of them mentioned the police investigation, and I didn't tell them. I phoned Nona to see if there was anything I could do, but there was no answer at Luke's home. It occurred to me she was probably at the funeral parlor making arrangements for the service. I remembered the frantic time after my daddy died, days filled with appointments with the funeral director, minister, the manager at the club where Lily would hold the gathering after his funeral. Finally I went upstairs and put on Luke's shirt and sat in the window, looking out at the sound. My body ached, as if I had been in a car accident or fallen down a flight of stairs. I had forgotten how grief could settle in you, cause physical pain. Make bone and muscles hurt.

THE FUNERAL was on Saturday. It was cool and overcast with rain in the forecast. Faye and I drove together to Luke's service. The funeral parlor was jammed, and we had to wait in line to sign the guest book. In the background, hymns were being played on an organ, and there was the sound of a woman sobbing in the distance. "I hate these things," I whispered to Faye. We saw Jim and Ginny, standing together on the other side of the room, and nodded to them. Rich Eldredge was there with a group of other men, all in dark, ill-fitting suits. We managed to find two seats toward the back of the room. The sobbing was louder now—a tanned blonde who sat in the first row of seats directly in front of the casket. I didn't recognize her.

"Poor Marcia," a woman beside me said to no one in particular.

Faye raised an eyebrow at me, and we both craned our necks to get a better look at Luke's ex-wife. A man and two women knelt by her side, attempting to comfort her as she held court like a grieving widow. Paige was among the missing, but Nona was there, sitting stiffly, separated from her ex-daughter-in-law by an empty chair. She wore a navy pantsuit, and her black hair was tightly permed. She stared straight at Luke's casket, which was closed. I was grateful for that. I don't think I could have endured it if it had been open. As it was, I began to shake—a shivering that took my whole body—then Faye reached over and clasped my hand, steadying me. I clung to her as if she were a life raft, and eventually Faye's warmth traveled through my fingers and up my arm, settling me. Without her, I could not have stayed.

The woman seated beside me chatted on. "Poor Nona," she said. "It's unnatural to bury your child. It goes against the natural order of things."

No, it doesn't, I wanted to tell her. It happens all the time.

The minister entered from a side vestibule, looked at his watch, crossed to Nona for a whispered conference, then approached the lectern. At that moment, Paige walked in, slightly unsteady on her feet and looking more like she was heading for a date than her father's funeral. She wore a lime green bustier, black satin pants as tight as skin, and a pair of fuck-me high heels.

"Holy Mother of God," a man behind us said.

"I'll second that," Faye murmured.

The service only lasted a half hour, but it was a half hour more than I thought I could take, even with Faye at my side, even with the Xanax I'd taken. Marcia and Paige wept loudly throughout. The minister—who it was soon clear had never met Luke—twice referred to him as Duke. Nona sat unmoving, and the sight of her—grief-shrunken and still—nearly broke my heart.

When we left, it had begun to rain—a light drizzle. Ginny and Jim waited in the parking lot.

"Are you going to the cemetery?" Ginny asked.

"No," Faye and I said in unison. Jim suggested we meet at the Wayside for a drink. They were taking the rest of the day off.

It was too early for the lunch crowd, and we were the only ones in the bar. Jim ordered a bourbon on the rocks, and we all followed his lead, as if the occasion demanded something more serious than wine. As if we were holding an Irish wake.

"How are you doing?" Ginny asked me while we waited for the drinks.

I shrugged, meaning okay under the circumstances. I was afraid if I attempted speech, I would start to cry again.

Jim shook his head. "I thought he had a few more weeks."

I stared down at the bar top, retreating to automatic pilot. The others talked a bit about Luke and Nona and the service, and eventually the topic switched to some of their other clients.

"Why?" I said, interrupting them.

"Why what, Jess?" Jim said.

"Why did he have to die?" It was a foolish question, a child's question.

The others exchanged a look. "Oh, honey," Ginny said. "That's a question there just isn't any answer to."

I remembered a night nurse on the oncology ward who sat with me when I was having a bad time, the sole time I had fallen into self-pity. *Why? Why me?* I'd asked her. She looked at me straight on and said, *Honey, life is not a problem to be solved but a mystery to be lived.*

THE DAY after the service, Nona moved back to her house in Wellfleet. I called her that morning and asked her if I could help out with anything, but she seemed preoccupied, distant. I put it down to grief—I could understand grief, the need for isolation—and after a few minutes, we hung up.

In the following days, I called her several times, but she was either not home or unavailable, and I left messages with whoever answered the phone. The calls were not returned. I drove by Luke's home. The shades were drawn on the windows. The grass needed cutting. His truck was gone, and in the side yard, the boat cradle was empty. I tried the front door, but it was locked. With nowhere to go, I headed back to the cottage. The State Police detective was waiting for me there.

"What can I do for you?" I said.

"We're continuing to talk to anyone who saw the Luke Ryder on the last day of his life," he said. He asked a few questions, some of them the same ones he'd asked the first time he came around, some not. Had Luke ever mentioned suicide? Had I had access to drugs? Did I have any plans to leave town? When I said I didn't, he told me to let his office know if I changed my mind.

"Am I a suspect?" I said, smiling to show it was a joke.

"You are a person of interest," he said, not smiling.

A person of interest. What the hell did that mean?

I CALLED Faye as soon as he left.

"I suspect this is Paige's doing," Faye said.

"Paige? Why would she call the police?"

Faye explained that Ginny had heard that Paige was telling everyone that her father had been given a deliberate overdose and had demanded an autopsy. Ginny and Jim had been questioned, too.

"Why didn't you tell me?"

"I thought this whole thing would die. To tell you the truth, I'm surprised they're continuing to investigate. Paige isn't the most credible person in the world."

"The detective told me not to leave town."

There was a long pause on Faye's end of the line. Then she suggested that I think about hiring an attorney.

"What for?"

"To deal with the police. Keep yourself from being harassed."

I WANTED to hire a woman, but Faye insisted I talk to Gage Fisk. "Forget being PC," she said. "You want the best, and he's the best. A shark. Sharpest lawyer on Cape Cod."

I remained unconvinced. "Maybe I should get someone from Boston."

Faye made a *pifff* sound of annoyance, the way she did when anyone insisted on going into Boston for a knee or hip replacement instead of the hospital in Hyannis. "At least talk to him. Promise me that."

At the first meeting, I wasn't impressed. Gage Fisk didn't look like anyone's idea of a successful defense attorney. He was short, soft, and wore a cheap suit and honest-to-God alligator shoes with lifts. I estimated he was pushing seventy.

His office was a disaster, with clutter everywhere. He would have had to clean the place for a week to raise the disorder up a notch to a simple mess. A diploma from some college in Iowa I'd never heard of hung on the wall behind his desk. He called me—and every other woman in sight—sweetheart. I was horrified by both him and his office, and for a brief paranoid moment, I wondered if Faye was sabotaging me by suggesting I hire him. The paranoia was not without cause. I had begun to receive phone calls accusing me of killing Luke. A woman's voice. Whoever it was sounded drunk. Paige, I thought.

When I reported my negative impression of Gage Fisk back to Faye, she advised me to ignore the trappings. He was the man for the job, she said, citing a half dozen tough cases he had won in the past year. So I hired him, partly because I didn't have the strength to search for another lawyer and partly for practical reasons. I figured he was probably cheaper than any Boston lawyer, and even with help from Ashley, I could be repaying legal fees for years if things spiraled. Fisk's retainer alone started at fifteen grand. The whole thing was turning into a nightmare. I had no idea it was just beginning.

THE
BEGINNING

twenty-two

BY EIGHT IN the morning, the commuter parking lot off Exit 6 of the Mid-Cape was packed, but I managed to find a spot on the far side and waited for one of Gage Fisk's paralegals to pick me up, an arrangement we had made after the first day of the trial, when I had been sandbagged by reporters upon arriving at the courthouse.

It was one of those beautiful days in late September that residents claimed as their reward for surviving the summer of tourists—sunny and clear, warm enough for a last-of-the-season swim, in fact a day very much like the one exactly a year before when I had arrived at the Harwich Port cottage, hoping to find some answers that would point me to the rest of my life. Now that day seemed impossibly remote. As did the person I had been. But why should I have been surprised at how much had changed in twelve months? As Faye so often reminded me, life could be transformed in a day. A minute. The time it took to strike a match.

I was dressed in a taupe linen suit, an ice blue shell beneath the jacket, and wore a pair of sling-back pumps, all chosen to strike the note Gage Fisk had suggested: neat, attractive (thinking of the males on the jury), but nonthreatening (so as not to alienate the women). Ashley had driven up two weeks before to offer moral support and help me shop for the clothes. The taupe suit was one of three we had purchased, figuring I could interchange scarves and tops for different looks. Ashley had offered to stay on, even to move up with the boys for the duration of the trial, but I had refused, trying to make it sound like this was all a colossal mistake, one that would be straightened out quickly, just the formalities to go through. My sister didn't question me too closely, unusual for Ashley, and I was left with the impression she was afraid of what she might hear. She had driven back to Richmond after extracting a promise that I would call if I needed anything. *Anything,* she had said. She still disagreed with my decision not to tell Lily about the trial, but I saw no reason to interrupt our mama's extended stay in the Azores. Lily had spent enough time worrying about me when they discovered the tumor. I didn't want to put her through any more. "I'm protecting her," I had said.

"Protecting her or punishing her?" Ashley had asked.

Ashley thought I was still angry because Lily had taken both of us by surprise and married Jan after they'd completed the Atlantic crossing. Lily maintained that it was a spur-of-the-moment decision, although I was convinced that had been the plan all along. It would explain the big party at the club. A prenuptial reception.

Mama had called me on one of the worst days. Just moments after the police had charged me with Luke's death, she was on the line, calling from Europe. I thought at first she knew about my problems by some mother's instinct, but the joy in her voice as she announced the nuptials quickly showed me how wrong I had been. Still reeling from being formally charged, I was too numb to do more than offer token congratulations.

"Be happy for us, Jess," she had said. "I want you to be happy."

"I am," I said in a dead voice. I had never felt more abandoned.

I LOCKED the Toyota and joined the throng waiting near the shelter for a bus to Boston. In those first days of the trial, my face was not yet widely recognizable, and while I waited for my ride, I wondered what the commuters saw when they glanced my way. A professional heading in to work, I supposed, or a woman treating herself to a day of shopping in the city and perhaps a lunch date with a friend, and I thought about the false comfort we found in believing that a person's appearance could disclose essential truths.

Irene, the older of the paralegals, pulled up to the curb in an unremarkable gray sedan, indistinguishable from scores of others in the lot, which I gathered was the idea. The last thing I needed was to be chauffeured in something flashy. I slid in, and Irene handed me a cup of coffee she had just picked up at a fast-food drive-through. Cream, no sugar. It struck me that I knew little more about Irene than I had the first day we had met back in August in Gage's office, but the paralegal knew all about me, including my preference for coffee.

"How are you doing?" Irene asked, the same question I had heard yesterday from Robin, Gage's other paralegal.

"Fine," I said. We rode in silence the rest of the way to the Barnstable County Court House, a handsome granite building that sat high on a hill overlooking Cape Cod Bay, the most impressive edifice in a complex that included the county jail and the district and probate courts. TV trucks from all three Boston stations were already in the lot. Bunched near them were the protesters. It was a small group in those opening days, but before the trial was over, it would grow to a fair-size crowd. Irene drove past and parked in front of the courthouse entrance.

"Are you ready?" she asked.

"As ready as I'll ever be." I handed her back the coffee, barely touched.

"Good luck," Irene said. "Gage will meet you inside."

"Thanks," I said. My hand trembled as I reached for the door handle. Yesterday, I had managed to slip inside unnoticed, but today the reporters were prepared. I sensed the flurry of their approach, saw in my peripheral vision microphones extended, heard my name called out. *JessieJessieJessieHeyJessieoverhere.*

Gage had advised me to nod or in some way politely acknowledge the reporters—get them on my side—but I was as repelled by them as I would have been by a crowd of drunks or a rabid dog and did not care if they liked me. Of course, it was stupid not to try to charm them, but I was to come to that understanding too late.

Also, as I look back with the clarity of hindsight, I see I spent most of those days in a stupor and had to bring deliberate focus to the most routine of tasks, like eating or brushing my teeth. Much later, whenever I would hear a reporter proclaim a defendant without feeling or expression, I would wonder if they might consider this: It's shock.

As soon as the reporters started calling my name, the protesters crowded in. A few carried signs of the right-to-life variety, something that had caught me off guard the first day I saw them. Gage had maintained all along that he could make this all go away. He'd said that the DA wasn't too thrilled to be prosecuting someone for the manslaughter of a person who'd been days away from dying anyway, and a lot of people were sympathetic. Then an organized group from the Christian Right had started busing people in to protest, which raised the profile of the case. I would later learn that some of them came from as far away as Ohio. That morning, I deliberately ignored them. Then a woman's voice rose, separate from the others. "I hope you die," the woman shouted, the words filled with such venom that I actually could feel them in my body, as if the protester had thrown rocks. I shouldn't have looked her way, of course, but was unable not to. Our eyes locked. The woman's face was twisted with hate and righteousness, an image similar to those I had seen on the front pages of newspapers in famous photos reprinted on the anniversaries of Selma or Birmingham, or the antibusing protests in Boston. Or more recently during antiabortion demonstrations. It always shocked me to see such hatred on the face of a woman, just as it always seemed more appalling to hear about a mother who had abused or killed her children, as if women were supposed to be innately more compassionate, less capable of violence.

"I hope you die!" the woman screamed again. I froze, suddenly terrified. Those were the kind of people who killed doctors at women's clinics. Insanely, in the nanosecond it took for an entire soap opera to play in the mind, I saw the woman raise a gun, heard a shot, pictured myself falling. If she killed me, would people protest that, scream at her that she should die? Then a hand gripped my elbow, breaking my paralysis, and Gage was there, guiding me through the courthouse door, furious.

"Tell Nelson I want guards outside tomorrow," he barked at the officer who manned the security check, a heavyset man named Connolly with balding red hair and pitted skin.

Still shaken—*I hope you die*—I set my handbag on the belt, watched it disappear behind the flaps of the X-ray box, and stepped through the metal-detector gates. I didn't wear jewelry, anything that might set off the alarm and delay the process or give Connolly an opportunity to pull me aside for a more thorough search. Only two days in court, and already I had learned how to make it easier.

"Come on, sweetheart," Gage said. Somehow he'd managed to find a vacant conference room that morning, and he led me there.

The previous two days had been spent impaneling the jury. During preliminary questioning, Judge Fiona Savage—her name an omen that gave me nightmares—excused thirty jurors: five for medical reasons, two because of their age, and twenty-three because they either currently had a family member with cancer or had recently lost a close relative to a lengthy illness. That took care of one-third of the one hundred people who had been summoned to appear. Four jurors had asked to be excused, requests she had denied.

When the judge was satisfied with those remaining, the clerk drew numbers for twelve jurors, eight men and four women, and two alternates, both men. It had been nearly noon by then, so we had taken a lunch break. Gage had ham salad sandwiches sent in, but spent most of his time holed up in a corner on the phone. He made one call the second the door closed, and then a half hour later was back at it, this time taking notes. At one thirty, the court reconvened, and Gage and the DA had taken turns questioning individual jurors. Nelson, the DA, was trying the case himself instead of turning it over to one of the assistant DAs. He was good-looking and slender and everything Gage Fisk wasn't, and I was scared to death of him. He challenged two jurors, both women about my age. Gage exercised his arbitrary peremptory challenge only once: juror number sixty-seven, a middle-aged woman with neatly waved brown hair wearing a blue pantsuit. She had smiled at me from the box, and that quick smile had given me hope. When Gage challenged the woman, I tugged at his sleeve, bent my head to his, and told him I thought that was a mistake, that the prospective juror had smiled at me and that seemed a good sign. Without a word, Gage pushed his pad in front of me. I recognized it as the one he had used for notes during the lunch break. He pointed to the notes next to the number of the one he had challenged, juror sixty-seven, and I read the notations. She was a regular attendee of the Catholic Church and sent annual contributions to one of the extreme right-to-life organizations. "How did you find that out so fast?" I whispered. He only winked at me and turned back to the jury. For the first time since I had hired him, I felt confident I had not made a mistake. I took another glance at the pad as he rose to question another juror and noticed that number eighty-three, a woman named Martha Anderson, was a widow whose only son had died in a car accident when he was forty-six, almost the same age as Luke. I hadn't liked the coincidence, and when Gage sat down, I had underlined the name with my finger and raised an eyebrow.

"Not a problem," he had said. "Trust me."

What choice did I have?

THE PREVIOUS day, the third of the trial, Nelson had presented his opening statement, what Gage described as a road map of the state's case, a case that was in Gage's view circumstantial at best. Nelson had asked the jury to keep an open mind and had laid out the foundation of his case. After the first series of *You are going to hear . . .* and *You are going to see . . . ,* I had found myself drifting

off, strangely unconnected to it all, as if it were happening to another woman, as if I had shut down. During the following days, that
would happen a fair bit. One moment I would be listening to testimony, and a few minutes later I would be thinking about a movie
I'd seen or a book I'd read the summer before or a pattern I was
considering for a new necklace I'd been commissioned to make. So
the morning session had passed, and at noon, Judge Savage had adjourned so she could finish up some old business in the afternoon.

NOW, ON the fourth day, I still felt numb as Gage ushered me into
a conference room and closed the door. "How ya doing?" he asked.
"You okay? Sorry about that mess outside. I'll get that straightened
out." He strutted around the room in that roosterlike way some
short men possess. "It's the goddamned media. You better start
praying for a high-profile murder in the statehouse or a natural disaster or a scandal with cocaine or call girls in the governor's office,
get them off our back and on to the next dog and pony show."

Days before the trial, he warned me the media would be tough
because it would draw attention to the case, and what we wanted
was to slip under the radar. Without the media, everyone would be
happy if the case just disappeared. ("To tell you the truth," Gage
said one night, "Nelson would like this case to dry up and go away.
It's a no-win.") But with press attention, everything had changed.
"The case got sex appeal" was how Gage put it now. A handsome
young man dying of cancer. A pretty young defendant (Gage's
words). A grieving mother. A young daughter. And of course the
hot-button issue of assisted suicide. Or manslaughter, depending
on which paper you read. For Nelson, it had become a high-profile
prosecution right before an election. "It's all about politics," Gage
said. "It's always about politics. Never forget that."

"So here's what's happening today," he was saying. "The DA will
start calling his witnesses. Most of them will be familiar to you." He
checked a paper. "The first one on Nelson's list is the State Police

lieutenant who headed the investigation first," he said. "Lieutenant Moody. You remember him?"

I nodded. As if I could forget.

There was a rap on the door.

"Come," Gage barked.

A court officer poked his head in. "The judge is ready," he said.

twenty-three

UNTIL THE ARRAIGNMENT, I had never been inside a court-room in my life. (I had never even had a parking ticket, a fact that failed to impress either the prosecutor or the people picketing outside in the parking lot.) But by the second day of the trial, I had come to know every detail of the courtroom. It smelled like all other public buildings of a certain age—old shellac, dust, dreariness—and held the same faded but stately grandeur. The furniture was heavy, and four chandeliers hung from the frescoed ceiling; there were oil portraits of men hanging on the butter yellow walls and a grandfather clock by the judge's bench. Floral print carpeting covered the floors. The only odd note was a large gold cod that hung suspended from the ceiling. "The official state fish," Gage explained.

Back on Tuesday, Judge Savage had laid out the ground rules. One pool camera for the media. Everyone was to remain seated during the proceedings, and there was to be no standing at the back of the room or on the spiral stairs that led to the balcony. If a spectator was unable to find a seat, he had to leave, an announcement that had resulted in a throng of people crowding the corridors each day before the doors were opened. By the time the court convened each morning, the room was packed, every seat taken, including those in the balcony. Faye was there. And Ben and Muriel and Gordon. The others in my hospice group had stayed away.

This morning, the judge nodded to the bailiff, and the jury was ushered in. They were serious, stiff, and self-conscious. Several of the men wore jackets and neckties. At one time or another, each of them looked over at me with some curiosity. When one juror caught me looking at her, she averted her eyes, as if we had been caught doing something illegal. Mrs. Martha Anderson, mother of the deceased son, sat in the chair designated for the foreperson. Once they were settled in, the judge leaned her arms on the bench and peered out over the courtroom. She was easily the smallest person in the room—Gage told me that she sat on a stack of phone books—and if you passed her on the street, you might think she was a widow, someone who had never worked outside the home, but up there behind her bench, there was no doubt about her power. She turned to the DA.

"Mr. Nelson, is the commonwealth ready to proceed?"

"We are, Your Honor."

"You may call your first witness."

Nelson stood up. "The state calls Lieutenant Ralph Moody."

The bailiff left and moments later returned through a side door by the jury box with Moody, who was sworn in and seated. He was dressed in a navy suit, a little tight through the shoulders, and looked larger than I remembered.

"Would you please state your name and spell your last name for the record?" Nelson said.

"Lieutenant Ralph Moody, M-o-o-d-y."

"Where do you reside?"

"Yarmouth Port, Massachusetts."

"Lieutenant Moody, what is your occupation?"

"I am a State Police detective."

"For how long?"

"Approximately fourteen years."

I kept my hands folded in my lap, and I could see the pulse throbbing against my inner wrist. I fixed my attention on the witness stand, but in my peripheral vision, I was aware of one of the reporters sketching my profile. My cheeks flushed. My mouth went dry, in spite of the Xanax I'd taken earlier without telling Gage.

Speaking clearly and precisely and without referring to notes,

Nelson led Moody through his opening testimony. Moody told the jury that the commonwealth gave the DA's office the authority to investigate any unattended death and that he was an officer in the detective bureau assigned to the district attorney's office. He explained that earlier in the summer, the DA's office had received a call from the Chatham Police asking them to investigate the unattended death of a man named Luke Ryder.

"And did you respond to that call?"

"I did."

"Please tell the jury what you did."

"I went to the deceased's home on Sea Harbor Lane in West Chatham."

"And what did you discover about the deceased?"

"I learned that the deceased, Luke Ryder, had been dying of cancer."

"So what was your reaction to being called in to investigate?"

"I would say I was somewhat surprised."

"Did the Chatham Police give any further explanation as to why they had called you?"

"Yes. According to the officer, a member of the deceased's immediate family was convinced he had been given an overdose of morphine."

"Did the officer tell you who that was?"

"Yes. The deceased's daughter."

"And what did you do then?"

"I, along with State Police detective Peter Sakolosky, carried out a preliminary investigation."

"Please tell the jury what that involved."

"We called in Crime Scene Services. We videotaped the scene and took photos."

In response to Nelson's questions, Lieutenant Moody walked the jury through his procedure, explaining how the investigators had looked at the medications, written down the prescription strength, counted the pills. "We called the doctor who prescribed them, then bagged them as evidence. There was a morphine drip by the patient's bed, and we took that, too. We also checked and bagged the trash. We took down the names of anyone who had seen the deceased or been inside the house within the last twenty-four hours."

"What were you looking for?"

"Syringe, any meds not prescribed, any signs of a discarded package or empty vials or IV bags."

"Did you find anything?"

"Yes, sir. We found a single plastic bag in the garbage by the deceased's bed."

"What did you do with that?"

"We bagged it and brought it to the station."

"And what did you do next?"

"We interviewed several people who had seen the deceased prior to his death."

"And was the defendant one of the people you interviewed?"

"Yes, she was."

"Do you see the defendant in the courtroom today?"

"Yes, sir. I do."

"Would you point her out and describe her for the court?"

Moody raised an arm and pointed at me. "She is the redhead in the tan suit sitting next to the defense attorney."

"May the record indicate that Lieutenant Moody has identified the defendant, Jessica Long?"

"Yes, it may," Savage said.

The swooshing of my heart pounded in my ears like surf, and I grew light-headed. I swallowed and silently intoned a litany. *Don't faint. Don't faint. Don't faint.* That moment, with Moody singling me out, I knew terror, deep and pure and nothing like the anxiety I had until then thought was fear. This—this icy clutch of dread—was true fear.

"And what, if any, was the defendant's relationship to the deceased?"

"She was his hospice volunteer."

"Now, during your initial interview with the defendant," Nelson continued, "did you ask the defendant if Luke Ryder had ever discussed the possibility of suicide?"

"Yes, I did."

"And what did she say?"

"She said he never had."

"So, at this point, what were you thinking?"

"I had an open mind, but in the initial inquiry, we found nothing to substantiate the relative's accusation."

"But you kept the investigation open?"

"Yes."

"Why is that?"

"We continued to receive calls from the deceased's family. Particularly from his daughter."

Nelson looked down at his notes. "And that would be Miss Paige Ryder?"

"Yes, sir. She continued to insist that her father's death was not due to normal causes. She insisted that the police request an autopsy."

"And did you?"

"We told her that, as part of the investigation, we had sent urine and blood to the state crime lab and had requested a full toxicology report. We also sent the bottles of medications and the plastic bag we retrieved from the scene."

"And what else did you do while waiting for the report?"

"We pursued other avenues. We checked with the deceased's insurance company to see if there was an insurance angle, someone who would profit from his death."

"And what was the result of that line of inquiry?"

"We learned that the deceased did have a life insurance policy but that, during his illness, he had borrowed against it."

"And what else did you do?"

"We conducted background checks on everyone who was on our list."

"And did this check reveal anything of further interest?"

"No."

"And eventually you received the report back from the state lab."

"Yes."

"And what did the results disclose?"

"The toxicology report revealed that, at the time of death, there was a massive amount of narcotics in the system of the deceased, specifically Seconal. The cause of death was determined to be acute narcotic intoxication."

Nelson stopped the questioning to have the lab report marked and entered as evidence; several of the jurors looked over at me.

"Did you receive anything else from the state lab pertaining to this case?"

"Yes. We also received a report that the defendant's fingerprints were on both the medicine vials and the plastic bag we recovered from the scene. The bag also contained traces of Seconal."

Moody again stopped his questioning to enter the lab result as evidence. He took his time, waiting until after the clerk had completed the paperwork to resume questioning, and I saw how this gave the jury time to sit with the information about my fingerprints. Finally he turned back to Moody.

"And at this time, because of the lab results, what did you do?"

"We focused our investigation on the defendant."

"Did you have occasion to interview her a second time?"

"I did."

"Please tell the jury about this interview."

"Well, I asked her again if the deceased had ever mentioned taking his own life, and she said he never had."

"And what did you do next?"

"We procured a search warrant and searched the defendant's home."

"And what, if anything, did you find?"

I knew what was coming. Moody was about to present the evidence that convinced the grand jury to sign the bill of indictment. Don't worry about it, Gage told me back when we'd learned that I was to be indicted. "The grand jury rubber-stamps cases for the DA's office." He told me that their threshold for signing a bill was extremely low, lower even than reasonable doubt, that Nelson's case was completely circumstantial. Still, I worried how this jury would react to Moody's answer.

"We found several things of interest in the defendant's home: a man's shirt, later identified by the deceased's mother as belonging to him, and a small oil painting that was reported missing from the deceased's home."

Again I felt the weight of the jurors' eyes. My pulse throbbed against my wrist, at my throat, echoed in my ears.

"Was there anything else?"

"Yes, sir."

"What else?"

"In a drawer in an upstairs room, we found an envelope bearing the deceased's name and containing a lock of hair, which later DNA testing confirmed belonged to the deceased."

There was noise in the room, as if everyone had dragged a shoe across the floor at once. I swallowed.

"You found a lock of the deceased's *hair* in the defendant's home?"

Gage was on his feet. "Asked and answered."

"Move along, Mr. Nelson," Judge Savage said.

"After you found these articles, did you have a conversation with the defendant?"

"Yes, I did."

"Please recall that conversation for the jury."

"I asked her how these articles came to be in her possession, and she said the deceased had given them to her."

"Let me understand," Nelson said. "The defendant, a hospice volunteer, maintained the deceased *gave* her a lock of his hair, one of his shirts, and a painting?" Disbelief dripped from his voice.

"That is what she said, yes."

They have nothing, Gage had said again and again about the DA's case. Some fingerprints on a vial that everyone and his brother had touched. A shirt, a lock of hair, a painting. A plastic bag. I didn't dare even one glance at the jury box.

"I want to enter into evidence Exhibits 3, 4, and 5," Nelson said. He carried Luke's shirt and the painting and the glassine envelope to the clerk, who attached stickers to each; then he brought them to the witness stand.

"Are these the items you recovered from the defendant's home?"

Moody inspected each of the items. "Yes, they are."

The jurors stared at the envelope containing Luke's hair, as if it alone held the answers to the question of my guilt or innocence.

"And while executing the search warrant, did you discover anything else pertinent to the case?"

Moody nodded. "We found a notebook belonging to the defendant."

Nelson returned to his table, picked up my sketchbook, and handed it to Moody. "Is this the notebook you are referring to?"

Moody opened the book, leafed through the pages. "Yes, it is."

Nelson again went through the procedure of having the book admitted as evidence.

"Was there anything about the book in particular?"

"There was."

"And what was that?"

"Drawings of the deceased. Dozens of drawings the defendant had made of him."

Nelson retrieved the sketchbook and received permission from the judge to show it to the jury. Looking back later, I would see that that was the moment, three days into the trial, when Luke stopped being *the deceased* to the jury and became a man.

Nelson addressed his witness.

"Did you have further conversation with the defendant at that time?"

"No, I did not."

"One more question, Lieutenant Moody. In the course of your investigation, were you able to ascertain who was the last person to see Luke Ryder before his death?"

"We were."

"And who was that?"

"The defendant. Jessica Long."

"Thank you." Nelson turned away. "No further questions."

I still couldn't look at the jury, afraid of what I might see on their faces. My hands ached. Across each palm, I'd inscribed livid half-moons with my fingernails.

Judge Savage addressed Gage.

"Does the defense wish to cross-examine the witness?"

"Yes, Your Honor."

Gage stood up. "Lieutenant Moody, the deceased was dying of pancreatic cancer, was he not?"

"I'm not a doctor."

"But you talked to his doctor several times during the course of your investigation, did you not?"

"Yes."

"And what did you learn?"

"The patient had cancer, yes."

"And Mr. Ryder had been on pain medication for several months and recently the dosage had been increased, and at the time of his death, he was on a morphine drip, is that correct?"

"Yes, sir, I believe so."

"Believe so? Or know so?"

"Yes, sir, that is what the medical records revealed."

"So one might reasonably assume he would have massive amounts of painkiller in his system?"

Moody shrugged. "He would have some, yes."

"In your investigation, did you learn that Luke Ryder was under hospice care?"

"Yes."

"To qualify for hospice, a person has to have a doctor's statement they have six months or less to live, is that correct?"

"I believe so."

"How long had hospice been involved?"

"Since April."

"So it is safe to assume that the deceased was, in fact, dying?"

"Like I said, I'm not a doctor."

Gage didn't pursue the question. I knew that Luke's doctor was on his list of witnesses and would be called later to testify. He looked down at his notes. "Now you testified that you found a prescription vial in the home of the deceased, is that correct?"

"Yes."

"Where was the vial?"

"In the kitchen."

"In plain sight?"

"Yes."

"Where anyone might have seen it or touched it?"

"It was in plain sight, yes."

"Is it possible that, at some time during the weeks that Jessie Long came to his home, Luke Ryder might have asked her to bring it to him?"

"I guess it's possible."

"And wouldn't it be appropriate for Jessie, in her role as volunteer, to spend time tidying up the house for Mr. Ryder?"

"It might be."

"And in doing so, isn't it reasonable to assume she might have moved the bottle?"

"She might have."

"Were there any other fingerprints on the bottle?"

"Yes."

"How many?"

"A number of partial prints, some of which we couldn't identify."

"And the ones you identified. Who did they belong to?"

"The deceased's mother, the hospice health aide, the hospice nurse, a pharmacist, and the deceased."

"In your testimony, you mentioned also finding a plastic bag that contained Jessie's fingerprints. Were hers the only prints you recovered?"

"No. The deceased's prints were also on the bag."

"Any others?"

"Several we could not identify."

Gage switched gears. "Now, at one point in your investigation, you obtained a court order for a search warrant for the defendant's home, is that correct?"

"Yes."

"And on what basis did you obtain the warrant?"

"The request was granted based on the results from the lab indicating that the deceased's death was due to massive amounts of Seconal in his system, that the defendant's fingerprints were on one of the medication vials, and that the bag recovered from the scene contained trace evidence of Seconal."

"Did you seek warrants for any of the other people whose fingerprints were found on the bottles?"

"No."

"You did not?"

"No."

"Prior to your search of Jessie's home, did you have any knowledge of the missing shirt or the painting?"

Moody looked over at Nelson. The DA stared ahead.

"Lieutenant?" Gage said. I knew what was coming. Gage had learned from his mole in the system that Paige had hired a private detective who had at some point gone into my cottage and found Luke's shirt, the painting, and the envelope with Luke's hair. My notebook. I could still recall how ill it had made me to learn someone had been in my home, gone through my things. Gage had told me the search was illegal and none of those things could have been admitted without the police uncovering them independently, but during a pretrial motion, to Gage's astonishment and anger, the judge had allowed them.

"We received information that an unnamed person had gone into the defendant's home and found these things."

"Gone into her home or broken into it?"

"Our informant didn't specify."

"Who was your informant?"

"We never ascertained the identity."

"An anonymous caller?"

"Yes."

Gage gave the jury a look of astonishment, as if he was just learning this himself. "So on the basis of an *illegal* search by an *anonymous* person, you sought and received permission to search Jessica Long's home?"

"No. The warrant was granted on evidence we had in hand that pointed to the defendant. She was the last person to see the deceased alive. Her fingerprints were on the vial. He died of a Seconal overdose."

"And it had nothing to do with the information obtained in an *illegal* search by an *anonymous* person and relayed to you by *another* anonymous person?"

"That is correct."

"And you expect this jury to believe that?"

Nelson rose. "Object. Argumentative."

"Sustained."

"Approach, Your Honor," Gage said.

Judge Savage motioned for both attorneys to approach her for a whispered conference. I knew Gage was trying to get the evidence tossed out because it was based on knowledge gained during the illegal search, even though Savage had already ruled on this before the trial. Now she denied it again.

Gage returned to the witness, smiling and acting as if he had

won some point in the conference, although I didn't believe the
jury was fooled for a minute. "Lieutenant Moody, did you uncover
any proof that Miss Long actually was responsible for the things
you found? Could they have been placed there by the same anonymous person who made the call?" Of course, Gage should have quit
while he was ahead.

"We didn't believe so."

"And why not?"

"The defendant's handwriting was on the envelope that contained the deceased's hair."

"So you say," Gage said.

Nelson jumped up.

"Withdrawn."

"Any redirect, Mr. Nelson?"

"No, Your Honor."

Judge Savage excused Moody and recessed for lunch. The bailiff
led the jury out. Gage and I returned to a conference room. Irene
brought in coffee and sandwiches, but I couldn't eat. When Gage
was busy reviewing his notes, I popped another Xanax and mulled
over Moody's testimony, wondering when the small pile of coinci-
dences and circumstantial evidence had become a pile with a force
of its own. When we returned to the courtroom, my head was
throbbing.

"Call your next witness," Savage said to Nelson as soon as the
members of the jury were again settled in their box.

"The state calls Detective Peter Sakolosky," Nelson said.

According to Gage, Sakolosky was an ex-marine, and he looked
every inch of it, from his gray crew cut and erect posture to his
highly polished shoes. He was on the stand for the next half hour,
and his testimony corroborated Moody's. There were no surprises
for the jury. Eventually Sakolosky was excused, replaced by the
Chatham Police officer who had received the call from Paige and
had initially called in the State Police. When he was excused, the
judge directed the DA to call his next witness.

"The state calls Dr. James Wilber," Nelson said.

Wilber was quickly sworn in and seated. He was thin, with glasses, and was pale as a soda cracker, as if he lived and slept in his lab.

"Would you please state your name and spell it for the court?"

"Dr. James Wilber, W-i-l-b-e-r."

"And where do you live, Dr. Wilber?"

"Plymouth, Massachusetts."

"How are you employed?"

"I am the chief forensic pathologist for the Commonwealth of Massachusetts crime lab."

Nelson took him through his credentials, and then began the questions.

"In layman's terms," he said, "please tell the jury the cause of Luke Ryder's death?"

"Narcotic poisoning."

"We have heard that the deceased was taking morphine to relieve pain. Could that account for the narcotics you found in the toxicology screening?"

"At the time of his death, the deceased had not only morphine in his system but five times the lethal dose of Seconal."

"Beyond any reasonable amount ingested for pain or to induce sleep?"

"Five times the lethal dose," Wilber repeated.

Gage had told me that jurors usually found testimony by experts tedious and that they often nodded off, especially after lunch, but when I dared look over at the box, each of them looked alert. Not one appeared the least bit in danger of napping. "It was the lock of hair and the sketchbook that did it," Gage would tell me later. "That woke everyone up. Sexy."

It was after four by the time both Gage and Nelson finished with their examinations, much of it corroborating Moody's testimony. The fingerprints. The toxicology results. Nelson had more evidence marked as exhibits. Shortly before five, Judge Savage excused the jurors and instructed them not to discuss the case with anyone, and then she adjourned for the weekend. The court would reconvene at 9:00 on Monday morning.

Gage waited with me inside the courthouse while Irene went for the car. "Don't you worry," he said, his constant refrain. "It's all circumstantial."

twenty-four

ARLIER IN SEPTEMBER, I'd moved out of the cottage in the campground. I'd felt vulnerable there ever since I'd learned of the break-in by the *anonymous* person, Paige's detective. I had also become concerned about the effect of a trial on my neighbors, most of whose families had been vacationing on this street for generations. They knew Lily, and a good many of them remembered my daddy. Some of the oldest even remembered his daddy. They had been supportive throughout the days after I had been arraigned and indicted, but when reporters had began to come around and the *Cape Cod Times* had printed a photo of the house, I knew I would have to leave. I didn't want them to have to put up with the invasion.

An old friend of Faye's had gone to Bordeaux for several months and, through Faye, had offered me the use of his home. It was an old estate at the end of a private road in Dennis. A large multiacre parcel, overlooking Cape Cod Bay, it was one of the few remaining homesteads in the area that had not been subdivided. The mansion was a white Greek revival called the Captain's House, a name I thought apt since it had been built sometime in the 1800s by a sea captain before being passed along to a grandson who was a captain of industry, and then, most recently, to a well-known captain of commerce. This last captain had had the interior completely gutted, reinforced, and renovated. Spacious, awash with light, and filled with the owner's art collection, the result had been featured in an issue of *Architectural Digest*. Off to the side of the circular drive was a converted carriage house that the family used for overflow guests. A simple four-room cottage that had escaped the renovation plans, it contained a kitchen, living room with a fieldstone fireplace that took up an entire wall, two bedrooms, and a bath. There were wide pine floors throughout and pine paneling in the living room that had aged to a warm gold. Faye's friend had offered me either the mansion or the carriage house, and I chose the smaller of the two. It suited me perfectly and—looking back later—I would believe it saved my sanity. No one knew I was there except for Faye, Gage and his staff, and, of course, Ashley.

Those weeks I lived like a hermit. I prepared simple meals, worked on my jewelry, walked along the flats when the tide was low. It was a nunlike existence, as if I were serving penance. My sole human visitor was Faye, who occasionally stopped by to drop off my mail and a pot of homemade soup or a pie or a jar of beach plum jelly. My only other company was avian.

There was an old wooden feeder atop a post by the kitchen window, and on my second day there, I'd gone to the Bird Watcher's General Store in Orleans and bought five pounds of seed. Each morning I woke to birdcalls. I'd listen and try to identify them—chickadee, cardinal, finch—and I'd think about Luke. The clarity of my memory of him was fading, like a watercolor exposed to the sun. How fragile was the tissue of memory. One night I tried to sketch his image, but the drawing was poor. I would have given anything for one photo of him, *something*. I couldn't even hold the locket in which I'd hidden the curl of his hair. After the police had arrived with the search warrant and taken away his shirt and my sketchbook and the envelope containing his hair, I'd driven to Falmouth and rented a safe-deposit box in a savings bank and secreted it there, safely out of reach of Lieutenant Moody.

Luke. The missing underlay every moment—like a frigid underground lake—although I could speak of it to no one. The ever-present ache of sorrow lodged in my body, and I wondered what happened to grief that could not be expressed. Shakespeare had a line about that, but I couldn't recall it. I remembered what I had thought when Luke told me that birds sang for joy: *What do they do with their grief?*

AFTER THAT fourth day of the trial, I returned to my refuge in Dennis and tried not to think about the day's testimony, the expressions of the jurors, the hate-filled ugliness on the face of the protester who wished me dead. There was no cable hookup at the carriage house, and I was grateful for that, for I might have been tempted to watch the news, see what the pool television camera had recorded. Four days. On the first day, Gage estimated we would be through all the testimony in a week, but things were proceeding slower than he'd expected, and Nelson still had a number of witnesses to call before the state rested and Gage began my defense. I pushed these thoughts from my mind as I prepared a dinner of rice and steamed green beans. And tea. I'd stopped drinking alcohol weeks ago. Part of the penance. I wouldn't allow myself the easy escape of wine or gin. After dinner, I cleaned up the kitchen, and then placed my nightly call to Ashley.

"How did it go?" Ashley asked.

"Okay."

She wanted details, so I recounted as much as I could about the day's testimony. I tried to convey Gage's confidence, but, as always, Ashley could read me.

"I think I should come up," she said. "Someone should be there with you."

"What does Daniel say about that?"

"I haven't talked it over with him yet," she said after a hesitation. The pause was all the answer I needed.

"I don't think you should," I said, and repeated Gage's assertion that I didn't need to worry, that the entire case was circumstantial.

"He's been telling you that since the day you hired him."

"I believe him."

"Wake up and smell the fire, Jess. This is not going to go away, no matter what your runt lawyer says." Ashley had met Gage when she'd come up for the clothes-shopping expedition, and she hadn't been impressed. She wanted me to call Bill Miller. I told her I'd eat ground glass before I'd get him involved.

"It'll be over soon," I said, hoping I sounded optimistic.

"I wish you would tell Mama. Think how it'll be if she hears about it from someone else."

"She's in Italy. How is she going to hear about it? It will be over before she comes home." I hadn't told Ashley about the TV trucks, reporters, protesters, and she hadn't mentioned seeing anything in the news. If it hadn't reached Virginia, I doubted it would reach Italy.

"I'm here for you, sweetie," Ashley said.

"I know you are."

"If there is anything you want, anything I can do—"

"You've already done enough." I would be paying her and Daniel back for years.

"Oh, baby. I wish I could do more. I wish I could make this go away."

I closed my eyes. "Can I ask you something?"

"Sure."

"How come you've never asked me?"

"What's that?"

"If I did it. If I gave Luke an overdose."

"Oh, baby. There was no need to ask. I know you. I know you didn't do it."

Ashley's voice was sure, but I couldn't help wondering if the real reason she had never asked was because she hadn't wanted to hear the answer. "Give the boys my love."

"And ours to you."

We hung up. I climbed the stairs to the room where I'd set up my worktable and turned the radio on to the local NPR affiliate. A Bach concerto was playing. I began braiding and weaving the buttery blond hair from a woman in Seattle into a chain braid. A spider at work.

I know you didn't do it.

FROM THE moment I'd hired him, Gage Fisk never asked me if I'd given Luke an overdose. The only one who'd asked was Faye. "I need to know," she had said in a voice devoid of judgment. "I need to know what we are dealing with." I'd held her gaze and told her no. No, I had not given Luke an overdose. Faye had searched my face, seemed satisfied with what she saw there. "We'll beat this," she'd said. "Don't worry." The same thing Gage had said earlier when we left the courthouse.

twenty-five

T HE NORTH SHORE of the Cape fronts Cape Cod Bay. At high
tide, all is concealed, and you have to walk on soft sand that
gives beneath your feet. But when the tide is low, extensive sand
flats are exposed, and although the trick is not to get caught out
when the tide turns, it is possible to walk nearly a mile straight out
to the water's lip. Shellfishermen dig for clams then, and shorebirds
skitter around, leaving miniature prints in the damp sand. Things
are revealed in the intertidal zone, exposed. Ribs and masts of old
vessels; ropes; bleached shells; the shoaling of sands, all maternal
curves and swells; skate egg cases; horseshoe crabs; short, random
ribbons drawn by sandworms. Once I came upon the skeleton of a
seal, its fin bones alarmingly like those of a human hand.

Now I walked along the shore. I'd woken early. It was too cool
to go barefoot on those fall days, and I kept a pair of old beach-
walking sneakers, stiff with dried salt, by the back door. I stored a
walking stick there, too, a length of gray driftwood worn smooth
by sand and water that I'd found during the first week at the carriage house. I carried it as I headed out, east toward Brewster, poking holes in the sand as I went. I passed by houses, some occupied
by year-round residents. Inside, people were rising into the slow
unfolding of their days, measuring scoops of coffee, retrieving the
morning papers from front steps, taking vitamins. Ordinary lives.

Later, when I would look back on those weeks in the carriage
house, I would think of the days as a period when time stopped. As
if I had stepped outside of it. There were moments—mornings in
the first instants of waking or when I was walking along the beach,

my mind drifting, lulled by the running song of the water lapping at the shore—when I could almost believe I was caught up in a bad dream, as trite as this sounds, one from which I would wake and find myself back in Virginia or Chicago. But then a wave of pain would take hold, and I would remember. I'd think back to the year before and how I had come to the Cape, clear of cancer and full of hope, ready to begin anew. I'd run through all the things that had happened since then. And at the center of all the memories was Luke. I had believed I could block out grief, but of course I couldn't. It would take me at unexpected times, rocking me to my soul and bringing a terrible tightness to my throat, making it nearly impossible to swallow, let alone breathe.

As I WALKED toward the sunrise, I replayed the testimony thus far and was taken with a gnawing fear of what lay ahead. How could this have happened to me? As if, all evidence to the contrary, death, disaster, disease, freak accidents, befell only others. Or if they did happen, one would be rescued, cured, saved. I was swept with a sudden longing for my daddy, an aching that was as fierce as it was unexpected, and with it came an attendant pain I hadn't felt in years. Beneath the longing was anger. Fury born in betrayal. And, I suppose, grief.

WHEN, AS children, Ashley and I had vacationed on the Cape, we seldom went swimming on the bay side, where I walked that Saturday morning, preferring the deeper and more convenient waters of Nantucket Sound. Once or twice during the summer, our family would drive to Nauset Beach in Orleans and brave the icy Atlantic. These outings were all-day events that followed a ritualistic pattern. Lily would pack a picnic: tuna salad sandwiches, lemonade, and carrot sticks for Ashley and me; brie, French bread, olives, and wine for her and my daddy; white grapes and homemade cookies for the four of us. We would swim, sun, collect seashells, toss a Frisbee, or, if there was a decent breeze, launch a kite. Then, late in the afternoon, my daddy would walk to the snack shack to buy double orders of fried clams and onion rings, one of us tagging along on Lily's orders to ensure he wouldn't forget extra tartar sauce. Our fingers and lips shiny with grease, we would sit on the blanket and gorge. Ashley and I would fight over who'd get the last clam. Ashley usually won. Finally, tired and sunburned, we would pack up and return to the cottage, proclaiming the day the best of the summer.

The year I was eleven, my daddy taught me to bodysurf. He checked his tide charts, and when it was scheduled to be high at midday, he instructed Lily to pack a lunch and we headed for Nauset. Once we chose the spot—a science in itself: too close to the water and we would be forced to shift everything when the tide came in, too far back and Lily couldn't keep an eye on us while we swam—we claimed it as ours. My daddy set up the umbrella and unfolded the beach chairs; Lily spread the blanket, anchoring it at one corner with the cooler and at the other three with our sandals. Ashley and I stripped off our T-shirts and shorts to reveal our new suits (mine a pink halter-top one-piece; Ashley's a blue bikini, her first, bought after a sharp battle with Lily). Soon we were settled— Daddy with the *Boston Globe*, Lily with a paperback mystery, my sister on her towel. (Ashley had turned thirteen that summer and refused to sit with us, instead staking out her space several feet away so that any cute boy walking by would not connect her with us.) Immediately I commenced nagging her, begging her to come with me to find shells for our collections or to toss the Frisbee.

"Maybe later," she said, and began oiling her arms and legs, her newly exposed stomach, still virgin white.

"Please," I said. I kept it up until Ashley put on her earphones, flopped prone, and put on a pair of protective goggles, silly-looking things, white with black pupils painted on them. Determined to regain her attention, I kicked sand on her legs.

"Cut it out, stupid," Ashley screamed, as if I had splattered her with acid.

Our daddy set his paper aside. "Come on, Jess," he said. "Let's go for a swim. It's about time you learned how to bodysurf."

"Be careful," Lily said automatically, not looking up from her book.

As we walked down to the water, I saw women on other blankets watching him, confirming what I already knew—he was tall, good-looking, his middle-aged body muscular and fit, swim trunks revealing only the slightest thickening at the waist—and I slipped my hand possessively into his.

We were used to swimming in Nantucket Sound, where, by mid-August, it was as warm as pool water, and I always forgot how cold the Atlantic was. When the waves first licked and shocked, I screamed and hopped back, my feet and ankles numb. (I was always convinced I would never be able to go all the way in, but eventually I did, usually after I had been knocked flat by a wave I hadn't outrun.)

That day my daddy dove right in, but I inched in, jumping the waves as they came ashore, calling to him, my voice and his joining a cacophony I would forever associate with that time and place: the cries of seagulls, children's laughter, a shrill whistle coming from one of the lifeguard stands, music pouring from boom boxes. When I finally joined him, we swam out to the calm waters where the waves broke. He demonstrated the technique first. He looked over his shoulder, and when a wave started cresting several feet away, he raised his arms above his head in the diver's classic pose, and then, just as the wave was about to break over him, he dove, his body stiff, his legs flutter-kicking. The wave carried him all the way in to the beach.

It took a while for me to get the hang of it, but he was a patient teacher. Timing was everything. You had to catch the wave at the precise moment before it broke in order for the momentum to catch you and carry you in. Not *carry* you in so much as launch, as if you were no more substantial than seaweed.

I was on my fourth or fifth wave, waterlogged and groggy, when a wave caught me unprepared and I was sucked under. I panicked, swallowed saltwater, and then I felt his hands take hold of me, his arms lift me up. Choking, sputtering, eyes burning, I clung to the safety of him. I wanted to go back to the blanket after that, but he insisted I catch one more wave. I hung back, mute with fear.

"One more," he said. "Then we'll go in."

"I don't want to," I said.

"One more, Jess," he said.

"I'm afraid," I confessed.

"That's the worst reason in the world not to do something."

"But I almost drowned," I said.

"No, you didn't," he said. "I was right here."

I was close to tears, torn between my new fear of the water and my old fear of disappointing him, this handsome, strong man who was my daddy, who had lifted me high, who had never once struck me in anger.

"I won't let anything happen to you," he said.

"Promise?"

"Promise. I'll always be here for you, Jess. I'll never let anything happen to you. You can count on it."

How COULD parents promise things like that? I wondered now.

How could anyone?

twenty-six

SUNDAY, NEEDING ESCAPE, I drove to Boston for the day. I wandered through Quincy Market and the old burial grounds near Beacon Hill, ate dinner in an expensive Italian restaurant, and sometime after midnight, returned to the Cape and the reality of the trial.

Early Monday morning, I was again at the commuter parking lot, standing off to one side of the bus shelter, eyes averted from the others waiting there. I was watching for the gray sedan the paralegals drove when a green BMW swung in at the curb directly in front of me. The passenger's side window slid down, and the driver leaned over.

"Jessie?" a stranger said.

I drew back. The woman was smiling, but that didn't ease my apprehension. She was dressed in a purple sweat suit and wore false eyelashes and eye makeup in neon blue. Her hair was bleached nearly white and teased into a beehive that defied time and style. I looked around, taking comfort in the proximity of the commuters, thinking that no one, not even a right-to-life fanatic, would be stupid enough to shoot me in front of twenty witnesses.

"Hop in," the blonde said. "I'm supposed to give you a ride."

I wasn't about to get into the car. Those fanatic types were clever. One of the men waiting for the bus, sensing my discomfort, edged closer, his face questioning.

"It's okay," the blonde said. "Gage sent me."

"Where are Irene and Robin?"

"He's sent them out on errands."

I still hesitated.

"Everything okay?" the man asked. The other commuters stared.

"It's okay, Jessie. Really. I'm Gage's wife."

Gage's wife? "How do I know that?" I said.

The woman laughed—a short bark. "Do you think I'd lie about being married to a twerp like Gage Fisk? For Christ's sake, Jessie, just get in the goddamned car."

I slid in and was nearly knocked out by the smell of perfume and the scent of new leather. "Sorry," I said. "I just needed to be sure. I'm kind of freaked out by the protesters."

"Gage told me about them. He should have called and told you I'd be picking you up, but things like that just don't occur to him. Anyway, my name's Cecilia. Most people call me CeeCee."

"He could have tried to call," I said, suddenly needing to defend Gage. "I had the phone unplugged all weekend."

"Nah, he didn't try. The man expects everyone to be a fucking mind reader. By the way, no need to tell him I called him a twerp," she said. "I was just trying to get you in the car." She swung out of the lot and hooked a left toward 6A.

I had to smile. "Have you been married a long time?"

"Seven years."

I tried to picture them as a couple and failed.

"I'll tell you how we met," CeeCee said, as if I had asked this question. "A blind date. We went out to dinner, and then we went dancing. On the way home, he looked straight at me and said, 'I have to tell you, if I had hair like that, I wouldn't know whether to shave it or shoot it.'"

"You're kidding."

"As God is my witness."

"What did you say?"

"I told him, 'Yeah, well, now I've got a hair across my ass. And speaking of ass, I hope you don't think you're getting any.'" She threw back her head and howled at the memory.

"You didn't."

"Swear on the Bible. Yeah, you might say it was love at first date."

For the first time in days, I laughed.

GAGE'S COMMENT to the guard on Friday must have been relayed to Nelson, because when we pulled up at the courthouse, there were sawhorses set up to keep the protesters at a distance, enabling me to get out of the car. "Thanks for the ride," I said. "And everything."

"Good luck today, honey," CeeCee said. "And don't you worry about a thing. Gage hasn't lost a case since I've known him, and he doesn't plan on starting now."

She's his wife, I thought. What else is she going to say? But I felt more optimistic than I had in weeks.

Gage met me at the door. "I see you and CeeCee connected," he said, his voice thick with pride. "She's something, isn't she?"

I agreed with this assessment.

"This will be the tough day," he said. "Once we get through today, the worst of it will be over." On Friday, he'd readied me for what lay ahead—Paige and Nona were scheduled to testify—and I'd tried to prepare myself.

"There's something we got to discuss before we go in," he said, ushering me into a conference room.

"Okay."

"Something you need to be prepared for."

My heart stopped.

"The reason Irene couldn't get you this morning is because she and Robin were driving in to Logan to meet a plane. Your mother's here."

"Lily's here?" I looked around, as if my mama was hiding in a corner of the room.

"In the courtroom."

"Why?" I said, meaning how did she find out about the trial, how did she get here, and why hadn't Lily called me, why was I the last to know.

"I tried to get you all weekend," Gage said.

"I had the phone unplugged."

"Well, she called me Saturday morning when she couldn't reach you. Said she'd be here this morning, asked if I could have someone meet the plane."

"She called you?"

"Yeah. Anyway, I didn't want you to be caught off guard."

I SAW her as soon as I entered the courtroom. Lily was sitting right behind the bar that separated the defense table from the pewlike seats where the onlookers sat. I looked for Jan, but Lily was alone. Beneath the tan, she looked exhausted.

"Mama." The word was more sigh than sound.

Lily mouthed *I love you.*

And then the jury was led in.

NELSON CALLED Paige first. I hadn't seen her since the day of Luke's funeral, and I hardly recognized her as she entered the courtroom and took the stand. My granddaddy would have said Paige "cleaned up good." She had cut her hair and was dressed in a conservative skirt and sweater. No makeup. She looked young. Vulnerable. The grieving daughter. I cast a quick glance at the jury. Several of the women were offering Paige tender smiles. This was when I began to believe I might be totally screwed. As if reading my mind, Gage passed a note to me. *No problem,* it read. *Right,* I thought. I turned back to look at Lily, who nodded in encouragement, her eyes steady, her face filled with her belief in my innocence.

Nelson—dripping sympathy—led Paige through her testimony. If the jurors weren't empathetic when he started, they certainly were by the time he was finished. He established how difficult it had been for her to lose her father, portraying her as the dutiful daughter. Then Paige began on me. "We trusted her," she said. "We thought she would take care of my father."

"And was there a time when you felt that trust was abused?"

"Yes, several times," she said. She told the jurors about Easter, and how her grandmother had wanted to go to church and had asked if I would stay with Luke, but when she had stopped by later, her father had been all alone. She told them how I had left him to go out and buy cola and a pack of cigarettes. Together, she and Nelson gave the jury a portrayal of me: unreliable and selfish. Paige didn't testify that I'd gone to the store at Luke's request. I felt Lily's presence behind me and was both comforted by it and ashamed.

"During the months that the defendant came to your father's house, did you have opportunities to observe her with him?" Nelson asked.

"Yes, I did."

"And what was the defendant's relationship with your father?"

"He didn't have a relationship with her. But she was obsessed with him."

Gage was on his feet, yelling his objection. Judge Savage ordered the jury to disregard the witness's last response, but the word was now in the air. *Obsessed.* I could almost see it take root in the minds of the jurors. I thought of my notebook, filled with sketches of Luke. *Obsessed.* Nelson went on, as if there had been no interruption. "Paige, did your father at any time mention an intention of giving a painting to the defendant?"

"No. Never."

"Now, Paige, I know that this is difficult for you, but I have to ask, did your father ever, at any time, mention that he wanted to die?"

"No."

"Did he ever mention any intention of taking his own life?"

"No, of course not."

"Never, in the weeks prior to his death, did he have any conversation with you about ending his life?"

"No."

I stared at her. Luke told me he had shown her the pills. Why was she lying?

"Not once? In spite of his pain, in spite of the fact that death was inevitable, he never mentioned the possibility of an overdose?"

"He never would have done that. Never. We wanted to make use of what time he did have." Paige started to cry. "He wouldn't have left me before he had to."

Several of the jurors were wiping their eyes. *Screwed,* I thought.

"No further questions," Nelson said.

"She did it." Paige raised her hand, pointed directly at me. "She's the one who killed my father."

Judge Savage instructed the DA to get his witness under control and told the jury to disregard her outburst. Too late. How could you unsay words? Unring the bell? Paige's accusation echoed in the room. I didn't dare turn around and look at Lily.

"Cross-examine?" Savage asked Gage.

Gage tried, but he couldn't change the impression Paige had made on the jurors. He attempted to question her about her drinking and whether she had ever appeared at Luke's while drunk or hungover, but Nelson objected to every question and Savage sustained the objections.

When she left the stand, the air hung heavy in the room. Judge Savage adjourned until one.

DURING THE break, Gage left me alone with Lily in the conference room, saying he was going to the deli across the street to pick up the lunch order. Lily hugged me, kissed my cheeks, stroked my forehead, as if I were ten again.

"I'm sorry," I said.

"For what?"

"That you came all this way."

A look of irritation briefly replaced that of concern. "For heaven's sake, Jessie. Of course I want to be here."

"Ashley shouldn't have bothered you."

"She didn't. Jan read about the trial in an article online."

"Still, you shouldn't have come." *I'm grown-up,* I wanted to say. *You don't have to come in and rescue me.* I felt like I was back in high school, disappointing Lily yet again. Secretly I wondered if Lily was worried about what her friends would think when they heard about the trial.

Lily sighed and sat at the long table. I saw then how tired she was.

"How was the flight?"

Lily ignored the question. "Listen, Jessie, I have no intention of coming in and taking over. I only want to support you in this."

"But . . ."

"Well, are you sure this lawyer knows what he's doing? How did you find him, anyway?"

"Faye."

"Oh," she said, her voice suddenly flat. "Faye." An expression I couldn't read flitted across my mama's face.

"Where's Jan?" I asked.

"He's still in Italy," Lily said.

"He didn't come with you?"

"He wanted to, but I told him to stay with the *Odyssey*. He sent his love."

"God, I'm sorry, Mama. You shouldn't have come all this way."

"You don't have one earthly thing to be sorry for, Jessie."

For a moment, I felt her love and knew it to be strong and true.

Then Gage returned. The three of us ate soggy sandwiches and drank coffee, and then it was time to return to court.

NONA LOOKED old, beaten. Over the summer, she had lost more weight, and when she took the stand, she stumbled, suddenly frail. She wouldn't meet my eyes. She spoke softly as she identified herself, gave her address, answered the opening questions, and Nelson had to keep asking her to speak in a louder voice. After they had gone through the preliminary questions, he turned toward the easel that held the oil painting.

"Do you recognize this painting?" he said.

"Yes," Nona said, her voice suddenly firm.

"Would you identify it for the jury?"

"That's Luke's."

"Are you positive?"

"Absolutely," Nona said. "That is Luke's painting. His college roommate painted it."

Next Nelson picked up the green plaid shirt. "And do you recognize this?"

Nona reached for the shirt, scrunched the fabric between her fingers, pressed it against her abdomen, whispered, "Yes, this is my son's."

"Are you certain?"

"Yes."

"Forgive me for asking this, Mrs. Ryder, but how can you be absolutely certain that this shirt belonged to Luke?"

Nona stroked the shirt, her eyes closed.

"Mrs. Ryder?"

Slowly Nona opened her eyes. She turned the shirt inside out, held it up for Nelson to see. "Here," she said. "You see here where the stitches are red along this seam? It's where I mended it for him. I had run out of green thread."

NONA STAYED on the stand for more than an hour while Nelson led her through the months of Luke's illness up to the last day of his life, all of it captured by the news camera and the reporters. She told the jurors how she had gone to take a nap, leaving him in my care, how when she'd woken up, I had told her he was sleeping, how later when she'd gone in, he seemed to be asleep and she hadn't wanted to disturb him since he'd had a bad night, and how, finally, later in the evening when the health aide arrived, they had gone in together and found that Luke had passed.

"And to the best of your knowledge, who was the last person to see him alive?"

Nona finally looked at me. "She was," she said. "Jessie."

"Mrs. Ryder, during these last months of his life," Nelson said, "was your son alone?"

"Alone? I'm not sure what you mean."

"Was he isolated?"

"Oh, he was never alone. We made sure of that."

"Who was with him?"

"Well, I was always there. And Rocker. His dog. Until Luke got very sick and felt Rocker would get better care if his friend Rich looked after him. And Paige stopped by when she could. And of course the hospice people."

"Who were the hospice people?"

"There was Ginny, his nurse."

Nelson checked his notes. "That would be Virginia Reiser?"

"Yes. She came about twice a week to check on him, monitor his medications. And Jim came three times a week, more toward the end."

"By Jim, you mean Jim Robbins, the home health aide?"

"Yes. He would help with Luke's personal care. Washing him, things like that."

Nelson looked back at his notes.

Without waiting for his next question, Nona continued. "I was always glad when he came. Luke was, too. Jim always made him laugh." A hint of a smile crossed her face.

"He made him laugh?" Nelson turned to the jury as he repeated her words.

"Yes."

"Can you tell us more about that?"

"Well, Jim would tell these jokes. Silly, really, but they'd make us all laugh. Luke always seemed better after he left."

Nelson paused, making sure the jury digested this last bit. The dying man *laughed*. "And the defendant, Jessica Long, she also came to the house."

"Yes."

"As a volunteer?"

"Yes."

"And what was her role in his care?"

I thought that Nona would look at me then, would remember the cups of coffee we had shared, the hours we had spent together, remember, too, how I'd cared for Luke, how she had told me I was good for him.

"She was supposed to help us out," Nona said, staring straight ahead.

"How was she supposed to help?"

"She was supposed to stay with Luke if I had to go to the store or to the dentist. Things like that. So Luke wouldn't be alone."

"How long would you be away?"

"Not long. No more than an hour. I didn't like to be away from him for long."

"And during the times that the defendant was there, did she ever encourage you to stay away for longer periods of time?"

"Yes."

"Please tell the jury what she said."

"Well, once she said I should go back to my home overnight. She said she would stay with Luke until I got back."

"Did she say why you should go home?"

"She said I should get my hair done."

One of the jurors made a noise, not quite a gasp. It wasn't like that, I wanted to tell them. Not like what it sounds like. Nona had been exhausted and had wanted to go home, had missed her house. How easily things could be taken out of context, twisted. I started to say something to Gage, but he motioned for me to be quiet.

Judge Savage asked Nona if she would like to take a short break, but she said she would continue. The bailiff offered her water. Even from the defense table, I could see Nona's hand shake when she reached for the glass.

Nelson flipped through his notes. When he resumed, he asked Nona to describe for the jurors what a typical day had been for Luke, how he had occupied himself.

"He watched TV," she said. "And did the crossword. And he liked to sit by the window and listen to the birds."

I could see all too clearly the portrait of Luke the jurors must have had in their minds. A man loved and cared for, sitting in his room—perhaps as they themselves had, when recovering from a cold or the flu—watching television, reading the paper, laughing at jokes. Listening to birds. There was no place in this vision for vomiting; cruel, unending pain; despair.

"Mrs. Ryder," Nelson said, "did your son ever speak to you about ending his life?"

"No," she whispered.

"Could you repeat that, please? I'm not sure the jurors could hear."

"No," Nona said, her voice stronger, sure. "No, he did not. Not once."

Nelson turned to Gage. "Your witness."

Gage kept his cross to a minimum, basically trying to counter the DA's picture of Luke with one of a very sick and dying man, drawing a reluctant admission from Nona that, during the time she had been napping, it was possible Luke had another visitor on the afternoon of his death, but the damage had been done.

Nona's testimony hadn't been as dramatic as Paige's. She hadn't cried or shouted accusations or displayed contempt for me. She just broke the jurors' hearts.

And that ended the fifth day of the trial.

twenty-seven

CeeCee insisted on staying with me at the commuter parking lot while I waited for Lily, who had driven over to Hyannis with Irene to pick up a rental car. Earlier, we had made plans hurriedly in the courthouse corridor, agreeing to meet at the Barnstable lot, and then Lily would follow me home.

I had started to explain that I was no longer at our cottage, but of course Lily knew that.

"Ashley probably told you," I said.

"No, Faye did," Lily said, her voice strangely flat. She had already rejected the thought of staying at the Harwich Port cottage, put off by the idea of reporters tracking her there, and had mentioned getting a room at a B and B, but I insisted she stay with me. Of course that was what she wanted all along, and so did I.

We made a brief detour by a market so Lily could run in for some groceries. She suggested we go out to dinner, but I couldn't face the possibility of being recognized, and the end result was that we agreed to eat in but Lily would cook. I told her I had some soup and other leftovers—she was exhausted by the flight and the day at court—but she insisted on cooking. While she shopped, I waited in the car, growing edgy, suddenly feeling defensive about the evening ahead. When we finally arrived at the house, Lily proclaimed it "charming," sounding for a moment like her old pre-Jan self. I cleared the worktable and supplies from the second bedroom and suggested she take a nap before dinner, but she said no and went off to the kitchen. I changed out of my suit and took a quick shower, a vain attempt to wash the courtroom from my body. I heard her on the phone to Jan despite the time difference, which would make it later in the night for him. When I came downstairs, the house was filled with the scent of onions and some spice I couldn't identify. Coriander? Cumin? Lily was in the living room, kneeling in front of the fieldstone fireplace, breaking kindling and laying logs. I saw a thin circle of pink on the crown of her head where her hair was beginning to thin.

"Shall we take a walk before dinner?" she asked.

"If you want," I said.

We donned sweaters and Windbreakers and walked down the cliff to the beach, heading west, into the setting sun. As if by a mutual pact, we did not speak for a long time. Lily was the first to break the silence.

"Are you sure about this lawyer of yours?"

I knew what she must think of Gage, with his baggy suits and those ridiculous lizard elevated shoes. "I trust him," I said. "He's savvy." I told her about the day of the jury selection and how Gage had information on each juror and challenged the woman who had seemed friendly to me but had donated to a Christian Right cause.

"I'm not criticizing, Jessie. Just concerned."

"I don't want to talk about any of it right now. Okay?"

"Okay, then, whenever you're ready."

We walked along, the silence heavy. Again Lily was the first one to break it. "Tell me what this year has been like for you."

I thought she was curious about my plans for the future: Had I gotten a job, gotten myself straightened out, made good use of her largesse, the sabbatical?

"I don't have a job yet." Again I felt like the fuckup of the century. "So the year hasn't done what it was supposed to, if that's what you want to know," I said, hearing and hating the defensive sound of my voice. I waited for Lily's lecture.

She turned and looked at me. "Oh, I think it has," she said.

I didn't have the first clue what she meant by that but felt we could easily edge into an argument, slip into an old pattern. I switched the conversation away from myself. "Tell me about the trip."

"Well, you know how long those overseas flights are. But it wasn't bad, considering. Jan insisted I fly business class."

"Not the flight over. Last summer's trip. The transatlantic sail."

Lily smiled. She looked pretty, then, less tired. "Oh, Jess, it was fantastic," she said. "Didn't you read the e-mails Jan sent?"

"Yes." I didn't have a computer, but Ashley had printed out the messages Jan had written each day and mailed them to me. I recalled some of the details: storms, life at sea, how Lily had found the hardest thing was boiling water for pasta.

"It's something I'll never, ever forget. I wish you could have been there. The things we saw. Dolphins and whales. A loggerhead turtle. And birds. When there was nothing else, there was always seabirds. Once we saw a Dole pineapple cargo ship heading to Europe. Some nights, the skies were clear and motionless. And there were phosphorescent bubbles in the wake of the boat. They looked like fireflies in tall grass."

I remembered reading something in one of the letters about storms and recalled my own terror at the thought of Lily in the middle of the ocean, unprotected. I'd had to stop reading.

"Were you ever afraid?" I asked.

"Oh yes. But Jan would remind me that the boat was built to handle all kinds of deep-ocean weather."

"Did you get seasick?"

"More than once. And bored. And tired. But I never once regretted it."

"But why did you go? I never understood that."

"Lots of reasons."

"So give me one."

"Sometimes you have to take a journey to find yourself."

"I didn't know you were lost," I said, a lame joke.

Lily slowed her steps—she'd set the pace when we started out, and we had covered a lot of ground—and then continued as if I hadn't spoken.

"I wanted my life to get bigger," she said.

"I don't understand."

"I looked at my friends and saw their lives gradually shrinking. I thought about my mama and daddy and how, before they died, the territory of their days grew smaller and smaller. Your granddaddy Earl used to hike the Blue Ridge, and in the end, he was afraid to take a trip to the store without your grandma Rose. Neither of them would even go into the city. I didn't want that to happen to me."

"It wouldn't have," I said automatically.

She shook her head. "It happens so subtly, Jessie. You get a little uncomfortable driving at night, so you stop. You no longer like going to the movies or out to dinner alone, so it gets easier to stay home. In increments, so tiny you don't even notice, you give your life away. I wanted my life to get bigger, not smaller."

I felt a surge of jealousy. And then, unexpectedly, pride. I slid my hand into Lily's, suddenly feeling close to her in a way I seldom had growing up. Then we mostly fought. And even when I was in my twenties, we never really shared. Ashley was the one Lily usually traded confidences with. This conversation was deeper than most we'd had. Had crossing the ocean caused this change in Lily? Or had Jan? Or was I the one who had changed?

"Mama?" I said.

"Yes, Jess."

"I'm glad you married Jan."

She turned to me, surprised. "You are?"

"I am," I said. "Totally." And I was. It had been foolish to feel shame about something as incidental as the difference in their ages, to fear that Jan was using her. I understood now that, like everyone else, they only wanted love. I understood that love was a gift, whenever and however it came.

"Thank you, Jessie. You don't know how happy it makes me to

hear you say that." She was poking at the sand with the walking stick, flicking aside shells and small pieces of driftwood. Then she nudged a gelatinous mass—a small jellyfish, I thought. It adhered to the end of the stick, and we both realized at the same time that she had hooked a condom.

"Gross," I said, embarrassed for her.

She surprised me by laughing and deftly dislodged it with the toe of her shoe. "We saw those on the beach all the time in the Azores. The place is awash with them. I think the national pastime is fucking."

I had never heard her use that word.

"Tell me what he was like," she said suddenly.

"Who?"

"Luke. Tell me about him."

Something shifted in my chest, the scrape of bone on bone.

"You would have liked him." Five words. All I could manage.

"Did you love him?"

I thought about Paige's testimony. *Obsessed*. Was that what she was thinking?

"Yes." Sorrow pressed inside. I made a small noise. It circled, orbiting my grief.

She turned and opened her arms, held me. "I'm so sorry, Jess."

"I can't talk about it." The words were muffled against her shoulder.

"It's all right, baby. It's all right."

FINALLY I slipped from the embrace, but when we resumed walking, I slid my hand back into hers. "Thank you, Mama. For coming, I mean. I'm glad you're here."

"Me, too."

"I'm sorry I didn't call you and tell you. I should have."

"Shhh, baby. It's all right."

A sandpiper skittered along in front of us, and we watched him for a minute.

"After Daddy died," I said, "how did you go on?" This was as close as I could come to talking about Luke.

She sighed. "Oh, Jess, that was such a long time ago."

"Please, Mama. I need to know."

"Well, I was pretty busy. Taking care of the house and you and Ashley was about all I could manage."

"Did you miss him?"

"Terribly. At first, I didn't think I would be able to stand it. The nights—alone in the bed—were bad. Sometimes I had to sleep on the couch."

I remembered the mornings when Ashley and I would wake to find her on the living room sofa. We'd think she'd fallen asleep watching television. It never occurred to us it had anything to do with a bed grown too big for one.

"And evenings when you girls were out or asleep, the loneliness was like an illness. There was no one to talk to. Those days felt like a long, endless tunnel," she continued. "And just when I'd think I was going to reach the end, something would take me by surprise. A letter would arrive addressed to him, and just the sight of his name on the envelope would level me. Or I'd see something—a rainbow, the first bulbs in spring, it could be anything—and I'd think, Oh, I must tell Lowell. Then, of course, I'd remember, and the pain would be as raw as in the beginning. It was a long, long time before I could bring myself to the task of tending to his clothes. I kept thinking he would need them when he came back."

"Why didn't you ever tell us?"

"It was mine to deal with. Not your burden."

But it was my burden, I wanted to say. It weighted down my days, left a hole no one could fill. "We never talked about the important things."

"No. I guess we didn't."

"I won't be able to forget him, Mama." I meant Luke.

"Oh, you will. The mind protects us. We would drown in memories if it didn't."

I pictured Luke, remembered lying next to him, his last kiss. My belly softened and I felt desire, as swift and sharp as it was unexpected. I remembered, too, my daddy, slumped over the steering wheel, the picture as clear as if I'd seen it yesterday. "Some things you don't forget," I said.

"I'm not sure that's true," she said. "You know, the memory of pain is one of the first things we let go of."

I had heard this before. "I don't believe it," I said.

"It's true. Our brains are wired to release painful memories. Life would be intolerable if it didn't. Take childbirth. You'd be surprised how quickly you forget the pain of giving birth." Lily gave a quick laugh. "And it's a good thing, too. If that memory didn't recede, most women wouldn't have more than one child. I think that eventually, when we try to recall suffering, pain is the word we use for the experience, not the memory itself."

And then she said something that I wasn't to understand until much later. "People think memories are all we have, Jessie, but what we forget is just as important as what we remember."

"I—"

"Oh, Jess, look," she said.

The sun was near the horizon, painting it with bands of rose beneath the darkening sky and scattered banks of clouds. We both stopped.

"It's because of the clouds, you know, the color," she said.

I did know, but I let her continue.

"The colors of the sunset are beautiful because the clouds give the sun's rays something to reflect off of. We saw some of the most spectacular sunsets when we were at sea. Like nothing I'd ever seen before. Oh, I wish you could have been with us."

"He makes you happy," I said.

"More than happy," she said. "He makes me want to live."

The sun was sinking into the horizon. "We should probably turn back," I said, but we stayed, staring.

"The lavender hour," she said.

"What?"

"That's what your grandma used to call this time of evening."

"It does look sort of violet," I said. "And rose."

"She didn't mean the color," Lily said. "She meant because the day is dying. Your grandma said most people think black is the color of death, but its true color is lavender."

I thought instantly of Luke's house, the lavender door.

"You know, when your father died, I thought I was in the lavender hour, that my life had ended, too. Then I learned that grief and loss are just one note in the song of life."

"You're turning into a romantic," I said, surprised at the edge in my voice.

"I always was," she said.

I was suddenly annoyed; the connection with Lily—tentative after all—was severed. My mama was still the old pre-Jan Lily, putting a pretty face on the facts, as she had tried to teach her daughters to do, romanticizing things, transforming even death into a Technicolor movie.

"We'd better get back," I said abruptly. We returned to the house in silence, just as we had started out.

twenty-eight

IN THE MORNING, Nelson called more witnesses. Luke's doc- tor; Ginny Reiser, the hospice nurse. Jim Robbins. All rein- forced the picture of Luke as a man who was dying, but who had said nothing about intending to end his life. They gave a picture of a man still hungry to live fully in the time he had left. On cross, Gage got the doctor to say that the dosage for Luke's medication had recently been increased, that his pain had intensified, that body functions had begun to break down, that the quality of his life had diminished dramatically. Paige, sitting next to Nona, wept during the testimonies. *This is a disaster,* I thought. "Smile," Gage whis- pered to me. "Don't look so glum." I did my best.

Faye was the last witness Nelson called to testify. She approached the stand with grace, met my eye across the courtroom, and smiled.

"Please tell the jury your name," Nelson began.

"Faye Wilson, W-i-l-s-o-n."

"And where do you reside?"

"In Harwich Port."

"What is your occupation?"

"I am the hospice volunteer coordinator for the Bayberry Hos- pice of Cape Cod." She spoke distinctly. Inspiring trust is her gift, I thought.

"What does your job entail?"

"I select candidates to work as volunteers. I oversee their train- ing. I work with them when they are on a case."

"Please tell the jury about the training."

Faye turned toward the jurors, told them about the weeks during which the volunteers met, the many aspects of the training.

"And during their training, are the volunteers given set rules that they must follow?" Nelson asked.

"Not rules," Faye said, smiling slightly. "Guidelines."

"Please tell the jury what these guidelines are."

"Mostly common sense," Faye said. Again she faced the jury. "Volunteers are there primarily to help the client and the family. What they do varies depending on the individual situations. Sometimes they play cards or read books, run errands. Sometimes they simply provide a listening ear."

"Mrs. Wilson, are volunteers allowed to give medications?"

"They are not supposed to."

"So during their training, they are specifically told not to administer drugs to the clients? Is that right?"

"Yes."

"And they understand this."

"I would think so. Yes."

"Is it usual for volunteers to spend the nights with their patients?"

"Not usual, no."

"Really? In fact, they are specifically told not to, isn't that right?"

"There's no rule forbidding it."

"But you discourage it."

"We don't encourage it."

"Were you aware that the defendant stayed overnight with Luke Ryder?"

"Yes."

"In fact, didn't the defendant spend the night there on several occasions?"

"I believe she stayed with Luke twice. Once when there was a family emergency. His mother had been taken to the hospital. Jessie stayed there so Luke wouldn't be alone."

I silently thanked Faye for calling me by name, for refusing the term *the defendant*.

"Did she notify you to tell you she was staying there?" Nelson said.

"No."

"If she had, what would you have said?"

Gage stood. "Calls for speculation."

Before Savage could rule, Nelson changed the phrasing. "In your position as hospice coordinator, if a volunteer phoned to tell you that she was staying overnight at a patient's home because of an emergency, what would you tell that volunteer?"

Faye paused. "I would suggest that she call a hospice nurse to come in."

"To the best of your knowledge, did the defendant even attempt to call a nurse to stay with Luke when his mother went to the hospital?"

"Not to my knowledge, no."

"Now, Mrs. Wilson, in your role as coordinator, do you frequently have conversations with the volunteers about their patients?"

"Yes. We have meetings with the team during which we discuss the case."

"And during these meetings, did the defendant ever express concern about Luke Ryder's state of mind or convey to you that he was becoming suicidal or that he had mentioned any intention of ending his own life?"

Faye hesitated, looked over at me.

"Mrs. Ryder?"

"No, she did not."

"She never once mentioned this to you?"

"No."

"Would it be reasonable to assume that if a patient had expressed such thoughts, a volunteer, out of concern, would share those thoughts with you?"

Faye looked straight at Nelson. "Over the years, I have learned never to assume anything."

Nelson changed direction. "And were you aware that, during these weeks, the defendant was becoming overly attached to the deceased?"

Faye smiled. "All our volunteers become attached to their clients, Mr. Nelson. In fact, it is nearly inevitable. Their capacity for compassion is what draws them to this work and makes them so well suited for it."

Bless you, I thought. I dared a look at the jury. Several members nodded as Faye spoke. I could see that they liked her.

"Wasn't it clear to you that she had come to care about Luke Ryder?"

"Yes," Faye said. "That is what made her so valuable. You know, the founder of hospice said that hospice workers were 'missing an outer layer of skin,' meaning that they were especially compassionate. Jessie was unusually compassionate."

"Let me rephrase," Nelson said. "During those weeks prior to his death, did you have any indication that the defendant was becoming obsessed with Luke Ryder?"

Even before Gage got to his feet, Nelson withdrew the question.

"Thank you. No further questions at this time."

"MRS. WILSON," Gage began, "what kind of volunteer would you say Jessie was?"

Faye smiled. "She was conscientious. Dependable. Thoughtful."

"In what way?"

"I know she brought flowers to Nona Ryder. Gave up extra time when Nona called and asked her to come over."

"Did you at any time worry about her being overly involved?"

"No. There was no sign of that."

"Not even when she bent a guideline and stayed overnight at her patient's home?"

Faye turned to me, smiled. "I'm sure Jessie's only intention was to provide help and relief for the family during an emergency."

"Mrs. Wilson, how long have you served in your present job?"

"I have been the volunteer coordinator for fifteen years."

"In that time, how many volunteers have you assigned?"

"I'm not certain."

"More than a hundred?"

"Yes, I would say so."

"So it is fair to say you have extensive experience working with volunteers?"

"Yes."

"Has there ever been an occasion when you have had to remove a volunteer from a case?"

"Yes."

"Please tell the jury why."

"In one particular incident, a volunteer asked to be relieved because the client was a chain-smoker and she couldn't stand the smoke. And another time, it became apparent that the work had become too heavy a burden for the volunteer, who had developed his own health problems."

"Did you ever have any concerns that Jessie was anything but a dedicated volunteer?"

"No."

"At any time did you think it might be in her best interests or those of Luke Ryder or his family to remove her from the case?"

"No."

"No more questions."

Faye smiled at me as she left the stand.

"Mr. Nelson," Judge Savage said, "do you have any further witnesses you wish to call?"

"No, Your Honor. At this time, the commonwealth rests."

Then Judge Savage checked her watch and, following her usual instructions to the jury, adjourned until the morning, when Gage would begin his defense.

. . .

I WAITED inside the courthouse for Irene, Lily at my side, who was fuming at the protesters gathered outdoors. *Dirt-eating vultures,* she said, fierce and protective on my behalf. *They raise my blood.* For a moment, I feared Lily would storm into the parking lot and confront them, but Gage hurried us along to the cars and we escaped without incident.

Lily and I followed the routine of the previous afternoon. We stopped for groceries on the way to the carriage house, and then changed out of our court clothes and headed out to the bay, walking until we were forced to return by a darkness that fell earlier each day. This evening we shared no confidences, no talk of death. We ate on trays in front of the fireplace, a scene so comfortably domestic, it struck me as absurdly normal given the circumstances. We didn't discuss the events of the courtroom until we had finished dinner and had poured the brandy. With Lily's arrival, my self-imposed monasticism had come to an end.

"At least Nelson is finished with the prosecution," I said. I was unutterably relieved that this part of the trial was over.

"Faye certainly didn't do you any favors," Lily said.

"I thought she was strong. The jury liked her."

"That isn't the point. The one the jury needs to like is you."

"Actually, Mama, what they need to do is find me not guilty."

"Well, Faye could have been more of a help."

"She just told the truth, Mama. What else could she have said?"

"She could have fought for you."

"I think she did fight for me. I don't know why you're on her case, anyway, Mama. She's been good to me this year."

"And what have you given her?"

"What do you mean?"

"I don't think Faye gives anything without expecting something in return."

"You're wrong. Besides, what in the world do I have that Faye could want?"

"Good question. I've wondered that all winter," Lily said.

"You don't like her," I said, surprised by this sudden realization.

Lily didn't answer.

"Why?" I pressed. "What has Faye ever done to you?"

Lily stared into the fire. "Some people don't change."

"Mama, Faye has been wonderful to me. She's treated me like a daughter."

"Exactly," Lily said.

"Meaning what?"

"She takes what she wants."

"I don't understand."

"She always wanted children, you know."

I stared at her. "What? Are you *jealous* of Faye?"

Lily gazed at the fire.

"That's crazy," I said.

"After your daddy died," Lily said, "I always felt I failed you."

"How could you think that?"

"You and Lowell always had a special relationship."

"Like you and Ashley," I said.

Lily ignored this. "I wanted to reach out to you, but after he died, I didn't know how. So, yes, I guess I am jealous of Faye."

"But why?"

"She's taught you things this year, things I should have. She's mothered you in a way I couldn't."

"She's just been a friend, Mama. That's all."

Lily splashed more brandy in her glass, held the bottle toward me.

"I'd better not. Tomorrow Gage is putting me on the stand."

Lily read the fear in my voice. "You'll do fine, Jessie."

"I don't know."

"You will. Just sit tall and proud, like your daddy taught you. Tell the truth."

I swallowed. The room had turned dark, but I didn't switch on a lamp, welcoming the dark. "The truth," I said.

"Yes."

I looked through the shadows at Lily. "The truth is, I lied, Mama."

Lily set her glass down, drew a breath. "Tell me," she said.

I searched my mama's face. "I lied. To the police."

She waited for me to go on.

"I lied when I told them Luke never mentioned suicide. He wanted to die."

"He told you this?"

I nodded. "Yes."

"Did he tell you he intended to take an overdose?"

"Oh, Mama, it was awful at the end. He was wasting away. He said he didn't want to go like that. He said he had it planned. He had a bottle of Seconal. And something to take to avoid vomiting."

"Jessie, why didn't you tell this to the police?"

I shrugged. "I don't know. I guess I wanted to protect Nona. He didn't want her to know. I don't think it ever occurred to him there would be an investigation. Why would there be? He was dying."

"Does Gage know this? Or Faye?"

"No. I didn't tell anyone."

"Well, now you have to."

"Do you think anyone will believe me? They'll think I'm making it up to save my skin."

"Jessie Lynn, tomorrow you get on that stand and you tell the truth."

The truth. I searched Lily's face. Was anyone ever prepared to face the truth?

twenty-nine

G AGE OPENED THE defense by calling Rich. He looked uncomfortable as he made his way to the stand. He was dressed
in the same suit he'd worn to Luke's funeral.

"Please state and spell your name for the court."

"Richard Eldredge. E-l-d-r-e-d-g-e."

"What is your occupation?"

"I own a landscape business."

"Please tell the court where you live."

"Chatham, Massachusetts."

"Mr. Eldredge, were you acquainted with Luke Ryder?"

"Yes, I was."

"What was your relationship?"

"We were friends."

"Good friends?"

"Yes. I'd say Luke was one of my best friends."

"Please tell the court how long you had been friends."

Rich paused, considered. "Ever since Luke moved to Chatham.
Twenty-three years. I was best man at his wedding."

"Had you seen Luke in recent months?"

"Yes."

"How many times?"

"Twice. Maybe three times."

"You were good friends, best friends, and you only saw him a
few times?"

"Well, I wanted to."

"But you didn't?"

"You have to understand. When he got really sick, he didn't want to see his friends."

"He was clear about that?"

Rich nodded. "Well, at first, he'd still drive around town, go down to the shore, look me up where I was doing a job, but after he got real bad, he stayed pretty much at home." He looked over at the jury. "I don't think Luke wanted people to see him like he was."

"How was that?"

"He looked pretty bad, you know?"

"No, Mr. Eldredge. I don't know. Please tell us."

"Well, he'd lost a lot of weight. He was real thin. And sickly looking. Yellow. I think he was kind of embarrassed. He'd been so strong."

"Now, shortly before he died, you had occasion to see Luke twice, is that correct?"

Rich nodded.

"I need a yes or no, Mr. Eldredge."

"Yes."

"Please tell the jury about the first of those two times."

"Well, I was stopping by to check on Nona. I tried to do that about once a week. See if there was anything I could do to help her out, pick up the trash for her, that kind of thing. When I pulled up, Luke was in front of the house. He was getting out of Jessie's car."

"You are referring to Jessie Long?" Gage gestured to where I sat.

"Yes."

"And what, if anything, happened next?"

"He was sick, puking on the lawn."

"Anything else?"

Rich looked down, embarrassed. "And he . . . he shit his—"

Judge Savage cleared her throat.

Rich reddened. "Excuse me, Your Honor. I mean he, you know, defecated in his pants."

"Outside? On the lawn?"

"Yes. I mean, he was trying to make it to the house but couldn't."

"Did you help him?"

"No. There was someone there with him, helping him. And it was pretty clear he didn't want me there, you know, seeing him like that. I know I would be. I mean, Christ, shitting himself like that."

"And did you see him after that?"

"Yes. A couple of days later, he called and asked if I would come over."

"He called you, after not wanting to see you for months?"

"Yes. He asked if I'd come over."

"Did he say why he wanted to see you?"

"Yes. After I got there, he told me he wanted me to take Rocker for him."

"Rocker was his dog?"

"Yes."

"Did he say why?"

"He didn't have to."

"Why was that?"

"Well, earlier in the winter, when he knew what was wrong with him, he asked me if I'd take Rocker for him after he died. He was real worried about that dog, ya know? He didn't want it going to Animal Rescue or anything."

"You mean after he died?"

"Yes."

"So he was making arrangements for his death?"

Nelson leaped up.

"Withdrawn," Gage said. "No more questions."

"MR. ELDREDGE," Nelson began on cross, "you have given testimony that you were one of Luke Ryder's best friends."

"Yes."

"So close he trusted you with his dog?"

"He gave him to me, yes."

"And did your close friend ever once mention any intention of wanting to end his life?"

"No."

"Did he in any way hint that he planned on taking an overdose?"

"No."

"Not even the day when he asked you to take his dog?"

"No."

"Mr. Eldredge, are you familiar with the defendant?"

"Like I said, I've seen her at Luke's."

"Is that all?"

"Maybe a couple of times around town."

"Please tell the jury where you have seen her."

He hesitated. "Well, I saw her once at the Squire."

"That would be a bar in town?"

"Yeah. A bar and restaurant."

"And please tell the jury the nature of your relationship with the defendant."

"I just knew who she was."

"Didn't you have a romantic involvement with the defendant?"

Rich glanced at me. "No."

"Did you ever have a date with her?"

"No."

"Mr. Eldredge, remembering you are under oath, please tell the jury if you ever remember kissing the defendant."

I felt my cheeks grow hot, regretted that Lily was there, sitting behind me. Was she remembering the times she'd accused me of kissing anything that would stand still?

"It was just the once. I guess we'd both had a little too much to drink."

Paige, I realized. I now understood the queer smile of triumph.

"CALL YOUR next witness," Judge Savage told Gage after Rich left the stand.

Gage turned toward me, smiled. "The defense calls Jessica Long."

I had taken a Xanax, but it might as well have been an aspirin the way my heart was pounding. My palms were slick with sweat. As I crossed to the witness stand, my knees trembled.

"Please tell the court your name."

"Jessie Long," I said. "Jessica Lynn Long."

"Where do you currently reside?"

"Harwich Port, Massachusetts."

"And before that?"

"In Virginia. Richmond, Virginia."

"Please tell the court your occupation."

"Well, I make jewelry. And I'm a schoolteacher."

"What do you teach?"

"High school art."

"Do you like teaching?" Gage was smiling at me, his voice friendly, curious.

"Yes."

"What do you like about it?"

"The students. I really like the students."

"Now please tell the court if you are currently employed."

"No. I'm not presently teaching."

Methodically, Gage led me through the questions that we had reviewed during pretrial preparations. This is your chance to gain the jury's sympathy, he'd told me. Make them imagine that it could be one of their daughters up there. I told the jury about my job being downsized, about moving to the Cape for the year, about how I had come to volunteer for hospice, about the training. He led me finally to the first day I had gone to Luke's home. I told the jury about staying with Luke while Nona went out.

"How did you feel about Nona?" Gage asked.

I looked over to the seats directly behind the table where Nelson sat with two assistant DAs. Nona and Paige stared up at me.

"I loved Nona."

"And Luke?"

I fell silent.

"Jessie."

"I cared about Luke. Of course."

"Jessie, we have heard the state's witnesses testify that your fingerprints were found on medicine vials in Luke Ryder's home. Do you have any explanation for that?"

I remembered Gage's cross-examination of the detective, his suggestion that I might have moved the bottles while straightening up the kitchen. I looked over at Lily. Tell the truth, my mama had said.

"Yes," I said. "A couple of times, when Luke was in pain, he asked me to get his medication for him."

"And you did?"

"Yes."

"Even though you had been told volunteers weren't supposed to?"

"Yes." I turned to the jury. "He was in pain. It didn't make any sense. Why should he have to wait around for someone who was allowed to give it to him? I'd do it again, if I had to."

Gage nodded. "Now, Jessie, in the last days of Luke's life, during the hours that you spent alone together, did he confide in you?"

"Yes."

"What did he tell you?"

"He told me he was ready to die. He said he wanted to die, that he'd saved some pills. He showed me where he kept them. In the bottom drawer of a desk."

Paige shot to her feet. "She's lying."

Judge Savage rapped her gavel. Nelson turned and motioned for Paige to sit down.

"Any further outbursts and I'll have you removed from the courtroom," Judge Savage said to Paige. "Is that clear?"

Paige nodded, sat down.

Gage ignored this interchange. He swept his hand through the air, a theatrical gesture. "Luke Ryder was dying. We have heard his own doctor testify he had only weeks, perhaps days, to live. Why would he choose to take his life?"

"He was in so much pain. Even with the morphine drip." I turned again to the jury. I needed them to see Luke as he was in the end, not as the man sitting looking out at backyard bird feeder and laughing at Jim's jokes. "He had begun to lose control of his bowels. He didn't want his daughter to see him like that, to have to clean him up, to remember him like that. He said he didn't want to die like that, bit by bit."

Gage's next question wasn't something we had covered during the preparations for my testimony, and it took me by surprise. "Jessie, please tell the jury why you became a hospice volunteer."

"I guess I wanted to help," I said. I looked over at Lily. "My mama always told us how important it was to help others."

"But why hospice, Jessie?"

"I . . ."

"Take your time," Gage said.

I paused, swallowed. I felt stripped bare. "It was something I heard," I said.

"Go on."

"At this lecture I went to with Faye."

"That would be Faye Wilson?"

"Yes. During the lecture, the doctor said that we learn how to live from the dying. I guess I wanted to learn the lessons the dying can teach."

Gage stood closer to the jury, looked at them, then at me. "So you became a volunteer because you wanted to help and because you thought the dying have something to teach the rest of us?"

"Yes."

"And did you learn anything from Luke?"

I smiled. "Yes. Yes, I did."

"What did you learn from Luke?"

"I learned that dying, you know, slow like that, requires a lot of courage. Luke taught me that. He said most people go through life not realizing what they have." A deep sigh of loss escaped my lips. I swallowed, concentrated on staying in control. My throat ached with tears held back.

"Anything else?" Gage said.

"He showed me how to appreciate the little things."

"Like what?"

"Everything, really. The birds. Their song. He was teaching me how to recognize the individual birds by their calls." I stopped, unable to go on.

Again Gage surprised me. "Jessie, are your parents alive?"

I looked over at Lily. "My mama is."

"In fact, she's right here in the courtroom, is she not?"

"Yes, she is." I pointed to Lily. The jurors turned and looked. Lily held her head proud, smiled at me.

"And your father?" Gage asked.

"No," I whispered. "He's dead."

"In fact, your father died when you were fourteen. Is that correct?"

"Yes," I said. Where was he going with this?

"How did he die, Jessie?"

"A heart attack."

Nelson leaned forward, as if to object, then settled back.

"Was he alone when he died?"

I raised my hand to my throat. "No," I whispered.

"In fact, you were with him when he died, weren't you?"

Daddy. Daddy, what's wrong? "Yes."

"Please tell the jury what happened."

I couldn't do this. *Couldn't.*

"Jessie?"

"I—could I have some water?"

An officer brought me a glass.

"Miss Long," Judge Savage said, "do you need to take a break?"

I shook my head. I wanted only for this to end. "He was driving," I began. "He was driving me to soccer practice." *One of Daddy's*

Sinatra tapes was playing, and he was singing along. We caught the red light. Shit, I said. I was already late. The coach would be mad. Then he made that odd coughing sound; he slumped over the wheel. Daddy. Daddy, what's wrong?

The tears I'd managed to hold back flowed down my cheeks. I'd vowed I would not do that, would not break down on the stand. Why was Gage doing this?

"Jessie," he said, "knowing what it feels like to lose a parent, could you ever, for whatever good reason, take the life of someone else's father?"

I looked over at Paige. "No," I said. "No. I couldn't."

He nodded, handed me a tissue, stroked my hand. "Your witness," he said to Nelson.

Nelson took his time rising from his seat.

"Miss Long, you have testified that you make jewelry. Is that correct?"

"Yes."

"Please tell the jury what kind of jewelry you make."

"Necklaces. Rings. Pins."

"Silver jewelry? Gold?"

"No."

"What material do you use?"

"Hair," I said.

He leaned forward. "Would you repeat that so that the members of the jury can hear your answer?"

"Hair."

"Human hair?"

"Yes."

A sound—no more than a whisper—came from the jury box. I understood how easy it was to take a single fact and present it so it shadowed a person. I wanted to explain about my jewelry, but Nelson didn't give me time.

"Is that why you took Luke Ryder's hair? To make jewelry?"

I could have lied then, said I had taken it to make a keepsake for

Nona or Paige—perhaps I should have lied, but my mama's eyes were on me. "No. I took it to have something of Luke's."

"Just like you took his shirt and his painting?"

"He gave me the painting," I said.

"Did anyone see him give you the painting?"

"No."

"Did you tell anyone he gave you the painting?"

"No."

"When did this occur?"

"The last day," I said. "The day he died."

"Let's talk about that day," Nelson said. "Luke Ryder's final day."

I looked out over the courtroom, found Lily, searched for Faye. I felt Nona's eyes on me.

"You were alone with Luke that afternoon, is that correct?"

"Yes."

"And where was his mother?"

"Upstairs. She went up to her room to take a nap."

"And you would have this jury believe that while his mother was upstairs, asleep, Luke told you he intended to take an overdose?"

"Yes."

"Was that the first time he had mentioned this to you?"

"No. He'd brought it up before."

"And did you mention this to anyone?"

"No."

"And that final day, when you say he again brought up the subject, what did you do?"

I looked down, bit my lip. "I left him," I whispered.

"I'm sorry. I can't hear you."

"I left him."

"Left him alone after he told you he wanted to take an overdose, without saying a word to his mother?"

I forced myself to look at Nona. "Yes."

"Did you believe that Luke Ryder was serious?"

"Yes."

"Were you concerned?"

"Yes. Of course."

"And out of this *concern,* did you make one phone call, tell one person what you say Luke Ryder told you he intended?"

"No."

"Not one? Not to his daughter?"

"No."

"Not to his doctor?"

"No."

"Or the hospice nurse?"

"No."

"Not to Faye Wilson?"

"No."

"So you kept this crucial information secret?"

Gage stood. "Your Honor—"

"Move along, Mr. Nelson," Judge Savage said. "Miss Long has answered the question."

"That is not the only information you kept secret, is it?"

"I don't know what you mean."

"Miss Long, you yourself have been treated for cancer, isn't that true?"

I looked immediately over to where Faye sat, saw the surprise on her face.

"Yes," I said. "Five years ago. I don't have it now."

"What kind of cancer did you have?"

"It's called schwannoma."

"Schwannoma," Nelson said. "And that is a tumor on the brain, is it not?"

How had he discovered all this? "Yes."

"Your Honor," Gage said, "I don't see the relevance of this line of questioning."

"Goes to opportunity, Your Honor," Nelson said.

"Overruled."

"Miss Long, during the period prior to treatment and in the five years following, did you ever have a prescription for Seconal?"

I looked over at Gage. "Yes."

"I have nothing further for this witness," Nelson said.

"You DID great," Lily told me later.

Mother boilerplate, I thought. What else could she say?

thirty

I N THE MORNING, Judge Savage called for closing arguments. She reminded the jury that these arguments were not evidence in the case.

Gage, dressed in a new suit, spoke first. He clasped my shoulder as he rose and approached the jurors. He started out softly. He thanked the judge and turned to the jury, all but bowing.

"I do not envy you your task," he said. "You have the hardest job there is, the heaviest burden. You must decide what the truth is.

"Now if, in the following minutes, Mr. Nelson or I say something to you that doesn't comport with your memory of the evidence, please disregard it. Your memory is what controls the proceedings once you enter deliberations.

"Later, after I and Mr. Nelson have talked to you a little while, Judge Savage is going to instruct you about presumption of innocence and the burden of proof and reasonable doubt. She will do a far better job than I can, and I am not going to waste your time now. But I want to talk a bit about reasonable doubt. Reasonable doubt is just that. It means a reasonable person can listen to the testimonies, review the evidence, and find cause to doubt the guilt of the defendant. The doubt does not have to be absolute. Only reasonable.

"I just mentioned evidence, and I want to talk to you about that. You must decide the case not on conjecture or emotion—although there has been plenty of both—but on evidence. Hard evidence. Evidence that convinces you without reasonable doubt that Jessie Long is solely responsible for Luke Ryder's death.

"Now, as you have heard, Mr. Ryder was dying. His passing was inevitable. No one disputes that fact. You have heard testimony that he was in pain. He was losing dignity. He confided to Jessie Long that he no longer wanted to be a burden to his family. That he didn't want his daughter to have to clean his body, change his soiled sheets. We can understand this. Who among us would wish that on our child?" He paused, let the jury think about that.

"Let's review what Mr. Nelson has presented as the facts of the commonwealth's case.

"You have heard testimony that Jessie's fingerprints were on a vial of medication. Her fingerprints and those belonging to half a dozen other people. Jessie could have lied to you, could have told you that she moved the bottle while performing a routine household chore. Instead, she chose to tell you the truth, that when she was alone and when Luke Ryder was in great pain and in need of relief, she did what I think any compassionate person would do. She gave him his medication. Why didn't Jessie lie to you? Because she tells the truth. Just as she has told you the truth when she testified that she did not give Luke Ryder an overdose.

"Let's talk about motive, a subject about which Mr. Nelson has remained silent.

"You heard my client say how attached she had grown to Luke and his family. Why would she give him an overdose? What possible motive could she have had?

"Earlier, you heard Paige Ryder testify that she believes that Jessie is responsible for her father's death. I sympathize with Paige, as I am sure most of you do. She has lost her father. Jessie Long sympathizes with this girl. As you heard during Jessie's testimony, her own father died when she was fourteen. She has only compassion and sympathy for Paige. She understands that, in her anger and grief, Paige wants to find someone to blame. But that person should not be my client.

"Luke Ryder was trying to spare his family further pain. That was his single objective. He knew he was dying. Why didn't he tell his mother or daughter of his plans? Again, he wanted to save them from pain. Just as Jessie wanted to save them from pain when she didn't tell them what Luke confided in her.

"Luke Ryder did not know there would be an investigation. He had no reason to believe there would be an autopsy or a toxicology screen. He intended to slip away, having seen to the care of his dog. He intended to take control of his own death. Jessie Long had absolutely nothing to do with his death. She is an innocent and unintended victim of Luke's final decision. Jessie Long is innocent."

NELSON LOOKED rested, confident, as he stood to present his closing argument.

"Thank you, Your Honor. Madam Clerk, Counsel, good morning, ladies and gentlemen of the jury. I want to take this opportunity to thank you for the attention that you've paid to this case and to the testimony and evidence presented over the past few days.

"I know you don't remember word for word the testimonies you have heard, and no one expects you to. What we do expect you to do, what you are charged to do, is to render your decision based not on passion, prejudice, or personal beliefs but on the facts.

"Mr. Fisk has asked that you look at the facts. Here are the facts.

"Luke Ryder was dying. As defense counsel pointed out, there is no argument about that. But even in his last days, surrounded by his beloved family and his dog, he still found enjoyment in life. You have heard from several witnesses that Luke found meaning in life's simple pleasures, just as you or I might. Baseball games, a good joke, the birds that flocked to the feeders in his yard.

"I want you to picture for a moment the daily life of Luke Ryder, a healthy fisherman in the prime of his life who suddenly learned he was dying of cancer. Into his family, hit with the worst tragedy a family can withstand, came the defendant. At this vulnerable time in their lives, they opened their home and their hearts to her. They trusted her.

"How did she repay that trust?

"She stole from the dying man. Took his shirt. A painting. She took a piece of his hair. And ultimately she took his life.

"Now, the defense will have you believe that Luke Ryder died by his own hand, with an overdose he himself took. But did he ever mention this intention to his beloved daughter or mother or his friend of twenty-three years? Did he mention it to any of the people charged with his care? No. The fact is that he didn't say one word of this to the people closest to him. Are we to believe he told it to a woman he had known only weeks? A woman who has lied? Because, despite what opposing counsel will have you believe, Jessie Long lies. This fact is not in dispute. You heard Lieutenant Moody testify that Jessie Long told him on the day after Luke Ryder died that Luke never once mentioned suicide. When Lieutenant Moody interviewed her weeks later, he again asked her that question, and again Jessie Long told him that Luke had never mentioned the possibility of taking his own life. Yet on the stand, with her own future at stake, the defendant now tells us that Luke did tell her he intended to take his own life. So the question, ladies and gentlemen, is not if the defendant is a liar. She has given two conflicting statements, only one of which can be true. The other has to be a lie. The question for you is, which story do you believe? The one she told to the investigating officer shortly after Luke's death or the one she told here in this courtroom when she was on trial?

"You have heard testimony from Dr. Wilber about the toxicology results. Luke Ryder did not die of cancer. His death was caused by acute narcotic intoxication. A fatal dose of barbiturates. Five times the lethal dose.

"You heard testimony that the defendant's fingerprints were on a medicine vial in Luke Ryder's home. You heard testimony that, in her training, she had specifically been told that volunteers were not to dispense medications, and yet she herself said that she gave Luke narcotics. You have heard testimony that her fingerprints were on a plastic bag found in the trash at Mr. Ryder's house.

"Jessie Long had opportunity. She herself testified that she had been prescribed Seconal. She testified that, on the final day of Luke Ryder's life, she spent the afternoon with him while his mother slept upstairs. She alone was the last person to see him alive before his mother went to him later that night and found that he was dead.

"The opposing counsel has asked what Jessie Long's motive could possibly be. Why would this woman, who entered the deceased's home promising to help—why would she give Luke Ryder a lethal dose of Seconal?"

Nelson shrugged. "I do not know. We cannot know. Only she can know. Perhaps she believed it was an act of mercy. Perhaps, in fact, it was merciful. But it was not her decision to make, and I will not talk about the morality of this decision. That is not the question we are here today to debate, and, regardless of your personal beliefs, it should play no role in your deliberations. We will stick to the letter of the law, and in the Commonwealth of Massachusetts, it is against the law to cause the death of another person or to assist that person in his death. Clear and simple, it is manslaughter. In a few minutes, you are going to be receiving instructions from Judge Savage regarding the law.

"And then you will begin your deliberations, and you will return with a verdict. The word *verdict* comes from the Latin and means 'to speak the truth.' The search for truth is now in your hands. And I suggest to you that, when you find the truth in this case, you will find the defendant guilty. Guilty beyond a reasonable doubt."

thirty-one

WORD SPREAD THAT the jury had gone into deliberation, and the crowd outside the courthouse grew. Reporters milled around, cameras trained on the protesters and on a second, smaller group who had gathered in support of me. As I left the courthouse flanked by Gage and Lily, the crowd surged toward me. Gage waved aside the microphones thrust at us. "We'll have a statement later," he said, as he hustled me toward the car.

"Where are we going?" I asked.

"Lunch," he said. "I've reserved a table at Abbicci."

"I can't eat," I said.

"Relax," Gage said. "There's no way the jury can find you guilty."

I wished I could share his confidence. Nelson's closing had seemed frighteningly persuasive.

"How long do you think it will take to reach a verdict?" Lily asked.

"Juries are hard to predict," Gage said. "Some of them come right back in an hour, and others like to go over every bit of the testimony. Depends on whether we've got a nitpicker in there."

"What's your sense?" Lily asked.

"I think they'll come back today."

"Today?" I said.

"Before five."

I clutched Lily's hand. "Please," I said to Gage. "I need to go home."

Lily's brow creased with concern. "Are you all right, Jess?"

"No. I don't think so."

"You probably need food," Gage said.

I felt the air closing in. My voice was suddenly frantic. "No. I need to get out of here. I need to go home."

"Okay," Lily said, her tone calm, soothing. "Take it easy, Jess. We'll get you home."

"Stay with her," I heard Gage say to Lily. "And stay by the phone. I'll call you as soon as the jury returns."

GAGE WAS mistaken. It was another two days before the jury reached a decision.

As they filed into the courtroom, they did not look over at the defense table. I couldn't remember what I had heard. Did the jury avoid looking at me if they thought I was innocent, or was it the other way around?

The foreperson, the mother who had lost a forty-six-year-old son, handed the verdict to the clerk, who passed it up to Judge Savage, who read it, her face impassive, and then handed it back to the clerk. She asked me to stand. Before the verdict was read, I dared one glance at the jurors. I was surprised to see that several of them were crying.

epilogue

OFTEN, THESE DAYS, I think about the conversations I had with Lily as we walked along the bay side shore each day during the trial. There is one thing in particular she said that stays in my mind.

What we forget is as important as what we remember.

I can't know with certainty if this is true, but I believe it to be. I believe that one day I will no longer be haunted by the torment of the trial. I believe that the intensity of my grief will dim and I will remember the joy that love can bring. I believe what will stay with me is the power of connection and friendship.

I recall what Luke told me on the day that he died——*You care this much now, and you will care this much again*——and I pray that this is so. I hope that eventually I will remember not the pain of his death but the many lessons I was taught from his dying, the hard ones that crack your heart wide open in the learning.

After the trial was over, I received calls from several national organizations offering help if I decided to appeal. Lily thought I should fight. And Gage told me there were certainly grounds for appeal. Only Faye seemed to understand my willingness to accept both the verdict and Judge Savage's ruling. I was given a one-year suspended sentence, fifty hours of community service, and forbidden to ever again work for hospice.

When I refused to appeal, Lily thought it was because I was tired and didn't have the stomach for a fight. The truth is, I thought the verdict just. I was not guilt-free.

I had made foolish choices and had not taken responsibility for them. I had not been honest with Faye. I had broken rules. I had been lost in my own need to find love, believing it possible to enter someone's life and take what you needed without considering what it cost them. I had loved not too much but too wrongly.

Although I had taken the plastic bag from the desk and given it to Luke, had opened the capsules when he couldn't manage the task, had dissolved them in ginger ale, I had not given him the fatal dose of Seconal. I stayed with him that afternoon until he fell asleep, sat with him through the very final moments, something I would not have believed I was capable of doing, but as I sat there, I kept hearing Faye. *No one should have to die alone,* she had told me that spring. *We are stronger than we think,* she had said.

But I had been weak, too. I know now I should not have left Nona alone with Luke that afternoon, knowing that he was gone. I should have woken her earlier and told her what Luke intended, made her a part of his death, as she had been of his birth. She was his mother and deserved that. I really believe she would have understood what he wanted to do and would have supported his choice. If I had found the courage to wake her and bring her to Luke's room, everything that followed would have been different.

Faye told me once that regret was a futile emotion, but I will forever regret not telling Nona.

"You were afraid," Faye said, when I finally confessed to her.

Looking back now, I see that, for most of my life, I have been clenched in the steely jaws of fear. Afraid to commit, to fight for a job, to take chances, to stand with the man I had grown to care so deeply about.

As I look back, I am grateful for where I am now. I am living my second chance. I have been changed by the things that transform us all: Love, incalculable loss. And death, that most eloquent of teachers. Most of all, I have been altered by Luke.

DURING THE trial, Gage asked me what I had learned from Luke. Courage, I told him. I meant, of course, courage for the hard work that dying requires. But I also meant I had learned not that the cost of bravery is high but that the price we pay for weakness is much greater.

I learned that it takes strength to love and that love is as indestructible as the hair on ancient mummies and can lead us to strange places. To grief, joy, and loss. To deception, betrayal, and redemption. It can bring us to our knees. Strand us in the shallows or lead us across an ocean. I learned that the very thing that breaks our hearts can be the necessary thing that heals us.

I LEARNED, too, from Paige. After the trial, others asked me if I harbored resentment toward her, for her actions. At first, I did, and then I realized that we were not so dissimilar, Paige and I. She, too, had lost a father and had felt abandoned by her mother. She was fighting to hold on in the only way she knew how. How could I blame her for that? How could I not love her for that?

WHEN THE year of my sentence was over, I stayed on the Cape. I am teaching again, a new beginning in a small private school with students I adore. Lily maintains that I am living in a state of radical hope.

I continue to rise early, as I did those mornings at the Harwich Port cottage. At dawn, I walk outside with my coffee, and I listen to the calls and songs of the birds. I remember when Luke told me that they sing out of joy, and as I listen to them, I wonder: If they can sing out of one emotion, why not more? And who is to say they don't? There is so much else to give voice to. Grief. Envy. Regret. Longing and loss.

Even in the lavender hour of sorrow, there is song.

THE
LAVENDER
HOUR

ANNE LeCLAIRE

A Reader's Guide

A CONVERSATION WITH ANNE LeCLAIRE

N. M. Kelby (Nicole Mary Kelby) is a former print and television journalist and the author of three novels: In the Company of Angels, Theater of the Stars, *and most recently,* Whale Season. *She met Anne LeClaire while in residence at the Ragdale Foundation in Lake Forest, Illinois, where both have been named Distinguished Fellows.*

NMK: *The Lavender Hour* strikes me as a book that puts death in its place in the cycle of life—it allows readers to embrace it as a part of life, to overcome their fear of it, and allow for the lessons it brings.

AL: I don't know if most of us ever actually overcome our fear of death. I sense we are hardwired with that fear, but by witnessing it, in fiction as well as in fact, we are cracked open to the gift of its significant lessons.

NMK: I find that most writers write from a dark place in their heart. Much of my work, including my comedic novel *Whale Season,* has been influenced by the death of my daughter. I write out of the need to find hope in darkness. Your work feels crafted along a similar path. Does writing provide you a way to own your private sorrow and to re-create it?

AL: Writing provides me with a way to try to make sense of things. And to delve into issues like loss and grief and disconnection as well as to explore the role these things play in our lives. I am not re-creating a specific personal sorrow but draw on my experiences to inform the sorrows of the characters. The one step removed gives me just the distance I need to explore. I don't think of the writing as coming from a dark place in my heart but from a center of hope. As Flannery O'Connor once responded to a reader who accused her of being a pessimist that only an optimist dares look life fully in the face. And her answer to people who complained that the novelist painted a picture of a world that is unbearable was "People without hope do not write novels."

I do know that experiencing grief and exploring it through my stories has made me passionate about finding and celebrating joy. And life.

NMK: What inspired you to write this particular story?

AL: One sentence in a novel I was reading. I don't remember the name of the book or much about it except that a minor character in it was a hospice volunteer, and when I read that, I had the "solar plexus hit" I get when the germ of a story strikes. I thought about how people often envision hospice work as being about endings, but it can be about beginnings, too. I also recalled a sentence I heard during a lecture by Dr. Bernie Siegel: "We learn how to live from the dying." That seemed a wonderful premise for a book about a hospice volunteer, and eventually it landed in Jessie's narrative. What can we learn? What are the costs of the lessons? How do we heal?

NMK: Jessie, your heroine, is an amazing creation. As a reader, I felt both great sympathy and great antipathy toward her—and at times, she really made me mad. As a writer, I admire your skill in drawing such a flawed creature and applaud the choice. But what I really want to know is, do you like her? Would you take her out for girl talk, a glass of wine, and some steamers?

AL: Oh, I just love Jessie. I feel such compassion for her. She is the part of all of us that urgently wants to connect—and isn't that exactly all we ever long for?—and then keeps messing it up. This is the question I wanted to spend time with and in fact have been playing with for the last three books (*Entering Normal, Leaving Eden,* and *The Law of Bound Hearts*). If we long for connection, why do we keep messing it up? Of course, the answer is fear. I recently read somewhere that fear and longing are the two predominant emotions and motivating forces. In Jessie, they are in conflict with each other. And conflict in the human heart is always worth writing about.

As to hanging with her, I've just spent nearly two years with her and wouldn't mind some more, especially now that she has a lot of hard-earned wisdom to share.

A perfect day with Jessie would be to go for a long walk in the dunes at the National Seashore, then have those steamers, and cap the day by dancing at the Squire. And I'd love a piece of her jewelry.

NMK: Just between you and me, why do you really think Jessie was attracted to Luke? Did it have something to do with her cancer?

AL: Oh my, yes. At first, she was attracted to his looks and that sense she had of "I know you." And then she fell in love with the person. It was such a daring thing for her to fall in love with someone who was going to leave her. Loving is always courting the possibility of loss, and with Luke, it was a sure thing.

NMK: Lily, Jessie's mother, is so wonderful. Her "rebirth" after years of widowhood—finding a rich younger love (a dentist, no less!), letting her hair go gray, and jaunting away on a transatlantic sail with her lover—makes us all say "You go, girl!" It's interesting that Jessie has such a difficult time with her mother's new life.

AL: Well, change can be such a threat and a challenge, especially when it occurs in someone close to us. Jessie wanted Lily to continue as she always was, her dependable foundation, and the glorious thing about Lily refusing the role is that it forced Jessie to set down her own roots.

NMK: At one point, you have Lily tell her daughter, "Sometimes you have to take a journey to find yourself." What journey did you take when you wrote *The Lavender Hour*?

AL: What a great question. Obviously I took a journey into grief and loss and the arena of the dying. Years ago, when I was writing *Entering Normal,* I came across a quote by Oscar Wilde: "Where there is sorrow there is holy ground." I just love this quote and keep it by my computer. I think what Wilde meant was that it is in the times when we are brought to our knees with grief, absolutely humbled by loss, that we are doing soul work. That is when the heart cracks open and all our defenses are useless. You know this better than most, Nicole.

NMK: The human heart is an unwieldy thing—I think that's what I'll admit to. Everybody knows sorrow. As I always say, "Life is a morbid adventure—so let's try to have some fun."

AL: I'm with you there, sister.

NMK: You know, when I write, I always fall in love with my characters. After spending day after day with them, making them real, they seem real to me. I sometimes even dream of them. So I really hate killing them—even if they deserve it.

Was there ever a time in the process of writing this book that you found yourself pained over Luke's looming death? Or maybe regret the pain you cause his mother, Nona?

AL: Only every day. I kept thinking, there must be a way to save him. But as a wise editor once told me, you can't save them all. And she was right.

Being a mother myself, I felt Nona's pain deeply, but I couldn't rescue her either. Giving people the dignity of their own pain is a tough thing to do, in writing and in life.

NMK: The shades of grief that are portrayed in this book are amazing. From Paige, Luke's in-denial daughter, to his exhausted caretaking mother to his tough-guy best friend, it seems as if you've touched on every possible reaction to the death of a loved one. After my daughter died, I spent many years trying to avoid my grief. Only when I discovered the transformative power of writing, a decade later, did I begin to understand what I can learn from her death and how that loss enriched me as a person. Only since then have I been able to properly grieve. Do you see Luke's loved ones ever coming to grips with their grief?

AL: Yes. Especially Nona. It will take Paige longer, I suspect. None of us would choose to go through the kind of devastating loss that you experienced, nor would we wish it on anyone. But loss is inevitable for all of us. It is the human condition.

I suspect it wasn't only your writing that transformed you but your experience. Even when you thought you were avoiding grief, you were living with it. Like the crucible in a science lab class, it burned away the crust and left you with the essence.

NMK: I think you're right. That "essence" throws the rest of life into relief—it makes the joys more profound and the pleasures richer.

AL: It awakens us to life.

NMK: You seem to have done a good deal of research on hospice volunteers.

AL: I was fortunate in that a number of people with extraordinarily generous hearts gave me insight into their experiences. I have also had three friends die and have witnessed the key role hospice workers played during their last months.

NMK: In this book, you provide the reader with a wealth of information on the Victorian practice of making jewelry from hair. The poet in me loves the idea that our heroine makes hair jewelry and some of her clients are cancer patients—it seems such a wonderful and gripping artistic expression for her. However, the shopper in me says "ick."

Of course, I think this is what you were going for—that lovely conflicted feeling we have for Jessie—but I had to ask myself, what drew you, as a writer, to make this particular choice? Do you know someone who actually does make hair jewelry for people going through chemo?

AL: I don't know of anyone who makes the jewelry for people in chemo, but through the Internet, I found a wonderful woman named Jeanenne Bell, author of *Collector's Encyclopedia of Hairwork Jewelry,* who gave me tons of information.

The aversion we have toward hair jewelry is fairly recent and reflects the conflicted feelings we have about death and our bodies. For centuries and centuries—well before the Victorian age so often associated with the craft—people have been making hair jewelry.

And, of course, as a symbol, hair is so rich, so absolutely loaded.

NMK: You set your story in Cape Cod. You obviously have some strong feelings about the healing powers of place.

AL: You yourself know the power of place, in life and in fiction. And you use it beautifully in your work. That is one of the things I loved about *Whale Season.*

Certainly there are sacred spots we are drawn to for healing, and I think Cape Cod is one.

NMK: In *Whale Season,* the unspoiled subtropical beauty that was once Florida does heal and transform. It's a shame those places don't exist anymore. At least the Cape still has that mystic power. I remember the first time I drove out through the dunes, I turned to my husband and said, "It looks like the moon dreaming of itself."

AL: Jeez, Nicole, that line deserves a poem. I don't think I'll ever again walk a dune without recalling it.

NMK: I know that both you and your husband are pilots. How does flying, maintaining that delicate balance between life and death, inform your writing?

AL: Flying requires a certain healthy detachment that is a good thing to nurture. And looking down on the land provides a pilot with perspective, the visual reminder that there is always a larger picture to be seen, one we miss when we are absorbed by the closer surrounds. In writing, it is key to remember the larger scope—the humanscape and the landscape—within which the story takes place.

Paying attention, rigorous preparation, faith, trust—all things required of a pilot—are also required of the writer. And, like writing, flying is exhilarating exactly because it requires dancing on the edge.

NMK: That's true. As writers, we all dance on the edge—of our hearts.

AL: More poetry!

NMK: And more love! Seems like you, and your work, inspire that reaction in people—so, many thanks for that. Can't have enough love and poetry in the world. Lots of pizza is good, too.

1. Why does Jessie call her mother by her first name? What does this say about their relationship? Does your family have nicknames or use specific names in different contexts?

2. Jessie is disappointed with her first visit to Luke's, much of which she spends alone: "I sipped the coffee, bitter, and felt . . . What? Let down? This was so *not* what I expected" (p. 10). What do you think Jessie did expect out of her work with hospice? Why do you think she joined?

3. What do you think first attracts Jessie to Luke? Why do you think she has such an intense reaction when she sees his photograph?

4. Have you ever felt connected to a person simply by seeing his or her photo, as Jessie was in the novel?

5. Why does Jessie have such a strong aversion to her mother's relationship with Jan? Why, in particular, is she so opposed to her mother's transatlantic trip? How does this particular attitude reflect her own romantic insecurities? Her fears of death? Her belated grief for her father?

6. While she is on the Cape, Jessie's close friendships are with two older women—first Faye, then Nona. Why does she gravitate toward these two women? How do her relationships with each differ? How are they the same?

7. Jessie says, after Luke gets sick on their outing to Dairy Queen, "Later I would see that, from the beginning, I wanted too much.

Wanted too much in a fierce and violent way that could only lead to trouble" (p. 105). What does she mean by this?

8. The use of hair as a metaphor threads through much of the book. Faye points out that hair, out of which Jessie makes her jewelry, is actually already dead. She says, "Odd, then, that that part of us which is dead will outlast the living—the blood, body, bones" (p. 28). Later, on the first night they spend together, Jessie tells Luke a story about a woman who is saved by her own hair. Finally, a piece of Luke's hair that Jessie had clipped is used as evidence against her. What do you think hair represents in the novel? Why is it so important?

9. When Jessie is first questioned by the police, she is still overwhelmed with grief for Luke. How does this harm her case? How, if at all, does the trial help her deal with Luke's death?

10. Luke's daughter, Paige, becomes the linchpin in Jessie's trial. How would you describe Paige's relationship with her father? How, if at all, are she and Jessie alike? Why do you think she is so interested in pursuing the investigation?

11. Why does Jessie choose to stay on the Cape, after it has caused her so much pain? What does it hold for her that Virginia does not?

12. Faye tells Jessie, "The dying can teach us how to die. . . . Maybe that serves as a model for how to live" (p. 18). How is that true for Jessie and Luke's relationship? What does Luke teach Jessie?

13. Was Jessie guilty of a crime?

14. Have you ever been close to someone throughout the dying process? How did your experience differ from Jessie's?

PHOTO: © JENNIFER ELDREDGE STELLO

ANNE LECLAIRE is the author of eight novels, including the critically acclaimed *Leaving Eden* and *Entering Normal.* Her books have been published in twenty countries and translated into eighteen languages. She lives on Cape Cod with her husband, a black cat, and fifteen chickens.

Visit the author's website at www.anneleclaire.com.

Join the Reader's Circle
to enhance your book club or
personal reading experience.

Our FREE monthly e-newsletter gives you:

- Sneak-peak excerpts from our newest titles

- Exclusive interviews with your favorite authors

- Fun ideas to spice up your book club meetings: creative activities, outings, and discussion topics

- Opportunities to invite an author to your next book club meeting

- Anecdotes and pearls of wisdom from other book group members . . . and the opportunity to share your own!

- Special offers and promotions giving you access to advance copies of books, our Reader's Circle catalog, and much more

To sign up, visit our website at
www.thereaderscircle.com
or send a blank e-mail to
Sub_rc@info.randomhouse.com

 When you see this seal on the outside, there's a great book club read inside.